"Run, Eleni!" Connor T[...] sword and bearing down o[...]

Of all that Connor had cri[...] word "drow." The young man's attitude and intent could not be mistaken, though, for Connor charged straight between Drizzt and Eleni, his sword tip pointed Drizzt's way. Eleni managed to get to her feet behind her brother, but she did not flee. She, too, had heard of the evil dark elves, and she would not leave Connor to face one alone.

"Turn away, dark elf," Connor growled. "I am an expert swordsman and much stronger than you."

Drizzt held his hands out, not understanding a word.

"Turn away!" Connor yelled.

On impulse, Drizzt replied in the silent code of his people, an intricate language of hand and facial gestures.

"He's casting a spell!" Eleni cried, and she dove into the blueberries. Connor charged, his sword leading the way.

Before Connor even knew of the counter, Drizzt grabbed him by the forearm, used his other hand to twist the boy's wrist and take away the sword, spun the crude weapon three times over Connor's head, flipped it in his slender hand, then handed it, hilt first, back to the boy.

Drizzt held his arms out wide and smiled. In drow custom, such a show of superiority without injury signaled a desire for friendship. To the oldest son of farmer Thistledown, the drow's display brought only terror.

Connor stood, mouth agape, for a long moment. His sword fell from his hand; his pants, soiled, clung uncomfortably to his thighs, but he didn't notice.

A scream erupted from somewhere within Connor and he grabbed Eleni, who joined in his scream, and they fled back to the grove to collect the others, then farther, running until they crossed the threshold of their own home.

Drizzt was left, his smile fast fading and his arms out wide, standing all alone in the blueberry patch.

———————
————

Books by
R. A. Salvatore

THE ICEWIND DALE TRILOGY

THE DARK ELF TRILOGY

FORGOTTEN REALMS
FANTASY ADVENTURE ®

SOJOURN

R. A. Salvatore

Cover Art by
JEFF EASLEY

TSR Inc.™

It is time for me to acknowledge the two people whose belief in me and whose creative influence helped to make Drizzt's tales possible. I dedicate Sojourn to Mary Kirchoff and J. Eric Severson, editors and friends, with all my thanks.

SOJOURN

First Printing: May, 1991
Printed in the United States of America.
Library of Congress Catalog Card Number: 90-71499

9 8 7 6 5 4

ISBN: 1-56076-047-8

TSR, Inc.
P.O. Box 756
Lake Geneva,
WI 53147 U.S.A.

TSR Ltd.
120 Church End, Cherry Hinton
Cambridge CB1 3LB
United Kingdom

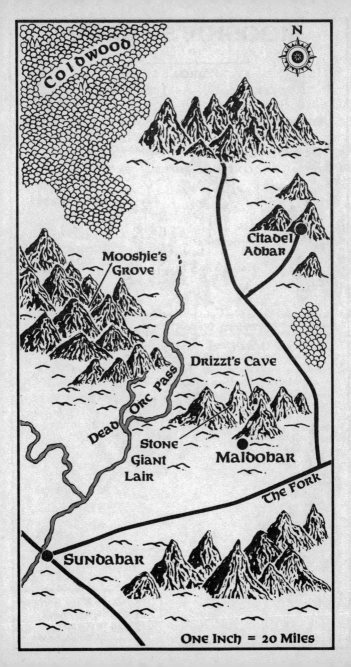

N

Coldwood

Mooshie's
Grove

Citadel
Adbar

Drizzt's Cave

Dead Orc Pass

Stone
Giant
Lair

Maldobar

The Fork

Sundabar

ONE INCH = 20 MILES

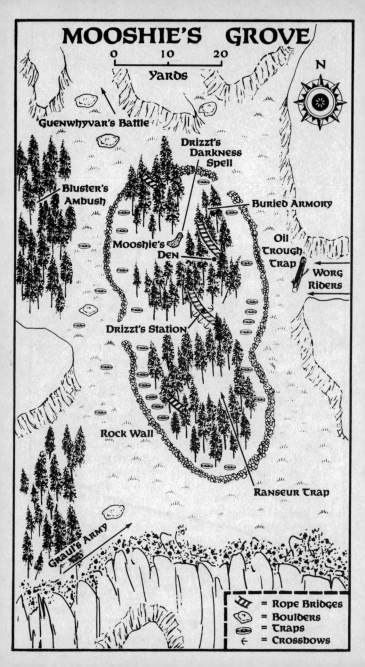

❧ Prelude ❧

The dark elf sat on the barren mountainside, watching anxiously as the line of red grew above the eastern horizon. This would be perhaps his hundredth dawn, and he knew well the sting the searing light would bring to his lavender eyes—eyes that had known only the darkness of the Underdark for more than four decades.

The drow did not turn away, though, when the upper rim of the flaming sun crested the horizon. He accepted the light as his purgatory, a pain necessary if he was to follow his chosen path, to become a creature of the surface world.

Gray smoke wafted up before the drow's dark-skinned face. He knew what it meant without even looking down. His *piwafwi*, the magical drow-made cloak that had so many times in the Underdark shielded him from probing enemy eyes, had finally succumbed to the daylight. The magic in the cloak had begun fading weeks before, and the fabric itself was simply melting away. Wide holes appeared as patches of the garment dissolved, and the drow pulled his arms in tightly to salvage as much as he could.

It wouldn't make any difference, he knew; the cloak was doomed to waste away in this world so different from where it had been created. The drow clung to it desperately, somehow viewing it as an analogy to his own fate.

The sun climbed higher and tears rolled out of the drow's squinting lavender eyes. He could not see the smoke anymore, could see nothing beyond the blinding glare of that terrible ball of fire. Still he sat and watched, right through the dawn.

To survive, he had to adapt.

He pushed his toe painfully down against a jag in the stone and focused his attention away from his eyes, from the dizziness that threatened to overcome him. He thought of how thin his finely woven boots had become and knew that they, too, would soon dissipate into nothingness.

Then his scimitars, perhaps? Would those magnificent drow weapons, which had sustained him through so many trials, be no more? What fate awaited Guenhwyvar, his magical panther companion? Unconsciously the drow dropped a hand into his pouch to feel the marvelous figurine, so perfect in every detail, which he used to summon the cat. Its solidity reassured him in that moment of doubt, but if it, too, had been crafted by the dark elves, imbued with the magic so particular to their domain, would Guenhwyvar soon be lost?

"What a pitiful creature I will become," the drow lamented in his native tongue. He wondered, not for the first time and certainly not for the last, about the wisdom of his decision to leave the Underdark, to forsake the world of his evil people.

His head pounded; sweat rolled into his eyes, heightening the sting. The sun continued its ascent and the drow could not endure. He rose and turned toward the small cave he had taken as his home, and he again put a hand absently on the panther figurine.

His *piwafwi* hung in tatters about him, serving as meager protection from the mountain winds' chill bite. There was no wind in the Underdark except for slight currents rising off pools of magma, and no chill except for the icy touch of an undead monster. This surface world, which the drow had known for several months, showed him many differences, many variables—too many, he often believed.

Drizzt Do'Urden would not surrender. The Underdark was the world of his kin, of his family, and in that darkness he would find no rest. Following the demands of his principles, he had struck out against Lloth, the Spider Queen, the evil deity his people revered above life itself. The dark elves, Drizzt's family, would not forgive his blasphemy, and the Underdark had no holes deep enough to escape their long reach.

Even if Drizzt believed that the sun would burn him away, as it burned away his boots and his precious *piwafwi*, even if he became no more than insubstantial, gray smoke blowing away in the chill mountain breeze, he would retain his principles and dignity, those elements that made his life worthwhile.

Drizzt pulled off his cloak's remains and tossed them down a deep chasm. The chilly wind nipped against his sweat-beaded brow, but the drow walked straight and proud, his jaw firm and his lavender eyes wide open.

This was the fate he preferred.

* * * * *

Along the side of a different mountain, not so far away, another creature watched the rising sun. Ulgulu, too, had left his birthplace, the filthy, smoking rifts that marked the plane of Gehenna, but this monster had not come of his own accord. It was Ulgulu's fate, his penance, to grow in this world until he attained sufficient strength to return to his home.

Ulgulu's lot was murder, feeding on the life force of the weak mortals around him. He was close now to attaining his maturity: huge and strong and terrible.

Every kill made him stronger.

❧ Part 1 ❧
Sunrise

It burned at my eyes and pained every part of my body. It destroyed my piwafwi and boots, stole the magic from my armor, and weakened my trusted scimitars. Still, every day, without fail, I was there, sitting upon my perch, my judgment seat, to await the arrival of the sunrise.

It came to me each day in a paradoxical way. The sting could not be denied, but neither could I deny the beauty of the spectacle. The colors just before the sun's appearance grabbed my soul in a way that no patterns of heat emanations in the Underdark ever could. At first, I thought my entrancement a result of the strangeness of the scene, but even now, many years later, I feel my heart leap at the subtle brightening that heralds the dawn.

I know now that my time in the sun—my daily penance—was more than mere desire to adapt to the ways of the surface world. The sun became the symbol of the difference between the Underdark and my new home. The society that I had run away from, a world of secret dealings and treacherous conspiracies, could not exist in the open spaces under the light of day.

This sun, for all the anguish it brought me physically, came to represent my denial of that other, darker world. Those rays of revealing light reinforced my principles as surely as they weakened the drow-made magical items.

In the sunlight, the piwafwi, the shielding cloak that defeated probing eyes, the garment of thieves and assassins, became no more than a worthless rag of tattered cloth.

—Drizzt Do'Urden

❧ 1 ❧

Poignant Lessons

Drizzt crept past the shielding shrubs and over the flat and bare stone that led to the cave now serving as his home. He knew that something had crossed this way recently— very recently. There were no tracks to be seen, but the scent was strong.

Guenhwyvar circled on the rocks up above the hillside cave. Sight of the panther gave the drow a measure of comfort. Drizzt had come to trust Guenhwyvar implicitly and knew that the cat would flush out any enemies hiding in ambush. Drizzt disappeared into the dark opening and smiled as he heard the panther come down behind, watching over him.

Drizzt paused behind a stone just inside the entrance, letting his eyes adjust to the gloom. The sun was still bright, though it was fast dipping into the western sky, but the cave was much darker—dark enough for Drizzt to let his vision slip into the infrared spectrum. As soon as the adjustment was completed, Drizzt located the intruder. The clear glow of a heat source, a living creature, emanated from behind another rock deeper in the one-chambered cave. Drizzt relaxed considerably. Guenhwyvar was only a few steps away now, and, considering the size of the rock, the intruder could not be a large beast.

Still, Drizzt had been raised in the Underdark, where every living creature, regardless of its size, was respected and considered dangerous. He signaled for Guenhwyvar to remain in position near the exit and crept around to get a better angle on the intruder.

Drizzt had never seen such an animal before. It appeared almost catlike, but its head was much smaller and more sharply pointed. The whole of it could not have weighed more than a few pounds. This fact, and the creature's bushy tail and thick fur, indicated that it was more a forager than a predator. It rummaged now through a pack of food, apparently oblivious to the drow's presence.

"Take ease, Guenhwyvar," Drizzt called softly, slipping his scimitars into their sheaths. He took a step toward the intruder for a better look, though he kept a cautious distance so as not to startle it, thinking that he might have found another companion. If he could only gain the animal's trust . . .

The small animal turned abruptly at Drizzt's call, its short front legs quickly backing it against the wall.

"Take ease," Drizzt said quietly, this time to the intruder. "I'll not harm you." Drizzt took another step in and the creature hissed and spun about, its small hind feet stamping down on the stone floor.

Drizzt nearly laughed aloud, thinking that the creature meant to push itself straight through the cave's back wall. Guenhwyvar bounded over then, and the panther's immediate distress stole the mirth from the drow's face.

The animal's tail came up high; Drizzt noticed in the faint light that the beast had distinctive stripes running down its back. Guenhwyvar whimpered and turned to flee, but it was too late. . . .

About an hour later Drizzt and Guenhwyvar walked along the lower trails of the mountain in search of a new home. They had salvaged what they could, though that wasn't very much. Guenhwyvar kept a good distance to the side of Drizzt. Proximity made the stink only worse.

Drizzt took it all in stride, though the stench of his own body made the lesson a bit more poignant than he would have liked. He didn't know the little animal's name, of course, but he had marked its appearance keenly. He would know better the next time he encountered a skunk.

"What of my other companions in this strange world,"

Drizzt whispered to himself. It was not the first time the drow had voiced such concerns. He knew very little of the surface and even less of the creatures that lived here. His months had been spent in and about the cave, with only occasional forays down to the lower, more populated regions. There, in his foraging, he had seen some animals, usually at a distance, and had even observed some humans. He had not yet found the courage to come out of hiding, though, to greet his neighbors, fearing potential rejection and knowing that he had nowhere left to run.

The sound of rushing water led the reeking drow and panther to a fast-running brook. Drizzt immediately found some protective shade and began stripping away his armor and clothing, while Guenhwyvar moved downstream to do some fishing. The sound of the panther fumbling around in the water brought a smile to the drow's severe features. They would eat well this night.

Drizzt gingerly flipped the clasp of his belt and laid his crafted weapons beside his mesh chain mail. Truly, he felt vulnerable without the armor and weapons—he never would have put them so far from his reach in the Underdark—but many months had passed since Drizzt had found any need for them. He looked to his scimitars and was flooded by the bittersweet memories of the last time he had put them to use.

He had battled Zaknafein then, his father and mentor and dearest friend. Only Drizzt had survived the encounter. The legendary weapon master was gone now, but the triumph in that fight belonged as much to Zak as it did to Drizzt, for it was not really Zaknafein who had come after Drizzt on the bridges of an acid-filled cavern. Rather, it was Zaknafein's wraith, under the control of Drizzt's evil mother, Matron Malice. She had sought revenge upon her son for his denouncement of Lloth and of the chaotic drow society in general. Drizzt had spent more than thirty years in Menzoberranzan but had never accepted the malicious and cruel ways that were the norm in the drow city. He had been a constant embarrassment to House Do'Urden despite his considerable skill with weapons. When he ran from the city to live a life of exile in the wilds of the Underdark, he had placed his high priestess mother out of Lloth's favor.

Thus, Matron Malice Do'Urden had raised the spirit of Zaknafein, the weapon master she had sacrificed to Lloth, and sent the undead thing after her son. Malice had miscalculated, though, for there remained enough of Zak's soul within the body to deny the attack on Drizzt. In the instant that Zak managed to wrest control from Malice, he had cried out in triumph and leaped into the lake of acid.

"My father," Drizzt whispered, drawing strength from the simple words. He had succeeded where Zaknafein had failed; he had forsaken the evil ways of the drow where Zak had been trapped for centuries, acting as a pawn in Matron Malice's power games. From Zaknafein's failure and ultimate demise, young Drizzt had found strength; from Zak's victory in the acid cavern, Drizzt had found determination. Drizzt had ignored the web of lies his former teachers at the Academy in Menzoberranzan had tried to spin, and he had come to the surface to begin a new life.

Drizzt shuddered as he stepped into the icy stream. In the Underdark he had known fairly constant temperatures and unvarying darkness. Here, though, the world surprised him at every turn. Already he had noticed that the periods of daylight and darkness were not constant; the sun set earlier every day and the temperature—changing from hour to hour, it seemed—had steadily dipped during the last few weeks. Even within those periods of light and dark loomed inconsistencies. Some nights were visited by a silver-glowing orb and some days held a pall of gray instead of a dome of shining blue.

In spite of it all, Drizzt most often felt comfortable with his decision to come to this unknown world. Looking at his weapons and armor now, lying in the shadows a dozen feet from where he bathed, Drizzt had to admit that the surface, for all of its strangeness, offered more peace than anywhere in the Underdark ever could.

Drizzt was in the wilds now, despite his calm. He had

spent four months on the surface and was still alone, except when he was able to summon his magical feline companion. Now, stripped bare except for his ragged pants, with his eyes stinging from the skunk spray, his sense of smell lost within the cloud of his own pungent aroma, and his keen sense of hearing dulled by the din of rushing water, the drow was indeed vulnerable.

"What a mess I must appear," Drizzt mused, roughly running his slender fingers through the mat of his thick, white hair. When he glanced back to his equipment, though, the thought was washed quickly from Drizzt's mind. Five hulking forms straddled his belongings and undoubtedly cared little for the dark elf's ragged appearance.

Drizzt considered the grayish skin and dark muzzles of the dog-faced, seven-foot-tall humanoids, but more particularly, he watched the spears and swords that they now leveled his way. He knew this type of monster, for he had seen similar creatures serving as slaves back in Menzoberranzan. In this situation, however, the gnolls appeared much different, more ominous, than Drizzt remembered them.

He briefly considered a rush to his scimitars but dismissed the notion, knowing that a spear would skewer him before he ever got close. The largest of the gnoll band, an eight-foot giant with striking red hair, looked at Drizzt for a long moment, eyed the drow's equipment, then looked back to him.

"What are you thinking?" Drizzt muttered under his breath. Drizzt really knew very little about gnolls. At Menzoberranzan's Academy he had been taught that gnolls were of a goblinoid race, evil, unpredictable, and quite dangerous. He had been told that of the surface elves and humans as well, though—and, he now realized, of nearly every race that was not drow. Drizzt almost laughed aloud despite his predicament. Ironically, the race that most deserved that mantle of evil unpredictability was the drow themselves!

The gnolls made no other moves and uttered no commands. Drizzt understood their hesitancy at the sight of a dark elf, and he knew that he must seize that natural fear if he was to have any chance at all. Calling upon the innate abilities of his magical heritage, Drizzt waved his dark hand and outlined all five gnolls in harmless purple-glowing flames.

One of the beasts dropped immediately to the ground, as Drizzt had hoped, but the others halted at a signal from their more experienced leader's outstretched hand. They looked around nervously, apparently wondering about the wisdom of continuing this meeting. The gnoll chieftain, though, had seen harmless faerie fire before, in a fight with an unfortunate—now deceased—ranger, and knew it for what it was.

Drizzt tensed in anticipation and tried to determine his next move.

The gnoll chieftain glanced around at its companions, as if studying how fully they were limned by the dancing flames. Judging by the completeness of the spell, this was no ordinary drow peasant standing in the stream—or so Drizzt hoped the chieftain was thinking.

Drizzt relaxed a bit as the leader dipped its spear and signaled for the others to do likewise. The gnoll then barked a jumble of words that sounded like gibberish to the drow. Seeing Drizzt's obvious confusion, the gnoll called something in the guttural tongue of goblins.

Drizzt understood the goblin language, but the gnoll's dialect was so very strange that he managed to decipher only a few words, "friend" and "leader" being among them.

Cautiously Drizzt took a step toward the bank. The gnolls gave ground, opening a path to his belongings. Drizzt took another tentative step, then grew more at ease when he noticed a black feline form crouched in the bushes a short distance away. At his command, Guenhwyvar, in one great spring, would come crashing into the gnoll band.

"You and I to walk together?" Drizzt asked the gnoll leader, using the goblin tongue and trying to simulate the creature's dialect.

The gnoll replied in a hurried shout, and the only thing that Drizzt thought he understood was the last word of the question: ". . . ally?"

Drizzt nodded slowly, hoping he understood the creature's full meaning.

"Ally!" the gnoll croaked, and all of its companions smiled and laughed in relief and patted each other on the back. Drizzt reached his equipment then, and immediately strapped on his scimitars. Seeing the gnolls distracted, the drow glanced at Guenhwyvar and nodded to the thick growth along the trail ahead. Swiftly and silently, Guenhwyvar took up a new position. No need to give all of his secrets away, Drizzt figured, not until he truly understood his new companions' intentions.

Drizzt walked along with the gnolls down the mountain's lower, winding passes. The gnolls kept far to the drow's sides, whether out of respect for Drizzt and the reputation of his race or for some other reason, he could not know. More likely, Drizzt suspected, they kept their distance simply because of his odor, which the bath had done little to diminish.

The gnoll leader addressed Drizzt every so often, accentuating its excited words with a sly wink or a sudden rub of its thick, padded hands. Drizzt had no idea of what the gnoll was talking about, but he assumed from the creature's eager lip-smacking that it was leading him to some sort of feast.

Drizzt soon guessed the band's destination, for he had often watched from jutting peaks high in the mountains, the lights of a small human farming community in the valley. Drizzt could only guess at the relationship between the gnolls and the human farmers, but he sensed that it was not a friendly one. When they neared the village, the gnolls dropped into defensive positions, followed lines of shrubs, and kept to the shadows as much as possible. Twilight was fast approaching as the troupe made its way around the village's central area to look down upon a secluded farmhouse off to the west.

The gnoll chieftain whispered to Drizzt, slowly rolling out each word so that the drow might understand. "One family," it croaked. "Three men, two women . . ."

"One young woman," another added eagerly.

The gnoll chieftain gave a snarl. "And three young males," it concluded.

Drizzt thought he now understood the journey's purpose, and the surprised and questioning look on his face prompted the gnoll to confirm it beyond doubt.

"Enemies," the leader declared.

Drizzt, knowing next to nothing of the two races, was in a dilemma. The gnolls were raiders—that much was clear—and they meant to swoop down upon the farmhouse as soon as the last daylight faded away. Drizzt had no intention of joining them in their fight until he had a lot more information concerning the nature of the conflict.

"Enemies?" he asked.

The gnoll leader crinkled its brow in apparent consternation. It spouted a line of gibberish in which Drizzt thought he heard "human . . . weakling . . . slave." All the gnolls sensed the drow's sudden uneasiness, and they began fingering their weapons and glancing to each other nervously.

"Three men," Drizzt said.

The gnoll jabbed its spear savagely toward the ground. "Kill oldest! Catch two!"

"Women?"

The evil smile that spread over the gnoll's face answered the question beyond doubt, and Drizzt was beginning to understand where he stood in the conflict.

"What of the children?" He eyed the gnoll leader squarely and spoke each word distinctly. There could be no misunderstanding. His final question confirmed it all, for while Drizzt could accept the typical savagery concerning mortal enemies, he could never forget the one time he had participated in such a raid. He had saved an elven child on that day, had hidden the girl under her mother's body to keep her from the wrath of his drow companions. Of all the many evils Drizzt had ever witnessed, the murder of children had been the worst.

The gnoll thrust its spear toward the ground, its dog-face

contorted in wicked glee.

"I think not," Drizzt said simply, fires springing up in his lavender eyes. Somehow, the gnolls noticed, his scimitars had appeared in his hands.

Again the gnoll's snout crinkled, this time in confusion. It tried to get its spear up in defense, not knowing what this strange drow would do next, but was too late.

Drizzt's rush was too quick. Before the gnoll's spear tip even moved, the drow waded in, scimitars leading. The other four gnolls watched in amazement as Drizzt's blades snapped twice, tearing the throat from their powerful leader. The giant gnoll fell backward silently, grasping futilely at its throat.

A gnoll to the side reacted first, leveling its spear and charging at Drizzt. The agile drow easily deflected the straightforward attack but was careful not to slow the gnoll's momentum. As the huge creature lumbered past, Drizzt rolled around beside it and kicked at its ankles. Off balance, the gnoll stumbled on, plunging its spear deep into the chest of a startled companion.

The gnoll tugged at the weapon, but it was firmly embedded, its barbed head hooked around the other gnoll's backbone. The gnoll had no concern for its dying companion; all it wanted was its weapon. It tugged and twisted and cursed and spat into the agonized expressions crossing its companion's face—until a scimitar bashed in the beast's skull.

Another gnoll, seeing the drow distracted and thinking it wiser to engage the foe from a distance, raised its spear to throw. Its arm went up high, but before the weapon ever started forward, Guenhwyvar crashed in, and the gnoll and panther tumbled away. The gnoll smashed heavy punches into the panther's muscled side, but Guenhwyvar's raking claws were more effective by far. In the split second it took Drizzt to turn from the three dead gnolls at his feet, the fourth of the band lay dead beneath the great panther. The fifth had taken flight.

Guenhwyvar tore free of the dead gnoll's stubborn grasp. The cat's sleek muscles rippled anxiously as it awaited the expected command. Drizzt considered the carnage around him, the blood on his scimitars, and the horrible expressions on the faces of the dead. He wanted to let it end, for he realized that he had stepped into a situation beyond his experience, had crossed the paths of two races that he knew very little about. After a moment of consideration, though, the single notion that stood out in the drow's mind was the gnoll leader's gleeful promise of death to the human children. Too much was at stake.

Drizzt turned to Guenhwyvar, his voice more determined than resigned. "Go get him."

* * * * *

The gnoll scrambled along the trails, its eyes darting back and forth as it imagined dark forms behind every tree or stone.

"Drow!" it rasped over and over, using the word itself as encouragement during its flight. "Drow! Drow!"

Huffing and panting, the gnoll came into a copse of trees stretching between two steep walls of bare stone. It tumbled over a fallen log, slipped, and bruised its ribs on the angled slope of a moss-covered stone. Minor pains would not slow the frightened creature, though, not in the least. The gnoll knew it was being pursued, sensed a presence slipping in and out of the shadows just beyond the edges of its vision.

As it neared the end of the copse, the evening gloom thick about it, the gnoll spotted a set of yellow-glowing eyes peering back at it. The gnoll had seen its companion taken down by the panther and could make a guess as to what now blocked its path.

Gnolls were cowardly monsters, but they could fight with amazing tenacity when cornered. So it was now. Realizing that it had no escape—it certainly couldn't turn back in the direction of the dark elf—the gnoll snarled and heaved its heavy spear.

The gnoll heard a shuffle, a thump, and a squeal of pain

as the spear connected. The yellow eyes went away for a moment, then a form scurried off toward a tree. It moved low to the ground, almost catlike, but the gnoll realized at once that his mark had been no panther. When the wounded animal got to the tree, it looked back and the gnoll recognized it clearly.

"Raccoon," the gnoll blurted, and it laughed. "I run from raccoon!" The gnoll shook its head and blew away all of its mirth in a deep breath. The sight of the raccoon had brought a measure of relief, but the gnoll could not forget what had happened back down the path. It had to get back to its lair now, back to report to Ulgulu, its gigantic goblin master, its god-thing, about the drow.

It took a step to retrieve the spear, then stopped suddenly, sensing a movement from behind. Slowly the gnoll turned its head. It could see its own shoulder and the moss-covered rock behind.

The gnoll froze. Nothing moved behind it, not a sound issued from anywhere in the copse, but the beast knew that something was back there. The goblinoid's breath came in short rasps; its fat hands clenched and opened at its sides.

The gnoll spun quickly and roared, but the shout of rage became a cry of terror as six hundred pounds of panther leaped down upon it from a low branch.

The impact laid the gnoll out flat, but it was not a weak creature. Ignoring the burning pains of the panther's cruel claws, the gnoll grasped Guenhwyvar's plunging head, held on desperately to keep the deadly maw from finding a hold on its neck.

For nearly a minute the gnoll struggled, its arms quivering under the pressure of the powerful muscles in the panther's neck. The head came down then and Guenhwyvar found a hold. Great teeth locked onto the gnoll's neck and squeezed away the doomed creature's breath.

The gnoll flailed and thrashed wildly; somehow it managed to roll back over the panther. Guenhwyvar remained viselike, unconcerned. The maw held firm.

In a few minutes, the thrashing stopped.

❧ 2 ❧

Questions of
Conscience

Drizzt let his vision slip into the infrared spectrum, the night vision that could see gradations of heat as clearly as he viewed objects in the light. To his eyes, his scimitars now shone brightly with the heat of fresh blood and the torn gnoll bodies spilled their warmth into the open air.

Drizzt tried to look away, tried to observe the trail where Guenhwyvar had gone in pursuit of the fifth gnoll, but, every time, his gaze fell back to the dead gnolls and the blood on his weapons.

"What have I done?" Drizzt wondered aloud. Truly, he did not know. The gnolls had spoken of slaughtering children, a thought that had evoked rage within Drizzt, but what did Drizzt know of the conflict between the gnolls and the humans of the village? Might the humans, even the human children, be monsters? Perhaps they had raided the gnolls' village and killed without mercy. Perhaps the gnolls meant to strike back because they had no choice, because they had to defend themselves.

Drizzt ran from the grizzly scene in search of Guenhwyvar, hoping he could get to the panther before the fifth gnoll was dead. If he could find the gnoll and capture it, he might be able to learn some of the answers that he desperately needed to know.

He moved with swift and graceful strides, making barely a rustle as he slipped through the brush along the trail. He found signs of the gnoll's passing easily enough, and he saw, to his fear, that Guenhwyvar had also discovered the trail. When he came at last to the narrow copse of trees, he fully expected that his search was at its end. Still, Drizzt's heart sank when he saw the cat, reclined beside the final kill.

Guenhwyvar looked at Drizzt curiously as he approached, the drow's stride obviously agitated.

"What have we done, Guenhwyvar?" Drizzt whispered. The panther tilted its head as though it did not understand.

"Who am I to pass such judgment?" Drizzt went on, talking to himself more than to the cat. He turned from Guenhwyvar and the dead gnoll and moved to a leafy bush, where he could wipe the blood from his blades. "The gnolls did not attack me, but they had me at their mercy when they first found me in the stream. And I repay them by spilling their blood!"

Drizzt spun back on Guenhwyvar with the proclamation, as if he expected, even hoped, that the panther would somehow berate him, somehow condemn him and justify his guilt. Guenhwyvar hadn't moved an inch and did not now, and the panther's saucer eyes, shining greenish yellow in the night, did not bore into Drizzt, did not incriminate him for his actions in any way.

Drizzt started to protest, wanting to wallow in his guilt, but Guenhwyvar's calm acceptance would not be shaken. When they had lived out alone in the wilds of the Underdark, when Drizzt had lost himself to savage urges that relished killing, Guenhwyvar had sometimes disobeyed him, had even returned to the Astral Plane once without being dismissed. Now, though, the panther showed no signs of leaving or of disappointment. Guenhwyvar rose to its feet, shook the dirt and twigs from its sleek, black coat, and walked over to nuzzle against Drizzt.

Gradually Drizzt relaxed. He wiped his scimitars once more, this time on the thick grass, and slipped them back into their sheaths, then he dropped a thankful hand onto Guenhwyvar's huge head.

"Their words marked them as evil," the drow whispered to reassure himself. "Their intentions forced my action." His own words lacked conviction, but, at that moment, Drizzt had to believe them. He took a deep breath to steady himself and looked inward to find the strength he knew he would need. Realizing then that Guenhwyvar had been at his side for a long time and needed to return to the Astral Plane to rest, he reached into the small pouch at his side.

Before Drizzt ever got the onyx figurine out of his pouch, though, the panther's paw came up and batted it from his grasp. Drizzt looked at Guenhwyvar curiously, and the cat leaned heavily into him, nearly taking him from his feet.

"My loyal friend," Drizzt said, realizing that the weary panther meant to stay beside him. He pulled his hand from the pouch and dropped to one knee, locking Guenhwyvar in a great hug. The two of them, side by side, then walked from the copse.

Drizzt slept not at all that night, but watched the stars and wondered. Guenhwyvar sensed his anxiety and stayed close throughout the rise and set of the moon, and when Drizzt moved out to greet the next dawn, Guenhwyvar plodded along, drawn and tired, at his side. They found a rocky crest in the foothills and sat back to watch the coming spectacle.

Below them the last lights faded from the windows of the farming village. The eastern sky turned to pink, then crimson, but Drizzt found himself distracted. His gaze lingered on the farmhouses far below; his mind tried to piece together the routines of this unknown community and tried to find in that some justification for the previous day's events.

The humans were farmers, that much Drizzt knew, and diligent workers, too, for many of them were already out tending their fields. While those facts brought promise, however, Drizzt could not begin to make sweeping assumptions as to the human race's overall demeanor.

Drizzt came to a decision then, as the daylight stretched wide, illuminating the wooden structures of the town and the wide fields of grain. "I must learn more, Guenhwyvar," he said softly. "If I—if we—are to remain in this world, we must come to understand the ways of our neighbors."

Drizzt nodded as he considered his own words. It had already been proven, painfully proven, that he could not remain a neutral observer to the goings-on of the surface world. Drizzt was often called to action by his conscience, a force he had no power to deny. Yet with so little knowledge of the races sharing this region, his conscience could easily lead him astray. It could wreak damage against the innocent, thereby defeating the very principles Drizzt meant to champion.

Drizzt squinted through the morning light, eyeing the distant village for some hint of an answer. "I will go there," he told the panther. "I will go and watch and learn."

Guenhwyvar sat silently through it all. If the panther approved or disapproved, or even understood Drizzt's intent, Drizzt could not tell. This time, though, Guenhwyvar made no move of protest when Drizzt reached for the onyx figurine. A few moments later, the great panther was running off through the planar tunnel to its astral home, and Drizzt moved along the trails leading to the human village and his answers. He stopped only once, at the body of the lone gnoll, to take the creature's cloak. Drizzt winced at his own thievery, but the chill night had reminded him that the loss of his *piwafwi* could prove serious.

To this point, Drizzt's knowledge of humans and their society was severely limited. Deep in the bowels of the Underdark, the dark elves had little communication with, or interest in, those of the surface world. The one time in Menzoberranzan that Drizzt had heard anything of humans at all was during his tenure in the Academy, the six months he had spent in Sorcere, the school of wizards. The drow masters had warned the students against using magic "like a human would," implying a dangerous recklessness generally associated with the shorter-lived race.

"Human wizards," the masters had said, "have no fewer ambitions than drow wizards, but while a drow may take five centuries accomplishing those goals, a human has only a few short decades."

Drizzt had carried the implications of that statement with him for a score of years, particularly over the last few months, when he had looked down upon the human village almost daily. If all humans, not just wizards, were as ambitious as so many of the drow—fanatics who might spend the better part of a millennium accomplishing their goals—would they be consumed by a single-mindedness that bordered on hysteria? Or perhaps, Drizzt hoped, the stories he had heard of humans at the Academy were just more of the typical lies that bound his society in a web of intrigue and paranoia. Perhaps humans set their goals at more reasonable levels and found enjoyment and satisfaction in the small pleasures of the short days of their existence.

Drizzt had met a human only once during his travels through the Underdark. That man, a wizard, had behaved irrationally, unpredictably, and ultimately dangerously. The wizard had transformed Drizzt's friend from a pech, a harmless little humanoid creature, into a horrible monster. When Drizzt and his companions went to set things aright at the wizard's tower, they were greeted by a roaring blast of lightning. In the end, the human was killed and Drizzt's friend, Clacker, had been left to his torment.

Drizzt had been left with a bitter emptiness, an example of a man who seemed to confirm the truth of the drow masters' warnings. So it was with cautious steps that Drizzt now traveled toward the human settlement, his steps weighted by the growing fear that he had erred in killing the gnolls.

Drizzt chose to observe the same secluded farmhouse on the western edge of town that the gnolls had selected for their raid. It was a long and low log structure with a single door and several shuttered windows. An open-sided, roofed porch ran the length of the front. Beside it stood a barn, two-stories high, with wide and high doors that would admit a large wagon. Fences of various makes and sizes dotted the immediate yard, many holding chickens or pigs, one corralling a goat, and others encircling straight rows of leafy plants that Drizzt did not recognize.

The yard was bordered by fields on three sides, but the back of the house was near the mountain slopes' thick brush and boulders. Drizzt dug in under the low branches of a pine tree to the side of the house's rear corner, affording him a view of most of the yard.

The three adult men of the house—three generations, Drizzt guessed by their appearances—worked the fields, too far from the trees for Drizzt to discern many details. Closer to the house, though, four children, a daughter just coming into womanhood and three younger boys, quietly went about their chores, tending to the hens and pigs and pulling weeds from a vegetable garden. They worked separately and with minimum interaction for most of the morning, and Drizzt learned little of their family relationships. When a sturdy woman with the same wheat-colored hair as all five children came out on the porch and rang a giant bell, it seemed as if all the spirit that had been cooped up within the workers burst beyond control.

With hoots and shouts, the three boys sprinted for the house, pausing just long enough to toss rotted vegetables at their older sister. At first, Drizzt thought the bombing a prelude to a more serious conflict, but when the young woman retaliated in kind, all four howled with laughter and he recognized the game for what it was.

A moment later, the youngest of the men in the field, probably an older brother, charged into the yard, shouting and waving an iron hoe. The young woman cried encouragement to this new ally and the three boys broke for the porch. The man was quicker, though, and he scooped up the trailing imp in one strong arm and promptly dropped him into the pig trough.

And all the while, the woman with the bell shook her head helplessly and issued an unending stream of exasperated grumbling. An older woman, gray-haired and stick-thin, came out to stand next to her, waving a wooden spoon ominously. Apparently satisfied, the young man draped one arm over the young woman's shoulders and they followed the first two boys into the house. The remaining youngster pulled himself from the murky water and moved to follow, but the wooden spoon kept him at bay.

Drizzt couldn't understand a word of what they were

saying, of course, but he figured that the women would not let the little one into the house until he had dried off. The rambunctious youngster mumbled something at the spoon-wielder's back as she turned to enter the house, but his timing was not so great.

The other two men, one sporting a thick, gray beard and the other clean-shaven, came in from the field and sneaked up behind the boy as he grumbled. Up into the air the boy went again and landed with a *splash!* back in the trough. Congratulating themselves heartily, the men went into the house to the cheers of all the others. The soaking boy merely groaned again and splashed some water into the face of a sow that had come over to investigate.

Drizzt watched it all with growing wonderment. He had seen nothing conclusive, but the family's playful manner and the resigned acceptance of even the loser of the game gave him encouragement. Drizzt sensed a common spirit in this group, with all members working toward a common goal. If this single farm proved a reflection of the whole village, then the place surely resembled Blingdenstone, a communal city of the deep gnomes, far more than it resembled Menzoberranzan.

The afternoon went much the same way as the morning, with a mixture of work and play evident throughout the farm. The family retired early, turning down their lamps soon after sunset, and Drizzt slipped deeper into the thicket of the mountainside to consider his observations.

He still couldn't be certain of anything, but he slept more peacefully that night, untroubled by nagging doubts concerning the dead gnolls.

* * * * *

For three days the drow crouched in the shadows behind the farm, watching the family at work and at play. The closeness of the group became more and more evident, and whenever a true fight did erupt among the children, the nearest adult quickly stepped in and mediated it to a level of reasonableness. Invariably, the combatants were back at play together within a short span.

All doubts had flown from Drizzt. "Ware my blades, rogues," he whispered to the quiet mountains one night. The young drow renegade had decided that if any gnolls or goblins—or creatures of any other race at all—tried to swoop down upon this particular farming family, they first would have to contend with the whirling scimitars of Drizzt Do'Urden.

Drizzt understood the risk he was taking by observing the farm family. If the farmer-folk noticed him—a distinct possibility—they surely would panic. At this point in his life, though, Drizzt was willing to take that chance. A part of him may even have hoped to be discovered.

Early on the morning of the fourth day, before the sun had found its way into the eastern sky, Drizzt set out on his daily patrol, circumventing the hills and woodlands surrounding the lone farmhouse. By the time the drow returned to his perch, the work day on the farm was in full swing. Drizzt sat comfortably on a bed of moss and peered from the shadows into the brightness of the cloudless day.

Less than an hour later, a solitary figure crept from the farmhouse and in Drizzt's direction. It was the youngest of the children, the sandy-haired lad who seemed to spend nearly as much time in the trough as out of it, usually not of his own volition.

Drizzt rolled around the trunk of a nearby tree, uncertain of the lad's intent. He soon realized that the youngster hadn't seen him, for the boy slipped into the thicket, gave a snort over his shoulder, back toward the farmhouse, and headed off into the hilly woodland, whistling all the while. Drizzt understood then that the lad was avoiding his chores, and Drizzt almost applauded the boy's carefree attitude. In spite of that, though, Drizzt wasn't convinced of the small child's wisdom in wandering away from home in such dangerous terrain. The boy couldn't have been more than ten years old; he looked thin and delicate, with innocent, blue eyes peering out from under his amber locks.

Drizzt waited a few moments, to let the boy get a lead and to see if anyone would be following, then he took up the trail, letting the whistling guide him.

The boy moved unerringly away from the farmhouse, up into the mountains, and Drizzt moved behind him by a hundred paces or so, determined to keep the boy out of danger.

In the dark tunnels of the Underdark Drizzt could have crept right up behind the boy—or behind a goblin or practically anything else—and patted him on the rump before being discovered. But after only a half-hour or so of this pursuit, the movements and erratic speed changes along the trail, coupled with the fact that the whistling had ceased, told Drizzt that the boy knew he was being followed.

Wondering if the boy had sensed a third party, Drizzt summoned Guenhwyvar from the onyx figurine and sent the panther off on a flanking maneuver. Drizzt started ahead again at a cautious pace.

A moment later, when the child's voice cried out in distress, the drow drew his scimitars and threw out all caution. Drizzt couldn't understand any of the boy's words, but the desperate tone rang clearly enough.

"Guenhwyvar!" the drow called, trying to bring the distant panther back to his side. Drizzt couldn't stop and wait for the cat, though, and he charged on.

The trail wound up a steep climb, came out of the trees suddenly, and ended on the lip of a wide gorge, fully twenty feet across. A single log spanned the crevasse, and hanging from it near the other side was the boy. His eyes widened considerably at the sight of the ebony-skinned elf, scimitars in hand. He stammered a few words that Drizzt could not begin to decipher.

A wave of guilt flooded through Drizzt at the sight of the imperiled child; the boy had only landed in this predicament because of Drizzt's pursuit. The gorge was only about as deep as it was wide, but the fall ended on jagged rocks and brambles. At first, Drizzt hesitated, caught off guard by the sudden meeting and its inevitable implications, then the drow quickly put his own problems out of mind. He snapped his scimitars back into their sheaths and, folding his arms across his chest in a drow signal for peace, he put one foot out on the log.

The boy had other ideas. As soon as he recovered from the shock of seeing the strange elf, he swung himself to a ledge on the stone bank opposite Drizzt and pushed the log from its perch. Drizzt quickly backed off the log as it tumbled down into the crevasse. The drow understood then that the boy had never been in real danger but had pretended distress to flush out his pursuer. And, Drizzt presumed, if the pursuer had been one of the boy's family, as the boy no doubt had suspected, the peril might have deflected any thoughts of punishment.

Now Drizzt was the one in the predicament. He had been discovered. He tried to think of a way to communicate with the boy, to explain his presence and stave off panic. The boy didn't wait for any explanations, though. Wide-eyed and terror-stricken, he scaled the bank—via a path he obviously knew well—and darted off into the shrubbery.

Drizzt looked around helplessly. "Wait!" he cried in the drow tongue, though he knew the boy would not understand and would not have stopped even if he could.

A black feline form rushed out beside the drow and sprang into the air, easily clearing the crevasse. Guenhwyvar padded down softly on the other side and disappeared into the thicket.

"Guenhwyvar!" Drizzt cried, trying to halt the panther. Drizzt had no idea how Guenhwyvar would react to the child. To Drizzt's knowledge, the panther had only encountered one human before, the wizard that Drizzt's companions had subsequently killed. Drizzt looked around for some way to follow. He could scale down the side of the gorge, cross at the bottom, and climb back up, but that would take too long.

Drizzt ran back a few steps, then charged the gorge and leaped into the air, calling on his innate powers of levitation as he went. Drizzt was truly relieved when he felt his body pull free of the ground's gravity. He hadn't used his levitation spell since he had come to the surface. The spell served no purpose for a drow hiding under the open sky. Gradually, Drizzt's initial momentum carried him near the far bank. He began to concentrate on drifting down to the stone, but the spell ended abruptly and Drizzt plopped down hard. He ignored the bruises on his knee, and the questions of why his spell had faltered, and came up running, calling desperately for Guenhwyvar to stop.

Drizzt was relieved when he found the cat. Guenhwyvar sat calmly in a clearing, one paw casually pinning the boy facedown to the ground. The child was calling out again—for help, Drizzt assumed—but appeared unharmed.

"Come, Guenhwyvar," Drizzt said quietly, calmly. "Leave the child alone." Guenhwyvar yawned lazily and complied, padding across the clearing to stand at its master's side.

The boy remained down for a long moment. Then, summoning his courage, he moved suddenly, leaping to his feet and spinning to face the dark elf and the panther. His eyes seemed wider still, almost a caricature of terror, peeking out from his now dirty face.

"What are you?" the boy asked in the common human language.

Drizzt held his arms out to the sides to indicate that he did not understand. On impulse, he poked a finger into his chest and replied, "Drizzt Do'Urden." He noticed that the boy was moving slightly, secretly dropping one foot behind the other and then sliding the other back into place. Drizzt was not surprised—and he made certain that he kept Guenhwyvar in check this time—when the boy turned on his heel and sprinted away, screaming "Help! It's a drizzit!" with every stride.

Drizzt looked at Guenhwyvar and shrugged, and the cat seemed to shrug back.

❦ 3 ❦

The Whelps

Nathak, a spindle-armed goblin, made his way slowly up the steep, rocky incline, every step weighted with dread. The goblin had to report his findings—five dead gnolls could not be ignored—but the unfortunate creature seriously doubted that either Ulgulu or Kempfana would willingly accept the news. Still, what options did Nathak have? He could run away, flee down the other side of the mountain, and off into the wilderness. That seemed an even more desperate course, though, for the goblin knew well Ulgulu's taste for vengeance. The great purple-skinned master could tear a tree from the ground with his bare hands, could tear handfuls of stone from the cave wall, and could readily tear the throat from a deserting goblin.

Every step brought a shudder as Nathak moved beyond the concealing scrub into the small entry room of his master's cave complex.

"Bouts time yez isses back," one of the other two goblins in the room snorted. "Yez been gone fer two days!"

Nathak just nodded and took a deep breath.

"What're ye fer?" the third goblin asked. "Did ye finded the gnolls?"

Nathak's face blanched, and no amount of deep breathing could relieve the fit that came over the goblin. "Ulgulu in there?" he asked squeamishly.

The two goblin guards looked curiously at each other, then back to Nathak. "He finded the gnolls," one of them remarked, guessing the problem. "Dead gnolls."

"Ulgulu won'ts be glad," the other piped in, and they

moved apart, one of them lifting the heavy curtain that separated the entry room from the audience chamber.

Nathak hesitated and started to look back, as though reconsidering this whole course. Perhaps flight would be preferable, he thought. The goblin guards grabbed their spindly companion and roughly shoved him into the audience chamber, crossing their spears behind Nathak to prevent any retreat.

Nathak managed to find a measure of composure when he saw that it was Kempfana, not Ulgulu, sitting in the huge chair across the room. Kempfana had earned a reputation among the goblin ranks as the calmer of the ruling brothers, though Kempfana, too, had impulsively devoured enough of his minions to earn their healthy respect. Kempfana hardly took note of the goblin's entrance, instead busily conversing with Lagerbottoms, the fat hill giant that formerly claimed the cave complex as his own.

Nathak shuffled across the room, drawing the gazes of both the hill giant and the huge—nearly as large as the hill giant—scarlet-skinned goblinoid.

"Yes, Nathak," Kempfana prompted, silencing the hill giant's forthcoming protest with a simple wave of the hand. "What have you to report?"

"Me . . . me," Nathak stuttered.

Kempfana's large eyes suddenly glowed orange, a clear sign of dangerous excitement.

"Me finded the gnolls!" Nathak blurted. "Dead. Killded."

Lagerbottoms issued a low and threatening growl, but Kempfana clutched the hill giant's arm tightly, reminding him of who was in charge.

"Dead?" the scarlet-skinned goblin asked quietly.

Nathak nodded.

Kempfana lamented the loss of such reliable slaves, but the barghest whelp's thoughts at that moment were more centered on his brother's inevitably volatile reaction to the news. Kempfana didn't have long to wait.

"*Dead!*" came a roar that nearly split the stone. All three monsters in the room instinctively ducked and turned to the side, just in time to see a huge boulder, the crude door to another room, burst out and go skipping off to the side.

"Ulgulu!" Nathak squealed, and the little goblin fell face-down to the floor, not daring to look.

The huge, purple-skinned goblinlike creature stormed into the audience chamber, his eyes seething in orange-glowing rage. Three great strides took Ulgulu right up beside the hill giant, and Lagerbottoms suddenly seemed very small and vulnerable.

"Dead!" Ulgulu roared again in rage. As his goblin tribe had diminished, killed either by the humans of the village or by other monsters—or eaten by Ulgulu during his customary fits of anger—the small gnoll band had become the primary capturing force for the lair.

Kempfana cast an ugly glare at his larger sibling. They had come to the Material Plane together, two barghest whelps, to eat and grow. Ulgulu had promptly claimed dominance, devouring the strongest of their victims and, thus, growing larger and stronger. By the color of Ulgulu's skin, and by his sheer size and strength, it was apparent that the whelp would soon be able to return to the reeking valley rifts of Gehenna.

Kempfana hoped that day was near. When Ulgulu was gone, he would rule; he would eat and grow stronger. Then Kempfana, too, could escape his interminable weaning period on this cursed plane, could return to compete among the barghests on their rightful plane of existence.

"Dead," Ulgulu growled again. "Get up, wretched goblin, and tell me how! What did this to my gnolls?"

Nathak groveled a minute longer, then managed to rise to his knees. "Me no know," the goblin whimpered. "Gnolls dead, slashed and ripped."

Ulgulu rocked back on the heels of his floppy, oversized feet. The gnolls had gone off to raid a farmhouse, with orders to return with the farmer and his oldest son. Those two hardy human meals would have strengthened the great barghest considerably, perhaps even bringing Ulgulu to the level of maturation he needed to return to Gehenna.

Now, in light of Nathak's report, Ulgulu would have to send Lagerbottoms, or perhaps even go himself, and the sight of either the giant or the purple-skinned monstrosity could prompt the human settlement to dangerous, organized action. "Tephanis!" Ulgulu roared suddenly.

Over on the far wall, across from where Ulgulu had made his crashing entrance, a small pebble dislodged and fell. The drop was only a few feet, but by the time the pebble hit the floor, a slender sprite had zipped out of the small cubby he used as a bedroom, crossed the twenty feet of the audience hall, and run right up Ulgulu's side to sit comfortably atop the barghest's immense shoulder.

"You-called-for-me, yes-you-did, my-master," Tephanis buzzed, too quickly. The others hadn't even realized that the two-foot-tall sprite had entered the room. Kempfana turned away, shaking his head in amazement.

Ulgulu roared with laughter; he so loved to witness the spectacle of Tephanis, his most prized servant. Tephanis was a quickling, a diminutive sprite that moved in a dimension that transcended the normal concept of time. Possessing boundless energy and an agility that would shame the most proficient halfling thief, quicklings could perform many tasks that no other race could even attempt. Ulgulu had befriended Tephanis early in his tenure on the Material Plane—Tephanis was the only member of the lair's diverse tenants that the barghest did not claim rulership over—and that bond had given the young whelp a distinct advantage over his sibling. With Tephanis scouting out potential victims, Ulgulu knew exactly which ones to devour and which ones to leave to Kempfana, and knew exactly how to win against those adventurers more powerful than he.

"Dear Tephanis," Ulgulu purred in an odd sort of grating sound. "Nathak, poor Nathak,"—The goblin didn't miss the implications of that reference—"has informed me that my gnolls have met with disaster."

"And-you-want-me-to-go-and-see-what-happened-to-them, my-master," Tephanis replied. Ulgulu took a moment to decipher the nearly unintelligible string of words, then nodded eagerly.

"Right-away, my-master. Be-back-soon."

Ulgulu felt a slight shiver on his shoulder, but by the time he, or any of the others, realized what Tephanis had said, the heavy drape separating the chamber from the entry room was floating back to its hanging position. One of the goblins poked its head in for just a moment, to see if Kempfana or Ulgulu had summoned it, then returned to its station, thinking the drape's movement a trick of the wind.

Ulgulu roared in laughter again; Kempfana cast him a disgusted glare. Kempfana hated the sprite and would have killed it long ago, except that he couldn't ignore the potential benefits, assuming that Tephanis would work for him once Ulgulu had returned to Gehenna.

Nathak slipped one foot behind the other, meaning to silently retreat from the room. Ulgulu stopped the goblin with a look.

"Your report served me well," the barghest started.

Nathak relaxed, but only for the moment it took Ulgulu's great hand to shoot out, catch the goblin by the throat, and lift Nathak from the floor.

"But it would have served me better if you had taken the time to find out what happened to my gnolls!"

Nathak swooned and nearly fainted, and by the time half of his body had been stuffed into Ulgulu's eager mouth, the spindle-armed goblin wished he had.

* * * * *

"Rub the behind, ease the pain. Switch it brings it back again. Rub the behind, ease the pain. Switch it brings it back again," Liam Thistledown repeated over and over, a litany to take his concentration from the burning sensation beneath his britches, a litany that mischievous Liam knew all too well. This time was different, though, with Liam actually admitting to himself, after a while, that he had indeed run out on his chores.

"But the drizzit was true," Liam growled defiantly.

As if in answer to his statement, the shed's door opened just a crack and Shawno, the second youngest to Liam, and Eleni, the only sister, slipped in.

"Got yourself into it this time," Eleni scolded in her best big-sister voice. "Bad enough you run off when there's work to be done, but coming home with such tales!"

"The drizzit was true," Liam protested, not appreciating Eleni's pseudomothering. Liam could get into enough trouble with just his parents scolding him; he didn't need Eleni's ever-sharp hindsight. "Black as Connor's anvil and with a lion just as black!"

"Quiet, you both," Shawno warned. "If dad's to learn that we're out here talking such, he'll whip the lot of us."

"Drizzit," Eleni huffed doubtfully.

"True!" Liam protested too loudly, bringing a stinging slap from Shawno. The three turned, faces ashen, when the door swung open.

"Get in here!" Eleni whispered harshly, grabbing Flanny, who was a bit older than Shawno but three years Eleni's junior, by the collar and hoisting him into the woodshed. Shawno, always the worrier of the group, quickly poked his head outside to see that no one was watching, then softly closed the door.

"You should not be spying on us!" Eleni protested.

"How'd I know you was in here?" Flanny shot back. "I just came to tease the little one." He looked at Liam, twisted his mouth, and waved his fingers menacingly in the air. "Ware, ware," Flanny crooned. "I am the drizzit, come to eat little boys!"

Liam turned away, but Shawno was not so impressed. "Aw, shut up!" he growled at Flanny, emphasizing his point with a slap on the back of his brother's head. Flanny turned to retaliate, but Eleni stepped between them.

"Stop it!" Eleni cried, so loudly that all four Thistledown children slapped a finger over their lips and said, "Ssssh!"

"The drizzit was true," Liam protested again. "I can prove it–if you're not too scared!"

Liam's three siblings eyed him curiously. He was a notorious fibber, they all knew, but what now would be the gain? Their father hadn't believed Liam, and that was all that mattered as far as the punishment was concerned. Yet Liam was adamant, and his tone told them all that there was substance behind the proclamation.

"How can you prove the drizzit?" Flanny asked.

"We've no chores tomorrow," Liam replied. "We'll go blueberry picking in the mountains."

"Ma and Daddy'd never let us," Eleni put in.

"They would if we can get Connor to go along," said Liam, referring to their oldest brother.

"Connor'd not believe you," Eleni argued.

"But he'd believe you!" Liam replied sharply, drawing another communal "Ssssh!"

"I don't believe you," Eleni retorted quietly. "You're always making things up, always causing trouble and then lying to get out of it!"

Liam crossed his little arms over his chest and stamped one foot impatiently at his sister's continuing stream of logic. "But you will believe me," Liam growled, "if you get Connor to go!"

"Aw, do it," Flanny pleaded to Eleni, though Shawno, thinking of the potential consequences, shook his head.

"So we go up into the mountains," Eleni said to Liam, prompting him to continue and thus revealing her agreement.

Liam smiled widely and dropped to one knee, collecting a pile of sawdust in which to draw a rough map of the area where he had encountered the drizzit. His plan was a simple one, using Eleni, casually picking blueberries, as bait. The four brothers would follow secretly and watch as she feigned a twisted ankle or some other injury. Distress had brought the drizzit before; surely with a pretty young girl as bait, it would bring the drizzit again.

Eleni balked at the idea, not thrilled at being planted as a worm on a hook.

"But you don't believe me anyway," Liam quickly pointed out. His inevitable smile, complete with a gaping hole where a tooth had been knocked out, showed that her own stubbornness had cornered her.

"So I'll do it, then!" Eleni huffed. "And I don't believe in your drizzit, Liam Thistledown! But if the lion is real, and I get chewed, I'll tan you good!" With that, Eleni turned and stormed out of the woodshed.

Liam and Flanny spit in their hands, then turned daring glares on Shawno until he overcame his fears. Then the three brothers brought their palms together in a triumphant, wet slap. Any disagreements between them always seemed to vanish whenever one of them found a way to bother Eleni.

None of them told Connor about their planned hunt for the drizzit. Rather, Eleni reminded him of the many favors he owed her and promised that she would consider the debt paid in full—but only after Liam had agreed to take on Connor's debt if they didn't find the drizzit—if Connor would only take her and the boys blueberry picking.

Connor grumbled and balked, complaining about some shoeing that needed to be done to one of the mares, but he could never resist his little sister's batting blue eyes and wide, bright smile, and Eleni's promise of erasing his considerable debt had sealed his fate. With his parents' blessing, Connor led the Thistledown children up into the mountains, buckets in the children's hands and a crude sword belted on his hip.

*　*　*　*　*

Drizzt saw the ruse coming long before the farmer's young daughter moved out alone in the blueberry patch. He saw, too, the four Thistledown boys, crouched in the shadows of a nearby grove of maple trees, Connor, somewhat less than expertly, brandishing the crude sword.

The youngest had led them here, Drizzt knew. The day before, the drow had witnessed the boy being pulled out into the woodshed. Cries of "drizzit!" had issued forth after every switch, at least at the beginning. Now the stubborn lad wanted to prove his outrageous story.

The blueberry picker jerked suddenly, then fell to the ground and cried out. Drizzt recognized "Help!" as the same distress call the sandy-haired boy had used, and a smile widened across his dark face. By the ridiculous way the girl had fallen, Drizzt saw the game for what it was. The girl was not injured now; she was simply calling out for the drizzit.

With an incredulous shake of his thick white mane, Drizzt started away, but an impulse grabbed at him. He looked back to the blueberry patch, where the girl sat rubbing her ankle, all the while glancing nervously around or back toward her concealed brothers. Something pulled at Drizzt's heartstrings at that moment, an urge he could not resist. How long had he been alone, wandering without companionship? He longed for Belwar at that moment, the svirfneblin who had accompanied him through many trials in the wilds of the Underdark. He longed for Zaknafein, his father and friend. Seeing the interplay between the caring siblings was more than Drizzt Do'Urden could bear.

The time had come for Drizzt to meet his neighbors.

Drizzt hiked the hood of his oversized gnoll cloak up over his head, though the ragged garment did little to hide the truth of his heritage, and bounded across the field. He hoped that if he could at least deflect the girl's initial reaction to seeing him, he might find some way to communicate with her. The hopes were farfetched at best.

"The drizzit!" Eleni gasped under her breath when she saw him coming. She wanted to cry out loud but found no breath; she wanted to run, but her terror held her firmly.

From the copse of trees, Liam spoke for her. "The drizzit!" the boy cried. "I told you so! I told you so!" He looked to his brothers, and Flanny and Shawno were having the expected excited reactions. Connor's face, though, was locked into a look of dread so profound that one glance at it stole the joy from Liam.

"By the gods," the eldest Thistledown son muttered. Connor had adventured with his father and had been trained to spot enemies. He looked now to his three confused brothers and muttered a single word that explained nothing to the inexperienced boys. "Drow."

Drizzt stopped a dozen paces from the frightened girl, the first human woman he had seen up close, and studied her. Eleni was pretty by any race's standards, with huge, soft eyes, dimpled cheeks, and smooth, golden skin. Drizzt knew there would be no fight here. He smiled at Eleni and crossed his arms gently over his chest. "Drizzt," he corrected, pointing to his chest. A movement to the side turned him away from the girl.

"Run, Eleni!" Connor Thistledown cried, waving his sword and bearing down on the drow. "It is a dark elf! A drow! Run for your life!"

Of all that Connor had cried, Drizzt only understood the word "drow." The young man's attitude and intent could not be mistaken, though, for Connor charged straight between Drizzt and Eleni, his sword tip pointed Drizzt's way. Eleni managed to get to her feet behind her brother, but she did not flee as he had instructed. She, too, had heard of the evil dark elves, and she would not leave Connor to face one alone.

"Turn away, dark elf," Connor growled. "I am an expert swordsman and much stronger than you."

Drizzt held his hands out helplessly, not understanding a word.

"Turn away!" Connor yelled.

On an impulse, Drizzt tried to reply in the drow silent code, an intricate language of hand and facial gestures.

"He's casting a spell!" Eleni cried, and she dove down into the blueberries. Connor shrieked and charged.

Before Connor even knew of the counter, Drizzt grabbed him by the forearm, used his other hand to twist the boy's wrist and take away the sword, spun the crude weapon three times over Connor's head, flipped it in his slender hand, then handed it, hilt first, back to the boy.

Drizzt held his arms out wide and smiled. In drow custom, such a show of superiority without injuring the opponent invariably signaled a desire for friendship. To the oldest son of farmer Bartholemew Thistledown, the drow's blinding display brought only awe-inspired terror.

Connor stood, mouth agape, for a long moment. His sword fell from his hand, but he didn't notice; his pants, soiled, clung to his thighs, but he didn't notice.

A scream erupted from somewhere within Connor. He grabbed Eleni, who joined in his scream, and they fled back to the grove to collect the others, then farther, running until they crossed the threshold of their own home.

Drizzt was left, his smile fast fading and his arms out wide, standing all alone in the blueberry patch.

*   *   *   *   *

A set of dizzily darting eyes had watched the exchange in the blueberry patch with more than a casual interest. The unexpected appearance of a dark elf, particularly one wearing a gnoll cloak, had answered many questions for Tephanis. The quickling sleuth had already examined the gnoll corpses but simply could not reconcile the gnolls' fatal wounds with the crude weapons usually wielded by the simple village farmers. Seeing the magnificent twin scimitars so casually belted on the dark elf's hips and the ease with which the dark elf had dispatched the farm boy, Tephanis knew the truth.

The dust trail left by the quickling would have confused the best rangers in the Realms. Tephanis, never a straightforward sprite, zipped up the mountain trails, spinning circuits around some trees, running up and down the sides of others, and generally doubling, even tripling, his route. Distance never bothered Tephanis; he stood before the purple-skinned barghest whelp even before Drizzt, considering the implications of the disastrous meeting, had left the blueberry patch.

❧ 4 ❧

WORRIES

Farmer Bartholemew Thistledown's perspective changed considerably when Connor, his oldest son, renamed Liam's "drizzit" a dark elf. Farmer Thistledown had spent his entire forty-five years in Maldobar, a village fifty miles up the Dead Orc River north of Sundabar. Bartholemew's father had lived here, and his father's father before him. In all that time, the only news any Farmer Thistledown had ever heard of dark elves was the tale of a suspected drow raid on a small settlement of wild elves a hundred miles to the north, in Coldwood. That raid, if it was even perpetrated by the drow, had occurred more than a decade before.

Lack of personal experience with the drow race did not diminish Farmer Thistledown's fears at hearing his children's tale of the encounter in the blueberry patch. Connor and Eleni, two trusted sources old enough to keep their wits about them in a time of crisis, had viewed the elf up close, and they held no doubts about the color of his skin.

"The only thing I can't rightly figure," Bartholemew told Benson Delmo, the fat and cheerful mayor of Maldobar and several other farmers gathered at his house that night, "is why this drow let the children go free. I'm no expert on the ways of dark elves, but I've heard tell enough about them to expect a different sort of action."

"Perhaps Connor fared better in his attack than he believed," Delmo piped in tactfully. They had all heard the tale of Connor's disarming; Liam and the other Thistledown children, except for poor Connor, of course, particularly enjoyed retelling that part.

As much as he appreciated the mayor's vote of confidence, though, Connor shook his head emphatically at the suggestion. "He took me," Connor admitted. "Maybe I was too surprised at the sight of him, but he took me—clean."

"And no easy feat," Bartholemew put in, deflecting any forthcoming snickers from the gruff crowd. "We've all seen Connor at fighting. Just last winter, he took down three goblins and the wolves they were riding!"

"Calm, good Farmer Thistledown," the mayor offered. "We've no doubts of your son's prowess."

"I've my doubts about the truth o' the foe!" put in Roddy McGristle, a bear-sized and bear-hairy man, the most battle-seasoned of the group. Roddy spent more time up in the mountains than tending his farm, a recent endeavor he didn't particularly enjoy, and whenever someone offered a bounty on orc ears, Roddy invariably collected the largest portion of the coffers, often larger than the rest of the town combined.

"Put yer neck hairs down," Roddy said to Connor as the boy began to rise, a sharp protest obviously forthcoming. "I know what ye says ye seen, and I believe that ye seen what ye says. But ye called it a drow, an' that title carries more than ye can begin to know. If it was a drow ye found, my guess's that yerself an' yer kin'd be lying dead right now in that there blueberry patch. No, not a drow, by my guess, but there's other things in them mountains could do what ye says this thing did."

"Name them," Bartholemew said crossly, not appreciating the doubts Roddy had cast over his son's story. Bartholemew didn't much like Roddy anyway. Farmer Thistledown kept a respectable family, and every time crude and loud Roddy McGristle came to pay a visit, it took Bartholemew and his wife many days to remind the children, particularly Liam, about proper behavior.

Roddy just shrugged, taking no offense at Bartholemew's tone. "Goblin, troll—might be a wood elf that's seen too much o' the sun." His laughter, erupting after the last statement, rolled over the group, belittling their seriousness.

"Then how do we know for sure," said Delmo.

"We find out by finding it," Roddy offered. "Tomorrow mornin'," —he pointed around at each man sitting at Bartholemew's table—"we go out an' see what we can see." Considering the impromptu meeting at an end, Roddy slammed his hands down on the table and pushed himself to his feet. He looked back before he got to the farmhouse door, though, and cast an exaggerated wink and a nearly toothless smile back at the group. "And, boys," he said, "don't be forgettin' yer weapons!"

Roddy's cackle rolled back in on the group long after the rough-edged mountain man had departed.

"We could call in a ranger," one of the other farmers offered hopefully as the dispirited group began to depart. "I heard there's one in Sundabar, one of Lady Alustriel's sisters."

"A bit too early for that," Mayor Delmo answered, defeating any optimistic smiles.

"Is it ever too early when drow are involved?" Bartholemew quickly put in.

The mayor shrugged. "Let us go with McGristle," he replied. "If anyone can find some truth up in the mountains, it's him." He tactfully turned to Connor. "I believe your tale, Connor. Truly I do. But we've got to know for sure before we put out a call for such distinguished assistance as a sister of the Lady of Silverymoon."

The mayor and the rest of the visiting farmers departed, leaving Bartholemew, his father, Markhe, and Connor alone in the Thistledown kitchen.

"Wasn't no goblin or wood elf," Connor said in a low tone that hinted at both anger and embarrassment.

Bartholemew patted his son on the back, never doubting him.

* * * * *

Up in a cave in the mountains, Ulgulu and Kempfana, too, spent a night of worry over the appearance of a dark elf.

"If he's a drow, then he's an experienced adventurer," Kempfana offered to his larger brother. "Experienced enough, perhaps, to send Ulgulu into maturity."

"And back to Gehenna!" Ulgulu finished for his conniving brother. "You do so dearly desire to see me depart."

"You, too, hope for the day when you may return to the smoking rifts," Kempfana reminded him.

Ulgulu snarled and did not reply. The appearance of a dark elf prompted many considerations and fears beyond Kempfana's simple statement of logic. The barghests, like all intelligent creatures on nearly every plane of existence, knew of the drow and maintained a healthy respect for the race. While one drow might not be too much of a problem, Ulgulu knew that a dark elf war party, perhaps even an army, could prove disastrous. The whelps were not invulnerable. The human village had provided easy pickings for the barghest whelps and might continue to do so for some time if Ulgulu and Kempfana were careful about their attacks. But if a band of dark elves showed up, those easy kills could disappear quite suddenly.

"This drow must be dealt with," Kempfana remarked. "If he is a scout, then he must not return to report."

Ulgulu snapped a cold glare on his brother, then called to his quickling. "Tephanis," he cried, and the quickling was upon his shoulder before he had even finished the word.

"You-need-me-to-go-and-kill-the-drow, my-master," the quickling replied. "I-understand-what-you-need-me-to-do!"

"No!" Ulgulu shouted immediately, sensing that the quickling intended to go right out. Tephanis was halfway to the door by the time Ulgulu finished the syllable, but the quickling returned to Ulgulu's shoulder before the last note of the shout had died away.

"No," Ulgulu said again, more easily. "There may be a gain in the drow's appearance."

Kempfana read Ulgulu's evil grin and understood his brother's intent. "A new enemy for the townspeople," the smaller whelp reasoned. "A new enemy to cover Ulgulu's murders?"

"All things can be turned to advantage," the big, purple-skinned barghest replied wickedly, "even the appearance of a dark elf." Ulgulu turned back to Tephanis.

"You-wish-to-learn-more-of-the-drow, my-master," Tephanis spouted excitedly.

"Is he alone?" Ulgulu asked. "Is he a forward scout to a larger group, as we fear, or a lone warrior? What are his intentions toward the townspeople?"

"He-could-have-killed-the-children," Tephanis reiterated. "I-guess-him-to-desire-friendship."

"I know," Ulgulu snarled. "You have made those points before. Go now and learn more! I need more than your guess, Tephanis, and by all accounts, a drow's actions rarely hint at his true intent!"

Tephanis skipped down from Ulgulu's shoulder and paused, expecting further instructions.

"Indeed, dear Tephanis," Ulgulu purred. "Do see if you can appropriate one of the drow's weapons for me. It would prove usef—" Ulgulu stopped when he noticed the flutter in the heavy curtain blocking the entry room.

"An excitable little sprite," Kempfana noted.

"But with his uses," Ulgulu replied, and Kempfana had to nod in agreement.

* * * * *

Drizzt saw them coming from a mile away. Ten armed farmers followed the young man he had met in the blueberry patch on the previous day. Though they talked and joked, the set of their stride was determined and their weapons were prominently displayed, obviously ready to be put to use. Even more insidious, walking to the side of the main band came a barrel-chested, grim-faced man wrapped in thick skins, brandishing a finely crafted axe and leading two large and snarling yellow dogs on thick chains.

Drizzt wanted to make further contact with the villagers, wanted dearly to continue the events he had set in motion the previous day and learn if he might have, at long last, found a place he could call home, but this coming encounter, he realized, was not the place to make such gains. If the farmers found him, there would surely be trouble, and while Drizzt wasn't too worried for his own safety against the ragged band, even considering the grim-faced fighter, he did fear that one of the farmers might get hurt.

Drizzt decided that his mission this day was to avoid the group and to deflect their curiosity. The drow knew the perfect diversion to accomplish those goals. He set the onyx figurine on the ground before him and called to Guenhwyvar.

A buzzing noise off to the side, followed by the sudden rustle of brush, distracted the drow for just a moment as the customary mist swirled around the figurine. Drizzt saw nothing ominous approaching, though, and quickly dismissed it. He had more pressing problems, he thought.

When Guenhwyvar arrived, Drizzt and the cat moved down the trail beyond the blueberry patch, where Drizzt guessed that the farmers would begin their hunt. His plan was simple: He would let the farmers mill about the area for a while, let the farmer's son retell his story of the encounter. Guenhwyvar then would make an appearance along the edge of the patch and lead the group on a futile chase. The black-furred panther might cast some doubts on the farm boy's tale; possibly the older men would assume that the children had encountered the cat and not a dark elf and that their imaginations had supplied the rest of the details. It was a gamble, Drizzt knew, but, at the very least, Guenhwyvar would cast some doubts about the existence of the dark elf and would get this hunting party away from Drizzt for a while.

The farmers arrived at the blueberry patch on schedule, a few grim-faced and battle-ready but the majority of the group talking casually in conversations filled with laughter. They found the discarded sword, and Drizzt watched, nodding his head, as the farmer's son played through the events of the previous day. Drizzt noticed, too, that the large axe-wielder, listening to the story halfheartedly, circled the group with his dogs, pointing at various spots in the patch and coaxing the dogs to sniff about. Drizzt had no practical experience with dogs, but he knew that many creatures had superior senses and could be used to aid in a hunt.

"Go, Guenhwyvar," the drow whispered, not waiting for the dogs to get a clear scent.

The great panther loped silently down the trail and took up a position in one of the trees in the same grove where the boys had hidden the previous day. Guenhwyvar's sudden roar silenced the group's growing conversation in an instant, all heads spinning to the trees.

The panther leaped out into the patch, shot right past the stunned humans, and darted across the rising rocks of the mountain slopes. The farmers hooted and took up pursuit, calling for the man with the dogs to take the lead. Soon the whole group, dogs baying wildly, moved off and Drizzt went down into the grove near the blueberry patch to consider the day's events and his best course of action.

He thought that a buzzing noise followed him, but he passed it off as the hum of an insect.

* * * * *

By his dogs' confused actions, it didn't take Roddy McGristle long to figure out that the panther was not the same creature that had left the scent in the blueberry patch. Furthermore, Roddy realized that his ragged companions, particularly the obese mayor, even with his aid, had little chance of catching the great cat; the panther could spring across ravines that would take the farmers many minutes to circumvent.

"Go on!" Roddy told the rest of the group. "Chase the thing along this course. I'll take my dogs'n go far to the side and cut the thing off, turn it back to ye!" The farmers hooted their accord and bounded away, and Roddy pulled back the chains and turned his dogs aside.

The dogs, trained for the hunt, wanted to go on, but their master had another route in mind. Several thoughts bothered Roddy at that moment. He had been in these mountains for thirty years but had never seen, or even heard of, such a cat. Also, though the panther easily could have left its pursuers far behind, it always seemed to appear out in the open not too far away, as though it was leading the farmers on. Roddy knew a diversion when he saw it, and he had a good guess of where the perpetrator might be hiding. He muzzled the dogs to keep them silent and headed back the way he had come, back to the blueberry patch.

*　*　*　*　*

Drizzt rested against a tree in the shadows of the thick copse and wondered how he might further his exposure to the farmers without causing any more panic among them. In his days of watching the single farm family, Drizzt had become convinced that he could find a place among the humans, of this or of some other settlement, if only he could convince them that his intentions were not dangerous.

A buzz to Drizzt's left brought him abruptly from his contemplations. Quickly he drew his scimitars, then something flashed by him, too fast for him to react. He cried out at a sudden pain in his wrist, and his scimitar was pulled from his grasp. Confused, Drizzt looked down to his wound, expecting to see an arrow or crossbow bolt stuck deep into his arm.

The wound was clean and empty. A high-pitched laughter spun Drizzt to the right. There stood the sprite, Drizzt's scimitar casually slung over one shoulder, nearly touching the ground behind the diminutive creature, and a dagger, dripping blood, in his other hand.

Drizzt stayed very still, trying to guess the thing's next move. He had never seen a quickling, or even heard of the uncommon creatures, but he already had a good idea of his speedy opponent's advantage. Before the drow could form any plan to defeat the quickling, though, another nemesis showed itself.

Drizzt knew as soon as he heard the howl that his cry of pain had revealed him. The first of Roddy McGristle's snarling hounds crashed through the brush, charging in low at the drow. The second, a few running strides behind the first, came in high, leaping toward Drizzt's throat.

This time, though, Drizzt was the quicker. He slashed down with his remaining scimitar, cutting the first dog's head and bashing its skull. Without hesitation, Drizzt threw himself backward, reversing his grip on the blade and bringing it up above his face, in line with the leaping dog. The scimitar's hilt locked fast against the tree trunk, and the dog, unable to turn in its flight, drove hard into the set weapon's other end, impaling itself through the throat and chest. The wrenching impact tore the scimitar from Drizzt's hand, and dog and blade bounced away into some scrub to the side of the tree.

Drizzt had barely recovered when Roddy McGristle burst in.

"Ye killed my dogs!" the huge mountain man roared, chopping Bleeder, his large, battle-worn axe, down at the drow's head. The cut came deceptively swiftly, but Drizzt managed to dodge to the side. The drow couldn't understand a word of McGristle's continuing stream of expletives, and he knew that the burly man would not understand a word of any explanations Drizzt might try to offer.

Wounded and unarmed, Drizzt's only defense was to continue to dodge away. Another swipe nearly caught him, cutting through his gnoll cloak, but he sucked in his stomach, and the axe skipped off his fine chain mail. Drizzt danced to the side, toward a tight cluster of smaller trees, where he believed his greater agility might give him some advantage. He had to try to tire the enraged human, or at least make the man reconsider his brutal attack. McGristle's ire did not lessen, though. He charged right after Drizzt, snarling and swinging with every step.

Drizzt now saw the shortcomings of his plan. While he might keep away from the large human's bulky body in the tightly packed trees, McGristle's axe could dive between them quite deftly.

The mighty weapon came in from the side at shoulder level. Drizzt dropped flat down on the ground desperately, narrowly avoiding death. McGristle couldn't slow his swing in time, and the heavy—and heavily enscorceled—weapon smashed into the four-inch trunk of a young maple, felling the tree.

The tightening angle of the buckling trunk held Roddy's axe fast. Roddy grunted and tried to tear the weapon free, and did not realize his peril until the last minute. He managed to jump away from the main weight of the trunk but was buried under the maple's canopy. Branches ripped across his face and the side of his head forming a web around him and pinning him tightly to the ground. "Damn ye, drow!" McGristle roared, shaking futilely at his natural prison.

Drizzt crawled away, still clutching his wounded wrist. He found his remaining scimitar, buried to the hilt in the unfortunate dog. The sight pained Drizzt; he knew the value of animal companions. It took him several heartsick moments to pull the blade free, moments made even more dramatic by the other dog, which, merely stunned, was beginning to stir once again.

"Damn ye, drow!" McGristle roared again.

Drizzt understood the reference to his heritage, and he could guess the rest. He wanted to help the fallen man, thinking that he might make some inroads on opening some more civilized communication, but he didn't think that the awakening dog would be so ready to lend a paw. With a final glance around for the sprite that had started this whole thing, Drizzt dragged himself out of the grove and fled into the mountains.

*　*　*　*　*

"We should've got the thing!" Bartholemew Thistledown grumbled as the troupe returned to the blueberry patch. "If

McGristle had come in where he said he would, we'd've gotten the cat for sure! Where is that dog pack leader, anyhow?"

An ensuing roar of "Drow! Drow!" from the maple grove answered Bartholemew's question. The farmers rushed over to find Roddy still helplessly pinned by the felled maple tree.

"Damned drow!" Roddy bellowed. "Killed my dog! Damned drow!" He reached for his left ear when his arm was free but found that the ear was no longer attached. "Damned drow!' he roared again.

Connor Thistledown let everyone see the return of his pride at the confirmation of his oft-doubted tale, but the eldest Thistledown child was the only one pleased at Roddy's unexpected proclamation. The other farmers were older than Connor; they realized the grim implications of having a dark elf haunting the region.

Benson Delmo, wiping sweat from his forehead, made little secret of how he stood on the news. He turned immediately to the farmer by his side, a younger man known for his prowess in raising and riding horses. "Get to Sundabar," the mayor ordered. "Find us a ranger straightaway!"

In a few minutes, Roddy was pulled free. By this time, his wounded dog had rejoined him, but the knowledge that one of his prized pets had survived did little to calm the rough man.

"Damned drow!" Roddy roared for perhaps the thousandth time, wiping the blood from his cheek. "I'm gonna get me a damned drow!" He emphasized his point by slamming Bleeder, one-handed, into the trunk of another nearby maple, nearly felling that one as well.

❦ 5 ❦

The Stalk of Doom

The goblin guards dove to the side as mighty Ulgulu tore through the curtain and exited the cave complex. The open, crisp air of the chill mountain night felt good to the barghest, better still when Ulgulu thought of the task before him. He looked to the scimitar that Tephanis had delivered, the crafted weapon appearing tiny in Ulgulu's huge, dark-skinned hand.

Ulgulu unconsciously dropped the weapon to the ground. He didn't want to use it this night; the barghest wanted to put his own deadly weapons—claws and teeth—to use, to taste his victims and devour their life essence so that he could become stronger. Ulgulu was an intelligent creature, though, and his rationale quickly overruled the base instincts that so desired the taste of blood. There was purpose in this night's work, a method that promised greater gains and the elimination of the very real threat that the dark elf's unexpected appearance posed.

With a guttural snarl, a small protest from Ulgulu's base urges, the barghest grabbed the scimitar again and pounded down the mountainside, covering long distances with each stride. The beast stopped on the edge of a ravine, where a single narrow trail wound down along the sheer facing of the cliff. It would take him many minutes to scale down the dangerous trail.

But Ulgulu was hungry.

Ulgulu's consciousness fell back into itself, focusing on that spot of his being that fluctuated with magical energy. He was not a creature of the Material Plane, and extra-planar creatures inevitably brought with them powers that would seem magical to creatures of the host plane. Ulgulu's eyes glowed orange with excitement when he emerged from his trance just a few moments later. He peered down the cliff, visualizing a spot on the flat ground below, perhaps a quarter of a mile away.

A shimmering, multicolored door appeared before Ulgulu, hanging in the air beyond the lip of the ravine. His laughter sounding more like a roar, Ulgulu pushed open the door and found, just beyond its threshold, the spot he had visualized. He moved through, circumventing the material distance to the ravine's floor with a single extradimensional step.

Ulgulu ran on, down the mountain and toward the human village, ran on eagerly to set the gears of his cruel plan turning.

As the barghest approached the lowest mountain slopes, he again found that magical corner of his mind. Ulgulu's strides slowed, then the creature stopped altogether, jerking spasmodically and gurgling indecipherably. Bones ground together with popping noises, skin ripped and reformed, darkening nearly to black.

When Ulgulu started away again, his strides—the strides of a dark elf—were not so long.

* * * * *

Bartholemew Thistledown sat with his father, Markhe, and his oldest son that evening in the kitchen of the lone farmhouse on the western outskirts of Maldobar. Bartholemew's wife and mother had gone out to the barn to settle the animals for the night, and the four youngest children were safely tucked into their beds in the small room off the kitchen.

On a normal night the rest of the Thistledown family, all three generations, would also be snugly snoring in their beds, but Bartholemew feared that many nights would pass before any semblance of normalcy returned to the quiet farm. A dark elf had been spotted in the area, and while Bartholemew wasn't convinced that this stranger meant harm—the drow easily could have killed Connor and the other children—he knew that the drow's appearance would cause a stir in Maldobar for quite some time.

"We could get back to the town proper," Connor offered. "They'd find us a place, and all of Maldobar'd stand behind us then."

"Stand behind us?" Bartholemew responded with sarcasm. "And would they be leaving their farms each day to come out here and help us keep up with our work? Which of them, do ye think, might ride out here each night to tend to the animals?"

Connor's head drooped at his father's berating. He slipped one hand to the hilt of his sword, reminding himself that he was no child. Still, Connor was silently grateful for the supporting hand his grandfather casually dropped on his shoulder.

"Ye've got to think, boy, before ye make such calls," Bartholemew continued, his tone mellowing as he began to realize the profound effect his harsh words had on his son. "The farm's yer lifeblood, the only thing that matters."

"We could send the little ones," Markhe put in. "The boy's got a right to be fearing, with a dark elf about and all."

Bartholemew turned away and resignedly dropped his chin into his palm. He hated the thought of breaking apart the family. Family was their source of strength, as it had been through five generations of Thistledowns and beyond. Yet, here Bartholemew was berating Connor, even though the boy had spoken only for the good of the family.

"I should have thought better, Dad," he heard Connor whisper, and he knew that his own pride could not hold out against the realization of Connor's pain. "I am sorry."

"Ye needn't be," Bartholemew replied, turning back to the others. "I'm the one should apologize. All of us got our neck hairs up with this dark elf about. Ye're right in yer thinking, Connor. We're too far out here to be safe."

As if in answer came a sharp crack of breaking wood and

a muffled cry from outside the house, from the direction of the barn. In that single horrible moment, Bartholemew Thistledown realized that he should have come to his decision earlier, when the revealing light of day still offered his family some measure of protection.

Connor reacted first, running to the door and throwing it open. The farmyard was deathly quiet; not the chirp of a cricket disturbed the surrealistic scene. A silent moon loomed low in the sky, throwing long and devious shadows from every fencepost and tree. Connor watched, not daring to breathe, through the passing of a second that seemed like an hour.

The barn door creaked and toppled from its hinges. A dark elf walked out into the farmyard.

Connor shut the door and fell back against it, needing its tangible support. "Ma," he breathed to the startled faces of his father and grandfather. "Drow."

The older Thistledown men hesitated, their minds whirling through the tumult of a thousand horrible notions. They simultaneously leaped from their seats, Bartholemew going for a weapon and Markhe moving toward Connor and the door.

Their sudden action freed Connor from his paralysis. He pulled the sword from his belt and swung the door open, meaning to rush out and face the intruder.

A single spring of his powerful legs had brought Ulgulu right up to the farmhouse door. Connor charged over the threshold blindly, slammed into the creature—which only appeared like a slender drow—and bounced back, stunned, into the kitchen. Before any of the men could react, the scimitar slammed down onto the top of Connor's head with all the strength of the barghest behind it, nearly splitting the young man in half.

Ulgulu stepped unhindered into the kitchen. He saw the old man—the lesser remaining enemy—reaching out for him, and called upon his magical nature to defeat the attack. A wave of imparted emotion swept over Markhe Thistledown, a wave of despair and terror so great that he could not combat it. His wrinkled mouth shot open in a silent scream and he staggered backward, crashing into a wall and clutching helplessly at his chest.

Bartholemew Thistledown's charge carried the weight of unbridled rage behind it. The farmer growled and gasped unintelligible sounds as he lowered his pitchfork and bore down on the intruder that had murdered his son.

The slender, assumed frame that held the barghest did not diminish Ulgulu's gigantic strength. As the pitchfork's tips closed the last inches to the creature's chest, Ulgulu slapped a single hand on the weapon's shaft. Bartholemew stopped in his tracks, the butt end of the pitchfork driving hard into his belly, blowing away his breath.

Ulgulu raised his arm quickly, lifting Bartholemew clear off the floor and slamming the farmer's head into a ceiling beam with enough force to break his neck. The barghest casually tossed Bartholemew and his pitiful weapon across the kitchen and stalked over to the old man.

Perhaps Markhe saw him coming; perhaps the old man was too torn by pain and anguish to register any events in the room. Ulgulu moved to him and opened his mouth wide. He wanted to devour the old man, to feast on this one's life force as he had with the younger woman out in the barn. Ulgulu had lamented his actions in the barn as soon as the ecstasy of the kill had faded. Again the barghest's rationale displaced his base urges. With a frustrated snarl, Ulgulu drove the scimitar into Markhe's chest, ending the old man's pain.

Ulgulu looked around at his gruesome work, lamenting that he had not feasted on the strong young farmers but reminding himself of the greater gains his actions this night would yield. A confused cry led him to the side room, where the children slept.

*　*　*　*　*

Drizzt came down from the mountains tentatively the next day. His wrist, where the sprite had stabbed him, throbbed, but the wound was clean and Drizzt was confident that it would heal. He crouched in the brush on the hillside behind the Thistledown farm, ready to try another meeting with the children. Drizzt had seen too much of the human community, and had spent too much time alone, to give up. This was where he intended to make his home if he could get beyond the obvious prejudicial barriers, personified most keenly by the large man with the snarling dogs.

From this angle, Drizzt couldn't see the blasted barn door, and all appeared as it should on the farm in the predawn glow.

The farmers did not come out with the sun, however, and always before they had been out no later than its arrival. A rooster crowed and several animals shuffled around the barnyard, but the house remained silent. Drizzt knew this was unusual, but he figured that the encounter in the mountains on the previous day had sent the farmers into hiding. Possibly the family had left the farm altogether, seeking the shelter of the larger cluster of houses in the village proper. The thoughts weighed heavily on Drizzt; again he had disrupted the lives of those around him simply by showing his face. He remembered Blingdenstone, the city of svirfneblin gnomes, and the tumult and potential danger his appearance had brought to them.

The sunny day brightened, but a chill breeze blew down off the mountains. Still not a person stirred in the farmyard or within the house, as far as Drizzt could tell. The drow watched it all, growing more concerned with each passing second.

A familiar buzzing noise shook Drizzt from his contemplations. He drew his lone scimitar and glanced around. He wished he could call Guenhwyvar, but not enough time had passed since the cat's last visit. The panther needed to rest in its astral home for another day before it would be strong enough to walk beside Drizzt. Seeing nothing in his immediate area, Drizzt moved between the trunks of two large trees, a more defensible position against the sprite's blinding speed.

The buzzing was gone an instant later, and the sprite was nowhere to be seen. Drizzt spent the rest of that day moving about the brush, setting trip wires and digging shallow pits. If he and the sprite were to battle again, the drow was determined to change the outcome.

The lengthening shadows and crimson western sky brought Drizzt's attention back to the Thistledown farm. No candles were lighted within the farmhouse to defeat the deepening gloom.

Drizzt grew ever more concerned. The return of the nasty sprite had poignantly reminded him of the dangers in the region, and with the continuing inactivity in the farmyard, a fear budded within him, took root, and quickly grew into a sense of dread.

Twilight darkened into night. The moon rose and climbed steadily into the eastern sky.

Still not a candle burned in the house, and not a sound came through the darkened windows.

Drizzt slipped out of the brush and darted across the short back field. He had no intentions of getting close to the house; he just wanted to see what he might learn. Perhaps the horses and the farmer's small wagon would be gone, lending evidence to Drizzt's earlier suspicion that the farmers had taken refuge in the village.

When he came around the side of the barn and saw the broken door, Drizzt knew instinctively that this was not the case. His fears grew with every step. He peered through the barn door and was not surprised to see the wagon sitting in the middle of the barn and the stalls full of horses.

To the side of the wagon, though, lay the older woman, crumbled and covered in her own dried blood. Drizzt went to her and knew at once that she was dead, killed by some sharp-edged weapon. Immediately his thoughts went to the evil sprite and his own missing scimitar. When he found the other corpse, behind the wagon, he knew that some other monster, something more vicious and powerful, had been involved. Drizzt couldn't even identify this second, half-eaten body.

Drizzt ran from the barn to the farmhouse, throwing out all caution. He found the bodies of the Thistledown men in the kitchen and, to his ultimate horror, the children lying too still in their beds. Waves of revulsion and guilt rolled over the drow when he looked upon the young bodies. The word "drizzit" chimed painfully in his mind at the sight of the sandy-haired lad.

The tumult of Drizzt's emotions were too much for him. He covered his ears against that damning word, "drizzit!" but it echoed endlessly, haunting him, reminding him.

Unable to find his breath, Drizzt ran from the house. If he had searched the room more carefully, he would have found, under the bed, his missing scimitar, snapped in half and left for the villagers.

❧ Part 2 ❧

The Ranger

Does anything in all the world force a heavier weight upon one's shoulders than guilt? I have felt the burden often, have carried it over many steps, on long roads.

Guilt resembles a sword with two edges. On the one hand, it cuts for justice, imposing practical morality upon those who fear it. Guilt, the consequence of conscience, is what separates the goodly persons from the evil. Given a situation that promises gain, most drow can kill another, kin or otherwise, and walk away carrying no emotional burden at all. The drow assassin might fear retribution but will shed no tears for his victim.

To humans—and to surface elves, and to all of the other goodly races—the suffering imposed by conscience will usually far outweigh any external threats. Some would conclude that guilt—conscience—is the primary difference between the varied races of the Realms. In this regard, guilt must be considered a positive force.

But there is another side to that weighted emotion. Conscience does not always adhere to rational judgment. Guilt is always a self-imposed burden, but is not always rightly imposed. So it was for me along the road from Menzoberranzan to Icewind Dale. I carried out of Menzoberranzan guilt for Zaknafein, my father, sacrificed on my behalf. I carried into Blingdenstone guilt for Belwar Dissengulp, the svirfneblin my brother had maimed. Along the many roads there came many other burdens: Clacker, killed by the monster that hunted for me; the gnolls, slain by my own hand; and the farmers—most painfully—that simple farm family murdered by the barghest whelp.

Rationally I knew that I was not to blame, that the actions were beyond my influence, or in some cases, as with the gnolls, that I had acted properly. But rationale is little defense against the weight of guilt.

In time, bolstered by the confidence of trusted friends, I came to throw off many of those burdens. Others remain and always shall. I accept this as inevitable, and use the weight to guide my future steps.

This, I believe, is the true purpose of conscience.

—Drizzt Do'Urden

❧ 6 ❧

Sundabar

"Oh, enough, Fret," the tall woman said to the white-robed, white-bearded dwarf, batting his hands away. She ran her fingers through her thick, brown hair, messing it considerably.

"Tsk, tsk," the dwarf replied, immediately moving his hands back to the dirty spot on the woman's cloak. He brushed frantically, but the ranger's continual shifting kept him from accomplishing much. "Why, Mistress Falconhand, I do believe that you would do well to consult a few books on proper behavior."

"I just rode in from Silverymoon," Dove Falconhand replied indignantly, tossing a wink to Gabriel, the other fighter in the room, a tall and stern-faced man. "One tends to collect some dirt on the road."

"Nearly a week ago!" the dwarf protested. "You attended the banquet last night in this very cloak!" The dwarf then noticed that in his fuss over Dove's cloak he had smudged his own silken robes, and that catastrophe turned his attention from the ranger.

"Dear Fret," Dove went on, licking a finger and casually rubbing it over the spot on her cloak, "you are the most unusual of attendants."

The dwarf's face went beet red, and he stamped a shiny slipper on the tiled floor. "Attendant?" he huffed. "I should say . . ."

"Then do!" Dove laughed.

"I am the most—one of the most—accomplished sages in the north! My thesis concerning the proper etiquette of ra-

R. A. SALVATORE

cial banquets—"

"Or lack of proper etiquette—" Gabriel couldn't help but interrupt. The dwarf turned on him sourly—"at least where dwarves are concerned," the tall fighter finished with an innocent shrug.

The dwarf trembled visibly and his slippers played a respectable beat on the hard floor.

"Oh, dear Fret," Dove offered, dropping a comforting hand on the dwarf's shoulder and running it along the length of his perfectly trimmed, yellow beard.

"Fred!" the dwarf retorted sharply, pushing the ranger's hand away. "Fredegar!"

Dove and Gabriel looked at each other for one brief, knowing moment, then cried out the dwarf's surname in an explosion of laughter. "Rockcrusher!"

"Fredegar Quilldipper would be more to the point!" Gabriel added. One look at the fuming dwarf told the man that the time had passed for leaving, so he scooped up his pack and darted from the room, pausing only to slip one final wink Dove's way.

"I only desired to help." The dwarf dropped his hands into impossibly deep pockets and his head drooped low.

"So you have!" Dove cried to comfort him.

"I mean, you do have an audience with Helm Dwarffriend," Fret went on, regaining some pride. "One should be proper when seeing the Master of Sundabar."

"Indeed one should," Dove readily agreed. "Yet all I have to wear you see before you, dear Fret, stained and dirtied from the road. I am afraid that I shall not cut a very fine figure in the eyes of Sundabar's master. He and my sister have become such friends." It was Dove's turn to feign a vulnerable pout, and though her sword had turned many a giant into vulture food, the strong ranger could play this game better than most.

"Whatever shall I do?" She cocked her head curiously as she glanced at the dwarf. "Perhaps," she teased. "If only . . ."

Fret's face began to brighten at the hint.

"No," Dove said with a heavy sigh. "I could never impose

so upon you."

Fret verily bounced with glee, clapping his thick hands together. "Indeed you could, Mistress Falconhand! Indeed you could!"

Dove bit her lip to forestall any further demeaning laughter as the excited dwarf skipped out of the room. While she often teased Fret, Dove would readily admit that she loved the little dwarf. Fret had spent many years in Silverymoon, where Dove's sister ruled, and had made many contributions to the famed library there. Fret really was a noted sage, known for his extensive research into the customs of various races, both good and evil, and he was an expert on issues demihuman. He also was a fine composer. How many times, Dove wondered with sincere humility, had she ridden along a mountain trail, whistling a cheery melody composed by this very same dwarf?

"Dear Fret," the ranger whispered under her breath when the dwarf returned, a silken gown draped over one arm—but carefully folded so that it would not drag across the floor!—assorted jewelry and a pair of stylish shoes in his other hand, a dozen pins sticking out from between his pursed lips, and a measuring string looped over one ear. Dove hid her smile and decided to give the dwarf this one battle. She would tiptoe into Helm Dwarf-friend's audience hall in a silken gown, the picture of Ladydom, with the diminutive sage huffing proudly by her side.

All the while, Dove knew, the shoes would pinch and bite at her feet and the gown would find some place to itch where she could not reach. Alas for the duties of station, Dove thought as she stared at the gown and accessories. She looked into Fret's beaming face then and realized that it was worth all the trouble.

Alas for the duties of friendship, she mused.

* * * * *

The farmer had ridden straight through for more than a day; the sighting of a dark elf often had such effects on simple villagers. He had taken two horses out of Maldobar; one he had left a score of miles behind, halfway between the two towns. If he was lucky, he'd find the animal unharmed on the return trip. The second horse, the farmer's prized stallion, was beginning to tire. Still the farmer bent low in the saddle, spurring the steed on. The torches of Sundabar's night watch, high up on the city's thick stone walls, were in sight.

"Stop and speak your name!" came the formal cry from the captain of the gate guards when the rider approached, half an hour later.

* * * * *

Dove leaned on Fret for support as they followed Helm's attendant down the long and decorated corridor to the audience room. The ranger could cross a rope bridge without handrails, could fire her bow with deadly accuracy atop a charging steed, could scramble up a tree in full chain armor, sword and shield in hand. But she could not, for all of her experience and agility, manage the fancy shoes that Fret had squeezed her feet into.

"And this gown," Dove whispered in exasperation, knowing that the impractical garment would split in six or seven places if she had occasion to swing her sword while wearing it, let alone inhaled too abruptly.

Fret looked up at her, wounded.

"This gown is surely the most beautiful . . ." Dove stuttered, careful not to send the tidy dwarf into a tantrum. "Truly I can find no words suitable to my gratitude, dear Fret."

The dwarf's gray eyes shone brightly, though he wasn't sure that he believed a word of it. Either way, Fret figured that Dove cared enough about him to go along with his suggestions, and that fact was all that really mattered to him.

"I beg a thousand pardons, my lady," came a voice from behind. The whole entourage turned to see the captain of the night watch, a farmer by his side, trotting down the somber hallway.

"Good captain!" Fret protested at the violation of protocol. "If you desire an audience with the lady, you must make an introduction in the hall. Then, and only then, and only if the master allows, you may . . ."

Dove dropped a hand on the dwarf's shoulder to silence him. She recognized the urgency etched onto the men's faces, a look the adventuring heroine had seen many times. "Do go on, Captain," she prompted. To placate Fret, she added, "We have a few moments before our audience is set to begin. Master Helm will not be kept waiting."

The farmer stepped forward boldly. "A thousand pardons for myself, my lady," he began, fingering his cap nervously in his hands. "I am but a farmer from Maldobar, a small village north . . ."

"I know of Maldobar," Dove assured him. "Many times I have viewed the place from the mountains. A fine and sturdy community." The farmer brightened at her description. "No harm has befallen Maldobar, I pray."

"Not as yet, my lady," the farmer replied, "but we've sighted trouble, we're not to doubting." He paused and looked to the captain for support. "Drow."

Dove's eyes widened at the news. Even Fret, tapping his foot impatiently throughout the conversation, stopped and took note.

"How many?" Dove asked.

"Only one, as we have seen. We're fearing he's a scout or spy, and up to no good."

Dove nodded her agreement. "Who has seen the drow?"

"Children first," the farmer replied, drawing a sigh from Fret and setting the dwarf's foot impatiently tapping once again.

"Children?" the dwarf huffed.

The farmer's determination did not waver. "Then McGristle saw him," he said, eyeing Dove directly, "and McGristle's seen a lot!"

"What is a McGristle?" Fret huffed.

"Roddy McGristle," Dove answered, somewhat sourly, before the farmer could explain. "A noted bounty hunter and fur trapper."

"The drow killed one of Roddy's dogs," the farmer put in excitedly, "and nearly cut down Roddy! Dropped a tree right on him! He's lost an ear for the experience."

Dove didn't quite understand what the farmer was talking about, but she really didn't need to. A dark elf had been seen and confirmed in the region, and that fact alone set the ranger into motion. She flipped off her fancy shoes and handed them to Fret, then told one of the attendants to go straight off and find her traveling companions and told the other to deliver her regrets to the Master of Sundabar.

"But Lady Falconhand!" Fret cried.

"No time for pleasantries," Dove replied, and Fret could tell by her obvious excitement that she was not too disappointed at canceling her audience with Helm. Already she was wiggling about, trying to open the catch on the back of her magnificent gown.

"Your sister will not be pleased." Fret growled loudly over the tapping of his boot.

"My sister hung up her backpack long ago," Dove retorted, "but mine still wears the fresh dirt of the road!"

"Indeed," the dwarf mumbled, not in a complimentary way.

"Ye mean to come, then?" the farmer asked hopefully.

"Of course," Dove replied. "No reputable ranger could ignore the sighting of a dark elf! My three companions and I will set out for Maldobar this very night, though I beg that you remain here, good farmer. You have ridden hard—it is obvious—and need sleep." Dove glanced around curiously for a moment, then put a finger to her pursed lips.

"What?" the annoyed dwarf asked her.

Dove's face brightened as her gaze dropped down to Fret. "I have little experience with dark elves," she began, "and my companions, to my knowledge, have never dealt with one." Her widening smile set Fret back on his heels.

"Come, dear Fret," Dove purred at the dwarf. Her bare feet slapping conspicuously on the tiled floor, she led Fret, the captain, and the farmer from Maldobar down the hallway to Helm's audience room.

Fret was confused—and hopeful—for a moment by Dove's sudden change of direction. As soon as Dove began talking to Helm, Fret's master, apologizing for the unexpected inconvenience and asking Helm to send along one who might aid in the mission to Maldobar, the dwarf began to understand.

* * * * *

By the time the sun found its way above the eastern horizon the next morning, Dove's party, which included an elven archer and two powerful human fighters, had ridden more than ten miles from Sundabar's heavy gate.

"Ugh!" Fret groaned when the light increased. He rode a sturdy Adbar pony at Dove's side. "See how the mud has soiled my fine clothes! Surely it will be the end of us all! To die filthy on a gods-forsaken road!"

"Pen a song about it," Dove suggested, returning the widening smiles of her other three companions. "The Ballad of the Five Choked Adventurers, it shall be named."

Fret's angry glare lasted only the moment it took Dove to remind him that Helm Dwarf-friend, the Master of Sundabar himself, had commissioned Fret to travel along.

❧ 7 ❧

Simmering Rage

On the same morning that Dove's party left on the road to Maldobar, Drizzt set out on a journey of his own. The initial horror of his gruesome discovery the previous night had not diminished, and the drow feared that it never would, but another emotion had also entered Drizzt's thinking. He could do nothing for the innocent farmers and their children, nothing except avenge their deaths. That thought was not so pleasing to Drizzt; he had left the Underdark behind, and the savagery as well, he had hoped. With the images of the carnage still so horribly clear in his mind, and all alone as he was, Drizzt could look only to his scimitar for justice.

Drizzt took two precautions before he set out on the murderer's trail. First, he crept back down to the farmyard, to the back of the house, where the farmers had placed a broken plowshare. The metal blade was heavy, but the determined drow hoisted it and carried it away without a thought to the discomfort.

Drizzt then called Guenhwyvar. As soon as the panther arrived and took note of Drizzt's scowl, it dropped into an alert crouch. Guenhwyvar had been around Drizzt long enough to recognize that expression and to believe that they would see battle before it returned to its astral home.

They moved off before dawn, Guenhwyvar easily following the barghest's clear trail, as Ulgulu had hoped. Their pace was slow, with Drizzt hindered by the plowshare, but steady, and as soon as Drizzt caught the sound of a distant buzzing noise, he knew he had done right in collecting the cumbersome item.

Still, the remainder of the morning passed without incident. The trail led the companions into a rocky ravine and to the base of a high, uneven cliff. Drizzt feared that he might have to scale the cliff face—and leave the plowshare behind—but soon he spotted a single narrow trail winding up along the wall. The ascending path remained smooth as it wound around sheer bends in the cliff face, blind and dangerous turns. Wanting to use the terrain to his advantage, Drizzt sent Guenhwyvar far ahead and moved along by himself, dragging the plowshare and feeling vulnerable on the open cliff.

That feeling did nothing to quench the simmering fires in Drizzt's lavender eyes, though, which burned clearly from under the low-pulled cowl of his oversized gnoll cloak. If the sight of the ravine looming just to the side unnerved the drow, he needed only to remember the farmers. A short while later, when Drizzt heard the expected buzzing noise from somewhere lower on the narrow trail, he only smiled.

The buzz quickly closed from behind. Drizzt fell back against the cliff wall and snapped out his scimitar, carefully monitoring the time it took the sprite to close.

Tephanis flashed beside the drow, the quickling's little dagger darting and prodding for an opening in the defensive twists of the waving scimitar. The sprite was gone in an instant, moving up ahead of Drizzt, but Tephanis had scored a hit, nicking Drizzt on one shoulder.

Drizzt inspected the wound and nodded gravely, accepting it as a minor inconvenience. He knew he could not defeat the blinding attack, and he knew, too, that allowing this first strike had been necessary for his ultimate victory. A growl on the path up ahead put Drizzt quickly back on alert. Guenhwyvar had met the sprite, and the panther, with flashing paws that could match the quickling's speed, no doubt had turned the thing back around.

Again Drizzt put his back to the wall, monitoring the buzzing approach. Just as the sprite came around the corner, Drizzt jumped out onto the narrow path, his scimitar at the ready. The drow's other hand was less conspicuous and held steady a metal object, ready to tilt it out to block the opening.

The speeding sprite cut back in toward the wall, easily able, as Drizzt realized, to avoid the scimitar. But in his narrow focus on his target, the sprite failed to notice Drizzt's other hand.

Drizzt hardly registered the sprite's movements, but the sudden "Bong!" and the sharp vibrations in his hand as the creature smacked into the plowshare brought a satisfied grin to his lips. He let the plowshare drop and scooped up the unconscious sprite by the throat, holding it clear of the ground. Guenhwyvar bounded around the bend about the same time the sprite shook the dizziness from his sharp-featured head, his long and pointed ears nearly flopping right over the other side of his head with each movement.

"What creature are you?" Drizzt asked in the goblin tongue, the language that had worked for him with the gnoll band. To his surprise, he found that the sprite understood, though his high-pitched, blurred response came too quickly for Drizzt to even begin to understand.

He gave the sprite a quick jerk to silence him, then growled, "One word at a time! What is your name?"

"Tephanis," the sprite said indignantly. Tephanis could move his legs a hundred times a second, but they didn't do him much good while he was suspended in the air. The sprite glanced down to the narrow ledge and saw his small dagger lying next to the dented plowshare.

Drizzt's scimitar moved in dangerously. "Did you kill the farmers?" he asked bluntly. He almost struck in response to the sprite's ensuing chuckle.

"No," Tephanis said quickly.

"Who did?"

"Ulgulu!" the sprite proclaimed. Tephanis pointed up the path and blurted out a stream of excited words. Drizzt managed to make out a few, "Ulgulu . . . waiting . . . dinner," being the most disturbing of them.

Drizzt really didn't know what he would do with the captured sprite. Tephanis was simply too fast for Drizzt to safely handle. He looked to Guenhwyvar, sitting casually a few feet up the path, but the panther only yawned and stretched.

Drizzt was about to come back with another question, to try to figure out where Tephanis fit into the whole scenario, but the cocky sprite decided that he had suffered enough of the encounter. His hands moving too fast for Drizzt to react, Tephanis reached down into his boot, produced another knife, and slashed at Drizzt's already injured wrist.

This time, the cocky sprite had underestimated his opponent. Drizzt could not match the sprite's speed, could not even follow the tiny, darting dagger. As painful as the wounds were, though, Drizzt was too filled with rage to take note. He only tightened his grip on the sprite's collar and thrust his scimitar ahead. Even with such limited mobility, Tephanis was quick enough and nimble enough to dodge, laughing wildly all the while.

The sprite struck back, digging a deeper cut into Drizzt's forearm. Finally Drizzt chose a tactic that Tephanis could not counter, one that took the sprite's advantage away. He slammed Tephanis into the wall, then tossed the stunned creature off the cliff.

* * * * *

Some time later, Drizzt and Guenhwyvar crouched in the brush at the base of a steep, rocky slope. At the top, behind carefully placed bushes and branches, lay a cave, and, every so often, goblin voices rolled out.

Beside the cave, to the side of the sloping ground was a steep drop. Beyond the cave, the mountain climbed on at an even greater angle. The tracks, though they were sometimes scarce on the bare stone, had led Drizzt and Guenhwyvar to this spot; there could be no doubt that the monster who slaughtered the farmers was in the cave.

Drizzt again fought with his decision to avenge the farmers' deaths. He would have preferred a more civilized justice, a lawful court, but what was he to do? He certainly could not go to the human villagers with his suspicions, nor to anyone else. Crouching in the bush, Drizzt thought again of the farmers, of the sandy-haired boy, of the pretty girl, barely a woman, and of the young man he had disarmed in the blueberry patch. Drizzt fought hard to keep his breathing steady. In the wild Underdark he had sometimes given in to his instinctive urges, a darker side of himself that fought with brutal and deadly efficiency, and Drizzt could feel that alter-ego welling within him once again. At first, he tried to sublimate the rage, but then he remembered the lessons he had learned. This darker side was a part of him, a tool for survival, and was not altogether evil.

It was necessary.

Drizzt understood his disadvantage in the situation, however. He had no idea how many enemies he would encounter, or even what type of monsters they might be. He heard goblins, but the carnage at the farmhouse indicated that something much more powerful was involved. Drizzt's good judgment told him to sit and watch, to learn more of his enemies.

Another fleeting instant of remembrance, the scene at the farmhouse, threw that good judgment aside. Scimitar in one hand, the sprite's dagger in another, Drizzt stalked up the stony hill. He didn't slow when he neared the cave, but merely ripped the brush aside and walked straight in.

Guenhwyvar hesitated and watched from behind, confused by the drow's straightforward tactics.

* * * * *

Tephanis felt cool air brushing by his face and thought for a moment that he was enjoying some pleasant dream. The sprite came out of his delusion quickly, though, and realized that he was fast approaching the ground. Fortunately, Tephanis was not far from the cliff. He send his hands and feet spinning rapidly enough to produce a constant humming sound and clawed and kicked at the cliff in an effort to slow his descent. In the meantime, he began the incantations to a levitation spell, possibly the only thing that could save him.

A few agonizingly slow seconds passed before the sprite felt his body buoyed by the spell. He still hit the ground hard, but he realized that his wounds were minor.

Tephanis stood relatively slowly and dusted himself off. His first thought was to go and warn Ulgulu of the approaching drow, but he reconsidered at once. He could not levitate up to the cave complex in time to warn the barghest, and there was only one path up the cliff face—which the drow was on.

Tephanis had no desire to face that one again.

* * * * *

Ulgulu had not tried to cover his tracks at all. The dark elf had served the barghest's needs; now he planned to make a meal of Drizzt, one that might bring him into maturity and allow him to return to Gehenna.

Ulgulu's two goblin guards were not too surprised at Drizzt's entrance. Ulgulu had told them to expect the drow and to simply delay him out in the entry room until the barghest could come and attend to him. The goblins halted their conversation abruptly, dropped their spears in a blocking cross over the curtain, and puffed out their scrawny chests, foolishly following their boss's instructions as Drizzt approached.

"None can go in—" one of them began, but then, in a single swipe of Drizzt's scimitar, both the goblin and its companion staggered down, clutching at their opened throats. The spear barrier fell away and Drizzt never even slowed as he stalked through the curtain.

In the middle of the inner room, the drow saw his enemy. Scarlet-skinned and giant-sized, the barghest waited with crossed arms and a wicked, confident grin.

Drizzt threw the dagger and charged right in behind it. That throw saved the drow's life, for when the dagger passed harmlessly through his enemy's body, Drizzt recognized the trap. He came in anyway, unable to break his momentum, and his scimitar entered the image without finding anything tangible to cut into.

The real barghest was behind the stone throne at the back of the room. Using another power of his considerable magical repertoire, Kempfana had sent an image of himself into the middle of the room to hold the drow in place.

Immediately Drizzt's instincts told him that he had been set up. This was no real monster he faced but an apparition meant to keep him in the open and vulnerable. The room was sparsely furnished; nothing nearby offered any cover.

Ulgulu, levitating above the drow, came down quickly, lighting softly behind him. The plan was perfect and the target was right in place.

Drizzt, his reflexes and muscles trained and honed to fighting perfection, sensed the presence and dove forward into the image as Ulgulu launched a heavy blow. The barghest's huge hand only clipped Drizzt's flowing hair, but that alone nearly ripped the drow's head to the side.

Drizzt half-turned his body as he dove, rolling back to his feet facing Ulgulu. He met a monster even larger than the giant image, but that fact did nothing to intimidate the enraged drow. Like a stretched cord, Drizzt snapped straight back at the barghest. By the time Ulgulu even recovered from his unexpected miss, Drizzt's lone scimitar had poked him three times in the belly and had dug a neat little hole under his chin.

The barghest roared in rage but was not too badly hurt, for Drizzt's drow-made weapon had lost most of its magic in the drow's time on the surface and only magical weapons—such as Guenhwyvar's claws and teeth—could truly harm a creature from Gehenna's rifts.

The huge panther slammed onto the back of Ulgulu's head with enough force to drop the barghest facedown on the floor. Never had Ulgulu felt such pain as Guenhwyvar's claws raked across his head.

Drizzt moved to join in, when he heard a shuffle from the

back of the room. Kempfana came charging out from behind the throne, bellowing in protest.

It was Drizzt's turn to utilize some magic. He threw a globe of darkness in the scarlet-skinned barghest's path, then dove into it himself, crouching on his hands and knees. Unable to slow, Kempfana roared in, stumbled over the braced drow—kicking Drizzt with enough force to blast the air from his lungs—and fell heavily out the other side of the darkness.

Kempfana shook his head to clear it and planted his huge hands to rise. Drizzt was on the barghest's back in no time, hacking away wildly with his vicious scimitar. Blood matted Kempfana's hair by the time he was able to brace himself enough to throw the drow off. He staggered to his feet dizzily and turned to face the drow.

* * * * *

Across the room, Ulgulu crawled and tumbled, rolled and twisted. The panther was too quick and too sleek for the giant's lumbering counters. A dozen gashes scarred Ulgulu's face and now Guenhwyvar had its teeth clamped on the back of the giant's neck and all four paws raking at the giant's back.

Ulgulu had another option, though. Bones crackled and reformed. Ulgulu's scarred face became an elongated snout filled with wicked canine teeth. Thick hair sprouted from all over the giant, fending off Guenhwyvar's claw attacks. Flailing arms became kicking paws.

Guenhwyvar battled a gigantic wolf, and the panther's advantage was short-lived.

* * * * *

Kempfana stalked in slowly, showing Drizzt new respect.

"You killed them all," Drizzt said in the goblin tongue, his voice so utterly cold that it stopped the scarlet-skinned barghest in his tracks.

Kempfana was not a stupid creature. The barghest recognized the explosive rage in this drow and had felt the sharp bite of the scimitar. Kempfana knew better than to walk straight in, so again he called upon his otherworldly skills. In the blink of an orange-burning eye, the scarlet-skinned barghest was gone, stepping through an extradimensional door and reappearing right behind Drizzt.

As soon as Kempfana disappeared, Drizzt instinctively broke to the side. The blow from behind came quicker, though, landing squarely on Drizzt's back and launching him across the room. Drizzt crashed into the base of one wall and came up into a kneel, gasping for his breath.

Kempfana did stalk straight in this time; the drow had dropped his scimitar halfway to the wall, too far away for Drizzt to grasp.

*   *   *   *   *

The great barghest-wolf, nearly twice Guenhwyvar's size, rolled over and straddled the panther. Great jaws snapped near Guenhwyvar's throat and face, the panther batting wildly to hold them at bay. Guenhwyvar could not hope to win an even fight against the wolf. The only advantage the panther retained was mobility. Like a black-shafted arrow, Guenhwyvar darted out from under the wolf and toward the curtain.

Ulgulu howled and gave chase, ripping the curtain down and charging on, toward the waning daylight.

Guenhwyvar came out of the cave as Ulgulu tore through the curtain, pivoted instantly, and leaped straight up to the slopes above the entrance. When the great wolf came out, the panther again crashed down on Ulgulu's back and resumed its raking and slashing.

*   *   *   *   *

"Ulgulu killed the farmers, not I," Kempfana growled as he approached. He kicked Drizzt's scimitar across to the other side of the room. "Ulgulu wants you—you who killed his gnolls. But I shall kill you, drow warrior. I shall feast on your life force so that I may gain in strength!"

Drizzt, still trying to find his breath, hardly heard the words. The only thoughts that occurred to him were the images of the dead farmers, images that gave Drizzt courage. The barghest drew near and Drizzt snapped a vile gaze upon him, a determined gaze not lessened in the least by the drow's obviously desperate situation.

Kempfana hesitated at the sight of those narrowed, burning eyes, and the barghest's delay brought Drizzt all the time he needed. He had fought giant monsters before, most notably hook horrors. Always Drizzt's scimitars had ended those battles, but for his initial strikes, he had, every time, used only his own body. The pain in his back was no match for his mounting rage. He rushed out from the wall, remaining in a crouch, and dove through Kempfana's legs, spinning and catching a hold behind the barghest's knee.

Kempfana, unconcerned, lurched down to grab the squirming drow. Drizzt eluded the giant's grasp long enough to find some leverage. Still, Kempfana accepted the attacks as a mere inconvenience. When Drizzt put the barghest off balance, Kempfana willingly toppled, meaning to crush the wiry little elf. Again Drizzt was too quick for the barghest. He twisted out from under the falling giant, put his feet back under him, and sprinted for the opposite end of the chamber.

"No, you shall not!" Kempfana bellowed, crawling then running in pursuit. Just as Drizzt scooped up his scimitar, giant arms wrapped around him and easily lifted him off the ground.

"Crush you and bite you!" Kempfana roared, and indeed, Drizzt heard one of his ribs crack. He tried to wiggle around to face his foe, then gave up on the notion, concentrating instead on freeing his sword arm.

Another rib snapped; Kempfana's huge arms tightened. The barghest did not want to simply kill the drow, though, realizing the great gains toward maturity he could make by devouring so powerful an enemy, by feeding on Drizzt's life force.

"Bite you, drow." The giant laughed. "Feast!"

Drizzt grasped his scimitar in both hands with strength inspired by the images of the farmhouse. He tore the weapon loose and snapped it straight back over his head. The blade entered Kempfana's open, eager mouth and dove down the monster's throat.

Drizzt twisted it and turned it.

Kempfana whipped about wildly and Drizzt's muscles and joints nearly ripped apart under the strain. The drow had found his focus, though, the scimitar hilt, and he continued to twist and turn.

Kempfana went down heavily, gurgling, and rolled onto Drizzt, trying to squash the life out of him. Pain began to seep into Drizzt's consciousness.

"No!" he cried, grabbing at the image of the sandy-haired boy, slain in his bed. Still Drizzt twisted and turned the blade. The gurgling continued, a wheezing sound of air rising through choking blood. Drizzt knew that this battle was won when the creature above him no longer moved.

Drizzt wanted only to curl up and find his breath but told himself that he was not yet finished. He crawled out from under Kempfana, wiped the blood, his own blood, from his lips, unceremoniously ripped his scimitar free of Kempfana's mouth, and retrieved his dagger.

He knew that his wounds were serious, could prove fatal if he didn't attend to them immediately. His breath continued to come in forced, bloodied gasps. It didn't concern him, though, for Ulgulu, the monster who had killed the farmers, still lived.

* * * * *

Guenhwyvar sprang from the giant wolf's back, again finding a tenuous footing on the steep slope above the cave entrance. Ulgulu spun, snarling, and leaped up at the panther, clawing and raking at the stones in an effort to get higher.

Guenhwyvar leaped out over the barghest-wolf, pivoted immediately, and slashed at Ulgulu's backside. The wolf spun but Guenhwyvar leaped by, again to the slope.

The game of hit-and-run went on for several moments, Guenhwyvar striking, then darting away. Finally, though, the wolf anticipated the panther's dodge. Ulgulu brought the leaping panther down in his massive jaws. Guenhwyvar squirmed and tore free, but came up near the steep gorge. Ulgulu hovered over the cat, blocking any escape.

Drizzt exited the cave as the great wolf bore down, pushing Guenhwyvar back. Pebbles rolled out into the gorge; the panther's back legs slipped and then clawed back, trying to find a hold. Even mighty Guenhwyvar could not hold out against the weight and strength of the barghest-wolf, Drizzt knew.

Drizzt saw immediately that he could not get the great wolf off Guenhwyvar in time. He pulled out the onyx figurine and tossed it near the combatants. "Be gone, Guenhwyvar!" he commanded.

Guenhwyvar normally would not desert its master in a time of such danger, but the panther understood what Drizzt had in mind. Ulgulu bore in powerfully, determinedly driving Guenhwyvar from the ledge.

Then the beast was pushing only intangible vapors. Ulgulu lurched forward and scrambled wildly, kicking more stones and the onyx figurine into the gorge. Overbalanced, the wolf could not find a hold, and then Ulgulu was falling.

Bones popped again, and the canine fur thinned; Ulgulu could not enact a levitation spell in his canine form. Desperate, the barghest concentrated, reaching for his goblinoid form. The wolf maw shortened into a flat-featured face; paws thickened and reformed into arms.

The half-transformed creature didn't make it, but instead cracked into the stone.

Drizzt stepped off the ledge and into a levitation spell, moving down slowly and close to the rocky wall. As it had before, the spell soon died away. Drizzt bounced and clawed through the last twenty feet of the fall, coming to a hard stop at the rocky bottom. He saw the barghest twitching only a few feet away and tried to rise in defense, but darkness overwhelmed him.

*   *   *   *   *

Drizzt could not know how many hours had passed when a thunderous roar awakened him some time later. It was dark now and a cloudy night. Slowly the memories of the encounter came back to the dazed and injured drow. To his relief, he saw that Ulgulu lay still on the stone beside him, half a goblin and half a wolf, obviously quite dead.

A second roar, back up by the cave, turned the drow toward the ledge high above him. There stood Lagerbottoms, the hill giant, returned from a hunting trip and outraged by the carnage he had found.

Drizzt knew as soon as he managed to crawl to his feet that he could not fight another battle this day. He searched around for a moment, found the onyx figurine, and dropped it into his pouch. He wasn't too concerned for Guenhwyvar. He had seen the panther through worse calamities—caught in the explosion of a magical wand, pulled into the Plane of Earth by an enraged elemental, even dropped into a lake of hissing acid. The figurine appeared undamaged, and Drizzt was certain that Guenhwyvar was now comfortably at rest in its astral home.

Drizzt, however, could afford no such rest. Already the giant had begun picking its way down the rocky slope. With a final look to Ulgulu, Drizzt felt a sense of vengeance that did little to defeat the agonizing, bitter memories of the slaughtered farmers. He set off, moving farther into the wild mountains, running from the giant and from the guilt.

❧ 8 ❧

Clues and Riddles

More than a day had passed since the massacre when the first of the Thistledowns' neighbors rode out to their secluded farm. The stench of death alerted the visiting farmer to the carnage even before he looked in the house or barn.

He returned an hour later with Mayor Delmo and several other armed farmers at his side. They crawled through the Thistledown house and across the grounds cautiously, putting cloth over their faces to combat the terrible smell.

"Who could have done this?" the mayor demanded. "What monster?" As if in answer, one of the farmers walked out of the bedroom and into the kitchen, holding a broken scimitar in his hands.

"A drow weapon?" the farmer asked. "We should be getting McGristle."

Delmo hesitated. He expected the party from Sundabar to arrive any day and felt that the famed ranger Dove Falconhand would be better able to handle the situation than the volatile and uncontrollable mountain man.

The debate never really began, though, for the snarl of a dog alerted all in the house that McGristle had arrived. The burly, dirty man stalked into the kitchen, the side of his face horribly scarred and caked with brown, dried blood.

"Drow weapon!" he spat, recognizing the scimitar all too clearly. "Same as he used agin me!"

"The ranger will be in soon," Delmo began, but McGristle hardly listened. He stalked about the room and into the adjoining bedroom, gruffly tapping bodies with his foot and bending low to inspect some minor details.

"Saw the tracks outside," McGristle stated suddenly. "Two sets, I make 'em."

"The drow has an ally," the mayor reasoned. "More cause for us to wait for the party from Sundabar."

"Bah, ye hardly know if they're even comin'!" McGristle snorted. "Got to get after the drow now, while the trail's fine for my dog's nose!"

Several of the gathered farmers nodded their accord—until Delmo prudently reminded them of exactly what they might be facing.

"A single drow took you down, McGristle," the mayor said. "Now you think there's two of them, maybe more, and you want us to go and hunt them?"

"Bad fortune, it was, that took me down!" Roddy snapped back. He looked around, appealing to the now less-than-eager farmers. "I had that drow, had him cleaned an' dressed!"

The farmers milled nervously and whispered to each other as the mayor took Roddy by the arm and led him to the side of the room.

"Wait a day," Delmo begged. "Our chances will be much greater if the ranger comes."

Roddy didn't seem convinced. "My battle's my own to fight," he snarled. "He killed my dog an' left me ugly."

"You want him, and you'll have him," the mayor promised, "but there might be more on the table here than your dog or your pride."

Roddy's face contorted ominously, but the mayor was adamant. If a drow war party was indeed operating in the area, all of Maldobar was in imminent danger. The small group's greatest defense until help could arrive from Sundabar was unity, and that defense would fail if Roddy led a group of men—fighters who were scarce enough already—on a chase through the mountains. Benson Delmo was astute enough to know that he could not appeal to Roddy on those terms, though. While the mountain man had remained in Maldobar for a couple of years, he was, in essence, a drifter and owed no allegiance to the town.

Roddy turned away, deciding that the meeting was at its end, but the mayor boldly grabbed his arm and turned him back around. Roddy's dog bared its teeth and growled, but that threat was a small consideration to the fat man in light of the awful scowl that Roddy shot him.

"You'll have the drow," the mayor said quickly, "but wait for the help from Sundabar, I beg." He switched to terms that Roddy could truly appreciate. "I am a man of no small means, McGristle, and you were a bounty hunter before you got here, and still are, I'd expect."

Roddy's expression quickly changed from outrage to curiosity.

"Wait for the help, then go get the drow." The mayor paused, considering his forthcoming offer. He really had no experience in this sort of thing and, while he didn't want to come in too low and spoil the interest he had sparked, he didn't want to tax his own purse strings any more than was necessary. "A thousand gold for the drow's head."

Roddy had played this pricing game many times. He hid his delight well; the mayor's offer was five times his normal fee and he would have gone after the drow in any case, with or without payment.

"Two thousand!" the mountain man grumbled without missing a beat, suspecting that more could be exacted for his troubles. The mayor rocked back on his heels but reminded himself several times that the town's very existence might be at stake.

"And not a copper less!" Roddy added, crossing his burly arms over his chest.

"Wait for Mistress Falconhand," Delmo said meekly, "and you shall have your two thousand."

* * * * *

All through the night, Lagerbottoms followed the wounded drow's trail. The bulky hill giant was not yet certain how it felt about the death of Ulgulu and Kempfana, the unasked for masters who had taken over his lair and his life. While Lagerbottoms feared any enemy who could defeat those two, the giant knew that the drow was sorely wounded.

Drizzt realized he was being followed but could do little to hide his tracks. One leg, injured in his bouncing descent into the ravine, dragged painfully and Drizzt had all he could do to keep ahead of the giant. When dawn came, bright and clear, Drizzt knew that his disadvantage had increased. He could not hope to escape the hill giant through the long and revealing light of day.

The trail dipped into a small grouping of variously sized trees, sprouting up wherever they could find cracks between the numerous boulders. Drizzt meant to go straight through—he saw no option other than continuing his flight—but while he leaned on one of the larger trees for support to catch his breath, a thought came to him. The tree's branches hung limply, supple and cordlike.

Drizzt glanced back along the trail. Higher up and crossing a bare expanse of rock, the relentless hill giant plodded along. Drizzt drew his scimitar with the one arm that still seemed to work and hacked down the longest branch he could find. Then he looked for a suitable boulder.

The giant crashed into the copse about a half-hour later, its huge club swinging at the end of one massive arm. Lagerbottoms stopped abruptly when the drow appeared from behind a tree, blocking the path.

Drizzt nearly sighed aloud when the giant stopped, exactly at the appointed area. He had feared that the huge monster would just continue on and swat him down, for Drizzt, injured as he was, could have offered little resistance. Seizing the moment of the monster's hesitation, Drizzt shouted "Halt!" in the goblin language and enacted a simple spell, limning the giant in blue-glowing, harmless flames.

Lagerbottoms shifted uncomfortably but made no advance toward this strange and dangerous enemy. Drizzt eyed the giant's shuffling feet with more than a casual interest.

"Why do you follow me?" Drizzt demanded. "Do you desire to join the others in the sleep of death?"

Lagerbottoms ran his plump tongue over dry lips. So far, this encounter hadn't gone as expected. Now the giant thought past those first instinctual urges that had led him out here and tried to consider the options. Ulgulu and Kempfana were dead; Lagerbottoms had his cave back. But the gnolls and goblins, too, were gone, and that pesky little quickling sprite hadn't been around for a while. A sudden thought came to the giant.

"Friends?" Lagerbottoms asked hopefully.

Though he was relieved to find that combat might be avoided, Drizzt was more than a little skeptical at the offer. The gnoll band had given him a similar offer, to disastrous ends, and this giant was obviously connected to those other monsters that Drizzt had just killed, those who had slaughtered the farm family.

"Friends to what end?" Drizzt asked tentatively, hoping against all reason that he might find this creature to be motivated by some principles, and not just by blood lust.

"To kill," Lagerbottoms replied, as though the answer had been obvious.

Drizzt snarled and jerked his head about in angry denial, his white mane flying wildly. He snapped the scimitar out of its sheath, hardly caring if the giant's foot had found the loop of his snare.

"Kill you!" Lagerbottoms cried, seeing the sudden turn, and the giant lifted his club and took a huge stride forward, a stride shortened by the vinelike branch pulling tightly around his ankle.

Drizzt checked his desire to rush in, reminding himself that the trap had been set into motion, and reminding himself, too, that in his present condition he would be hard put to survive against the formidable giant.

Lagerbottoms looked down at the noose and roared in outrage. The branch wasn't really a proper cord and the noose wasn't so tight. If Lagerbottoms had simply reached down, the giant easily could have slipped the noose off his foot. Hill giants, however, were never known for their intelligence.

"Kill you!" the giant cried again, and it kicked hard against the strain of the branch. Propelled by the considerable force of the kick, the large rock tied to the branch's other end, behind the giant, pelted forward through the underbrush and sailed into Lagerbottoms's back.

Lagerbottoms had started to cry out a third time, but the menacing threat came out as a *whoosh!* of forced air. The heavy club dropped to the ground and the giant, clutching its kidney area, dropped to one knee.

Drizzt hesitated a moment, not knowing whether to run or finish the kill. He didn't fear for himself; the giant would not be coming after him anytime soon, but he could not forget the lurid expression on the giant's face when the monster had said that they might kill together.

"How many other families will you slaughter?" Drizzt asked in the drow tongue.

Lagerbottoms could not begin to understand the language. He just grunted and snarled through the burning pain.

"How many?" Drizzt asked again, his hand wrenching over the scimitar's pommel and his eyes narrowing menacingly.

He came in fast and hard.

* * * * *

To Benson Delmo's absolute relief, the party from Sundabar—Dove Falconhand, her three fighting companions, and Fret, the dwarven sage—came in later that day. The mayor offered the troupe food and rest, but as soon as Dove heard of the massacre at the Thistledown farm, she and her companions set straight out, with the mayor, Roddy McGristle, and several curious farmers close behind.

Dove was openly disappointed when they arrived at the secluded farm. A hundred sets of tracks obscured critical clues, and many of the items in the house, even the bodies, had been handled and moved. Still, Dove and her seasoned company moved about methodically, trying to decipher what they could of the gruesome scene.

"Foolish people!" Fret scolded the farmers when Dove and the others had completed their investigation. "You have aided our enemies!"

Several of the farmer-folk, even the mayor, looked around uncomfortably at the berating, but Roddy snarled and towered over the tidy dwarf. Dove quickly interceded.

"Your earlier presence here has marred some of the clues," Dove explained calmly, disarmingly, to the mayor as she prudently stepped between Fret and the burly mountain man. Dove had heard many tales of McGristle before, and his reputation was not one of predictability or calm.

"We didn't know," the mayor tried to explain.

"Of course not," Dove replied. "You reacted as anyone would have."

"Any novice," Fret remarked.

"Shut yer mouth!" McGristle growled, and so did his dog.

"Be at ease, good sir," Dove bade him. "We have too many enemies beyond the town to need some within."

"Novice?" McGristle barked at her. "I've hunted down a hunnerd men, an' I know enough o' this damned drow to find him."

"Do we know it was the drow?" Dove asked, genuinely doubting.

On a nod from Roddy, a farmer standing on the side of the room produced the broken scimitar.

"Drow weapon," Roddy said harshly, pointing to his scarred face. "I seen it up close!"

One look at the mountain man's jagged wound told Dove that the fine-edged scimitar had not caused it, but the ranger conceded the point, seeing no gain in further argument.

"And drow tracks," Roddy insisted. "The boot prints match close to the ones by the blueberry patch, where we seen the drow!"

Dove's gaze led all eyes to the barn. "Something powerful broke that door," she reasoned. "And the younger woman inside was not killed by any dark elf."

Roddy remained undaunted. "Drow's got a pet," he insisted. "Big, black panther. Damned big cat!"

Dove remained suspicious. She had seen no prints to match a panther's paws, and the way that a portion of the woman had been devoured, bones and all, did not fit any knowledge that she had of great cats. She kept her thoughts to herself, though, realizing that the gruff mountain man wanted no mysteries clouding his already-drawn conclusions.

"Now, if ye've had enough o' this place, let's get onto the trail," Roddy boomed. "My dog's got a scent, and the drow's got a lead big enough already!"

Dove flashed a concerned glance at the mayor, who turned away, embarrassed, under her penetrating gaze.

"Roddy McGristle's to go with you," Delmo explained, barely able to spit out the words, wishing that he had not made his emotionally inspired deal with Roddy. Seeing the coolheadedness of the woman ranger and her party, so drastically different from Roddy's violent temper, the mayor now thought it better that Dove and her companions handle the situation in their own way. But a deal was a deal.

"He'll be the only one from Maldobar joining your troupe," Delmo continued. "He is a seasoned hunter and knows this area better than any."

Again Dove, to Fret's disbelief, conceded the point.

"The day is fast on the wane," Dove said. She added pointedly to McGristle, "We go at first light."

"Drow's got too much of a lead already!" Roddy protested. "We should get after him now!"

"You assume that the drow is running," Dove replied, again calmly, but this time with a stern edge to her voice. "How many dead men once assumed the same of enemies?" This time, Roddy, perplexed, did not shout back. "The drow, or drow band, could be holed up nearby. Would you like to come upon them unexpectedly, McGristle? Would it please you to battle dark elves in the dark of night?"

Roddy just threw up his hands, growled, and stalked away, his dog close on his heels.

The mayor offered Dove and her troupe lodging at his own house, but the ranger and her companions preferred to remain behind at the Thistledown farm. Dove smiled as the farmers departed, and Roddy set up camp just a short distance away, obviously to keep an eye on her. She wondered just how much a stake McGristle had in all of this and suspected that there was more to it than revenge for a scarred face and a lost ear.

"Are you really to let that beastly man come with us?" Fret asked later on, as the dwarf, Dove, and Gabriel sat around the blazing fire in the farmyard. The elven archer and the other member of the troupe were out on perimeter guard.

"It is their town, dear Fret," Dove explained. "And I cannot refute McGristle's knowledge of the region."

"But he is so dirty," the dwarf grumbled. Dove and Gabriel exchanged smiles, and Fret, realizing that he would get nowhere with his argument, turned down his bedroll and slipped in, purposefully spinning away from the others.

"Good old Quilldipper," mumbled Gabriel, but he noted that Dove's ensuing smile did little to diminish the sincere concern on her face.

"You've a problem, Lady Falconhand?" he asked.

Dove shrugged. "Some things do not fit properly in the order of things here," she began.

"'Twas no panther that killed the woman in the barn," Gabriel remarked, for he, too, had noted some discrepancies.

"Nor did any drow kill the farmer, the one they named Bartholemew, in the kitchen," said Dove. "The beam that broke his neck was nearly snapped itself. Only a giant possesses such strength."

"Magic?" Gabriel asked.

Again Dove shrugged. "Drow magic is usually more subtle, according to our sage," she said, looking to Fret, who was already snoring quite loudly. "And more complete. Fret does not believe that drow magic killed Bartholemew or the woman, or destroyed the barn door. And there is another mystery on the matter of the tracks."

"Two sets," Gabriel said, "and made nearly a day apart."

"And of differing depths," added Dove. "One set, the second, might indeed have been those of a dark elf, but the other, the set of the killer, went too deep for an elf's light steps."

"An agent of the drow?" Gabriel offered. "Conjured denizen of the lower planes, perhaps? Might it be that the dark elf came down the next day to inspect its monster's work?" This time, Gabriel joined Dove in her confused shrug.

"So we shall learn," Dove said. Gabriel lit a pipe then, and Dove drifted off into slumber.

* * * * *

"Oh-master, my-master," Tephanis crooned, seeing the grotesque form of the broken, half-transformed barghest. The quickling didn't really care all that much for Ulgulu or the barghest's brother, but their deaths left some severe implications for the sprite's future path. Tephanis had joined Ulgulu's group for mutual gain. Before the barghests came along, the little sprite had spent his days in solitude, stealing whenever he could from nearby villages. He had done all right for himself, but his life had been a lonely and unexciting existence.

Ulgulu had changed all of that. The barghest army offered protection and companionship, and Ulgulu, always scheming for new and more devious kills, had provided Tephanis with unending important missions.

Now the quickling had to walk away from it all, for Ulgulu was dead and Kempfana was dead, and nothing Tephanis could do would change those simple facts.

"Lagerbottoms?" the quickling asked himself suddenly. He thought that the hill giant, the only member missing from the lair, might prove a fine companion. Tephanis saw the giant's tracks clearly enough, heading away from the cave area and out into the deeper mountains. He clapped his hands excitedly, perhaps a hundred times in the next second, then was off, speeding away to find a new friend.

* * * * *

Far up in the mountains, Drizzt Do'Urden looked upon the lights of Maldobar for the last time. Since he had come down from the high peaks after his unpleasant encounter with the skunk, the drow had found a world of savagery nearly equal to the dark realm he had left behind. Whatever hopes Drizzt had realized in his days watching the farming family were lost to him now, buried under the weight of guilt and the awful images of carnage that he knew would haunt him forever.

The drow's physical pain had lessened a bit; he could draw his breath fully now, though the effort sorely stung, and the cuts on his arms and legs had closed. He would survive.

Looking down at Maldobar, another place that he could never call home, Drizzt wondered if that might be a good thing.

✿9✿

The Chase

"What is it?" Fret asked, cautiously moving behind the folds of Dove's forest-green cape.

Dove, and even Roddy, also moved tentatively, for while the creature seemed dead, they had never seen anything quite like it. It appeared to be some strange, giant-sized mutation between a goblin and a wolf.

They gained in courage as they neared the body, convinced that it was truly dead. Dove bent low and tapped it with her sword.

"It has been dead for more than a day, by my guess," she announced.

"But what is it?" Fret asked again.

"Half-breed," Roddy muttered.

Dove closely inspected the creature's strange joints. She noted, too, the many wounds inflicted upon the thing—tearing wounds, like those caused by the scratching of a great cat.

"Shape-changer," guessed Gabriel, keeping watch at the side of the rocky area.

Dove nodded. "Killed halfway through."

"I never heared of any goblin wizards," Roddy protested.

"Oh, yes," Fret began, smoothing the sleeves of his soft-clothed tunic. "There was, of course, Grubby the Wiseless, pretended archmage, who . . ."

A whistle from high above stopped the dwarf. Up on the ledge stood Kellindil, the elven archer, waving his arms about. "More up here," the elf called when he had their attention. "Two goblins and a red-skinned giant, the likes of which I have never seen!"

Dove scanned the cliff. She figured that she could scale it, but one look at poor Fret told her that they would have to go back to the trail, a journey of more than a mile. "You remain here," she said to Gabriel. The stern-faced man nodded and moved off to a defensive position among some boulders, while Dove, Roddy, and Fret headed back along the ravine.

Halfway up the single winding path that moved along the cliff, they met Darda, the remaining fighter of the troupe. A short and heavily muscled man, he scratched his stubbly beard and examined what looked to be a plowshare.

"That's Thistledown's!" Roddy cried. "I seen it out back of his farm, set for fixing!"

"Why is it up here?" Dove asked.

"And why might it be bloodied?" added Darda, showing them the stains on the concave side. The fighter looked over the ledge into the ravine, then back to the plowshare. "Some unfortunate creature hit this hard," Darda mused, "then probably went into the ravine."

All eyes focused on Dove as the ranger pulled her thick hair back from her face, put her chin in her delicate but calloused hand, and tried to sort through this newest puzzle. The clues were too few, though, and a moment later, Dove threw her hands up in exasperation and headed off along the trail. The path wound in and left the cliff as it leveled near the top, but Dove walked back over to the edge, right above where they had left Gabriel. The fighter spotted her immediately and his wave told the ranger that all was calm below.

"Come," Kellindil bade them, and he led the group into the cave. Some answers came clear to Dove as soon as she glanced upon the carnage in the inner room.

"Barghest whelp!" exclaimed Fret, looking upon the scarlet-skinned, giant corpse.

"Barghest?" Roddy asked, perplexed.

"Of course," piped in Fret. "That does explain the wolf-giant in the gorge."

"Caught in the change," Darda reasoned. "Its many wounds and the stone floor took it before it could complete the transition."

"Barghest?" Roddy asked again, this time angrily, not appreciating being left out of a discussion he could not understand.

"A creature from another plane of existence," Fret explained. "Gehenna, it is rumored. Barghests send their whelps to other planes, sometimes to our own, to feed and to grow." He paused a moment in thought. "To feed," he said again, his tone leading the others.

"The woman in the barn!" Dove said evenly.

The members of Dove's troupe nodded their heads at the sudden revelation, but grim-faced McGristle held stubbornly to his original theory. "Drow killed 'em!" he growled.

"Have you the broken scimitar?" Dove asked. Roddy produced the weapon from beneath one of the many folds in his layered skin garments.

Dove took the weapon and bent low to examine the dead barghest. The blade unmistakably matched the beast's wounds, especially the fatal wound in the barghest's throat.

"You said that the drow wielded two of these," Dove remarked to Roddy as she held up the scimitar.

"The mayor said that," Roddy corrected, "on account of the story Thistledown's son told. When I seen the drow—" He took back the weapon—"he had just the one—the one he used to kill the Thistledown clan!" Roddy purposely didn't mention that the drow, while wielding just the one weapon, had scabbards for two scimitars on his belt.

Dove shook her head, doubting the theory. "The drow killed this barghest," she said. "The wounds match the blade, the sister blade to the one you hold, I would guess. And if you check the goblins in the front room, you will find that their throats were slashed by a similar curving scimitar."

"Like the wounds on the Thistledowns!" Roddy snarled.

Dove thought it best to keep her budding hypothesis quiet, but Fret, disliking the big man, echoed the thoughts of all but McGristle. "Killed by the barghest," the dwarf proclaimed, remembering the two sets of footprints at the farmyard. "In the form of the drow!"

Roddy glowered at him and Dove cast Fret a leading look, wanting the dwarf to remain silent. Fret misinterpreted the ranger's stare, though, thinking it astonishment of his reasoning power, and he proudly continued. "That explains the two sets of tracks, the heavier, earlier set for the bar—"

"But what of the creature in the gorge?" Darda asked Dove, understanding his leader's desire to shut Fret up. "Might its wounds, too, match the curving blade?"

Dove thought for a moment and managed to subtly nod her thanks to Darda. "Some, perhaps," she answered. "More likely, that barghest was killed by the panther—" She looked directly at Roddy—"the cat you claimed the drow kept as a pet."

Roddy kicked the dead barghest. "Drow killed the Thistledown clan!" he growled. Roddy had lost a dog and an ear to the dark elf and would not accept any conclusions that lessened his chances of claiming the two thousand gold piece bounty that the mayor had levied.

A call from outside the cave ended the debate—both Dove and Roddy were glad of that. After leading the troupe into the lair, Kellindil had returned outside, following up on some further clues he had discovered.

"A boot print," the elf explained, pointing to a small, mossy patch, when the others came out. "And here," he showed them scratches in the stone, a clear sign of a scuffle.

"My belief is that the drow went to the ledge," Kellindil explained. "And then over, perhaps in pursuit of the barghest and the panther, though on that point I am merely assuming."

After a moment of following the trail Kellindil had reconstructed, Dove and Darda, and even Roddy, agreed with the assumption.

"We should go back into the ravine," Dove suggested. "Perhaps we will find a trail beyond the stony gorge that will lead us toward some clearer answers."

Roddy scratched at the scabs on his head and flashed Dove a disdainful look that showed her his emotions. Roddy cared not a bit for any of the ranger's promised "clearer answers," having drawn all of the conclusions that he needed long ago. Roddy was determined—beyond anything else, Dove knew—to bring back the dark elf's head.

Dove Falconhand was not so certain about the murderer's identity. Many questions remained for both the ranger and for the other members of her troupe. Why hadn't the drow killed the Thistledown children when they had met earlier in the mountains? If Connor's tale to the mayor had been true, then why had the drow given the boy back his weapon? Dove was firmly convinced that the barghest, and not the drow, had slaughtered the Thistledown family, but why had the drow apparently gone after the barghest lair?

Was the drow in league with the barghests, a communion that fast soured? Even more intriguing to the ranger—whose very creed was to protect civilians in the unending war between the good races and monsters—had the drow sought out the barghest to avenge the slaughter at the farm? Dove suspected the latter was the truth, but she couldn't understand the drow's motives. Had the barghest, in killing the family, put the farmers of Maldobar on alert, thereby ruining a planned drow raid?

Again the pieces didn't fit properly. If the dark elves planned a raid on Maldobar, then certainly none of them would have revealed themselves beforehand. Something inside Dove told her that this single drow had acted alone, had come out and avenged the slain farmers. She shrugged it off as a trick of her own optimism and reminded herself that dark elves were rarely known for such rangerlike acts.

By the time the five got down the narrow path and returned to the sight of the largest corpse, Gabriel had already found the trail, heading deeper into the mountains. Two sets of tracks were evident, the drow's and fresher ones belonging to a giant, bipedal creature, possibly a third barghest.

"What happened to the panther?" Fret asked, growing a bit overwhelmed by his first field expedition in many years.

Dove laughed aloud and shook her head helplessly. Every answer seemed to bring so many more questions.

* * * * *

Drizzt kept on the move at night, running, as he had for so many years, from yet another grim reality. He had not killed the farmers—he had actually saved them from the gnoll band—but now they were dead. Drizzt could not escape that fact. He had entered their lives, quite of his own will, and now they were dead.

On the second night after his encounter with the hill giant, Drizzt saw a distant campfire far down the winding mountain trails, back in the direction of the barghest's lair. Knowing this sight to be more than coincidence, the drow summoned Guenhwyvar to his side, then sent the panther down for a closer look.

Tirelessly the great cat ran, its sleek, black form invisible in the evening shadows as it rapidly closed the distance to the camp.

* * * * *

Dove and Gabriel rested easily by their campfire, amused by the continuing antics of Fret, who busily cleaned his soft jerkin with a stiff brush and grumbled all the while.

Roddy kept to himself across the way, securely tucked into a niche between a fallen tree and a large rock, his dog curled up at his feet.

"Oh, bother for this dirt!" Fret groaned. "Never, never will I get this outfit clean! I shall have to buy a new one." He looked at Dove, who was futilely trying to hold a straight face. "Laugh if you will, Mistress Falconhand," the dwarf admonished. "The price will come out of your purse, do not doubt!"

"A sorry day it is when one must buy fineries for a

dwarf," Gabriel put in, and at his words, Dove burst into laughter.

"Laugh if you will!" Fret said again, and he rubbed harder with the brush, wearing a hole right through the garment. "Drat and bebother!" he cursed, then he threw the brush to the ground.

"Shut yer mouth!" Roddy groused at them, stealing the mirth. "Do ye mean to bring the drow down upon us?"

Gabriel's ensuing glare was uncompromising, but Dove realized that the mountain man's advice, though rudely given, was appropriate. "Let us rest, Gabriel," the ranger said to her fighting companion. "Darda and Kellindil will be in soon and our turn shall come for watch. I expect that tomorrow's road will be no less wearisome—" She looked at Fret and winked—"and no less dirty, than today's."

Gabriel shrugged, hung his pipe in his mouth, and clasped his hands behind his head. This was the life that he and all of the adventuring companions enjoyed, camping under the stars with the song of the mountain wind in their ears.

Fret, though, tossed and turned on the hard ground, grumbling and growling as he moved through each uncomfortable position.

Gabriel didn't need to look at Dove to know that she shared his smile. Nor did he have to glance over at Roddy to know that the mountain man fumed at the continuing noise. It no doubt seemed negligible to the ears of a city-living dwarf but rang out conspicuously to those more accustomed to the road.

A whistle from the darkness sounded at the same time Roddy's dog put its fur up and growled.

Dove and Gabriel were up and over to the side of the camp in a second, moving to the perimeter of the firelight in the direction of Darda's call. Likewise, Roddy, pulling his dog along, slipped around the large rock, out of the direct light so that their eyes could adjust to the gloom.

Fret, too involved with his own discomfort, finally noticed the movements. "What?" the dwarf asked curiously. "What?"

After a brief and whispered conversation with Darda, Dove and Gabriel split up, circling the camp in opposite directions to ensure the integrity of the perimeter.

"The tree," came a soft whisper, and Dove dropped into a crouch. In a moment, she sorted out Roddy, cleverly concealed between the rock and some brush. The big man, too, had his weapon readied, and his other hand held his dog's muzzle tightly, keeping the animal silent.

Dove followed Roddy's nod to the widespread branches of a solitary elm. At first, the ranger could discern nothing unusual among the leafy branches, but then came the yellow flash of feline eyes.

"Drow's panther," Dove whispered. Roddy nodded his agreement. They sat very still and watched, knowing that the slightest movement could alert the cat. A few seconds later, Gabriel joined them, falling into a silent position and following their eyes to the same darker spot on the elm. All three understood that time was their ally; even now, Darda and Kellindil were no doubt moving into position.

Their trap would surely have had Guenhwyvar, but a moment later, the dwarf crashed out of the campsite, stumbling right into Roddy. The mountain man nearly fell over, and when he reflexively threw his weaponless hand out to catch himself, his dog rushed out, baying wildly.

Like a black-shafted arrow, the panther bolted from the tree and flew off into the night. Fortune was not with Guenhwyvar, though, for it crossed straight by Kellindil's position, and the keen-visioned elven archer saw it clearly.

Kellindil heard the barking and shouting in the distance, back by the camp, but had no way of knowing what had transpired. Any hesitation the elf had, however, was quickly dispelled when one voice called out clearly.

"Kill the murdering thing!" Roddy cried.

Thinking then that the panther or its drow companion must have attacked the campsite, Kellindil let his arrow fly. The enchanted dart buried itself deeply into Guenhwyvar's flank as the panther rushed by.

Then came Dove's call, berating Roddy. "Do not!" the

ranger shouted. "The panther has done nothing to deserve our ire!"

Kellindil rushed out to the panther's trail. With his sensitive elven eyes viewing in the infrared spectrum, he clearly saw the heat of blood dotting the area of the hit and trailing off away from the camp.

Dove and the others came upon him a moment later. Kellindil's elven features, always angular and beautiful, seemed sharp as his angry glare fell over Roddy.

"You have misguided my shot, McGristle," he said angrily. "On your words, I shot a creature undeserving of an arrow! I warn you once, and once alone, to never do so again." After a final glare to show the mountain man how much he meant his words, Kellindil stalked off along the blood trail.

Angry fires welled in Roddy, but he sublimated them, understanding that he stood alone against the formidable foursome and the tidy dwarf. Roddy did let his glare drop upon Fret, though, knowing that none of the others could disagree with his judgment.

"Keep yer tongue in yer mouth when danger nears!" Roddy growled. "And keep yer stinkin' boots off my back!"

Fret looked around incredulously as the group began to move off after Kellindil. "Stinking?" the dwarf asked aloud. He looked down, wounded, to his finely polished boots. "Stinking?" he said to Dove, who paused to offer a comforting smile. "Dirtied by that one's back, more likely!"

* * * * *

Guenhwyvar limped back to Drizzt soon after the first rays of dawn peeked through the eastern mountains. Drizzt shook his head helplessly, almost unsurprised by the arrow protruding from Guenhwyvar's flank. Reluctantly, but knowing it a wise course, Drizzt drew out the dagger he had taken from the quickling and cut the bolt free.

Guenhwyvar growled softly through the procedure but lay still and offered no resistance. Then Drizzt, though he wanted to keep Guenhwyvar by his side, allowed the panther to return to its astral home, where the wound would heal faster. The arrow had told the drow all he needed to know about his pursuers, and Drizzt believed that he would need the panther again all too soon. He stood out on a rocky outcropping and peered through the growing brightness to the lower trails, to the expected approach of yet another enemy.

He saw nothing, of course; even wounded, Guenhwyvar had easily outdistanced the pursuit and, for a man or similar being, the campfire was many hours' travel.

But they would come, Drizzt knew, forcing him into yet another battle he did not want. Drizzt looked all around, wondering what devious traps he could set for them, what advantages he could gain when the encounter came to blows, as every encounter seemed to.

Memories of his last meeting with humans, of the man with the dogs and the other farmers, abruptly altered Drizzt's thinking. On that occasion, the battle had been inspired by misunderstanding, a barrier that Drizzt doubted he could ever overcome. Drizzt had fostered no desire then to fight against the humans and fostered none now, despite Guenhwyvar's wound.

The light was growing and the still-injured drow, though he had rested through the night, wanted to find a dark and comfortable hole. But Drizzt could afford no delays, not if he wanted to keep ahead of the coming battle.

"How far will you follow me?" Drizzt whispered into the morning breeze. He vowed in a somber but determined tone, "We shall see."

☙ 10 ☙

A Question of Honor

"The panther found the drow," Dove concluded after she and her companions had spent some time inspecting the region near the rocky outcropping. Kellindil's arrow lay broken on the ground, at about the same spot where the panther tracks ended. "And then the panther disappeared."

"So it would seem," Gabriel agreed, scratching his head and looking down at the confusing trail.

"Hell cat," Roddy McGristle growled. "Gone back to its filthy home!"

Fret wanted to ask, "Your house?" but he wisely held the sarcastic thought to himself.

The others, too, let the mountain man's proclamation slip by. They had no answers to this riddle, and Roddy's guess was as good as any of them could manage. The wounded panther and the fresh blood trail were gone, but Roddy's dog soon had Drizzt's scent. Baying excitedly, the dog led them on, and Dove and Kellindil, both skilled trackers, often discovered other evidence that confirmed the direction.

The trail lay along the side of the mountain, dipped through some thickly packed trees, and continued on across an expanse of bare stone, ending abruptly at yet another ravine. Roddy's dog moved right to the lip and even down to the first step on a rocky and treacherous descent.

"Damned drow magic," Roddy grumbled. He looked around and bounced a fist off his thigh, guessing that it would take him many hours to circumvent the steep wall.

"The daylight wanes," Dove offered. "Let us set camp here and find our way down in the morn."

Gabriel and Fret nodded their accord, but Roddy disagreed. "The trail's fresh now!" the mountain man argued. "We should get the dog down there and back on it, at least, before we're taking to our beds."

"That could take hours . . ." Fret began to protest, but Dove hushed the tidy dwarf.

"Come," the ranger bade the others, and she walked off to the west, to where the ground sloped at a steep, but climbable decline.

Dove did not agree with Roddy's reasoning, but she wanted no further arguments with Maldobar's appointed representative.

At the bottom of the ravine they found only more riddles. Roddy spurred his dog off in every direction but could find no trace of the elusive drow. After many minutes of contemplation, the truth sparked in Dove's mind and her smile revealed everything to her other seasoned companions.

"He doubled us!" Gabriel laughed, guessing the source of Dove's mirth. "He led us right to the cliff, knowing we would assume he used some magic to get down!"

"What're ye talkin' about?" Roddy demanded angrily, though the experienced bounty hunter understood exactly what had happened.

"You mean that we have to climb all the way back up there?" Fret asked, his voice a whine.

Dove laughed again but sobered quickly as she looked to Roddy and said, "In the morning."

This time the mountain man offered no objections.

By the time the next dawn had broken, the group had hiked to the top of the ravine and Roddy had his dog back on Drizzt's scent, backtracking the trail in the direction of the rocky outcropping where they had first picked it up. The trick had been simple enough, but the same question nagged at all of the experienced trackers: how had the drow broken away from his track cleanly enough to so completely fool the dog? When they came again into the thickly packed trees, Dove knew that they had their answer.

She nodded to Kellindil, who was already dropping off his heavy pack. The nimble elf picked a low-hanging branch and swung up into the trees, searching for possible routes that the climbing drow might have followed. The branches of many trees twined together, so the options seemed many, but after a while, Kellindil correctly guided Roddy and his dog to the new trail, breaking off to the side of the copse and circling back down the side of the mountain, back in the direction of Maldobar.

"The town!" cried a distressed Fret, but the others didn't seem concerned.

"Not the town," offered Roddy, too intrigued to hold his angry edge. As a bounty hunter, Roddy always enjoyed a worthy opponent, at least during the chase. "The stream," Roddy explained, thinking that now he had figured out the drow's mind-set. "Drow's headed for the stream, to follow it along an' break off clean, back out to the wilder land."

"The drow is a crafty adversary," Darda remarked, wholeheartedly agreeing with Roddy's conclusions.

"And now he has at least a day's lead over us," Gabriel remarked.

After Fret's disgusted sigh finally died away, Dove offered the dwarf some hope. "Fear not," she said. "We are well stocked, but the drow is not. He must pause to hunt or forage, but we can continue on."

"We sleep only when need be!" Roddy put in, determined to not be slowed by the group's other members. "And only for short times!"

Fret sighed heavily again.

"And we begin rationing our supplies immediately," Dove added, both to placate Roddy and because she thought it prudent. "We shall be put to it hard enough just to close on the drow. I do not want any delays."

"Rationing," Fret mumbled under his breath. He sighed for the third time and placed a comforting hand on his belly. How badly the tidy dwarf wished that he could be back in his neat little room in Helm's castle in Sundabar!

* * * * *

Drizzt's every intention was to continue deeper into the mountains until the pursuing party had lost its heart for the chase. He kept up his misdirecting tactics, often doubling back and taking to the trees to begin a second trail in an entirely different direction. Many mountain streams provided further barriers to the scent, but Drizzt's pursuers were not novices, and Roddy's dog was as fine a hunting hound as had ever been bred. Not only did the party keep true to Drizzt's trail, but they actually closed the gap over the next few days.

Drizzt still believed that he could elude them, but their continuing proximity brought other, more subtle, concerns to the drow. He had done nothing to deserve such dogged pursuit; he had even avenged the deaths of the farming family. And, despite Drizzt's angry vow that he would go off alone, that he would bring no more danger to anyone, he had known loneliness as too close a companion for too many years. He could not help but look over his shoulder, out of curiosity and not fear, and the longing did not diminish.

At last, Drizzt could not deny his curiosity for the pursuing party. That curiosity, Drizzt realized as he studied the figures moving about the campfire one dark night, might prove to be his downfall. Still, the realization, and the second-guessing, came too late for the drow to do anything about it. His needs had dragged him back, and now the campsite of his pursuers loomed barely twenty yards away.

The banter between Dove, Fret, and Gabriel tugged at Drizzt's heartstrings, though he could not understand their words. Any desire the drow felt to walk into the camp was tempered, though, whenever Roddy and his mean-tempered dog strolled by the light. Those two would never pause to hear any explanations, Drizzt knew.

The party had set two guards, one an elf and one a tall human. Drizzt had sneaked past the human, guessing correctly that the man would not be as adept as the elf in the darkness. Now, though, the drow, again against all caution, picked his way around to the other side of the camp, toward the elven sentry.

Only once before had Drizzt encountered his surface cousins. It had been a disastrous occasion. The raiding party for which Drizzt was a scout had slaughtered every member of a surface elf gathering, except for a single elven girl, whom Drizzt had managed to conceal. Driven by those haunting memories, Drizzt needed to see an elf again, a living and vital elf.

The first indication Kellindil had that someone else was in the area came when a tiny dagger whistled past his chest, neatly severing his bowstring. The elf spun about immediately and looked into the drow's lavender eyes. Drizzt stood only a few paces away.

The red glow of Kellindil's eyes showed that he was viewing Drizzt in the infrared spectrum. The drow crossed his hands over his chest in an Underdark signal of peace.

"At last we have met, my dark cousin," Kellindil whispered harshly in the drow tongue, his voice edged in obvious anger and his glowing eyes narrowing dangerously. Quick as a cat, Kellindil snapped a finely crafted sword, its blade glowing in a fiery red flame, from his belt.

Drizzt was amazed and hopeful when he learned that the elf could speak his language, and in the simple fact that the elf had not spoken loudly enough to alert the camp. The surface elf was Drizzt's size and similary sharp-featured, but his eyes were narrower and his golden hair wasn't as long or thick as Drizzt's white mane.

"I am Drizzt Do'Urden," Drizzt began tentatively.

"I care nothing for what you are called!" Kellindil shot back. "You are drow. That is all I need to know! Come then, drow. Come and let us learn who is the stronger!"

Drizzt had not yet drawn his blade and had no intention of doing so. "I have no desire to battle with you . . ." Drizzt's voice trailed away, as he realized his words were futile against the intense hatred the surface elf held for him.

Drizzt wanted to explain everything to the elf, to tell his

tale completely and be vindicated by some voice other than his own. If only another—particularly a surface elf—would learn of his trials and agree with his decisions, agree that he had acted properly through the course of his life in the face of such horrors, then the guilt would fly from Drizzt's shoulders. If only he could find acceptance among those who so hated—as he himself hated—the ways of his dark people, then Drizzt Do'Urden would be at peace.

But the elf's sword tip did not slip an inch toward the ground, nor did the grimace diminish on his fair elven face, a face more accustomed to smiles.

Drizzt would find no acceptance here, not now and probably not ever. Was he forever to be misjudged? he wondered. Or was he, perhaps, misjudging those around him, giving the humans and this elf more credit for fairness than they deserved?

Those were two disturbing notions that Drizzt would have to deal with another day, for Kellindil's patience had reached its end. The elf came at the drow with his sword tip leading the way.

Drizzt was not surprised—how could he have been? He hopped back, out of immediate reach, and called upon his innate magic, dropping a globe of impenetrable blackness over the advancing elf.

No novice to magic, Kellindil understood the drow's trick. The elf reversed direction, diving out the back side of the globe and coming up, sword at the ready.

The lavender eyes were gone.

"Drow!" Kellindil called out loudly, and those in the camp immediately exploded into motion. Roddy's dog started howling, and that excited and threatening yelp followed Drizzt back into the mountains, damning him to his continuing exile.

Kellindil leaned back against a tree, alert but not too concerned that the drow was still in the area. Drizzt could not know it at that time, but his words and ensuing actions—fleeing instead of fighting—had indeed put a bit of doubt in the kindly elf's not-so-closed mind.

* * * * *

"He will lose his advantage in the dawn's light," Dove said hopefully after several fruitless hours of trying to keep up with the drow. They were in a bowl-shaped, rocky vale now, and the drow's trail led up the far side in a high and fairly steep climb.

Fret, nearly stumbling with exhaustion at her side, was quick to reply. "Advantage?" The dwarf groaned. He looked at the next mountain wall and shook his head. "We shall all fall dead of weariness before we find this infernal drow!"

"If ye can't keep up, then fall an' die!" Roddy snarled. "We're not to be lettin' the stinking drow get away this time!"

It was not Fret, however, but another member of the troupe who unexpectedly went down. A large rock soared into the group suddenly, clipping Darda's shoulder with enough force to lift the man from the ground and spin him right over in the air. He never even got the chance to cry out before he fell facedown in the dust.

Dove grabbed Fret and rolled for a nearby boulder, Roddy and Gabriel doing likewise. Another stone, and then several more, thundered into the region.

"Avalanche?" the stunned dwarf asked when he recovered from the shock.

Dove, too concerned with Darda, didn't bother to answer, though she knew the truth of their situation and knew that it was no avalanche.

"He is alive," Gabriel called from behind his protective rock, a dozen feet across from Dove's. Another stone skipped through the area, narrowly missing Darda's head.

"Damn," Dove mumbled. She peeked up over the lip of her boulder, scanning both the mountainside and the lower crags at its base. "Now, Kellindil," she whispered to herself. "Get us some time."

As if in answer came the distant twang of the elf's re-strung bow, followed by an angry roar. Dove and Gabriel glanced over to each other and smiled grimly.

"Stone giants!" Roddy cried, recognizing the deep, grating timbre of the roaring voice.

Dove crouched and waited, her back to the boulder and her open pack in her hand. No more stones bounced into the area; rather, thunderous crashes began up ahead of them, near Kellindil's position. Dove rushed out to Darda and gently turned the man over.

"That hurt," Darda whispered, straining to smile at his obvious understatement.

"Do not speak," Dove replied, fumbling for a potion bottle in her pack. But the ranger ran out of time. The giants, seeing her out in the open, resumed their attack on the lower area.

"Get back to the stone!" Gabriel cried. Dove slipped her arm under the fallen man's shoulder to support Darda as, stumbling with every movement, he crawled for the rock.

"Hurry! Hurry!" Fret cried, watching them anxiously with his back flat against the large stone.

Dove leaned over Darda suddenly, flattening him down to the ground as another rock zipped by just above their ducking heads.

Fret started to bite his fingernails, then realized what he was doing and stopped, a disgusted look on his face. "Do hurry!" he cried again to his friends. Another rock bounced by, too close.

Just before Dove and Darda got to Fret, a stone landed squarely on the backside of the boulder. Fret, his back tight against the rock barrier, flew out wildly, easily clearing his crawling companions. Dove placed Darda down behind the boulder, then turned, thinking she would have to go out again and retrieve the fallen dwarf.

But Fret was already back up, cursing and grumbling, and more concerned with a new hole in his fine garment than in any bodily injury.

"Get back here!" Dove screamed at him.

"Drat and bebother these stupid giants!" was all that Fret replied, stomping purposefully back to the boulder, his fists clenched angrily against his hips.

The barrage continued, both up ahead of the pinned companions and in their area. Then Kellindil came diving in, slipping to the rock beside Roddy and his dog.

"Stone giants," the elf explained. "A dozen at the least." He pointed up to a ridge halfway up the mountainside.

"Drow set us up," Roddy growled, banging his fist on the stone.

Kellindil wasn't convinced, but he held his tongue.

* * * * *

Up on the peak of the rocky rise, Drizzt watched the battle unfolding. He had passed through the lower paths an hour earlier, before the dawn. In the dark, the waiting giants had been no obstacle for the stealthy drow; Drizzt had slipped through their line with little trouble.

Now, squinting through the morning light, Drizzt wondered about his course of action. When he had passed the giants, he fully expected that his pursuers would fall into trouble. Should he have somehow tried to warn them? he wondered. Or should he have veered away from the region, leading the humans and the elf out of the giants' path?

Again Drizzt did not understand where he fit in with the ways of this strange and brutal world. "Let them fight among themselves," he said harshly, as though trying to convince himself. Drizzt purposefully recalled his encounter of the previous night. The elf had attacked despite his proclamation that he did not want to fight. He recalled, too, the arrow he had dug out of Guenhwyvar's flank.

"Let them all kill each other," Drizzt said and he turned to leave. He glanced back over his shoulder one final time and noticed that some of the giants were on the move. One group remained at the ridge, showering the valley floor with a seemingly endless supply of rocks while two other groups, one to the left and one to the right, had fanned out, moving to encircle the trapped party.

Drizzt knew then that his pursuers would not escape. Once the giants had them flanked, they would find no protection against the cross fire.

Something stirred within the drow at that moment, the same emotions that had set him into action against the gnoll band. He couldn't know for certain, but, as with the gnolls and their plans to attack the farmhouse, Drizzt suspected that the giants were the evil ones in this fight.

Other thoughts softened Drizzt's determined grimace, memories of the human children at play on the farm, of the sandy-haired boy going into the water trough.

Drizzt dropped the onyx figurine to the ground. "Come, Guenhwyvar," he commanded. "We are needed."

* * * * *

"We're being flanked!" Roddy McGristle snarled, seeing the giant bands moving along the higher trails.

Dove, Gabriel, and Kellindil all glanced around and to each other, searching for some way out. They had battled giants many times in their travels, together and with other parties. Always before, they had gone into the fight eagerly, happy to relieve the world of a few troublesome monsters. This time, though, they all suspected that the result might be different. Stone giants were reputably the best rock-throwers in all the realms and a single hit could kill the hardiest of men. Also, Darda, though alive, could not possibly run away, and none of the others had any intentions of leaving him behind.

"Flee, mountain man," Kellindil said to Roddy. "You owe us nothing."

Roddy looked at the archer incredulously. "I don't run away, elf," he growled. "Not from nothin'!"

Kellindil nodded and fitted an arrow to his bow.

"If they get to the side, we're doomed," Dove explained to Fret. "I beg your forgiveness, dear Fret. I should not have taken you from your home."

Fret shrugged the thought away. He reached under his robes and produced a small but sturdy silver hammer. Dove smiled at the sight, thinking how odd the hammer seemed in the dwarf's soft hands, more accustomed to holding a quill.

* * * * * *

On the top ridge, Drizzt and Guenhwyvar shadowed the movements of the stone giant band circling to the trapped party's left flank. Drizzt was determined to help the humans, but he wasn't certain of how effective he could be against the likes of four armed giants. Still, he figured that with Guenhwyvar by his side, he could find some way to disrupt the giant group long enough for the trapped party to make a break.

The valley rolled out wider across the way and Drizzt realized that the giant band circling in the other direction, to the trapped party's right flank, was probably out of rock-throwing range.

"Come, my friend," Drizzt whispered to the panther, and he drew his scimitar and started down a descent of broken and jagged stone. A moment later, though, as soon as he noticed the terrain a short distance ahead of the giant band, Drizzt grabbed Guenhwyvar by the scruff and led the panther back up to the top ridge.

Here the ground was jagged and cracked but undeniably stable. Just ahead, however, great boulders and hundreds of loose smaller rocks lay strewn about the steeply sloping ground. Drizzt was not so experienced in the dynamics of a mountainside, but even he could see that the steep and loose landscape verged on collapse.

The drow and the cat rushed ahead, again getting above the giant band. The giants were nearly in position; some of them had even begun to launch rocks at the pinned party. Drizzt crept down to a large boulder and heaved against it, setting it into motion. Guenhwyvar's tactics were far less subtle. The panther charged down the mountainside, dislodging stones with every great stride, leaping onto the back side of rocks and springing away as they began tumbling.

Boulders bounced and bounded. Smaller rocks skipped between them, building the momentum. Drizzt, committed to the action, ran down into the midst of the budding avalanche, throwing stones, pushing against others—whatever he could do to add to the rush. Soon the very ground beneath the drow's feet was sliding and the whole section of the mountainside seemed to be coming down.

Guenhwyvar sped along ahead of the avalanche, a beacon of doom for the surprised giants. The panther sprang out over them, but they took note of the great cat only momentarily, as tons of bouncing rocks slammed into them.

Drizzt knew that he was in trouble; he was not nearly as quick and agile as Guenhwyvar and could not hope to outrun the slide, or to get out of its way. He leaped high into the air from the crest of a small ridge and called upon a levitation spell as he went.

Drizzt fought hard to hold his concentration on the effort. The spell had failed him twice before, and if he couldn't hold it now, if he dropped back into the rush of stones, he knew he would surely die.

Despite his determination, Drizzt felt increasingly heavy on the air. He waved his arms futilely, sought that magical energy within his drow body—but he was coming down.

* * * * *

"Th'only ones that can hit us are up in front!" Roddy cried as a thrown boulder bounced harmlessly short of the right flank. "The ones on the right're too far for throwing, and the ones on the left . . . !"

Dove followed Roddy's logic and his gaze to the rising dust cloud on their left flank. She stared hard and long at the cascading rocks, and at what might have been a dark-cloaked elven form. When she looked back at Gabriel, she knew that he, too, had seen the drow.

"We have to go now," Dove called to the elf.

Kellindil nodded and spun to the side of his barrier boulder, his bowstring taut.

"Quickly," Gabriel added, "before the group to the right gets back in range."

Kellindil's bow twanged once and then again. Ahead, a giant howled in pain.

"Stay here with Darda," Dove bade Fret, then she, Gabriel, and Roddy—holding his dog on a tight leash—darted out from their cover and charged the giants straight ahead. They rolled from rock to rock, cutting their course in confusing zigzags to prevent the giants from anticipating their movements. All the while, Kellindil's arrows soared above them, keeping the giants more concerned with ducking than with throwing.

Deep crags marked the mountainside's lower slopes, crags that offered cover but that also split the three fighters apart. Neither could they see the giants, but they knew the general direction and picked their separate ways as best they could.

Rounding a sharp bend between two walls of stone, Roddy came upon one of the giants. Immediately the mountain man freed his dog, and the vicious canine charged fearlessly and leaped high, barely reaching the twenty-foot-tall behemoth's waist.

Surprised by the sudden attack, the giant dropped its huge club and caught the dog in midflight. It would have crushed the troublesome mutt in an instant, except that Bleeder, Roddy's wicked axe, sliced into its thigh with all the force the burly mountain man could muster. The giant lurched and Roddy's dog squirmed loose, climbing and clawing, then snapping at the giant's face and neck. Below, Roddy hacked away, chopping the monster down as he would a tree.

* * * * *

Half-floating and half-dancing atop the bouncing stones, Drizzt rode the rock slide. He saw one giant emerge, stumbling, from the tumult, only to be met by Guenhwyvar. Wounded and stunned, the giant went down in a heap.

Drizzt had no time to savor his desperate plan's success. His levitation spell continued somewhat, keeping him light enough so that he could ride along. Even above the main slide, though, rocks bounced heavily into the drow and dust choked him and stung his sensitive eyes. Nearly blinded, he managed to spot a ridge that could provide some shelter, but the only way he could get to it would be to release his levitation spell and scramble.

Another rock nicked into Drizzt, nearly spinning him over in midair. He could sense the spell failing and knew that he had only that one chance. He regained his equilibrium, released his spell, and hit the ground running.

He rolled and scrambled, coming up in a dead run. A rock skipped into the knee of his already wounded leg, forcing him parallel to the ground. Drizzt was rolling again, trying however he could to get to the safety of the ridge.

His momentum ended far short. He came back up to his feet, meaning to thrust ahead over the final distance, but Drizzt's leg had no strength and it buckled immediately, leaving him stranded and exposed.

He felt the impact on his back and thought his life was at its end. A moment later, dazed, Drizzt realized only that he somehow had landed behind the ridge and that he was buried by something, but not by stones or dirt.

Guenhwyvar stayed on top of its master, shielding Drizzt until the last of the bouncing rocks had rolled to a stop.

* * * * *

As the crags gave way to more open ground, Dove and Gabriel came back in sight of each other. They noticed movement directly ahead, behind a loose-fitted wall of piled boulders a dozen feet high and about fifty feet long.

A giant appeared atop the wall, roaring in rage and holding a rock above its head, readied to throw. The monster had several arrows protruding from its neck and chest, but it seemed not to care.

Kellindil's next shot surely caught the giant's attention,

though, for the elf put an arrow squarely into the monster's elbow. The giant howled and clutched at its arm, apparently forgetting about its rock, which promptly dropped with a thud upon its head. The giant stood very still, dazed, and two more arrows knocked into its face. It teetered for a moment, then crashed into the dust.

Dove and Gabriel exchanged quick smiles, sharing their appreciation for the skilled elven archer, then continued their charge, going for opposite ends of the wall.

Dove caught one giant by surprise just around her corner. The monster reached for its club, but Dove's sword beat it to the spot and cleanly severed its hand. Stone giants were formidable foes, with fists that could drive a person straight into the ground and a hide nearly as hard as the rock that gave them their name. But wounded, surprised, and without its cudgel, the giant was no match for the skilled ranger. She sprang atop the wall, which put her even with the giant's face, and set her sword to methodical work.

In two thrusts, the giant was blinded. The third, a deft, sidelong swipe, cut a smile into the monster's throat. Then Dove went on the defensive, neatly dodging and parrying the dying monster's last desperate swings.

Gabriel was not as lucky as his companion. The remaining giant was not close to the corner of the piled rock wall. Though Gabriel surprised the monster when he came charging around, the giant had enough time—and a stone in hand—to react.

Gabriel got his sword up to deflect the missile, and the act saved his life. The stone blew the fighter's sword from his hands and still came on with enough force to throw Gabriel to the ground. Gabriel was a seasoned veteran, and the primary reason he was still alive after so very many battles was the fact that he knew when to retreat. He forced himself through that moment of blurring pain and found his footing, then bolted back around the wall.

The giant, with its heavy club in hand, came right behind. An arrow greeted the monster as it turned into the open, but it brushed the pesky dart away as no more than an inconvenience and bore down on the fighter.

Gabriel soon ran out of room. He tried to make it back to the broken paths, but the giant cut him off, trapping him in a small box canyon of huge boulders. Gabriel drew his dagger and cursed his ill luck.

Dove had dispatched her giant by this time and rushed out around the stone wall, immediately catching sight of Gabriel and the giant.

Gabriel saw the ranger, too, but he only shrugged, almost apologetically, knowing that Dove couldn't possibly get to him in time to save him.

The snarling giant took a step in, meaning to finish the puny man, but then came a sharp *crack!* and the monster halted abruptly. Its eyes darted about weirdly for a moment or two, then it toppled at Gabriel's feet, quite dead.

Gabriel looked up to the side, to the top of the boulder wall, and nearly laughed out loud.

Fret's hammer was not a large weapon—its head being only two inches across—but it was a solid thing, and in a single swing, the dwarf had driven it clean through the stone giant's thick skull.

Dove approached, sheathing her sword, equally at a loss.

Looking upon their amazed expressions, Fret was not amused.

"I am a dwarf, after all!" he blurted at them, crossing his arms indignantly. The action brought the brain-stained hammer in contact with Fret's tunic, and the dwarf lost his bluster in a fit of panic. He licked his stubby fingers and wiped at the gruesome stain, then regarded the gore on his hand with even greater horror.

Dove and Gabriel did laugh aloud.

"Know that you are paying for the tunic!" Fret railed at Dove. "Oh, you most certainly are!"

A shout to the side brought them from their momentary relief. The four remaining giants, having seen one group of their companions buried in an avalanche and another group cut down so very efficiently, had lost interest in the ambush and had taken flight.

Right behind them went Roddy McGristle and his howling dog.

* * * * *

A single giant had escaped both the avalanche's thunder and the panther's terrible claws. It ran wildly now across the mountainside, seeking the top ridge.

Drizzt set Guenhwyvar in quick pursuit, then found a stick to use as a cane and managed to get to his feet. Bruised, dusty, and still nursing wounds from the barghest battle—and now a dozen more from his mountain ride—Drizzt started away. A movement at the bottom of the slope caught his attention and held him, though. He turned to face the elf and, more pointedly, the arrow nocked in the elf's drawn bow.

Drizzt looked around but had nowhere to duck. He could place a globe of darkness somewhere between himself and the elf, possibly, but he realized that the skilled archer, having drawn a bead on him, would not miss him even with that obstacle. Drizzt steadied his shoulders and turned about slowly, facing the elf squarely and proudly.

Kellindil eased his bowstring back and pulled the arrow from its nock. Kellindil, too, had seen the dark-cloaked form floating above the rock slide.

"The others are back with Darda," Dove said, coming upon the elf at that moment, "and McGristle is chasing . . ."

Kellindil neither answered nor looked to the ranger. He nodded curtly, leading Dove's gaze up the slope to the dark form, which moved again up the mountainside.

"Let him go," Dove offered. "That one was never our enemy."

"I fear to let a drow walk free," Kellindil replied.

"As do I," Dove answered, "but I fear the consequences more if McGristle finds the drow."

"We will return to Maldobar and rid ourselves of that man," Kellindil offered, "then you and the others may return to Sundabar for your appointment. I have kin in these mountains; together they and I will watch out for our dark-skinned friend and see that he causes no harm."

"Agreed," said Dove. She turned and started away, and Kellindil, needing no further convincing, turned to follow.

The elf paused and looked back one final time. He reached into his backpack and produced a flask, then laid it out in the open on the ground. Almost as an afterthought, Kellindil produced a second item, this one from his belt, and dropped it to the ground next to the flask. Satisfied, he turned and followed the ranger.

* * * * *

By the time Roddy McGristle returned from his wild, fruitless chase, Dove and the others had packed everything together and were prepared to leave.

"Back after the drow," Roddy proclaimed. "He's gained a bit o' time, but we'll close on him fast."

"The drow is gone," Dove said sharply. "We shall pursue him no more."

Roddy's face crinkled in disbelief and he seemed on the verge of exploding.

"Darda is badly in need of rest!" Dove growled at him, not backing down a bit. "Kellindil's arrows are nearly exhausted, as are our supplies."

"I'll not so easily forget the Thistledowns!" Roddy declared.

"Neither did the drow," Kellindil put in.

"The Thistledowns have already been avenged," Dove added, "and you know it is true, McGristle. The drow did not kill them, but he most definitely slew their killers!"

Roddy snarled and turned away. He was an experienced bounty hunter and, thus, an experienced investigator. He had, of course, figured out the truth long ago, but Roddy couldn't ignore the scar on his face or the loss of his ear—or the heavy bounty on the drow's head.

Dove anticipated and understood his silent reasoning. "The people of Maldobar will not be so anxious to see the drow brought in when they learn the truth of the massacre," she said, "and not so willing to pay, I would guess."

Roddy snapped a glare at her, but again he could not dispute her logic. When Dove's party set out on the trail back to Maldobar, Roddy McGristle went with them.

* * * * *

Drizzt came back down the mountainside later that day, searching for something that would tell him his pursuers' whereabouts. He found Kellindil's flask and approached it tentatively, then relaxed when he noticed the other item lying next to it, the tiny dagger he had taken from the sprite, the same one he had used to sever the elf's bowstring on their first meeting.

The liquid within the flask smelled sweet, and the drow, his throat still parched from the rock dust, gladly took a quaff. Tingling chills ran through Drizzt's body, refreshing him and revitalizing him. He had barely eaten for several days, but the strength that had seeped from his now-frail form came rushing back in a sudden burst. His torn leg went numb for a moment, and Drizzt felt that, too, grow stronger.

A wave of dizziness washed over Drizzt then, and he shuffled over to the shade of a nearby boulder and sat down to rest.

When he awoke, the sky was dark and filled with stars, and he felt much better. Even his leg, so torn in the ride down the avalanche, would once again support his weight. Drizzt knew who had left the flask and dagger for him, and now that he understood the nature of the healing potion, his confusion and indecision only grew.

❦ Part 3 ❦
Montolio

To all the varied peoples of the world, nothing is so out of reach, yet so deeply personal and controlling, as the concept of god. My experience in my homeland showed me little of these supernatural beings beyond the influences of the vile drow deity, the Spider Queen, Lloth.

After witnessing the carnage of Lloth's workings, I was not so quick to embrace the concept of any god, of any being that could so dictate, codes of behavior and precepts of an entire society. Is morality not an internal force, and if it is, are principles then to be dictated or felt?

So follows the question of the gods themselves: Are these named entities, in truth, actual beings, or are they manifestations of shared beliefs? Are the dark elves evil because they follow the precepts of the Spider Queen, or is Lloth a culmination of the drow's natural evil conduct?

Likewise, when the barbarians of Icewind Dale charge across the tundra to war, shouting the name of Tempus, Lord of Battles, are they following the precepts of Tempus, or is Tempus merely the idealized name they give to their actions?

This I cannot answer, nor, I have come to realize, can anyone else, no matter how loudly they—particularly priests of certain gods—might argue otherwise. In the end, to a preacher's ultimate sorrow, the choice of a god is a personal one, and the alignment to a being is in accord with one's internal code of principles. A missionary might coerce and trick would-be disciples, but no rational being can truly follow the determined orders of any god-figure if those orders run contrary to his own tenets. Neither I, Drizzt Do'Urden, nor my father, Zaknafein, could ever have become disciples of the Spider Queen. And Wulfgar of Icewind Dale, my friend of later years, though he still might yell out to the battle god, does not please this entity called Tempus except on those occasions when he puts his mighty war hammer to use.

The gods of the realms are many and varied—or they are the many and varied names and identities tagged onto the same being.

I know not—and care not—which.

—Drizzt Do'Urden

❧ 11 ❧

Winter

Drizzt picked his way through the rocky, towering mountains for many days, putting as much ground between himself and the farm village—and the awful memories—as he could. The decision to flee had not been a conscious one; if Drizzt had been less out of sorts, he might have seen the charity in the elf's gifts, the healing potion and the returned dagger, as a possible lead to a future relationship.

But the memories of Maldobar and the guilt that bowed the drow's shoulders would not be so easily dismissed. The farming village had become simply one more stopover on the search to find a home, a search that he increasingly believed was futile. Drizzt wondered how he could even go down to the next village that he came upon. The potential for tragedy had been played out all too clearly for him. He didn't stop to consider that the presence of the barghests might have been an unusual circumstance, and that, perhaps, in the absence of such fiends, his encounter might have turned out differently.

At this low point in his life, Drizzt's entire thoughts focused around a single word that echoed interminably in his head and pierced him to his heart: "drizzit."

Drizzt's trail eventually led him to a wide pass in the mountains and to a steep and rocky gorge filled by the mist of some roaring river far below. The air had been getting colder, something that Drizzt did not understand, and the moist vapor felt good to the drow. He picked his way down the rocky cliff, a journey that took him the better part of the day, and found the bank of the cascading river.

Drizzt had seen rivers in the Underdark, but none to rival this. The Rauvin leaped across stones, throwing spray high into the air. It swarmed around great boulders, did a white-faced skip over fields of smaller stones, and dove suddenly into falls five times the drow's height. Drizzt was enchanted by the sight and the sound, but, more than that, he also saw the possibilities of this place as a sanctuary. Many culverts edged the river, still pools where water had deflected from the pull of the main stream. Here, too, gathered the fish, resting from their struggles against the strong current.

The sight brought a grumble from Drizzt's belly. He knelt down over one pool, his hand poised to strike. It took him many tries to understand the refraction of sunlight through the water, but the drow was quick enough and smart enough to learn this game. Drizzt's hand plunged down suddenly and came back up firmly grasping a foot-long trout.

Drizzt tossed the fish away from the water, letting it bounce about on the stones, and soon had caught another. He would eat well this night, for the first time since he had fled the region of the farm village, and he had enough clear and cold water to satisfy any thirst.

This place was called Dead Orc Pass by those who knew the region. The title was somewhat of a misnomer, however, for while hundreds of orcs had indeed died in this rocky valley in numerous battles against human legions, thousands more lived here still, lurking in the many mountain caves, poised to strike against intruders. Few people came here, and none of them wisely.

To naive Drizzt, with the easy supply of food and water and the comfortable mist to battle the surprisingly chilling air, this gorge seemed the perfect retreat.

The drow spent his days huddled in the sheltering shadows of the many rocks and small caves, preferring to fish and forage in the dark hours of night. He didn't view this nocturnal style as a reversion to anything he had once been. When he had first stepped out of the Underdark, he had determined that he would live among the surface dwellers as a surface dweller, and thus, he had taken great pains to acclimate himself to the daytime sun. Drizzt held no such illusions now. He chose the nights for his activities because they were less painful to his sensitive eyes and because he knew that the less exposure his scimitar had to the sun, the longer it would retain its edge of magic.

It didn't take Drizzt very long, however, to understand why the surface dwellers seemed to prefer the daylight. Under the sun's warming rays, the air was still tolerable, if a bit chill. During the night, Drizzt found that he often had to take shelter from the biting breeze that whipped down over the steep edges of the mist-filled gorge. Winter was fast approaching the northland, but the drow, raised in the seasonless world of the Underdark, couldn't know that.

On one of these nights, with the wind driving a brutal northern blast that numbed the drow's hands, Drizzt came to an important understanding. Even with Guenhwyvar beside him, huddled beneath a low overhang, Drizzt felt the severe pain growing in his extremities. Dawn was many hours away, and Drizzt seriously wondered if he would survive to see the sunrise.

"Too cold, Guenhwyvar," he stuttered through his chattering teeth. "Too cold."

He flexed his muscles and moved vigorously, trying to restore lost circulation. Then he mentally prepared himself, thinking of times past when he was warm, trying to defeat the despair and trick his own body into forgetting the cold. A single thought stood out clearly, a memory of the kitchens in Menzoberranzan's Academy. In the ever-warm Underdark, Drizzt had never even considered fire as a source of warmth. Always before, Drizzt had seen fire as merely a method of cooking, a means of producing light, and an offensive weapon. Now it took on even greater importance for the drow. As the winds continued to blow colder and colder, Drizzt realized, to his horror, that a fire's heat alone could keep him alive.

He looked about for kindling. In the Underdark, he had burned mushroom stalks, but no mushrooms grew large enough on the surface. There were plants, though, trees that grew even larger than the Underdark's fungus.

"Get me . . . limb," Drizzt stuttered to Guenhwyvar, not knowing any words for wood or tree. The panther regarded him curiously.

"Fire," Drizzt begged. He tried to rise but found his legs and feet numb.

Then the panther did understand. Guenhwyvar growled once and sprinted out into the night. The great cat nearly tripped over a pile of branches and twigs that had been set—by whom, Guenhwyvar did not know—just outside the doorway. Drizzt, too concerned with his survival at the time, did not even question the cat's sudden return.

Drizzt tried unsuccessfully to strike a fire for many minutes, smacking his dagger against a stone. Finally he understood that the wind prevented the sparks from catching, so he moved the setup to a more sheltered area. His legs ached now, and his own saliva froze along his lips and chin.

Then a spark took hold in the dry pile. Drizzt carefully fanned the tiny flame, cupping his hands to prevent the wind from coming in too strongly.

* * * * *

"The flames are up," an elf said to his companion.

Kellindil nodded gravely, still not certain if he and his fellow elves had done right in aiding the drow. Kellindil had come right back out from Maldobar, while Dove and the others had set off for Sundabar, and had met with a small elven family, kinfolk of his, who lived in the mountains near Dead Orc Pass. With their expert aid, the elf had little trouble locating the drow, and together he and his kin had watched, curiously, over the last few weeks.

Drizzt's innocuous lifestyle had not dispelled all of the wary elf's doubts, though. Drizzt was a drow, after all, dark-skinned to view and dark-hearted by reputation.

Still, Kellindil's sigh was one of relief when he, too, noted the slight, distant glow. The drow would not freeze; Kellindil believed that this drow did not deserve such a fate.

* * * * *

After his meal later that night, Drizzt leaned on Guenhwyvar—and the panther gladly accepting the shared body heat—and looked up at the stars, twinkling brightly in the cold air. "Do you remember Menzoberranzan?" he asked the panther. "Do you remember when we first met?"

If Guenhwyvar understood him, the cat gave no indication. With a yawn, Guenhwyvar rolled against Drizzt and dropped its head between two outstretched paws.

Drizzt smiled and roughly rubbed the panther's ear. He had met Guenhwyvar in Sorcere, the wizard school of the Academy, when the panther was in the possession of Masoj Hun'ett, the only drow that Drizzt had ever killed. Drizzt purposely tried not to think of that incident now; with the fire burning brightly, warming his toes, this was no night for unpleasant memories. Despite the many horrors he had faced in the city of his birth, Drizzt had found some pleasures there and had learned many useful lessons. Even Masoj had taught him things that now aided him more than he ever would have believed. Looking back to the crackling flames, Drizzt mused that if it had not been for his apprenticeship duties of lighting candles, he would not even have known how to build a fire. Undeniably, that knowledge had saved him from a chilling death.

Drizzt's smile was short-lived as his thoughts continued along those lines. Not so many months after that particularly useful lesson, Drizzt had been forced to kill Masoj.

Drizzt lay back again and sighed. With neither danger nor confusing companionship apparently imminent, this was perhaps the most simple time of his life, but never had the complexities of his existence so fully overwhelmed him.

He was brought from his tranquility a moment later, when a large bird, an owl with tufted, hornlike feathers on its rounded head, rushed suddenly overhead. Drizzt laughed at his own inability to relax; in the second it had taken him to recognize the bird as no threat, he had leaped to his feet and drawn his scimitar and dagger. Guenhwyvar, too, had reacted to the startling bird, but in a far different manner. With Drizzt suddenly up and out of the way, the panther rolled closer to the heat of the fire, stretched languidly, and yawned again.

* * * * *

The owl drifted silently on unseen breezes, rising with the mist out of the river valley opposite the wall that Drizzt had originally descended. The bird rushed on through the night to a thick grove of evergreens on the side of a mountain, coming to rest on a wood-and-rope bridge constructed across the higher boughs of three of the trees. After a few moments preening itself, the bird rang a little silver bell, attached to the bridge for just such occasions.

A moment later, the bird rang the bell again.

"I am coming," came a voice from below. "Patience, Hooter. Let a blind man move at a pace that best suits him!" As if it understood, and enjoyed, the game, the owl rang the bell a third time.

An old man with a huge and bristling gray mustache and white eyes appeared on the bridge. He hopped and skipped his way toward the bird. Montolio was formerly a ranger of great renown, who now lived out his final years—by his own choice—secluded in the mountains and surrounded by the creatures he loved best (and he did not consider humans, elves, dwarves, or any of the other intelligent races among them). Despite his considerable age, Montolio remained tall and straight, though the years had taken their toll on the hermit, crinkling one hand up so that it resembled the claw of the bird he now approached.

"Patience, Hooter," he mumbled over and over. Anyone watching him nimbly pick his way across the somewhat treacherous bridge never would have guessed that he was blind, and those who knew Montolio certainly would not describe him that way. Rather, they might have said that his eyes did not function, but they quickly would have added that he did not need them to function. With his skills and knowledge, and with his many animal friends, the old ranger "saw" more of the world around him than most of those with normal sight.

Montolio held out his arm, and the great owl promptly hopped onto it, carefully finding its footing on the man's heavy leather sleeve.

"You have seen the drow?" Montolio asked.

The owl responded with a *whoo*, then went off into a complicated series of chattering hoots and *whoo*s. Montolio took it all in, weighing every detail. With the help of his friends, particularly this rather talkative owl, the ranger had monitored the drow for several days, curious as to why a dark elf had wandered into the valley. At first, Montolio had assumed that the drow was somehow connected to Graul, the chief orc of the region, but as time went on, the ranger began to suspect differently.

"A good sign," Montolio remarked when the owl had assured him that the drow had not yet made contact with the orc tribes. Graul was bad enough without having any allies as powerful as dark elves!

Still, the ranger could not figure out why the orcs had not sought out the drow. Possibly they had not caught sight of him; the drow had gone out of his way to remain inconspicuous, setting no fires (before this very night) and only coming out after sunset. More likely, Montolio mused as he gave the matter more thought, the orcs had seen the drow but had not yet found the courage to make contact.

Either way, the whole episode was proving a welcome diversion for the ranger as he went about the daily routines of setting up his house for the coming winter. He did not fear the drow's appearance—Montolio did not fear much of anything—and if the drow and the orcs were not allies, the resulting conflict might well be worth the watching.

"By my leave," the ranger said to placate the complaining owl. "Go and hunt some mice!" The owl swooped off immediately, circled once under then back over the bridge, and headed out into the night.

"Just take care not to eat any of the mice I have set to watching the drow!" Montolio called after the bird, and then he chuckled, shook his wild-grown gray locks, and turned back toward the ladder at the end of the bridge. He vowed, as he descended, that he would soon strap on his sword and find out what business this particular dark elf might have in the region.

The old ranger made many such vows.

* * * * *

Autumn's warning blasts gave way quickly to the onslaught of winter. It hadn't taken Drizzt long to figure out the significance of gray clouds, but when the storm broke this time, in the form of snow instead of rain, the drow was truly amazed. He had seen the whiteness along the tops of the mountains but had never gone high enough to inspect it and had merely assumed that it was a coloration of the rocks. Now Drizzt watched the white flakes descend on the valley; they disappeared in the rush of the river but gathered on the rocks.

As the snow began to mount and the clouds hung ever lower in the sky, Drizzt came to a dreadful realization. Quickly he summoned Guenhwyvar to his side.

"We must find better shelter," he explained to the weary panther. Guenhwyvar had only been released to its astral home the previous day. "And we must stock it with wood for our fires."

Several caves dotted the valley wall on this side of the river. Drizzt found one, not only deep and dark but sheltered from the blowing wind by a high stone ridge. He entered, pausing just inside to let his eyes adapt from the snow's glaring brightness.

The cave floor was uneven and its ceiling was not high. Large boulders were scattered randomly about, and off to the side, near one of these, Drizzt noticed a darker gloom, indicating a second chamber. He placed his armful of kindling down and started toward it, then halted suddenly, both he and Guenhwyvar sensing another presence.

Drizzt drew his scimitar, slipped to the boulder, and peered around it. With his infravision, the cave's other inhabitant, a warm-glowing ball considerably larger than the drow, was not hard to spot. Drizzt knew at once what it was, though he had no name for it. He had seen this creature from afar several times, watching it as it deftly—and with amazing speed, considering its bulk—snatched fish from the river.

Whatever it might be called, Drizzt had no desire to fight with it over the cave; there were other holes in the area, more easily attainable.

The great brown bear, though, seemed to have different ideas. The creature stirred suddenly and came up to its rear legs, its avalanche growl echoing throughout the cave and its claws and teeth all too noticeable.

Guenhwyvar, the astral entity of the panther, knew the bear as an ancient rival, and one that wise cats took great care to avoid. Still the brave panther sprang right in front of Drizzt, willing to take on the larger creature so that its master might escape.

"No, Guenhwyvar!" Drizzt commanded, and he grabbed the cat and pulled himself back in front.

The bear, another of Montolio's many friends, made no move to attack, but it held its position fiercely, not appreciating the interruption of its long-awaited slumber.

Drizzt sensed something here that he could not explain—not a friendship with the bear, but an eerie understanding of the creature's viewpoint. He thought himself foolish as he sheathed his blade, yet he could not deny the empathy he felt, almost as though he was viewing the situation through the bear's eyes.

Cautiously, Drizzt stepped closer, drawing the bear fully into his gaze. The bear seemed almost surprised, but gradually it lowered its claws and its snarling grimace became an expression that Drizzt understood as curiosity.

Drizzt slowly reached into his pouch and took out a fish that he had been saving for his own supper. He tossed it over to the bear, which sniffed it once, then swallowed it down with hardly a chew.

Another long moment of staring ensued, but the tension was gone. The bear belched once, rolled back down, and was soon snoring contentedly.

Drizzt looked at Guenhwyvar and shrugged helplessly, having no idea of how he had just communicated so profoundly with the animal. The panther had apparently understood the connotations of the exchange, too, for Guenhwyvar's fur was no longer ruffled.

For the rest of the time that Drizzt spent in that cave, he took care, whenever he had spare food, to drop a morsel by the slumbering bear. Sometimes, particularly if Drizzt had dropped fish, the bear sniffed and awakened just long enough to gobble the meal. More often, though, the animal ignored the food altogether, rhythmically snoring and dreaming about honey and berries and female bears, and whatever else sleeping bears dreamed about.

* * * * *

"He took up his home with Bluster?" Montolio gasped when he learned from Hooter that the drow and the ornery bear were sharing the two-chambered cave. Montolio nearly fell over—and would have if he hadn't been so close to the supporting tree trunk. The old ranger leaned there, stunned, scratching at the stubble on his face and pulling at his moustache. He had known the bear for several years, and even he wasn't certain that he would be willing to share quarters with it. Bluster was an easily riled creature, as many of Graul's stupid orcs had learned over the years.

"I guess Bluster is too tired to argue," Montolio rationalized, but he knew that something more was brewing here. If an orc or a goblin had gone into that cave, Bluster would have swatted it dead without a second thought. Yet the drow and his panther were in there, day after day, setting their fires in the outer chamber while Bluster snored contentedly in the inner.

As a ranger, and knowing many other rangers, Montolio had seen and heard of stranger things. Up to now, though, he had always considered that innate ability to mentally connect with wild animals the exclusive domain of those surface elves, sprites, halflings, gnomes, and humans who had trained in the woodland way.

"How would a dark elf know of a bear?" Montolio asked aloud, still scratching at his beard. The ranger considered two possibilities: Either there was more to the drow race than he knew, or this particular dark elf was not akin to his kin. Given the elf's already strange behavior, Montolio assumed the latter, though he greatly wanted to find out for sure. His investigation would have to wait, though. The first snow had already fallen, and the ranger knew the second, and the third, and many more, would not be far behind. In the mountains around Dead Orc Pass, little moved once the snows had begun.

* * * * *

Guenhwyvar proved to be Drizzt's salvation through the coming weeks. On those occasions when the panther walked the Material Plane, Guenhwyvar went out into the frigid, deep snows continually, hunting and, more importantly, bringing back wood for the life-giving fire.

Still, things were not easy for the displaced drow. Every day Drizzt had to go down to the river and break up the ice that formed in the slower pools, Drizzt's fishing pools, along its bank. It was not a far walk, but the snow was soon deep and treacherous, often sliding down the slope behind Drizzt to bury him in a chilling embrace. Several times, Drizzt stumbled back to his cave, all feeling gone from his hands and legs. He learned quickly to get the fires blazing before he went out, for on his return, he had no strength to hold the dagger and stone to strike a spark.

Even when Drizzt's belly was full and he was surrounded

by the glow of the fire and Guenhwyvar's fur, he was cold and utterly miserable. For the first time in many weeks, the drow questioned his decision to leave the Underdark, and as his desperation grew, he questioned his decision to leave Menzoberranzan.

"Surely I am a homeless wretch," he often complained in those no-longer-so-rare moments of self-pity. "And surely I will die here, cold and alone."

Drizzt had no idea of what was going on in the strange world around him. Would the warmth that he found when he first came to the surface world ever return to the land? Or was this some vile curse, perhaps aimed at him by his mighty enemies back in Menzoberranzan? This confusion led Drizzt to a troublesome dilemma: Should he remain in the cave and try to wait out the storm (for what else could he call the wintry season)? Or should he set out from the river valley and seek a warmer climate?

He would have left, and the trek through the mountains most assuredly would have killed him, but he noticed another event coinciding with the harsh weather. The hours of daylight had lessened and the hours of night had increased. Would the sun disappear completely, engulfing the surface in an eternal darkness and eternal cold? Drizzt doubted that possibility, so, using some sand and an empty flask that he had in his pack, he began measuring the time of light and of darkness.

His hopes sank every time his calculations showed an earlier sunset, and as the season deepened, so did Drizzt's despair. His health diminished as well. He was a wretched thing indeed, thin and shivering, when he first noticed the seasonal turn-around, the winter solstice. He hardly believed his findings—his measurements were not so precise—but after the next few days, Drizzt could not deny what the falling sand told him.

The days were growing longer.

Drizzt's hope returned. He had suspected a seasonal variance since the first cool winds had begun to blow months before. He had watched the bear fishing more diligently as the weather worsened, and now he believed that the creature had anticipated the cold and had stored up its fat to sleep it out.

That belief, and his findings about the daylight, convinced Drizzt that this frozen desolation would not endure.

The solstice did not bring any immediate relief, though. The winds blew harder and the snow continued to pile. But Drizzt grew determined again, and more than a winter would be needed to defeat the indomitable drow.

Then it happened—almost overnight, it seemed. The snows lessened, the river ran freer of ice, and the wind shifted to bring in warmer air. Drizzt felt a surge of vitality and hope, a release from grief and from guilt that he could not explain. Drizzt could not realize what urges gripped him, had no name or concept for it, but he was as fully caught up in the timeless spring as all of the natural creatures of the surface world.

One morning, as Drizzt finished his meal and prepared for bed, his long-dormant roommate plodded out of the side chamber, noticeably more slender but still quite formidable. Drizzt watched the ambling bear carefully, wondering if he should summon Guenhwyvar or draw his scimitar. The bear paid him no heed, though. It shuffled right by him, stopped to sniff at and then lick the flat stone Drizzt had used as a plate, and then ambled out into the warm sunlight, stopping at the cave exit to give a yawn and a stretch so profound that Drizzt understood that its winter nap was at an end. Drizzt understood, too, that the cave would grow crowded very quickly with the dangerous animal up and about, and he decided that perhaps, with the more hospitable weather, the cave might not be worth fighting for.

Drizzt was gone before the bear returned, but, to the bear's delight, he had left one final fish meal. Soon Drizzt was setting up in a more shallow and less protected cave a few hundred yards down the valley wall.

☙ 12 ☙

To Know Your Enemies

Winter gave way as quickly as it had come. The snows lessened daily and the southern wind brought air that had no chill. Drizzt soon settled into a comfortable routine; the biggest problem he faced was the daytime glare of the sun off the still snow-covered ground. The drow had adapted quite well to the sun in his first few months on the surface, moving about—even fighting—in the daylight. Now, though, with the white snow throwing the glaring reflection back in his face, Drizzt could hardly venture out.

He came out only at night and left the daytime to the bear and other such creatures. Drizzt was not too concerned; the snow would be gone soon, he believed, and he could return to the easy life that had marked the last days before winter.

Well fed, well rested, and under the soft light of a shining, alluring moon one night, Drizzt glanced across the river, to the far wall of the valley.

"What is up there?" the drow whispered to himself. Although the river ran strong with the spring melt, earlier that night Drizzt had found a possible way across it, a series of large and closely spaced rocks poking up above the rushing water.

The night was still young; the moon was not halfway up in the sky. Filled with the wanderlust and spirit so typical of the season, Drizzt decided to have a look. He skipped down to the riverbank and jumped lightly and nimbly out onto the stones. To a man or an orc—or most of the other races of the world—crossing on the wet, unevenly spaced, and often rounded stones might have seemed too difficult and treacherous to even make the attempt, but the agile drow managed it quite easily.

He came down on the other bank running, springing over or around the many rocks and crags without a thought or care. How different his demeanor might have been if he had known that he was now on the side of the valley belonging to Graul, the great orc chieftain!

* * * * *

An orc patrol spotted the prancing drow before he was halfway up the valley wall. The orcs had seen the drow before, on occasions when Drizzt was fishing out at the river. Fearful of dark elves, Graul had ordered its minions to keep their distance, thinking the snows would drive the intruder away. But the winter had passed and this lone drow remained, and now he had crossed the river.

Graul wrung his fat-fingered hands nervously when he was told the news. The big orc was comforted a bit by the belief that this drow was alone and not a member of a larger band. He might be a scout or a renegade; Graul could not know for sure, and the implications of either did not please the orc chieftain. If the drow was a scout, more dark elves might follow, and if the drow was a renegade, he might look upon the orcs as possible allies.

Graul had been chieftain for many years, an unusually long tenure for the chaotic orcs. The big orc had survived by taking no chances, and Graul meant to take none now. A dark elf could usurp the leadership of the tribe, a position Graul coveted dearly. This, Graul would not permit. Two orc patrols slipped out of dark holes shortly thereafter, with explicit orders to kill the drow.

* * * * *

A chill wind blew above the valley wall, and the snow was deeper up here, but Drizzt didn't care. Great patches of evergreens rolled out before him, darkening the mountainous valleys and inviting him, after a winter cooped up in the cave, to come and explore.

He had put nearly a mile behind him when he first realized that he was being pursued. He never actually saw anything, except perhaps a fleeting shadow out of the corner of his eye, but those intangible warrior senses told Drizzt the truth beyond doubt. He moved up the side of a steep incline, climbed above a copse of thick trees, and sprinted for the high ridge. When he got there, he slipped behind a boulder and turned to watch.

Seven dark forms, six humanoid and one large canine, came out of the trees behind him, following his trail carefully and methodically. From this distance, Drizzt couldn't tell their race, though he suspected that they were humans. He looked all about, searching for his best course of retreat, or the best defensible area.

Drizzt hardly noticed that his scimitar was in one hand, his dagger in the other. When he realized fully that he had drawn the weapons, and that the pursuing party was getting uncomfortably close, he paused and pondered.

He could face the pursuers right here and hit them as they scaled the last few treacherous feet of the slippery climb.

"No," Drizzt growled, dismissing that possibility as soon as it came to him. He could attack, and probably win, but then what burden would he carry away from the encounter? Drizzt wanted no fight, nor did he desire any contact at all. He already carried all the guilt he could handle.

He heard his pursuers' voices, guttural strains similar to the goblin tongue. "Orcs," the drow mouthed silently, matching the language with the creatures' human size.

The recognition did nothing to change the drow's attitudes, though. Drizzt had no love for orcs—he had seen enough of the smelly things back in Menzoberranzan—but neither did he have any reason, any justification, for battling this band. He turned and picked a path and sped off into the night.

The pursuit was dogged; the orcs were too close behind for Drizzt to shake them. He saw a problem developing, for if the orcs were hostile, and, by their shouts and snarls, Drizzt believed that to be the case, then Drizzt had missed his opportunity to fight them on favorable ground. The moon had set long ago and the sky had taken on the blue tint of predawn. Orcs did not favor sunlight, but with the glare of the snow all about him, Drizzt would be nearly helpless in it.

Stubbornly the drow ignored the battle option and tried to outrun the pursuit, circling back toward the valley. Here Drizzt made his second error, for another orc band, this one accompanied by both a wolf and a much larger form, a stone giant, lay in wait.

The path ran fairly level, one side of it dropping steeply down a rocky slope to the drow's left and the other climbing just as steeply and over ground just as rocky to his right. Drizzt knew his pursuers would have little trouble following him over such a predetermined course, but he relied solely on speed now, trying to get back to his defensible cave before the blinding sun came up.

A snarl warned him a moment before a huge bristle-haired wolf, called a worg, bounded around the boulders just above him and cut him off. The worg sprang at him, its jaws snapping for his head. Drizzt dipped low, under the assault, and his scimitar came out in a flash, slashing across to further widen the beast's huge maw. The worg tumbled down heavily behind the turning drow, its tongue lapping wildly at its own gushing blood.

Drizzt whacked it again, dropping it, but the six orcs came rushing in, brandishing spears and clubs. Drizzt turned to flee, then ducked again, just in time, as a hurled boulder flew past, skipping down the rocky decline.

Without a second thought, Drizzt brought a globe of darkness down over his own head.

The four leading orcs plunged into the globe without realizing it. Their remaining two comrades held back, clutching spears and glancing nervously about. They could see nothing inside the magical darkness, but from the rushing thumps of blades and clubs and the wild shouting, it sounded as if an entire army battled in there. Then another sound issued from the darkness, a growling, feline sound.

The two orcs backed away, looking over their shoulders and wishing the stone giant would hurry up and get down to them. One of their orc comrades, and then another, came tearing out of the blackness, screaming in terror. The first sped past its startled kin, but the second never made it.

Guenhwyvar latched on to the unfortunate orc and drove it to the ground, tearing the life from it. The panther hardly slowed, leaping out and taking down one of the waiting two as it frantically stumbled to get away. Those remaining outside the globe scrambled and tripped over the rocks, and Guenhwyvar, having finished the second kill, leaped off in pursuit.

Drizzt came out the other side of the globe unscathed, with both his scimitar and dagger dripping orc blood. The giant, huge and square-shouldered, with legs as large as tree trunks, stepped out to face him, and Drizzt never hesitated. He sprang to a large stone, then leaped off, his scimitar leading the way.

His agility and speed surprised the stone giant; the monster never even got its club or its free hand up to block. But luck was not with the drow this time. His scimitar, enchanted in the magic of the Underdark, had seen too much of the surface light. It drove against the stonelike skin of the fifteen-foot giant, bent nearly in half, and snapped at the hilt.

Drizzt bounced back, betrayed for the first time by his trusted weapon.

The giant howled and lifted its club, grinning evilly until a black form soared over its intended victim and crashed into its chest, raking with four cruel claws.

Guenhwyvar had saved Drizzt again, but the giant was hardly finished. It clubbed and thrashed until the panther flew free. Guenhwyvar tried to pivot and come right back in, but the panther landed on the down slope and its momentum broke away the sheet of snow. The cat slid and tumbled, and finally broke free of the slide, unharmed, but far down the mountainside from Drizzt and the battle.

The giant offered no smile this time. Blood seeped from a dozen deep scratches across its chest and face. Behind it, down the trail, the other orc group, led by a second howling worg, was quickly closing.

Like any wise warrior so obviously outnumbered, Drizzt turned and ran.

If the two orcs who had fled from Guenhwyvar had come right back down the slope, they could have cut the drow off. Orcs had never been known for bravery, though, and those two had already crested the ridge of the slope and were still running, not even looking back.

Drizzt sped along the trail, searching for some way he might descend and rejoin the panther. Nowhere on the slope seemed promising, though, for he would have to pick his way slowly and carefully, and no doubt with a giant raining boulders down at him. Going up seemed just as futile with the monster so close behind, so the drow just ran on, along the trail, hoping it wouldn't end anytime soon.

The sun peeked over the eastern horizon then, just another problem—suddenly one of many—for the desperate drow.

Understanding that fortune had turned against him, Drizzt somehow knew, even before he turned the trail's latest sharp corner, that he had come to the end of the road. A rock slide had long ago blocked the trail. Drizzt skidded to a halt and pulled off his pack, knowing that time was against him.

The worg-led orc band caught up to the giant, both gaining confidence in the presence of the other. Together they charged on, with the vicious worg sprinting out to take the lead.

Around a sharp bend the creature sped, stumbling and trying to stop when it tangled suddenly in a looped rope. Worgs were not stupid creatures, but this one didn't fully comprehend the terrible implications as the drow pushed a rounded stone over the ledge. The worg didn't understand, that is, until the rope snapped taut and the stone pulled the beast, flying, down behind.

The simple trap had worked to perfection, but it was the only advantage Drizzt could hope to gain. Behind him, the trail was fully blocked, and, to the sides, the slopes climbed and dropped too abruptly for him to flee. When the orcs and the giant came around the corner, tentatively after watching their worg go for a rather bumpy ride, Drizzt stood to face them with only a dagger in his hand.

The drow tried to parlay, using the goblin tongue, but the orcs would hear nothing of it. Before the first word left Drizzt's mouth, one of them had launched its spear.

The weapon came in a blur at the sun-blinded drow, but it was a curving shaft thrown by a clumsy creature. Drizzt easily sidestepped and then returned the throw with his dagger. The orc could see better than the drow, but it was not as quick. It caught the dagger cleanly, right in the throat. Gurgling, the orc went down, and its closest comrade grabbed at the knife and tore it free, not to save the other orc, but merely to get its hands on so fine a weapon.

Drizzt scooped up the crude spear and planted his feet firmly as the stone giant stalked in.

An owl swooped down above the giant suddenly and gave a hoot, hardly distracting the determined monster. A moment later, though, the giant jerked forward, moved by the weight of an arrow that had suddenly thudded into its back.

Drizzt saw the quivering, black-feathered shaft as the angry giant spun about. The drow didn't question the unexpected aid. He drove his spear with all his strength right into the monster's backside.

The giant would have turned to respond, but the owl swooped in again and hooted and, on cue, another arrow whistled in, this one digging into the giant's chest. Another hoot, and another arrow found the mark.

The stunned orcs looked all about for the unseen assailant, but the glaring brightness of the morning sun on the snow offered little assistance to the nocturnal beasts. The giant, struck through the heart, only stood and stared blankly, not even realizing that its life was at an end. The drow drove his spear in again from behind, but that action only served to tumble the monster away from Drizzt.

The orcs looked to each other and all around, wondering which way they could flee.

The strange owl dove in again, this time above an orc, and gave a fourth hoot. The orc, understanding the implications, waved its arms and shrieked, then fell silent with an arrow protruding from its face.

The four remaining orcs broke ranks and fled, one up the slope, another running back the way it had come, and two rushing toward Drizzt.

A deft spin of the spear sent its butt end slamming into the face of one orc, then Drizzt fully completed the spinning motion to deflect the other orc's spear tip toward the ground. The orc dropped the weapon, realizing that it could not get it back in line in time to stop the drow.

*　*　*　*　*

The orc climbing the slope understood its doom as the signaling owl closed on it. The terrified creature dove behind a rock upon hearing one hoot, but if it had been a smarter thing, it would have realized its error. By the angle of the shots that had felled the giant, the archer had to be somewhere up on this slope.

An arrow knocked into its thigh as it crouched, dropping it, writhing, to its back. With the orc's growling and thrashing, the unseen and unseeing archer hardly needed the owl's next hoot to place his second shot, this one catching the orc squarely in the chest and silencing it forever.

*　*　*　*　*

Drizzt reversed his direction immediately, clipping the second orc with the spear's butt end. In the blink of an eye, the drow reversed his grip a third time and drove the spear tip into the creature's throat, digging upward into its brain.

The first orc that Drizzt had hit reeled and shook its head violently, trying to reorient itself to the battle. It felt the drow's hands grab at the front of its dirty bearskin tunic, then it felt a rush of air as it flew out over the ledge, taking the same route as the previously trapped worg.

* * * * *

Hearing the screams of its dying companions, the orc on the trail put its head down and sped on, thinking itself quite clever in taking this route. It changed its mind abruptly, though, when it turned a bend and ran straight into the waiting paws of a huge black panther.

* * * * *

Drizzt leaned back, exhausted, against the stone, holding his spear ready for a throw as the strange owl floated back down the mountainside. The owl kept its distance, though, alighting on the outcropping that forced the trail's sharp bend a dozen steps away.

Movement up above caught the drow's attention. He could hardly see in the blinding light, but he did make out a humanlike form picking a careful path down toward him.

The owl set off again, circling above the drow and calling, and Drizzt crouched, alert and unnerved, as the man slipped down to a position behind the rocky spur. No arrow whistled out to the owl's hooting, though. Instead came the archer.

He was tall, straight, and very old, with a huge gray moustache and wild gray hair. Most curious of all were his milky white and pupil-less eyes. If Drizzt had not witnessed the man's archery display, he would have believed the man blind. The old man's limbs seemed quite frail, too, but Drizzt did not let appearances deceive him. The expert archer kept his heavy longbow bowed and ready, an arrow firmly nocked, with hardly any effort. The drow did not have to look far to see the deadly efficiency with which the human could put the powerful weapon to use.

The old man said something in a language that Drizzt could not understand, then in a second tongue, then in goblin, which Drizzt understood. "Who are you?"

"Drizzt Do'Urden," the drow replied evenly, taking some hope in the fact that he could at least communicate with this adversary.

"Is that a name?" the old man asked. He chuckled and shrugged. "Whatever it is, and whoever you might be, and whyever you might be here, is of minor consequence."

The owl, noticing movement, started hooting and swooping wildly, but it was too late for the old man. Behind him, Guenhwyvar slunk around the bend and closed to within an easy spring, ears flattened and teeth bared.

Seemingly oblivious to the peril, the old man finished his thought. "You are my prisoner now."

Guenhwyvar issued a low, throaty growl and the drow grinned broadly.

"I think not," Drizzt replied.

~13~

Montolio

"Friend of yours?" the old man asked calmly.

"Guenhwyvar," Drizzt explained.

"Big cat?"

"Oh, yes," Drizzt answered.

The old man eased his bowstring straight and let the arrow slowly slip, point down. He closed his eyes, tilted his head back, and seemed to fall within himself. A moment later, Drizzt noticed that Guenhwyvar's ears came up suddenly, and the drow understood that this strange human was somehow making a telepathic link to the panther.

"Good cat, too," the old man said a moment later. Guenhwyvar walked out from around the outcropping—sending the owl flapping away in a frenzy—and casually stalked past the old man, moving to stand beside Drizzt. Apparently, the panther had relinquished all concerns that the old man was an enemy.

Drizzt considered Guenhwyvar's actions curious, viewing them in the same manner as he had his own empathic agreement with the bear in the cave a season ago.

"Good cat," the old man said again.

Drizzt leaned back against the stone and relaxed his grip on the spear.

"I am Montolio," the old man explained proudly, as though the name should carry some weight with the drow. "Montolio DeBrouchee."

"Well met and fare well," Drizzt said flatly. "If we are done with our meeting, then we may go our own ways."

"We may," Montolio agreed, "if we both choose to."

"Am I to be your . . . prisoner . . . once more?" Drizzt asked with a bit of sarcasm in his voice.

The sincerity of Montolio's ensuing laughter brought a smile to the drow's face despite his cynicism. "Mine?" the old man asked incredulously. "No, no, I believe we have settled that issue. But you have killed some minions of Graul this day, a deed that the orc king will want punished. Let me offer you a room at my castle. The orcs will not approach the place." He showed a wry smile and bent over toward Drizzt to whisper, as if to keep his next words a secret between them. "They will not come near me, you know." Montolio pointed to his strange eyes. "They believe me to be bad magic because of my . . ." Montolio struggled for the word that would convey the thought, but the guttural language was limited and he soon grew frustrated.

Drizzt silently recounted the course of the battle, then his jaw drooped open in undeniable amazement as he realized the truth of what had transpired. The old man was indeed blind! The owl, circling over enemies and hooting, had led his shots. Drizzt looked around at the slain giant and orc and his jaw did not close; the old man hadn't missed.

"Will you come?" Montolio asked. "I would like to gain the" — Again he had to search for an appropriate term— "purposes . . . a dark elf would have to live a winter in a cave with Bluster the bear."

Montolio cringed at his own inability to converse with the drow, but from the context, Drizzt could pretty much understand what the old man meant, even figuring out unfamiliar terms such as "winter" and "bear."

"Orc king Graul has ten hundred more fighters to send against you," Montolio remarked, sensing that the drow was having a difficult time considering the offer.

"I will not come with you," Drizzt declared at length. The drow truly wanted to go, wanted to learn a few things about this remarkable man, but too many tragedies had befallen those who had crossed Drizzt's path.

Guenhwyvar's low growl told Drizzt that the panther did not approve of his decision.

"I bring trouble," Drizzt tried to explain to the old man, to the panther, and to himself. "You would be better served, Montolio DeBrouchee, to keep away from me."

"Is this a threat?"

"A warning," Drizzt replied. "If you take me in, if you even allow me to remain near to you, then you will be doomed, as were the farmers in the village."

Montolio perked his ears up at the mention of the distant farming village. He had heard that one family in Maldobar had been brutally killed and that a ranger, Dove Falconhand, had been called in to help.

"I do not fear doom," Montolio said, forcing a smile. "I have lived through many . . . fights, Drizzt Do'Urden. I have fought in a dozen bloody wars and spent an entire winter trapped on the side of a mountain with a broken leg. I have killed a giant with only a dagger and . . . befriended . . . every animal for five thousand steps in any direction. Do not fear for me." Again came that wry, knowing smile. "But, then," Montolio said slowly, "It is not for me that you fear."

Drizzt felt confused and a bit insulted.

"You fear for yourself," Montolio continued, undaunted. "Self-pity? It does not fit one of your prowess. Dismiss it and come along with me."

If Montolio had seen Drizzt's scowl, he would have guessed the forthcoming answer. Guenhwyvar did notice it, and the panther bumped hard into Drizzt's leg.

From Guenhwyvar's reaction, Montolio understood the drow's intent. "The cat wants you to come along," he remarked. "It'll be better than a cave," he promised, "and better food than half-cooked fish."

Drizzt looked down at Guenhwyvar and again the panther bumped him, this time voicing a louder and more insistent growl with the action.

Drizzt remained adamant, reminding himself pointedly by conjuring an image of carnage in a farmhouse far away. "I will not come," he said firmly.

"Then I must name you as an enemy, and a prisoner!" Montolio roared, snapping his bow back to a ready position. "Your cat will not aid you this time, Drizzt Do'Urden!" Montolio leaned in and flashed his smile and whispered, "The cat agrees with me."

It was too much for Drizzt. He knew that the old man wouldn't shoot him, but Montolio's flaky charm soon wore away the drow's mental defenses, considerable though they were.

What Montolio had described as a castle turned out to be a series of wooden caves dug around the roots of huge and tightly packed evergreens. Lean-tos of woven sticks furthered the protection and somewhat linked the caves together, and a low wall of stacked rocks ringed the whole complex. As Drizzt neared the place, he noticed several rope-and-wood bridges crossing from tree to tree at various heights, with rope ladders leading up to them from the ground level and with crossbows securely mounted at fairly regular intervals.

The drow didn't complain that the castle was of wood and dirt, though. Drizzt had spent three decades in Menzoberranzan living in a wondrous castle of stone and surrounded by many more breathtakingly beautiful structures, but none of them seemed as welcoming as Montolio's home.

Birds chittered their welcome at the old ranger's approach. Squirrels, even a raccoon, hopped excitedly among the tree branches to get near him—though they kept their distance when they noticed that a huge panther accompanied Montolio.

"I have many rooms," Montolio explained to Drizzt. "Many blankets and much food." Montolio hated the limited goblin tongue. He had so many things he wanted to say to the drow, and so many things he wanted to learn from the drow. This seemed impossible, if not overly tedious, in a language so base and negative in nature, not designed for complex thoughts or notions. The goblin tongue sported more than a hundred words for killing and for hatred, but not a one for higher emotions such as compassion. The goblin word for friendship could be translated to mean either a temporary military alliance or servitude to a stronger goblin, and neither definition fit Montolio's intentions toward the lone dark elf.

The first task then, the ranger decided, was to teach this drow the common tongue.

"We cannot speak" — There was no word for "properly" in Goblin, so Montolio had to improvise—". . . well . . . in this language," he explained to Drizzt, "but it will serve us as I teach you the tongue of humans—if you wish to learn."

Drizzt remained tentative in his acceptance. When he had walked away from the farming village, he had decided that his lot in life would be as a hermit, and thus far he had done pretty well—better than he had expected. The offer was tempting, though, and on a practical level, Drizzt knew that knowing the common language of the region might keep him out of trouble. Montolio's smile nearly took in the ranger's ears when the drow accepted.

Hooter, the owl, however, seemed not so pleased. With the drow—or, more particularly, with the drow's panther—about, the owl would be spending less time in the comforts of the evergreens' lower boughs.

* * * * *

"Cousin, Montolio DeBrouchee has taken the drow in!" an elf cried excitedly to Kellindil. All the group had been out searching for Drizzt's trail since the winter had broken. With the drow gone from Dead Orc Pass, the elves, particularly Kellindil, had feared trouble, had feared that the drow had perhaps taken in with Graul and his orc minions.

Kellindil jumped to his feet, hardly able to grasp the startling news. He knew of Montolio, the legendary if somewhat eccentric ranger, and he knew, too, that Montolio, with all of his animal contacts, could judge intruders quite accurately.

"When? How?" Kellindil asked, barely knowing where to begin. If the drow had confused him through the previous months, the surface elf was thoroughly flustered now.

"A week ago," the other elf answered. "I know not how it

came about, but the drow now walks in Montolio's grove, openly and with his panther beside him."

"Is Montolio . . ."

The other elf interrupted Kellindil, seeing where his line of concern was heading. "Montolio is unharmed and in control," he assured Kellindil. "He has taken in the drow of his own accord, it would seem, and now it appears that the old ranger is teaching the dark elf the common tongue."

"Amazing," was all that Kellindil could reply.

"We could set a watch over Montolio's grove," the other elf offered. "If you fear for the old ranger's safety—"

"No," Kellindil replied. "No, the drow once again has proven himself no enemy. I have suspected his friendly intentions since I encountered him near Maldobar. Now I am satisfied. Let us get on with our business and leave the drow and the ranger to theirs."

The other elf nodded his agreement, but a diminutive creature listening outside Kellindil's tent was not so certain.

Tephanis came into the elven camp nightly, to steal food and other items that would make him more comfortable. The sprite had heard of the dark elf a few days earlier, when the elves had resumed their search for Drizzt, and he had taken great pains to listen to their conversation ever since, as curious as any about the whereabouts of the one who had destroyed Ulgulu and Kempfana.

Tephanis shook his floppy-eared head violently. "Drat-the-day-that-that-one-returned!" he whispered, sounding somewhat like an excited bumblebee. Then he ran off, his little feet barely touching the ground. Tephanis had made another connection in the months since Ulgulu's demise, another powerful ally that he did not want to lose.

Within minutes he found Caroak, the great, silver-haired winter wolf, on the high peak that they called their home.

"The-drow-is-with-the-ranger," Tephanis spouted, and the canine beast seemed to understand. "Beware-of-that-one-I-say! It-was-he-who-killed-my-former-masters. Dead!"

Caroak looked down the wide expanse to the mountain that held Montolio's grove. The winter wolf knew that place well, and he knew well enough to stay away from it. Montolio DeBrouchee was friends with all sorts of animals, but winter wolves were more monster than animal, and no friend of rangers.

Tephanis, too, looked Montolio's way, worried that he might again have to face the sneaky drow. The mere thought of encountering that one again made the little sprite's head ache (and the bruise from the plowshare had never completely gone away).

* * * * *

As winter eased into spring over the next few weeks, so did Drizzt and Montolio ease into their friendship. The common tongue of the region was not so very different from the goblin tongue, more a shift of inflection than an alteration of complete words, and Drizzt caught on to it quickly, even learning how to read and write. Montolio proved a fine teacher, and by the third week, he spoke to Drizzt exclusively in the common tongue and scowled impatiently every time Drizzt reverted to using goblin to get a point across.

For Drizzt, this was a fun time, a time of easy living and shared pleasures. Montolio's collection of books was extensive, and the drow found himself absorbed in adventures of the imagination, in dragon lore, and accounts of epic battles. Any doubts Drizzt might have had were long gone, as were his doubts about Montolio. The shelter in the evergreens was indeed a castle, and the old man as fine a host as Drizzt had ever known.

Drizzt learned many other things from Montolio during those first weeks, practical lessons that would aid him for the rest of his life. Montolio confirmed Drizzt's suspicions about a seasonal weather change, and he even taught Drizzt how to anticipate the weather from day to day by watching the animals, the sky, and the wind.

In this, too, Drizzt caught on quickly, as Montolio had suspected he would. Montolio never would have believed it until he had witnessed it personally, but this unusual drow possessed the demeanor of a surface elf, perhaps even the heart of a ranger.

"How did you calm the bear?" Montolio asked one day, a question that had nagged at him since the very first day he had learned that Drizzt and Bluster were sharing a cave.

Drizzt honestly did not know how to answer, for he still did not understand what had transpired in that meeting. "The same way you calmed Guenhwyvar when first we met," the drow offered at length.

Montolio's grin told Drizzt that the old man understood better than he. "Heart of a ranger," Montolio whispered as he turned away. With his exceptional ears, Drizzt heard the comment, but he didn't fully comprehend.

Drizzt's lessons came faster as the days rolled along. Now Montolio concentrated on the life around them, the animals and the plants. He showed Drizzt how to forage and how to understand the emotions of an animal simply by watching its movements. The first real test came soon after, when Drizzt, shifting the outward branches of a berry bush, found the entrance to a small den and was promptly confronted by an angry badger.

Hooter, in the sky above, issued a series of cries to alert Montolio, and the ranger's first instinct was to go and help his drow friend. Badgers were possibly the meanest creatures in the region, even above the orcs, quicker to anger than Bluster the bear and quite willing to take the offensive against any opponent, no matter how large. Montolio stayed back, though, listening to Hooter's continuing descriptions of the scene.

Drizzt's first instinct sent his hand flashing to his dagger. The badger reared and showed its wicked teeth and claws, hissing and sputtering a thousand complaints.

Drizzt eased back, even put his dagger back in its sheath. Suddenly, he viewed the encounter from the badger's point of view, knew that the animal felt overly threatened. Somehow, Drizzt then further realized that the badger had chosen this den as a place to raise its soon-coming litter of pups.

The badger seemed confused by the drow's deliberate motions. Late in term, the expectant mother did not want a fight, and as Drizzt carefully slipped the berry bush back in place to conceal the den, the badger eased down to all fours, sniffed the air so that it could remember the dark elf's scent, and went back into its hole.

When Drizzt turned around, he found Montolio smiling and clapping. "Even a ranger would be hard put to calm a riled badger," the old man explained.

"The badger was with pups," Drizzt replied. "She wanted to fight less than I."

"How do you know that?" Montolio asked, though he did not doubt the drow's perceptions.

Drizzt started to answer, then realized that he could not. He looked back to the berry bush, then to Montolio helplessly.

Montolio laughed loudly and returned to his work. He, who had followed the ways of the goddess Mielikki for so many years, knew what was happening, even if Drizzt did not.

"The badger could have ripped you, you do know," the ranger said wryly when Drizzt moved beside him.

"She was with pups," Drizzt reminded him, "and not so large a foe."

Montolio's laughter mocked him. "Not so large?" the ranger echoed. "Trust me, Drizzt, you would rather tangle with Bluster than with a mother badger!"

Drizzt only shrugged in response, having no arguments for the more experienced man.

"Do you really believe that puny knife would have been any defense against her?" Montolio asked, now wanting to take the discussion in a different direction.

Drizzt regarded the dagger, the one he had taken from the sprite. Again he could not argue; the knife was indeed puny. He laughed both to and at himself. "It is all that I have, I fear," he replied.

"We shall see about that," the ranger promised, then said no more about it. Montolio, for all his calm and confidence, knew well the dangers of the wild, mountainous region.

The ranger had come to trust in Drizzt without reservations.

* * * * *

Montolio roused Drizzt shortly before sunset and led the drow to a wide tree in the northern end of the grove. A large hole, almost a cave, lay at the base of the tree, cunningly concealed by shrubs and a blanket colored to resemble the tree trunk. As soon as Montolio pushed this aside, Drizzt understood the secrecy.

"An armory?" the drow asked in amazement.

"You fancy the scimitar," Montolio replied, remembering the weapon Drizzt had broken on the stone giant. "I have a good one, too." He crawled inside and fished about for a while, then returned with a fine, curving blade. Drizzt moved in to the hole to survey the marvelous display of weapons as the ranger exited. Montolio possessed a huge variety of weapons, from ornamental daggers to great bardiche axes to crossbows, light and heavy, all polished and cared for meticulously. Set against the back of the inner tree trunk, running right up into the tree, were a variety of spears, including one metal-shafted ranseur, a ten-foot-long pike with a long and pointed head and two smaller barbs sticking out to the sides near the tip.

"Do you prefer a shield, or perhaps a dirk, for your other hand?" Montolio asked when the drow, muttering to himself in sincere admiration, reappeared. "You may have any but those bearing the taloned owl. That shield, sword, and helmet are my own."

Drizzt hesitated a moment, trying to imagine the blind ranger so outfitted for close melee. "A sword," he said at length, "or another scimitar if you have one."

Montolio looked at him curiously. "Two long blades for fighting," he remarked. "You would likely tangle yourself up in them, I would guess."

"It is not so uncommon a fighting style among the drow,"

Drizzt said.

Montolio shrugged, not doubting, and went back in. "This one is more for show, I fear," he said as he returned, bearing an overly ornamented blade. "You may use it if you choose, or take a sword. I've a number of those."

Drizzt took the scimitar to measure its balance. It was a bit too light and perhaps a bit too fragile. The drow decided to keep it, though, thinking its curving blade a better compliment to his other scimitar than a straight and cumbersome sword.

"I will care for these as well as you have," Drizzt promised, realizing how great a gift the human had given him. "And I will use them," he added, knowing what Montolio truly wanted to hear, "only when I must."

"Then pray that you may never need them, Drizzt Do'Urden," Montolio replied. "I have seen peace and I have seen war, and I can tell you that I prefer the former! Come now, friend. There are so many more things I wish to show you."

Drizzt regarded the scimitars one final time, then slipped them into the sheaths on his belt and followed Montolio.

With summer fast approaching and with such fine and exciting companionship, both the teacher and his unusual student were in high spirits, anticipating a season of valuable lessons and wondrous events.

* * * * *

How diminished their smiles would have been if they had known that a certain orc king, angered at the loss of ten soldiers, two worgs, and a valued giant ally, had its yellow, bloodshot eyes scanning the region, searching for the drow. The big orc was beginning to wonder if Drizzt had gone back to the Underdark or had taken in with some other group, perhaps with the small elven bands known to be in the region, or with the damnable blind ranger, Montolio.

If the drow was still in the area, Graul meant to find him. The orc chieftain took no chances, and the mere presence of the drow constituted a risk.

❧ 14 ❧

Montolio's Test

.

"Well, I have waited long enough!" Montolio said sternly late one afternoon. He gave the drow another shake.

"Waited?" Drizzt asked, wiping the sleep from his eyes.

"Are you a fighter or a wizard?" Montolio went on. "Or both? One of those multitalented types? The elves of the surface are known for that."

Drizzt's expression twisted in confusion. "I am no wizard," he said with a laugh.

"Keeping secrets, are you?" Montolio scolded, though his continuing smirk lessened his gruff facade. He pointedly straightened himself outside of Drizzt's bedroom hole and folded his arms over his chest. "That will not do. I have taken you in, and if you are a wizard, I must be told!"

"Why do you say that?" asked the perplexed drow. "Wherever did you—"

"Hooter told me!" Montolio blurted. Drizzt was truly confused. "In the fight when first we met," Montolio explained, "you darkened the area around yourself and some orcs. Do not deny it, wizard. Hooter told me!"

"That was no wizard's spell," Drizzt protested helplessly, "and I am no wizard."

"No spell?" echoed Montolio. "A device then? Well, let me see it!"

"Not a device," Drizzt replied, "an ability. All drow, even the lowest ranking, can create globes of darkness. It is not such a difficult task."

Montolio considered the revelation for a moment. He had no experience with dark elves before Drizzt had come into his life. "What other 'abilities' do you possess?"

"Faerie fire," Drizzt replied. "It is a line of—"

"I know of the spell," Montolio said to him. "It is commonly used by woodland priests. Can all drow create this as well?"

"I do not know," Drizzt answered honestly. "Also, I am—or was—able to levitate. Only drow nobles can accomplish that feat. I fear that the power is lost to me, or soon shall be. That ability has begun to fail me since I came to the surface, as my *piwafwi*, my boots, and my drow-crafted scimitars have failed me."

"Try it," Montolio offered.

Drizzt concentrated for a long moment. He felt himself growing lighter, then he lifted off the ground. As soon as he got up, though, his weight returned and he settled back to his feet. He rose no more than three inches.

"Impressive," Montolio muttered.

Drizzt only laughed and shook his white mane. "May I go back to sleep now?" he asked, turning back to his bedroll.

Montolio had other ideas. He had come to further feel out his companion, to find the limits of Drizzt's abilities, wizardly and otherwise. A new plan came to the ranger, but he had to set it into motion before the sun went down.

"Wait," he bade Drizzt. "You can rest later, after sunset. I need you now, and your 'abilities.' Could you summon a globe of darkness, or must you take time to contemplate the spell?"

"A few seconds," Drizzt replied.

"Then get your armor and weapons," Montolio said, "and come with me. Be quick about it. I do not want to lose the advantage of daylight."

Drizzt shrugged and got dressed, then followed the ranger to the grove's northern end, a little used section of the woodland complex.

Montolio dropped to his knees and pulled Drizzt down beside him, pointing out a small hole on the side of a grassy mound.

"A wild boar has taken to living in there," the old ranger explained. "I do not wish to harm it, but I fear to get close enough to make contact with the thing. Boars are unpredictable at best."

A long moment of silence passed. Drizzt wondered if Montolio simply meant to wait for the boar to emerge.

"Go ahead then," the ranger prompted.

Drizzt turned on him incredulously, thinking that Montolio expected him to walk right up and greet their uninvited and unpredictable guest.

"Do it," the ranger continued. "Enact your darkness globe—right in front of the hole—if you please."

Drizzt understood, and his relieved sigh made Montolio bite his lip to hide his revealing chuckle. A moment later, the area before the grassy mound disappeared in blackness. Montolio motioned for Drizzt to wait behind and headed in.

Drizzt tensed, watching and listening. Several high-pitched squeals issued forth suddenly, then Montolio cried out in distress. Drizzt leaped up and charged in headlong, nearly tripping over his friend's prostrate form.

The old ranger groaned and squirmed and did not answer any of the drow's quiet calls. With no boar to be heard anywhere about, Drizzt dropped down to find out what had happened and recoiled when he found Montolio curled up, clutching at his chest.

"Montolio," Drizzt breathed, thinking the old man seriously wounded. He leaned over to speak directly into the ranger's face, then straightened quicker than he had intended as Montolio's shield slammed into the side of his head.

"It is Drizzt!" the drow cried, rubbing his developing bruise. He heard Montolio jump up before him, then heard the ranger's sword come out of its scabbard.

"Of course it is!" Montolio cackled.

"But what of the boar?"

"Boar?" Montolio echoed. "There is no boar, you silly drow. There never was one. We are the opponents here. The time has come for some fun!"

Now Drizzt fully understood. Montolio had manipulated

him to use his darkness merely to take away his advantage of sight. Montolio was challenging him, on even terms. "Flat of the blade!" Drizzt replied, quite willing to play along. How Drizzt had loved such tests of skill back in Menzoberranzan with Zaknafein!

"For the sake of your life!" Montolio retorted with a laugh that came straight from his belly. The ranger sent his sword arcing in, and Drizzt's scimitar drove it harmlessly wide.

Drizzt countered with two rapid and short strokes straight up the middle, an attack that would have defeated most foes but did no more than play a two-note tune on Montolio's well-positioned shield. Certain of Drizzt's location, the ranger shield-rushed straight ahead.

Drizzt was pushed back on his heels before he managed to get out of the way. Montolio's sword came in again from the side, and Drizzt blocked it. The old man's shield slammed straight ahead again, and Drizzt deflected its momentum, digging his heels in stubbornly.

The crafty old ranger thrust the shield up high then, taking one of Drizzt's blades, and a good measure of the drow's balance, along with it, then sent his sword screaming across at Drizzt's midsection.

Drizzt somehow sensed the attack. He leaped back on his toes, sucked in his gut, and threw his rump out behind him. For all his desperation, he still felt the rush as the sword whisked past.

Drizzt went to the offensive, launching several cunning and intricate routines that he believed would end this contest. Montolio anticipated each one, though, for all of Drizzt's efforts were rewarded with the same sound of scimitar on shield. The ranger came on then and Drizzt was sorely pressed. The drow was no novice to blind-fighting, but Montolio lived every hour of every day as a blind man and functioned as well and as easily as most men with perfect vision.

Soon Drizzt realized that he could not win in the globe. He thought of moving the ranger out of the spell's area, but then the situation changed suddenly as the darkness expired. Thinking the game over, Drizzt backed up several steps, feeling his way with his feet up a rising tree root.

Montolio regarded his opponent curiously for a moment, noting the change in fighting attitude, then came on, hard and low.

Drizzt thought himself very clever as he dove headlong over the ranger, meaning to roll to his feet behind Montolio and come back in from one side or the other as the confused human spun about, disoriented.

Drizzt didn't get what he expected, though. Montolio's shield met the drow's face as he was halfway over, and Drizzt groaned and fell heavily to the ground. By the time he shook the dizziness away, he became aware that Montolio was sitting comfortably on his back, sword resting across Drizzt's shoulders.

"How . . ." Drizzt started to ask.

Montolio's voice was as sharp-edged as Drizzt had ever heard it. "You underestimated me, drow. You considered me blind and helpless. Never do that again!"

Drizzt honestly wondered, for just a split second, if Montolio meant to kill him, so angry was the ranger. He knew that his condescension had wounded the man, and he realized then that Montolio DeBrouchee, so confident and able, carried his own weight upon his old shoulders. For the first time since he had met the ranger, Drizzt considered how painful it must have been for the man to lose his sight. What else, Drizzt wondered, had Montolio lost?

"So obvious," Montolio said after a short pause. His voice had softened again. "With me charging in low, as I did."

"Obvious only if you sensed that the darkness spell had ended," Drizzt replied, wondering how disabled Montolio truly was. "I would never have attempted the diving maneuver in the darkness, without my eyes to guide me, yet how could a blind man know that the spell was no more?"

"You told me yourself!" Montolio protested, still making no move to get off Drizzt's back. "In attitude! The sudden shuffle of your feet—too lightly to be made in absolute blackness—and your sigh, drow! That sigh belied your relief, though you knew by then that you could not best me without your sight."

Montolio got up from Drizzt, but the drow remained prone, digesting the revelations. He realized how little he knew about his companion, how much he had taken for granted where Montolio was concerned.

"Come along, then," Montolio said. "This night's first lesson is ended. It was a valuable one, but there are other things we must accomplish."

"You said that I could sleep," Drizzt reminded him.

"I had thought you more competent," Montolio replied immediately, casting a smirk the prone drow's way.

*　*　*　*　*

While Drizzt eagerly absorbed the many lessons Montolio set out for him, that night and in the days that followed, the old ranger gathered his own information about the drow. Their work was most concerned with the present, Montolio teaching Drizzt about the world around him and how to survive in it. Invariably one or the other, usually Drizzt, would slip in some comment about his past. It became almost a game between the two, remarking on some distant event, more to measure the shocked expression of the other than to make any relevant point. Montolio had some fine anecdotes about his many years on the road, tales of valorous battles against goblins and humorous pranks that the usually serious-minded rangers often played on one another. Drizzt remained a bit guarded about his own past, but still his tales of Menzoberranzan, of the sinister and insidious Academy and the savage wars pitting family against family, went far beyond anything Montolio had ever imagined.

As great as the drow's tales were, though, Montolio knew that Drizzt was holding back, was carrying some great burden on his shoulders. The ranger didn't press Drizzt at first. He kept his patience, satisfied that he and Drizzt shared principles and—as he came to know with the drastic improvement of Drizzt's ranger skills—a similar way of viewing the world.

One night, beneath the moon's silvery light, Drizzt and Montolio rested back in wooden chairs that the ranger had constructed high in the boughs of a large evergreen. The brightness of the waning moon, as it dipped and dodged behind fast-moving, scattered clouds, enchanted the drow.

Montolio couldn't see the moon, of course, but the old ranger, with Guenhwyvar comfortably draped across his lap, enjoyed the brisk night no less. He rubbed a hand absently through the thick fur on Guenhwyvar's muscled neck and listened to the many sounds carried on the breeze, the chatter of a thousand creatures that the drow never even noticed, even though Drizzt's hearing was superior to Montolio's. Montolio chuckled every now and again, once when he heard a field mouse squealing angrily at an owl—Hooter probably—for interrupting its meal and forcing it to flee into its hole.

Looking at the ranger and Guenhwyvar, so at ease and accepting of one another, Drizzt felt the pangs of friendship and guilt. "Perhaps I should never have come," he whispered, turning his gaze back to the moon.

"Why?" Montolio asked quietly. "You do not like my food?" His smile disarmed Drizzt as the drow turned back to him somberly.

"To the surface, I mean," Drizzt explained, managing a laugh in spite of his melancholy. "Sometimes I think my choice a selfish act."

"Survival usually is," Montolio replied. "I have felt that way myself on some occasions. I was once forced to drive my sword into a man's heart. The harshness of the world brings great remorse, but mercifully it is a passing lament and certainly not one to carry into battle."

"How I wish it would pass," Drizzt remarked, more to himself or to the moon than to Montolio.

But the remark hit Montolio squarely. The closer he and Drizzt had become, the more the ranger shared Drizzt's unknown burden. The drow was young by elf standards but was already world-wise and skilled in battle beyond most professional soldiers. Undeniably one of Drizzt's dark heritage would find barriers in an unaccepting surface world. By Montolio's estimation, though, Drizzt should be able to get through these prejudices and live a long and prosperous life, given his considerable talents. What was it, Montolio wondered, that so burdens this elf? Drizzt suffered more than he smiled and punished himself more than he should.

"Is yours an honest lament?" Montolio asked him. "Most are not, you know. Most self-imposed burdens are founded on misperceptions. We—at least we of sincere character—always judge ourselves by stricter standards than we expect others to abide by. It is a curse, I suppose, or a blessing, depending on how one views it." He cast his sightless gaze Drizzt's way. "Take it as a blessing, my friend, an inner calling that forces you to strive to unattainable heights."

"A frustrating blessing," Drizzt replied casually.

"Only when you do not pause to consider the advances that the striving has brought to you," Montolio was quick to reply, as though he had expected the drow's words. "Those who aspire to less accomplish less. There can be no doubt. It is better, I think, to grab at the stars than to sit flustered because you know you cannot reach them." He shot Drizzt his typical wry smile. "At least he who reaches will get a good stretch, a good view, and perhaps even a low-hanging apple for his effort!"

"And perhaps also a low-flying arrow fired by some unseen assailant," Drizzt remarked sourly.

Montolio tilted his head helplessly against Drizzt's unending stream of pessimism. It pained him deeply to see the good-hearted drow so scarred. "He might indeed," Montolio said, a bit more harshly than he had intended, "but the loss of life is only great to those who chance to live it! Let your arrow come in low and catch the huddler on the ground, I say. His death would not be so tragic!"

Drizzt could not deny the logic, nor the comfort the old ranger gave to him. Over the last few weeks, Montolio's offhanded philosophies and way of looking at the world—

pragmatically yet heavily edged with youthful exuberance, put Drizzt more at ease than he had been since his earliest training days in Zaknafein's gymnasium. But Drizzt also could not deny the inevitably short life span of that comfort. Words could soothe, but they could not erase the haunting memories of Drizzt's past, the distant voices of dead Zaknafein, dead Clacker, and the dead farmers. A single mental echo of "drizzit" vanquished hours of Montolio's well-intended advice.

"Enough of this cockeyed banter," Montolio went on, seeming perturbed. "I call you friend, Drizzt Do'Urden, and I hope you call me the same. What sort of friend might I be against this weight that stoops your shoulders unless I know more of it? I am your friend, or I am not. The decision is yours, but if I am not, then I see no purpose in sharing nights as wondrous as this beside you. Tell me, Drizzt, or be gone from my home!"

Drizzt could hardly believe that Montolio, normally so patient and relaxed, had put him on such a spot. The drow's first reaction was to recoil, to build a wall of anger in the face of the old man's presumptions and cling to that which he considered personal. As the moments passed, though, and Drizzt got beyond his initial surprise and took the time to sift through Montolio's statement, he came to understand one basic truth that excused those presumptions: He and Montolio had indeed become friends, mostly through the ranger's efforts.

Montolio wanted to share in Drizzt's past, so that he might better understand and comfort his new friend.

"Do you know of Menzoberranzan, the city of my birth and of my kin?" Drizzt asked softly. Even speaking the name pained him. "And do you know the ways of my people, or the Spider Queen's edicts?"

Montolio's voice was somber as he replied. "Tell me all of it, I beg."

Drizzt nodded—Montolio sensed the motion even if he could not see it—and relaxed against the tree. He stared at the moon but actually looked right past it. His mind wandered back through his adventures, back down that road to Menzoberranzan, to the Academy, and to House Do'Urden. He held his thoughts there for a while, lingering on the complexities of drow family life and on the welcomed simplicity of his times in the training room with Zaknafein.

Montolio watched patiently, guessing that Drizzt was looking for a place to begin. From what he had learned from Drizzt's passing remarks, Drizzt's life had been filled with adventure and turbulent times, and Montolio knew that it would be no easy feat for Drizzt, with his still limited command of the common tongue, to accurately recount all of it. Also, given the burdens, the guilt and the sorrow, the drow obviously carried, Montolio suspected that Drizzt might be hesitant.

"I was born on an important day in the history of my family," Drizzt began. "On that day, House Do'Urden eliminated House DeVir."

"Eliminated?"

"Massacred," Drizzt explained. Montolio's blind eyes revealed nothing, but the ranger's expression was clearly one of revulsion, as Drizzt had expected. Drizzt wanted his companion to understand the horrible depths of drow society, so he pointedly added, "And on that day, too, my brother Dinin drove his sword through the heart of our other brother, Nalfein."

A shudder coursed up Montolio's spine and he shook his head. He realized that he was only just beginning to understand the burdens Drizzt carried.

"It is the drow way," Drizzt said calmly, matter-of-factly, trying to impart the dark elves' casual attitude toward murder. "There is a strict structure of rank in Menzoberranzan. To climb it, to attain a higher rank, whether as an individual or a family, you simply eliminate those above you."

A slight quiver in his voice betrayed Drizzt to the ranger. Montolio clearly understood that Drizzt did not accept the evil practices, and never had.

Drizzt went on with his story, telling it completely and accurately, at least for the more than forty years he had spent in the Underdark. He told of his days under the strict tutelage of his sister Vierna, cleaning the house chapel endlessly and learning of his innate powers and his place in drow society. Drizzt spent a long time explaining that peculiar social structure to Montolio, the hierarchies based on strict rank, and the hypocrisy of drow "law," a cruel facade screening a city of utter chaos. The ranger cringed as he heard of the family wars. They were brutal conflicts that allowed for no noble survivors, not even children. Montolio cringed even more when Drizzt told him of drow "justice," of the destruction wreaked upon a house that had failed in its attempt to eradicate another family.

The tale was less grim when Drizzt told of Zaknafein, his father and dearest friend. Of course, Drizzt's happy memories of his father became only a short reprieve, a prelude to the horrors of Zaknafein's demise. "My mother killed my father," Drizzt explained soberly, his deep pain evident, "sacrificed him to Lloth for my crimes, then animated his corpse and sent it out to kill me, to punish me for betraying the family and the Spider Queen."

It took a while for Drizzt to resume, but when he did, he again spoke truthfully, even revealing his own failures in his days alone in the wilds of the Underdark. "I feared that I had lost myself and my principles to some instinctive, savage monster," Drizzt said, verging on despair. But then the emotional wave that had been his existence rose again, and a smile found his face as he recounted his time beside Belwar, the most honored svirfneblin burrow-warden, and Clacker, the pech who had been polymorphed into a hook horror. Expectedly, the smile proved short-lived, for Drizzt's tale eventually led him to where Clacker fell to Matron Malice's undead monster. Another friend had died on Drizzt's behalf.

Appropriately, by the time Drizzt came to his exit from the Underdark, the dawn peeked through the eastern mountains. Now Drizzt picked his words more carefully, not ready to divulge the tragedy of the farming family for fear that Montolio would judge him and blame him, destroying their newfound bond. Rationally, Drizzt could remind himself that he had not killed the farmers, had even avenged their deaths, but guilt was rarely a rational emotion, and Drizzt simply could not find the words—not yet.

Montolio, aged and wise and with animal scouts throughout the region, knew that Drizzt was concealing something. When they had first met, the drow had mentioned a doomed farming family, and Montolio had heard of a family slaughtered in the village of Maldobar. Montolio didn't believe for a minute that Drizzt could have done it, but he suspected that the drow was somehow involved. He didn't press Drizzt, though. Drizzt had been more honest, and more complete, than Montolio had expected, and the ranger was confident that the drow would fill in the obvious holes in his own time.

"It is a good tale," Montolio said at length. "You have been through more in your few decades than most elves will know in three hundred years. But the scars are few, and they will heal."

Drizzt, not so certain, put a lamenting look upon him, and Montolio could only offer a comforting pat on the shoulder as he rose and headed off for bed.

* * * * *

Drizzt was still asleep when Montolio roused Hooter and tied a thick note to the owl's leg. Hooter wasn't so pleased at the ranger's instructions; the journey could take a week, valuable and enjoyable time at this height of the mousing and mating season. For all its whining hoots, however, the owl would not disobey.

Hooter ruffled its feathers, caught the first gust of wind, and soared effortlessly across the snow-covered range to the passes that would take it to Maldobar—and beyond that to Sundabar, if need be. A certain ranger of no small fame, a sister of the Lady of Silverymoon, was still in the region, Montolio knew through his animal connections, and he charged Hooter with seeking her out.

* * * * *

"Will-there-be-no-end-to-it?" the sprite whined, watching the burly human pass along the trail. "First-the-nasty-drow-and-now-this-brute!   Am-I-never-to-be-rid-of-these-trouble-makers?" Tephanis slapped his head and stamped his feet so rapidly that he dug himself a little hole.

Down on the trail, the big, scarred yellow dog growled and bared its teeth, and Tephanis, realizing that his pouting had been too loud, zipped in a wide semicircle, crossing the trail far behind the traveler and coming up on the other flank. The yellow dog, still looking in the opposite direction, cocked its head and whimpered in confusion.

❧ 15 ❧

A Shadow Over Sanctuary

Drizzt and Montolio said nothing of the drow's tale over the next couple of days. Drizzt brooded over painfully re-kindled memories, and Montolio tactfully gave him the room he needed. They went about their daily business methodically, farther apart, and with less enthusiasm, but the distance was a passing thing, which they both realized.

Gradually they came closer together, leaving Drizzt with hopes that he had found a friend as true as Belwar or even Zaknafein. One morning, though, the drow was awakened by a voice that he recognized all too well, and Drizzt thought at once that his time with Montolio had come to a crashing end.

He crawled to the wooden wall that protected his dugout chamber and peered through.

"Drow elf, Mooshie," Roddy McGristle was saying, holding a broken scimitar out for the old ranger to see. The burly mountain man, looming even larger in the many layers of furs he wore, sat atop a small but muscled horse just outside of the rock wall surrounding the grove. "Ye seen him?"

"Seen?" Montolio echoed sarcastically, giving an exaggerated wink of his milky-white eyes. Roddy was not amused.

"Ye know what I mean!" he growled. "Ye see more'n the rest of us, so don't ye be playin' dumb!" Roddy's dog, showing a wicked scar from where Drizzt had struck it, caught a familiar scent then and started sniffing excitedly and darting back and forth along the paths of the grove.

Drizzt crouched at the ready, a scimitar in one hand and a look of dread and confusion on his face. He had no desire to fight—he did not even want to strike the dog again.

"Get your dog back to your side!" Montolio huffed.

McGristle's curiosity was obvious. "Seen the dark elf, Mooshie?" he asked again, this time suspiciously.

"Might that I have," Montolio replied. He turned and let out a shrill, barely audible whistle. Immediately, Roddy's dog, hearing the ranger's clear ire in no uncertain terms, dropped its tail between its legs and slunk back to stand beside its master's horse.

"I've a brood of fox pups in there," the ranger lied angrily. "If your dog sets on them . . ." Montolio let the threat hang at that, and apparently Roddy was impressed. He dropped a noose down over the dog's head and pulled it tight to his side.

"A drow, must be the same one, came through here before the first snows," Montolio went on. "You will have a hard hunt for that one, bounty hunter." He laughed. "He had some trouble with Graul, by my knowledge, then set out again, back for his dark home, I would guess. Do you mean to follow the drow down into the Underdark? Certainly your reputation would grow considerably, bounty hunter, though your very life might prove the cost!"

Drizzt relaxed at the words; Montolio had lied for him! He could see that the ranger did not hold McGristle in high regard, and that fact, too, brought comfort to Drizzt. Then Roddy came back forcefully, laying out the story of the tragedy in Maldobar in a blunt and warped way that put Drizzt and Montolio's friendship to a tough test.

"The drow killed the Thistledowns!" Roddy roared at the ranger's smug smile, which vanished in the blink of an eye. "Slaughtered them, and his panther ate one o' them. Ye knew Bartholemew Thistledown, ranger. Shame on ye for talkin' lightly on his murderer!"

"Drow killed them?" Montolio asked grimly.

Roddy held out the broken scimitar once more. "Cut 'em down," he growled. "There's two thousand gold pieces on that one's head—I'll give ye back five hunnerd if ye can find out more for me."

"I have no need of your gold," Montolio quickly replied.

"But do ye have need to see the killer brought in?" Roddy shot back. "Do ye mourn for the deaths o' the Thistledown clan, as fine a family as any?"

Montolio's ensuing pause led Drizzt to believe that the ranger might turn him in. Drizzt decided then that he would not run, whatever Montolio's decision. He could deny the bounty hunter's anger, but not Montolio's. If the ranger accused him, Drizzt would have to face him and be judged.

"Sad day," Montolio muttered. "Fine family, indeed. Catch the drow, McGristle. It would be the best bounty you ever earned."

"Where to start?" Roddy asked calmly, apparently thinking he had won Montolio over. Drizzt thought so, too, especially when Montolio turned and looked back toward the grove.

"You have heard of Morueme's Cave?" Montolio asked.

Roddy's expression visibly dropped at the question. Morueme's Cave, on the edge of the great desert Anauroch, was so named for the family of blue dragons that lived there. "Hunnerd an' fifty miles," McGristle groaned. "Through the Nethers—a tough range."

"The drow went there, or about there, early in the winter," Montolio lied.

"Drow went to the dragons?" Roddy asked, surprised.

"More likely, the drow went to some other hole in that region," Montolio replied. "The dragons of Morueme could possibly know of him. You should inquire there."

"I'm not so quick to bargain with dragons," Roddy said somberly. "Too risky, and even goin', well, it costs too much!"

"Then it seems that Roddy McGristle has missed his first catch," Montolio said. "A good try, though, against the likes of a dark elf."

Roddy reined in his horse and spun the beast about. "Don't ye put yer bets against me, Mooshie!" he roared back over his shoulder. "I'll not let this one get away, if I have to search every hole in the Nethers myself!"

"Seems a bit of trouble for two thousand gold," Montolio remarked, not impressed.

"Drow took my dog, my ear, and give me this scar!" Roddy countered, pointing to his torn face. The bounty hunter realized the absurdity of his actions—of course, the blind ranger could not see him—and spun back, setting his horse charging out of the grove.

Montolio waved a hand disgustedly at McGristle's back, then turned to find the drow. Drizzt met him on the edge of the grove, hardly knowing how to thank Montolio.

"Never liked that one," Montolio explained.

"The Thistledown family was murdered," Drizzt admitted bluntly.

Montolio nodded.

"You knew?"

"I knew before you came here," the ranger answered. "Honestly, I wondered if you did it, at first."

"I did not," Drizzt said.

Again Montolio nodded.

The time had come for Drizzt to fill in the details of his first few months on the surface. All the guilt came back to him when he recounted his battle with the gnoll group, and all the pain came rushing back, focused on the word "drizzit," when he told of the Thistledowns and his gruesome discovery. Montolio identified the speedy sprite as a quickling but was quite at a loss to explain the giant goblin and wolf creatures that Drizzt had battled in the cave.

"You did right in killing the gnolls," Montolio said when Drizzt had finished. "Release your guilt for that act and let it fall to nothingness."

"How could I know?" Drizzt asked honestly. "All of my learning ties to Menzoberranzan and still I have not sorted the truth from the lies."

"It has been a confusing journey," Montolio said, and his sincere smile relieved the tension considerably. "Come along, and let me tell you of the races, and of why your scimitars struck for justice when they felled the gnolls."

As a ranger, Montolio had dedicated his life to the unending struggle between the good races—humans, elves, dwarves, gnomes, and halflings being the most prominent members—and the evil goblinoids and giantkind, who lived only to destroy as a bane to the innocent.

"Orcs are my particular unfavorites," Montolio explained. "So now I content myself with keeping an eye—an owl's eye, that is—on Graul and his smelly kin."

So much fell into perspective for Drizzt then. Comfort flooded through the drow, for Drizzt's instincts had proven correct and he could now, for a while and to some measure at least, be free from the guilt.

"What of the bounty hunter and those like him?" Drizzt asked. "They do not seem to fit so well into your descriptions of the races."

"There is good and bad in every race," Montolio explained. "I spoke only of the general conduct, and do not doubt that the general conduct of goblinoids and giantkind is an evil one!"

"How can we know?" Drizzt pressed.

"Just watch the children," Montolio answered. He went on to explain the not-so-subtle differences between children of the goodly races and children of the evil races. Drizzt heard him, but distantly, needing no clarification. Always it seemed to come down to the children. Drizzt had felt better concerning his actions against the gnolls when he had looked upon the Thistledown children at play. And back in Menzoberranzan, what seemed like only a day ago and a thousand years ago at the same time, Drizzt's father had expressed similar beliefs. "Are all drow children evil?" Zaknafein had wondered, and through all of his beleaguered life, Zaknafein had been haunted by the screams of dying children, drow nobles caught in the fire between warring families.

A long, silent moment ensued when Montolio finished, both friends taking the time to digest the day's many revelations. Montolio knew that Drizzt was comforted when the drow, quite unexpectedly, turned to him, smiled widely, and abruptly changed the grim subject.

"Mooshie?" Drizzt asked, recalling the name McGristle had tagged on Montolio at the rock wall.

"Montolio DeBrouchee." The old ranger cackled, tossing a grotesque wink Drizzt's way. "Mooshie, to my friends, and to those like McGristle, who struggle so with any words bigger than 'spit,' 'bear,' or 'kill!'"

"Mooshie," Drizzt mumbled under his breath, taking some mirth at Montolio's expense.

"Have you no chores to do, Drizzit?" the old ranger huffed.

Drizzt nodded and started boisterously away. This time, the ring of "drizzit" did not sting so very badly.

*　*　*　*　*

"Morueme's Cave," Roddy griped. "Damned Morueme's Cave!" A split second later, a small sprite sat atop Roddy's horse, staring the stunned bounty hunter in the face. Tephanis had watched the exchange at Montolio's grove and had cursed his luck when the ranger had turned the bounty hunter away. If Roddy could catch Drizzt, the quickling figured, they'd both be out of his way, a fact that did not alarm Tephanis.

"Surely-you-are-not-so-stupid-as-to-believe-that-old-liar?" Tephanis blurted.

"Here!" Roddy cried, grabbing clumsily at the sprite, who merely hopped down, darted back, past the startled dog, and climbed up to sit behind Roddy.

"What in the Nine Hells are you?" the bounty hunter roared. "And sit still!"

"I am a friend," Tephanis said as slowly as he could.

Roddy eyed him cautiously over one shoulder.

"If-you-want-the-drow, you-are-going-the-wrong-way," the sprite said smugly.

A short while later, Roddy crouched in the high bluffs south of Montolio's grove and watched the ranger and his dark-skinned guest going about their chores.

"Good-hunting!" Tephanis offered, then he was gone, back to Caroak, the great wolf that smelled better than this particular human.

Roddy, his eyes fixed upon the distant scene, hardly noticed the quickling's departure. "Ye'll pay for yer lies, ranger," he muttered under his breath. An evil smile spread over his face as he thought of a way to get at the companions. It would be a delicate feat. But then, dealing with Graul always was.

* * * * *

Montolio's messenger returned two days later with a note from Dove Falconhand. Hooter tried to recount the ranger's response, but the excitable owl was completely inept at conveying such long and intricate tales. Flustered and having no other option, Montolio handed the letter to Drizzt and told the drow to read it aloud, and quickly. Not yet a skilled reader, Drizzt was several lines through the creased paper before he realized what it was. The note detailed Dove's accounts of what had happened in Maldobar and along the subsequent chase. Dove's version struck near to the truth, vindicating Drizzt and naming the barghest whelps as the murderers.

Drizzt's relief was so great that he could hardly utter the words as the letter went on to express Dove's pleasure and gratitude that the "deserving drow" had taken in with the old ranger.

"You get your due in the end, my friend," was all that Montolio needed to say.

❧ Part 4 ❧

Resolutions

I now view my long road as a search for truth—truth in my own heart, in the world around me, and in the larger questions of purpose and of existence. How does one define good and evil?

I carried an internal code of morals with me on my trek, though whether I was born with it or it was imparted to me by Zaknafein—or whether it simply developed from my perceptions—I cannot ever know. This code forced me to leave Menzoberranzan, for though I was not certain of what those truths might have been, I knew beyond doubt that they would not be found in the domain of Lloth.

After many years in the Underdark outside of Menzoberranzan and after my first awful experiences on the surface, I came to doubt the existence of any universal truth, came to wonder if there was, after all, any purpose to life. In the world of drow, ambition was the only purpose, the seeking of material gains that came with increased rank. Even then, that seemed a little thing to me, hardly a reason to exist.

I thank you, Montolio DeBrouchee, for confirming my suspicions. I have learned that the ambition of those who follow selfish precepts is no more than a chaotic waste, a finite gain that must be followed by infinite loss. For there is indeed a harmony in the universe, a concordant singing of common weal. To join that song, one must find inner harmony, must find the notes that ring true.

There is one other point to be made about that truth: Evil creatures cannot sing.

—Drizzt Do'Urden

☙ 16 ☙

Of Gods and Purpose

The lessons continued to go quite well. The old ranger had lessened the drow's considerable emotional burden, and Drizzt picked up on the ways of the natural world better than anyone Montolio had ever seen. But Montolio sensed that something still bothered the drow, though he had no idea of what it might be.

"Do all humans possess such fine hearing?" Drizzt asked him suddenly as they dragged a huge fallen branch out of the grove. "Or is yours a blessing, perhaps, to make up for your blindness?"

The bluntness of the question surprised Montolio for just the moment it took him to recognize the drow's frustration, an uneasiness caused by Drizzt's failure to understand the man's abilities.

"Or is your blindness, perhaps, a ruse, a deception you use to gain the advantage?" Drizzt pressed relentlessly.

"If it is?" Montolio replied offhandedly.

"Then it is a good one, Montolio DeBrouchee," Drizzt replied. "Surely it aids you against enemies . . . and friends alike." The words tasted bitter to Drizzt, and he suspected that he was letting his pride get the best of him.

"You have not often been bested in battle," Montolio replied, recognizing the source of Drizzt's frustrations as their sparring match. If he could have seen the drow then, Drizzt's expression would have revealed much.

"You take it too hard," Montolio continued after an uneasy silence. "I did not truly defeat you."

"You had me down and helpless."

"You beat yourself," Montolio explained. "I am indeed blind, but not as helpless as you seem to think. You underestimated me. I knew that you would, too, though I hardly believed that you could be so blind."

Drizzt stopped abruptly, and Montolio stopped on cue as the drag on the branch suddenly increased. The old ranger shook his head and cackled. He then pulled out a dagger, spun it high into the air, caught it, and, yelling, "Birch!" heaved it squarely into one of the few birch trees by the evergreen grove.

"Could a blind man do that?" Montolio asked rhetorically.

"Then you can see," Drizzt stated.

"Of course not," Montolio retorted sharply. "My eyes have not functioned for five years. But neither am I blind, Drizzt, especially in this place I call my home!

"Yet you thought me blind," the ranger went on, his voice calm again. "In our sparring, when your spell of darkness expired, you believed that you had gained the edge. Did you think that all of my actions—effective actions, I must say—both in the battle against the orcs and in our fight were simply prepared and rehearsed? If I were as crippled as Drizzt Do'Urden believes me, how should I survive another day in these mountains?"

"I did not . . ." Drizzt began, but his embarrassment silenced him. Montolio spoke the truth, and Drizzt knew it. He had, at least on an unconscious level, thought the ranger less than whole since their very first meeting. Drizzt felt he showed his friend no disrespect—indeed, he thought highly of the man—but he had taken Montolio for granted and thought the ranger's limitations greater than his own.

"You did," Montolio corrected, "and I forgive you that. To your credit, you treated me more fairly than any who knew me before, even those who had traveled beside me through uncounted campaigns. Sit now," he bade Drizzt. "It is my turn to tell my tale, as you have told yours.

"Where to begin?" Montolio mused, scratching at his chin. It all seemed so distant to him now, another life that he had left behind. He retained one link to his past, though:

his training as a ranger of the goddess Mielikki. Drizzt, similarly instructed by Montolio, would understand.

"I gave my life to the forest, to the natural order, at a very young age," Montolio began. "I learned, as I have begun to teach you, the ways of the wild world and decided soon enough that I would defend that perfection, that harmony of cycles too vast and wonderful to be understood. That is why I so enjoy battling orcs and the like. As I have told you before, they are the enemies of natural order, the enemies of trees and animals as much as of men and the goodly races. Wretched things, all in all, and I feel no guilt in cutting them down!"

Montolio then spent many hours recounting some of his campaigns, expeditions in which he acted singly or as a scout for huge armies. He told Drizzt of his own teacher, Dilamon, a ranger so skilled with a bow that he had never seen her miss, not once in ten thousand shots. "She died in battle," Montolio explained, "defending a farmhouse from a raiding band of giants. Weep not for Mistress Dilamon, though, for not a single farmer was injured and not one of the few giants who crawled away ever showed its ugly face in that region again!"

Montolio's voice dropped noticeably when he came to his more recent past. He told of the Rangewatchers, his last adventuring company, and of how they came to battle a red dragon that had been marauding the villages. The dragon was slain, as were three of the Rangewatchers, and Montolio had his face burned away.

"The clerics fixed me up well," Montolio said somberly. "Hardly a scar to show for my pain." He paused, and Drizzt saw, for the first time since he had met the old ranger, a cloud of pain cross Montolio's face. "They could do nothing for my eyes, though. The wounds were beyond their abilities."

"You came out here to die," Drizzt said, more accusingly than he intended.

Montolio did not refute the claim. "I have suffered the breath of dragons, the spears of orcs, the anger of evil men, and the greed of those who would rape the land for their own gain," the ranger said. "None of those things wounded as deeply as pity. Even my Rangewatcher companions, who had fought beside me so many times pitied me. Even you."

"I did not . . ." Drizzt tried to interject.

"You did indeed," Montolio retorted. "In our battle, you thought yourself superior. That is why you lost! The strength of any ranger is wisdom, Drizzt. A ranger understands himself, his enemies, and his friends. You thought me impaired, else you never would have attempted so brash a maneuver as to jump over me. But I understood you and anticipated the move." That sly smile flashed wickedly. "Does your head still hurt?"

"It does," Drizzt admitted, rubbing the bruise, "though my thoughts seem to be clearing."

"As to your original question," Montolio said, satisfied that his point had been made, "there is nothing exceptional about my hearing, or any of my other senses. I just pay more attention to what they tell than do other folks, and they guide me quite well, as you now understand. Truly, I did not know of their abilities myself when I first came out here, and you are correct in your guess as to why I did. Without my eyes, I thought myself a dead man, and I wanted to die here, in this grove that I had come to know and love in my earlier travels.

"Perhaps it was due to Mielikki, the Mistress of the Forest—though more likely it was Graul, an enemy so close at hand—but it did not take me long to change my intentions concerning my own life. I found a purpose out here, alone and crippled—and I was crippled in those first days. With that purpose came a renewal of meaning in my life, and that in turn led me to realize again my limits. I am old now, and weary, and blind. If I had died five years ago, as I had intended, I would have died with my life incomplete. I never would have known how far I could go. Only in adversity, beyond anything Montolio DeBrouchee had ever imagined, could I have come to know myself and my goddess so well."

Montolio stopped to consider Drizzt. He heard a shuffle

at the mention of his goddess, and he took it to be an uncomfortable movement. Wanting to explore this revelation, Montolio reached inside his chain mail and tunic and produced a pendant shaped like a unicorn's head.

"Is it not beautiful?" he pointedly asked.

Drizzt hesitated. The unicorn was perfectly crafted and marvelous in design, but the connotations of such a pendant did not sit easily with the drow. Back in Menzoberranzan Drizzt had witnessed the folly of following the commands of deities, and he liked not at all what he had seen.

"Who is your god, drow?" Montolio asked. In all the weeks he and Drizzt had been together, they had not really discussed religion.

"I have no god," Drizzt answered boldly, "and neither do I want one."

It was Montolio's turn to pause.

Drizzt rose and walked off a few paces.

"My people follow Lloth," he began. "She, if not the cause, is surely the continuation of their wickedness, as this Gruumsh is to the orcs, and as other gods are to other peoples. To follow a god is folly. I shall follow my heart instead."

Montolio's quiet chuckle stole the power from Drizzt's proclamation. "You have a god, Drizzt Do'Urden," he said.

"My god is my heart," Drizzt declared, turning back to him.

"As is mine."

"You named your god as Mielikki," Drizzt protested.

"And you have not found a name for your god yet," Montolio shot back. "That does not mean that you have no god. Your god is your heart, and what does your heart tell you?"

"I do not know," Drizzt admitted after considering the troubling question.

"Think then!" Montolio cried. "What did your instincts tell you of the gnoll band, or of the farmers in Maldobar? Lloth is not your deity—that much is certain. What god or goddess then fits that which is in Drizzt Do'Urden's heart?"

Montolio could almost hear Drizzt's continuing shrugs.

"You do not know?" the old ranger asked. "But I do."

"You presume much," Drizzt replied, still not convinced.

"I observe much," Montolio said with a laugh. "Are you of like heart with Guenhwyvar?"

"I have never doubted that fact," Drizzt answered honestly.

"Guenhwyvar follows Mielikki."

"How can you know?" Drizzt argued, growing a bit perturbed. He didn't mind Montolio's presumptions about him, but Drizzt considered such labeling an attack on the panther. Somehow to Drizzt, Guenhwyvar seemed to be above gods and all the implications of following one.

"How can I know?" Montolio echoed incredulously. "The cat told me, of course! Guenhwyvar is the entity of the panther, a creature of Mielikki's domain."

"Guenhwyvar does not need your labels," Drizzt retorted angrily, moving briskly to sit again beside the ranger.

"Of course not," Montolio agreed. "But that does not change the fact of it. You do not understand, Drizzt Do'Urden. You grew up among the perversion of a deity."

"And yours is the true one?" Drizzt asked sarcastically.

"They are all true, and they are all one, I fear," Montolio replied. Drizzt had to agree with Montolio's earlier observation: He did not understand.

"You view the gods as entities without," Montolio tried to explain. "You see them as physical beings trying to control our actions for their own ends, and thus you, in your stubborn independence, reject them. The gods are within, I say, whether one has named his own or not. You have followed Mielikki all of your life, Drizzt. You merely never had a name to put on your heart."

Suddenly Drizzt was more intrigued than skeptical.

"What did you feel when you first walked out of the Underdark?" Montolio asked. "What did your heart tell you when first you looked upon the sun or the stars, or the forest green?"

Drizzt thought back to that distant day, when he and his drow patrol had come out of the Underdark to raid an elven gathering. Those were painful memories, but within them loomed one sense of comfort, one memory of wondrous elation at the feel of the wind and the scents of newly bloomed flowers.

"And how did you talk to Bluster?" Montolio continued. "No easy feat, sharing a cave with that bear! Admit it or not, you've the heart of a ranger. And the heart of a ranger is a heart of Mielikki."

So formal a conclusion brought back a measure of Drizzt's doubts. "And what does your goddess require?" he asked, the angry edge returned to his voice. He began to stand again, but Montolio slapped a hand over his legs and held him down.

"Require?" The ranger laughed. "I am no missionary spreading a fine word and imposing rules of behavior! Did I not just tell you that gods are within? You know Mielikki's rules as well as I. You have been following them all of your life. I offer you a name for it, that is all, and an ideal of behavior personified, an example that you might follow in times that you stray from what you know is true." With that, Montolio took up the branch and Drizzt followed.

Drizzt considered the words for a long time. He did not sleep that day, though he remained in his den, thinking.

"I wish to know more of your . . . our . . . goddess," Drizzt admitted that next night, when he found Montolio cooking their supper.

"And I wish to teach you," Montolio replied.

* * * * *

A hundred sets of yellow, bloodshot eyes settled to stare at the burly human as he made his way through the encampment, reining his yellow dog tightly to his side. Roddy didn't enjoy coming here, to the fort of the orc king, Graul, but he had no intentions of letting the drow get away this time. Roddy had dealt with Graul several times over the last few years; the orc king, with so many eyes in the wild mountains had proven an invaluable, though expensive, ally in hunting bounties.

Several large orcs purposely crossed Roddy's path, jostling him and angering his dog. Roddy wisely kept his pet still, though he, too, wanted to set upon the smelly orcs. They played this game every time he came in, bumping him, spitting at him, anything to provoke a fight. Orcs were always brave when they outnumbered opponents a hundred to one.

The whole group swept up behind McGristle and followed him closely as he covered the last fifty yards, up a rocky slope, to the entrance of Graul's cave. Two large orcs jumped out of the entrance, brandishing spears, to intercept the intruder.

"Why has yous come?" one of them asked in their native tongue. The other held out its hand, as if expecting payment.

"No pay this time," Roddy replied, imitating their dialect perfectly. "This time Graul pay!"

The orcs looked to each other in disbelief, then turned on Roddy and issued snarls that were suddenly cut short when an even larger orc emerged from the cave.

Graul stormed out and threw his guards aside, striding right up to put his oozing snout only an inch from Roddy's nose. "Graul pay?" he snorted, his breath nearly overwhelming Roddy.

Roddy's chuckle was purely for the sake of those excited orc commoners closest to him. He couldn't show any weakness here; like vicious dogs, orcs were quick to attack anyone who did not stand firm against them.

"I have information, King Graul," the bounty hunter said firmly. "Information that Graul would wish to know."

"Speak," Graul commanded.

"Pay?" Roddy asked, though he suspected that he was pushing his luck.

"Speak!" Graul growled again. "If yous wordses has value, Graul will let yous live."

Roddy silently lamented that it always seemed to work this way with Graul. It was difficult to strike any favorable bargain with the smelly chieftain when he was surrounded by a hundred armed warriors. Roddy remained undaunted, though. He hadn't come here for money—though he had hoped he might extract some—but for revenge. Roddy wouldn't openly strike against Drizzt while the drow was with Mooshie. In these mountains, surrounded by his animal friends, Mooshie was a formidable force, and even if Roddy managed to get past him to the drow, Mooshie's many allies, veterans such as Dove Falconhand, would surely avenge the action.

"There be a dark elf in yer domain, mighty orc king!" Roddy proclaimed. He didn't get the shock he had hoped for.

"Rogue," Graul clarified.

"Ye know?" Roddy's wide eyes betrayed his disbelief.

"Drow killed Graul's fighters," the orc chieftain said grimly. All the gathered orcs began stamping and spitting, cursing the dark elf.

"Then why does the drow live?" Roddy asked bluntly. The bounty hunter's eyes narrowed as he came to suspect that Graul did not now know the drow's location. Perhaps he still had something to bargain with.

"Me scouts cannot finds him!" Graul roared, and it was true enough. But any frustration the orc king showed was a finely crafted piece of acting. Graul knew where Drizzt was, even if his scouts did not.

"I have found him!" Roddy roared, and all the orcs jumped and cried in hungry glee. Graul raised his arms to quiet them. This was the critical part, the orc king knew. He scanned the gathering to locate the tribe's shaman, the spiritual leader of the tribe, and found the red-robed orc watching and listening intently, as Graul had hoped.

On advice from that shaman, Graul had avoided any action against Montolio for all these years. The shaman thought the cripple who was not so crippled to be an omen of bad magic, and with their religious leader's warnings, all the orc tribe cowered whenever Montolio was near. But in allying with the drow, and, if Graul's suspicions were correct, in helping the drow to win the battle on the high ridge,

Montolio had struck where he had no business, had violated Graul's domain as surely as had the renegade drow. Now convinced that the drow was indeed a rogue—for no other dark elves were in the region—the orc king only awaited some excuse that might spur his minions to action against the grove. Roddy, Graul had been informed, might now provide that excuse.

"Speak!" Graul shouted in Roddy's face, to intercept any forthcoming attempts for payment.

"The drow isses with the ranger," Roddy replied. "He sits in the blind ranger's grove!" If Roddy had hoped that his proclamation would inspire another eruption of cursing, jumping, and spitting, he was surely disappointed. The mention of the blind ranger cast a heavy pall over the gathering, and now all the common orcs looked from the shaman to Graul and back again for some guidance.

It was time for Roddy to weave a tale of conspiracy, as Graul had been told he would.

"Ye must goes and gets them!" Roddy cried. "They're not fer . . ."

Graul raised his arms to silence both the muttering and Roddy. "Was it the blind ranger who killded the giant?" the orc king asked Roddy slyly. "And helped the drow to kill me fighters?"

Roddy, of course, had no idea what Graul was talking about, but he was quick enough to catch on to the orc king's intent.

"It was!" he declared loudly. "And now the drow and the ranger plot against ye all! Ye must bash them and smash them before they come and bash yerselves! The ranger'll be bringing his animals, and elveses—lots an' lots of elveses—and dwarveses, too, against Graul!"

The mention of Montolio's friends, particularly the elves and dwarves, which Graul's people hated above everything else in all the world, brought sour expressions on every face and caused more than one orc to look nervously over its shoulder, as if expecting the ranger's army to be encircling the camp even then.

Graul stared squarely at the shaman.

"He-Who-Watches must bless the attack," the shaman replied to the silent question. "On the new moon!" Graul nodded, and the red-robed orc turned about, summoned a score of commoners to his side, and set out to begin the preparations.

Graul reached into a pouch and produced a handful of silver coins for Roddy. Roddy hadn't provided any real information that the king did not already know, but the bounty hunter's declaration of a conspiracy against the orc tribe gave Graul considerable assistance in his attempt to rouse his superstitious shaman against the blind ranger.

Roddy took the pitiful payment without complaint, thinking it well enough that he had achieved his purpose, and turned to leave.

"Yous is to stay," Graul said suddenly at his back. On a motion from the orc king, several orc guards stepped up beside the bounty hunter. Roddy looked suspiciously at Graul.

"Guest," the orc king explained calmly. "Join in the fight."

Roddy wasn't left with many options.

Graul waved his guards aside and went alone back into his cave. The orc guards only shrugged and smiled at each other, having no desire to go back in and face the king's guests, particularly the huge silver-furred wolf.

When Graul had returned to his place within, he turned to speak to his other guest. "Yous was right," Graul said to the diminutive sprite.

"I-am-quite-good-at-getting-information." Tephanis beamed, and silently he added, and-creating-favorable-situations!

Tephanis thought himself clever at that moment, for not only had he informed Roddy that the drow was in Montolio's grove, but he had then arranged with King Graul for Roddy to aid them both. Graul had no love for the blind ranger, Tephanis knew, and with the drow's presence serving as an excuse, Graul could finally persuade his shaman to bless the attack.

"Caroak will help in the fight?" Graul asked, looking suspiciously at the huge and unpredictable silver wolf.

"Of-course," Tephanis said immediately. "It-is-in-our-interest,-too,-to-see-those-enemies-destroyed!"

Caroak, understanding every word the two exchanged, rose up and sauntered out of the cave. The guards at the entrance did not try to block his way.

"Caroak-will-rouse-the-worgs," Tephanis explained. "A-mighty-force-will-assemble-against-the-blind-ranger. Too-long-has-he-been-an-enemy-of-Caroak."

Graul nodded and mused privately about the coming weeks. If he could get rid of both the ranger and the drow, his valley would be more secure than it had been in many years—since before Montolio's arrival. The ranger rarely engaged the orcs personally, but Graul knew that it was the ranger's animal spies that always alerted the passing caravans. Graul could not remember the last time his warriors had caught a caravan unawares, the preferred orc method. If the ranger was gone, however . . .

With summer, the height of the trading season, fast approaching, the orcs would prey well this year.

All that Graul needed now was confirmation from the shaman, that He-Who-Watches, the orc god Gruumsh One-eye, would bless the attack.

The new moon, a holy time for the orcs and a time when the shaman believed he could learn of the god's pleasures, was more than two weeks away. Eager and impatient, Graul grumbled at the delay, but he knew that he would simply have to wait. Graul, far less religious than others believed, meant to attack no matter the shaman's decision, but the crafty orc king would not openly defy the tribe's spiritual leader unless it was absolutely necessary.

The new moon was not so far away, Graul told himself. Then he would be rid of both the blind ranger and the mysterious drow.

☘ 17 ☘

Outnumbered

"You seem troubled," Drizzt said to Montolio when he saw the ranger standing on a rope bridge the next morning. Hooter sat in a branch above him.

Montolio, lost in thought, did not immediately answer. Drizzt thought nothing of it. He shrugged and turned away, respecting the ranger's privacy, and took the onyx figurine out of his pocket.

"Guenhwyvar and I will go out for a short hunt," Drizzt explained over his shoulder, "before the sun gets too high. Then I will take my rest and the panther will share the day with you."

Still Montolio hardly heard the drow, but when the ranger noticed Drizzt placing the onyx figurine on the rope bridge, the drow's words registered more clearly and he came out of his contemplations.

"Hold," Montolio said, reaching a hand out. "Let the panther remain at rest."

Drizzt did not understand. "Guenhwyvar has been gone a day and more," he said.

"We may need Guenhwyvar for more than hunting before too long," Montolio began to explain. "Let the panther remain at rest."

"What is the trouble?" Drizzt asked, suddenly serious. "What has Hooter seen?"

"Last night marked the new moon," Montolio said. Drizzt, with his new understanding of the lunar cycles, nodded.

"A holy day for the orcs," Montolio continued. "Their camp is miles away, but I heard their cries last night."

Again Drizzt nodded in recognition. "I heard the strains of their song, but I wondered if it might be no more than the quiet voice of the wind."

"It was the wail of orcs," Montolio assured him. "Every month they gather and grunt and dance wildly in their typical stupor—orcs need no potions to induce it, you know. I thought nothing of it, though they seemed overly loud. Usually they cannot be heard from here. A favorable . . . unfavorable . . . wind carried the tune in, I supposed."

"You have since learned that there was more to the song?" Drizzt assumed.

"Hooter heard them, too," Montolio explained. "Always watching out for me, that one." He glanced at the owl. "He flew off to get a look."

Drizzt also looked up at the marvelous bird, sitting puffed and proud as though it understood Montolio's compliments. Despite, the ranger's grave concerns, though, Drizzt had to wonder just how completely Montolio could understand Hooter, and just how completely the owl could comprehend the events around it.

"The orcs have formed a war party," Montolio said, scratching at his bristled beard. "Graul has awakened from the long winter with a vengeance, it seems."

"How can you know?" Drizzt asked. "Can Hooter understand their words?"

"No, no, of course not!" Montolio replied, amused at the notion.

"Then how can you know?"

"A pack of worgs came in, that much Hooter did tell me," Montolio explained. "Orcs and worgs are not the best of friends, but they do get together when trouble is brewing. The orc celebration was a wild one last night, and with the presence of worgs, there can be little doubt."

"Is there a village nearby?" Drizzt asked.

"None closer than Maldobar," Montolio replied. "I doubt the orcs would go that far, but the melt is about done and caravans will be rolling through the pass, from Sundabar to Citadel Adbar and the other way around, mostly. There must be one coming from Sundabar, though I do not believe Graul would be bold enough, or stupid enough, to attack a caravan of heavily armed dwarves coming from Adbar."

"How many warriors has the orc king?"

"Graul could collect thousands if he took the time and had the mind to do it," Montolio said, "but that would take weeks, and Graul has never been known for his patience. Also, he wouldn't have brought the worgs in so soon if he meant to hold off while collecting his legions. Orcs have a way of disappearing while worgs are around, and the worgs have a way of getting lazy and fat with so many orcs around, if you understand my meaning."

Drizzt's shudder showed that he did indeed.

"I would guess that Graul has about a hundred fighters," Montolio went on, "maybe a dozen to a score worgs, by Hooter's count, and probably a giant or two."

"A considerable force to strike at a caravan," Drizzt said, but both the drow and the ranger had other suspicions in mind. When they had first met, two months before, it had been at Graul's expense.

"It will take them a day or two to get ready," Montolio said after an uncomfortable pause. "Hooter will watch them more closely tonight, and I shall call on other spies as well."

"I will go to scout on the orcs," Drizzt added. He saw concern cross Montolio's face but quickly dismissed it. "Many were the times that such duties fell on me as a patrol scout in Menzoberranzan," he said. "It is a task that I feel quite secure in performing. Fear not."

"That was in the Underdark," Montolio reminded him.

"Is the night so different?" Drizzt replied slyly, throwing a wink and a comforting smile Montolio's way. "We shall have our answers."

Drizzt said his "good days" then and headed off to take his rest. Montolio listened to his friend's retreating steps, barely a swish through the thickly packed trees, with sincere admiration and thought it a good plan.

The day passed slowly and uneventfully for the ranger. He busied himself as best he could in considering his defense plans for the grove. Montolio had never defended the place before, except once when a band of foolish thieves had stumbled in, but he had spent many hours formulating and testing different strategies, thinking it inevitable that one day Graul would grow weary of the ranger's meddling and find the nerve to attack.

If that day had come, Montolio was confident that he would be ready.

Little could be done now, though—the defenses could not be put in place before Montolio was certain of Graul's intent—and the ranger found the waiting interminable. Finally, Hooter informed Montolio that the drow was stirring.

"I will set off, then," Drizzt remarked as soon as he found the ranger, noting the sun riding low in the west. "Let us learn what our unfriendly neighbors are planning."

"Have a care, Drizzt," Montolio said, and the genuine concern in his voice touched the drow. "Graul may be an orc, but he is a crafty one. He may well be expecting one of us to come and look in on him."

Drizzt drew his still-unfamiliar scimitars and spun them about to gain confidence in their movement. Then he snapped them back to his belt and dropped a hand into his pocket, taking further comfort in the presence of the onyx figurine. With a final pat on the ranger's back, the scout started off.

"Hooter will be about!" Montolio cried after him. "And other friends you might not expect. Give a shout if you find more trouble than you can handle!"

* * * * *

The orc camp was not difficult to locate, marked as it was by a huge bonfire blazing into the night sky. Drizzt saw the forms, including one of a giant, dancing around the flames, and he heard the snarls and yips of large wolves, worgs, Montolio had called them. The camp was in a small dale, in a clearing surrounded by huge maples and rock walls. Drizzt could hear the orc voices fairly well in the quiet night, so he decided not to get in too close. He selected one massive tree and focused on a lower branch, summoning his innate levitation ability to get him up.

The spell failed utterly, so Drizzt, hardly surprised, slipped his scimitars into his belt and climbed. The trunk branched several times, down low and as high as twenty feet. Drizzt made for the highest break and was just about to start out on a long and winding branch when he heard an intake of breath. Cautiously, Drizzt slipped his head around the large trunk.

On the side opposite him, nestled comfortably in the nook of the trunk and another branch, reclined an orc sentry with its hands clasped behind its head and a blank, bored expression on its face. Apparently the creature was oblivious to the silent-moving dark elf perched less than two feet away.

Drizzt grasped the hilt of a scimitar, then gaining confidence that the stupid creature was too comfortable to even look around, changed his mind and ignored the orc. He focused instead on the events down in the clearing.

The orc language was similar to the goblin tongue in structure and inflection, but Drizzt, no master even at goblin, could only make out a few scattered words. Orcs were ever a rather demonstrative race, though. Two models, effigies of a dark elf and a thin, moustached human, soon showed Drizzt the clan's intent. The largest orc of the gathering, King Graul, probably, sputtered and cursed at the models. Then the orc soldiers and the worgs took turns tearing into them, to the glee of the frenzied onlookers, a glee that turned to sheer ecstacy when the stone giant walked over and flattened the fake dark elf to the ground.

It went on for hours, and Drizzt suspected it would continue until the dawn. Graul and several other large orcs moved away from the main host and began drawing in the dirt, apparently laying battle plans. Drizzt could not hope to get close enough to make out their huddled conversations and he had no intention of staying in the tree with the dawn's revealing light fast approaching.

He considered the orc sentry on the other side of the trunk, now breathing deeply in slumber, before he started down. The orcs meant to attack Montolio's home, Drizzt knew; shouldn't he now strike the first blow?

Drizzt's conscience betrayed him. He came down from the huge maple and fled from the camp, leaving the orc to its snooze in the comfortable nook.

* * * * *

Montolio, Hooter on his shoulder, sat on one of the rope bridges, waiting for Drizzt's return. "They are coming for us," the old ranger declared when the drow finally came in. "Graul has his neck up about something, probably a little incident at Rogee's Bluff." Montolio pointed to the west, toward the high ridge where he and Drizzt had met.

"Do you have a sanctuary secured for times such as this?" Drizzt asked. "The orcs will come this very night, I believe, nearly a hundred strong and with powerful allies."

"Run?" Montolio cried. He grabbed a nearby rope and swung down to stand by the drow, Hooter clutching his tunic and rolling along for the ride. "Run from orcs? Did I not tell you that orcs are my special bane? Nothing in all the world sounds sweeter than a blade opening an orc's belly!"

"Should I even bother to remind you of the odds?" Drizzt said, smiling in spite of his concern.

"You should remind Graul!" Montolio laughed. "The old orc has lost his wits, or grown an oversized set of fortitude, to come on when he is so obviously outnumbered!"

Drizzt's only reply, the only possible reply to such an outrageous statement, came as a burst of laughter.

"But then," Montolio continued, not slowing a beat, "I will wager a bucket of freshly caught trout and three fine stallions that old Graul won't come along for the fight. He will stay back by the trees, watching and wringing his fat hands, and when we blast his forces apart, he will be the first to flee! He never did have the nerve for the real fighting, not since he became king anyway. He's too comfortable,

I would guess, with too much to lose. Well, we'll take away a bit of his bluster!"

Again Drizzt could not find the words to reply, and he couldn't have stopped laughing at the absurdity anyway. Still, Drizzt had to admit the rousing and comforting effect Montolio's rambling imparted to him.

"You go and get some rest," Montolio said, scratching his stubbly chin and turning all about, again considering his surroundings. "I will begin the preparations—you will be amazed, I promise—and rouse you in a few hours."

The last mumblings the drow heard as he crawled into his blanket in a dark den put it all in perspective. "Yes, Hooter, I've been waiting for this for a long time," Montolio said excitedly, and Drizzt did not doubt a word of it.

* * * * *

It had been a peaceful spring for Kellindil and his elven kin. They were a nomadic group, ranging throughout the region and taking up shelter where they found it, in trees or in caves. Their love was the open world, dancing under the stars, singing in tune with rushing mountain rivers, hunting harts and wild boar in the thick trees of the mountainsides.

Kellindil recognized the dread, a rarely seen emotion among the carefree group, on his cousin's face as soon as the other elf walked into camp late one night.

All the others gathered about.

"The orcs are stirring," the elf explained.

"Graul has found a caravan?" Kellindil asked.

His cousin shook his head and seemed confused. "It is too early for the traders," he replied. "Graul has other prey in mind."

"The grove," several of the elves said together. The whole group turned to Kellindil then, apparently considering the drow his responsibility.

"I do not believe that the drow was in league with Graul," Kellindil answered their unspoken question. "With all of his scouts, Montolio would have known. If the drow is a friend to the ranger, then he is no enemy to us."

"The grove is many miles from here," one of the others offered. "If we wish to look more closely at the orc king's stirrings, and to arrive in time to aid the old ranger, then we must start out at once."

Without a word of dissent, the wandering elves gathered the necessary supplies, mostly their great long bows and extra arrows. Just a few minutes later, they set off, running through the woods and across the mountain trails, making no more noise than a gentle breeze.

*   *   *   *   *

Drizzt awakened early in the afternoon to a startling sight. The day had darkened with gray clouds but still seemed bright to the drow as he crawled out of his den and stretched. High above him he saw the ranger, crawling about the top boughs of a tall pine. Drizzt's curiosity turned to horror, when Montolio, howling like a wild wolf, leaped spread-eagled out of the tree.

Montolio wore a rope harness attached to the pine's thin trunk. As he soared out, his momentum bent the tree, and the ranger came down lightly, bending the pine nearly in two. As soon as he hit the ground, he scrambled to his feet and set the rope harness around some thick roots.

As the scene fully unfolded to Drizzt, he realized that several pines had been bent this way, all pointing to the west and all tied by interconnected ropes. As he carefully picked his way over to Montolio, Drizzt passed a net, several trip wires, and one particularly nasty rope set with a dozen or more double-bladed knives. When the trap was sprung and the trees snapped back up, so would this rope, to the peril of any creatures standing beside it.

"Drizzt?" Montolio asked, hearing the light footsteps. "Ware your steps, now. I would not want to have to rebend all these trees, though I will admit it is a bit of fun."

"You seem to have the preparations well under way,"

Drizzt said as he came to stand near the ranger.

"I have been expecting this day for a long time," Montolio replied. "I have played through this battle a hundred times in my mind and know the course it will take." He crouched and drew an elongated oval on the ground, roughly the shape of the pine grove. "Let me show you," he explained, and he proceeded to draw the landscape around the grove with such detail and accuracy that Drizzt shook his head and looked again to make sure the ranger was blind.

The grove consisted of several dozen trees, running north-south for about fifty yards and less than half that in width. The ground sloped at a gentle but noticeable incline, with the northern end of the grove being half a tree's height lower than the southern end. Farther to the north the ground was broken and boulder-strewn, with scraggly patches of grass and sudden drops, and crossed by sharply twisting trails.

"Their main force will come from the west," Montolio explained, pointing beyond the rock wall and across the small meadow to a pair of dense copses packed between the many rock ledges and cliff facings. "That is the only way they could come in together."

Drizzt took a quick survey of the surrounding area and did not disagree. Across the grove to the east, the ground was rough and uneven. An army charging from that direction would come into the field of tall grass nearly single-file, straight between two high mounds of stone, and would make an easy target for Montolio's deadly bow. South, beyond the grove, the incline grew steeper, a perfect place for orc spear-throwers and archers, except for the fact that just over the nearest ridge loomed a deep ravine with a nearly unclimbable wall.

"We'll not see any trouble from the south," Montolio piped in, almost as though he had read Drizzt's thoughts. "And if they come from the north, they'll be running uphill to get at us. I know Graul better than that. With such favorable odds, he will charge his host straight in from the west, trying to overrun us."

"Thus the trees," Drizzt remarked in admiration. "And the net and knife-set rope."

"Cunning," Montolio congratulated himself. "But remember, I have had five years to prepare for this. Come along now. The trees are just the beginning. I have duties for you while I finish with the tree trap."

Montolio led Drizzt to another secret, blanket-shielded den. Inside hung lines of strange iron items, resembling animal jaws with a strong chain connected to their bases.

"Traps," Montolio explained. "Pelt hunters set them in the mountains. Wicked things. I find them—Hooter is particularly skilled at spotting them—and take them away. I wish I had eyes to see the hunter scratching his head when he comes for them a week later!

"This one belonged to Roddy McGristle," Montolio continued, pulling down the closest of the contraptions. The ranger set it on the ground and carefully maneuvered his feet to pull the jaws apart until they set. "This should slow an orc," Montolio said, grabbing a nearby stick and patting around until he hit the plunger.

The trap's iron jaws snapped shut, the force of the blow breaking the stick cleanly and wrenching the remaining half right out of Montolio's hand. "I have collected more than a score of them," Montolio said grimly, wincing at the evil sound of the iron jaws. "I never thought to put them to use—evil things—but against Graul and his clan the traps might just amend some of the damage they have wrought."

Drizzt needed no further instructions. He brought the traps out into the western meadow, set and concealed them, and staked down the chains several feet away. He put a few just inside the rock wall, too, thinking that the pain they might cause to the first orcs coming over would surely slow those behind.

Montolio was done with the trees by this time; he had bent and tied off more than a dozen of them. Now the ranger was up on a rope bridge that ran north-south, fastening a line of crossbows along the western supports. Once set and loaded, either Montolio or Drizzt could merely trot down the line, firing as he went.

Drizzt planned to go and help, but first he had another trick in mind. He went back to the weapons cache and got the tall and heavy ranseur he had seen earlier. He found a sturdy root in the area where he planned to make his stand and dug a small hole out behind it. He laid the metal-shafted weapon down across this root, with only a foot or so of the butt sticking out over the hole, then covered the whole of it with grass and leaves.

He had just finished when the ranger called to him again.

"Here is the best yet," Montolio said, flashing his sly smile. He brought Drizzt to a split log, hollowed and burned smooth, and pitched to seal any cracks. "Good boat for when the river is high and slow," Montolio explained. "And good for holding Adbar brandy," he added with another smile.

Drizzt, not understanding, eyed him curiously. Montolio had shown Drizzt his kegs of the strong drink more than a week before, a gift the ranger had received for warning a Sundabar caravan of Graul's ambush intent, but the dark elf saw no purpose in pouring the drink into a hollowed log.

"Adbar brandy is powerful stuff," Montolio explained. "It burns brighter than all but the finest oil."

Now Drizzt understood. Together, he and Montolio carried the log out and placed it at the end of the only pass from the east. They poured in some brandy, then covered it with leaves and grass.

When they got back to the rope bridge, Drizzt saw that Montolio had already made the preparations on this end. A single crossbow was set facing east, its loaded quarrel headed by a wrapped, oil-soaked rag and a flint and steel resting nearby.

"You will have to sight it in," Montolio explained. "Without Hooter, I cannot be sure, and even with the bird, sometimes the height of my aim is off."

The daylight was almost fully gone now, and Drizzt's keen night vision soon located the split log. Montolio had built the supports along the rope bridge quite well and with just this purpose in mind, and with a few minor adjustments, Drizzt had the weapon locked on its target.

All of the major defenses were in place, and Drizzt and Montolio busied themselves finalizing their strategies. Every so often, Hooter or some other owl would rush in, chattering with news. One came in with the expected confirmation: King Graul and his band were on the march.

"You can call Guenhwyvar now," Montolio said. "They will come in this night."

"Foolish," said Drizzt. "The night favors us. You are blind anyway and in no need of daylight and I surely prefer the darkness."

The owl hooted again.

"The main host will come in from the west," Montolio told Drizzt smugly. "As I said they would. Scores of orcs and a giant besides! Hooter's watching another smaller group that split from the first."

The mention of the giant sent a shudder along Drizzt's spine, but he had every intention, and a plan already set, for fighting this one. "I want to draw the giant to me," he said.

Montolio turned to him curiously. "Let us see how the battle goes," the ranger offered. "There is only one giant—you or I will get it."

"I want to draw the giant to me," Drizzt said again, more firmly. Montolio couldn't see the set of the drow's jaw or the seething fires in Drizzt's lavender eyes, but the ranger couldn't deny the determination in Drizzt's voice.

"*Mangura bok woklok*," he said, and he smiled again, knowing that the strange utterance had caught the drow unaware.

"*Mangura bok woklok*," Montolio declared again. "'Stupid blockhead,' translated word by word. Stone giants hate that phrase—brings them charging in every time!"

"*Mangura bok woklok*," Drizzt mouthed quietly. He'd have to remember that.

❧ 18 ❧

The Battle of Mooshie's Grove

Drizzt noticed that Montolio looked more than a little troubled after Hooter, back with more news, departed.

"The split of Graul's forces?" he inquired.

Montolio nodded, his expression grim. "Worg-riding orcs—just a handful—circling around to the west."

Drizzt looked out beyond the rock wall, to the pass secured by their brandy trough. "We can stop them," he said.

Still the ranger's expression told of doom. "Another group of worgs—a score or more—is coming from the south." Drizzt did not miss the ranger's fear, as Montolio added, "Caroak is leading them. I never thought that one would fall in with Graul."

"A giant?" Drizzt asked.

"No, winter wolf," Montolio replied. At the words, Guenhwyvar flattened its ears and growled angrily.

"The panther knows," Montolio said as Drizzt looked on in amazement. "A winter wolf is a perversion of nature, a blight against creatures following the natural order, and thus, Guenhwyvar's enemy."

The black panther growled again.

"It's a large creature," Montolio went on, "and too smart for a wolf. I have fought Caroak before. Alone he could give us a time of it! With the worgs around him, and us busy fighting orcs, he might have his way."

Guenhwyvar growled a third time and tore the ground with great claws.

"Guenhwyvar will deal with Caroak," Drizzt remarked.

Montolio moved over and grabbed the panther by the

ears, holding Guenhwyvar's gaze with his own sightless expression. "Ware the wolf's breath," the ranger said. "A cone of frost, it is, that will freeze your muscles to your bones. I have seen a giant felled by it!" Montolio turned to Drizzt and knew that the drow wore a concerned expression.

"Guenhwyvar has to keep them away from us until we can chase off Graul and his group," the ranger said, "then we can make arrangements for Caroak." He released his hold on the panther's ears and swatted Guenhwyvar hard on the scruff of the neck.

Guenhwyvar roared a fourth time and darted off through the grove, a black arrow aimed at the heart of doom.

*   *   *   *   *

Graul's main attack force came, as expected, from the west, whooping and hollering and trampling the brush in its path. The troops approached in two groups, one through each of the dense copses.

"Aim for the group on the south!" Montolio called up to Drizzt, in position on the crossbow-laden rope bridge. "We've friends in the other!"

As if in confirmation of the ranger's decree, the northern copse erupted suddenly in orc cries that sounded more like terrified shrieks than battle calls. A chorus of throaty growls accompanied the screams. Bluster the bear had come to Montolio's call, Drizzt knew, and by the sounds in the copse, he had brought a number of friends.

Drizzt wasn't about to question their good fortune. He positioned himself behind the closest crossbow and let the quarrel fly as the first orcs emerged from the southern copse. Right down the line the drow ran, clicking off his shots in rapid succession. From down below, Montolio arced a few arrows over the wall.

In the sudden swarm of orcs, Drizzt couldn't tell how many of their shots actually hit, but the buzzing bolts did slow the orc charge and scattered their ranks. Several orcs dropped to their bellies; a few turned and headed straight back into the trees. The bulk of the group, though, and some running to join from the other copse, came on.

Montolio fired one last time, then felt his way back into a sheltered run behind the center of his bent tree traps, where he would be protected on three sides by walls of wood and trees. His bow in one hand, he checked his sword and then reached around to touch a rope at his other side.

Drizzt noticed the ranger moving into position twenty feet below him and to the side, and he figured that this might be his last free opportunity. He sorted out an object hanging above Montolio's head and dropped a spell over it.

The quarrels had brought minimum chaos to the field of charging orcs, but the traps proved more effective. First one, then another, orc stepped in, their cries rising over the din of the charge. As other orcs saw their companions' pain and peril, they slowed considerably or stopped altogether.

With the commotion growing in the field, Drizzt paused and carefully considered his final shot. He noticed a large, finely outfitted orc watching from the closest boughs of the northern copse. Drizzt knew this was Graul, but his attention shifted immediately to the figure standing next to the orc king. "Damn," the drow muttered, recognizing McGristle. Now he was torn, and he moved the crossbow back and forth between the adversaries. Drizzt wanted to shoot at Roddy, wanted to end his personal torment then and there. But Roddy was not an orc, and Drizzt found himself repulsed by the thought of killing a human.

"Graul is the more important target," the drow told himself, more to distract his inner torment than for any other reason. Quickly, before he could find any more arguments, he took aim and fired. The quarrel whistled long and far, knocking into the trunk of a tree just inches above Graul's head. Roddy promptly grabbed the orc king and pulled him back into the deeper shadows. In their stead came a roaring stone giant, rock in hand.

The boulder clipped the trees beside Drizzt, shaking the branches and bridge alike. A second shot followed at once, this one taking a supporting post squarely and dropping the front half of the bridge.

Drizzt had seen it coming, though he was amazed and horrified by the uncanny accuracy at so far a range. As the front half of the bridge fell away beneath him, Drizzt leaped out, catching a hold in a tangle of branches. When he finally sorted himself out, he was faced by a new problem. From the east came the worg-riders, brandishing torches.

Drizzt looked to the log trap, then to the crossbow. It and the post securing it had survived the boulder hit, but the drow could not hope to cross to it on the faltering bridge.

The leaders of the main host, now behind Drizzt, reached the rock wall then. Fortunately, the first orc leaping over landed squarely into another of the wicked jaw traps, and its companions were not so quick to follow.

* * * * *

Guenhwyvar leaped around and between the many broken crags of stone marking the descent to the north. The panther caught the distant first cries of battle back at the grove, but more intently, Guenhwyvar heard the ensuing howls of the approaching wolf pack. The panther sprang up to a low ledge and waited.

Caroak, the huge silver canine beast, led the charge. Focused on the distant grove, the winter wolf's surprise was complete when Guenhwyvar dropped upon it, scratching and raking wildly.

Clumps of silver fur flew about under the assault. Yelping, Caroak dove into a sidelong roll. Guenhwyvar rode the wolf as a lumberjack might foot-roll a log in a pool, slashing and kicking with each step. But Caroak was a wizened old wolf, a veteran of a hundred battles. As the monster rolled about to its back, a blast of icy frost came at the panther.

Guenhwyvar dodged aside, both from the frost and the onslaught of several worgs. The frost got the panther on the side of the face, though, numbing Guenhwyvar's jaw. Then the chase was on, with Guenhwyvar leaping and tumbling right around the wolf pack, and the worgs, and angry Caroak, nipping at the panther's heels.

* * * * *

Time was running out for Drizzt and Montolio. Above all else, the drow knew that he must protect their rear flank. In synchronous movements, Drizzt kicked off his boots, took the flint in one hand and put a piece of steel in his mouth, and leaped up to a branch that would take him out over the lone crossbow.

He got above it a moment later. Holding with one hand, he struck the flint hard. Sparks rolled down, close to the mark. Drizzt struck again and again, and finally, a spark hit the oil-soaked rags tipping the loaded quarrel squarely enough to ignite them.

Now the drow was not so lucky. He rocked and twisted but could not get his foot close enough to the trigger.

Montolio could see nothing, of course, but he knew well enough the general situation. He heard the approaching worgs at the back of the grove and knew that those in front had breached the wall. He sent another bow shot through the thick canopy of bent trees, just for good measure, and hooted loudly three times.

In answer, a group of owls swooped down from the pines, bearing down on the orcs along the rock wall. Like the traps, the birds could only cause minimal real damage, but the confusion bought the defenders a little more time.

* * * * *

To this point, the only clear advantage for the grove's defenders came in the northernmost copse, where Bluster and three of his closest and largest bear buddies had a dozen orcs down and a score more running about blindly.

One orc, in flight from a bear, came around a tree and nearly crashed into Bluster. The orc kept its wits enough to thrust its spear ahead, but the creature hadn't the strength to drive the crude weapon through Bluster's thick hide.

Bluster responded with a heavy swipe that sent the orc's head flying through the trees.

Another great bear ambled by, its huge arms wrapped in front of it. The only clue that the bear held an orc in the crushing hug was the orc's feet, which hung out and kicked wildly below the engulfing fur.

Bluster caught sight of another enemy, smaller and quicker than an orc. The bear roared and charged, but the diminutive creature was long gone before he ever got close.

Tephanis had no intentions of joining the battle. He had come with the northernmost group mostly to keep out of Graul's sight, and had planned all along to remain in the trees and wait out the fighting. The trees didn't seem so safe anymore, so the sprite lighted out, meaning to get into the southern copse.

About halfway to the other woods, the sprite's plans were foiled again. Sheer speed nearly got him past the trap before the iron jaws snapped closed, but the wicked teeth just caught the end his foot. The ensuing jolt blasted the breath from him and left him dazed, facedown in the grass.

* * * * *

Drizzt knew how revealing that little fire on the quarrel would prove, so he was hardly surprised when another giant-hurled rock thundered in. It struck Drizzt's bending branch, and with a series of cracks, the limb swung down.

Drizzt hooked the crossbow with his foot as he dropped, and he hit the trigger immediately, before the weapon was deflected too far aside. Then he stubbornly held his position and watched.

The fiery quarrel reached out into the darkness beyond the eastern rock wall. It skidded in low, sending sparks up through the tall grass, then thudded into the side—the outside—of the brandy-filled trough.

The first half of the worg-riders got across the trap, but the remaining three were not so lucky, bearing in just as flames licked over the side of the dugout. The brandy and kindling roared to life as the riders plunged through. Worgs and orcs thrashed about in the tall grass, setting other pockets of fire.

Those who had already come through spun about abruptly at the sudden conflagration. One orc rider was thrown heavily, landing on its own torch, and the other two barely kept their seats. Above all else, worgs hated fire, and the sight of three of their kin rolling about, furry balls of flame, did little to strengthen their resolve for this battle.

* * * * *

Guenhwyvar came to a small, level area dominated by a single maple. Onlookers to the panther's rush would have blinked incredulously, wondering if the vertical tree trunk was really a log lying on its side, so fast did Guenhwyvar run up it.

The worg pack came in soon after, sniffing and milling about, certain that the cat was up the tree but unable to pick out Guenhwyvar's black form among the dark boughs.

The panther showed itself soon enough, though, again dropping heavily to the back of the winter wolf, and this time taking care to lock its jaws onto Caroak's ear.

The winter wolf thrashed and yelped as Guenhwyvar's claws did their work. Caroak managed to turn about and Guenhwyvar heard the sharp intake of breath, the same as the one preceding the previous chilling blast.

Guenhwyvar's huge neck muscles flexed, forcing Caroak's open jaws to the side. The foul breath came anyway, blasting three charging worgs right in the face.

Guenhwyvar's muscles reversed and flexed again suddenly, and the panther heard Caroak's neck snap. The winter wolf plopped straight down, Guenhwyvar still atop it.

Those three worgs closest to Guenhwyvar, the three who had caught Caroak's icy breath, posed no threat. One lay on its side, gasping for air that would not move through its frozen lungs, another turned tight circles, fully blinded, and the last stood perfectly still, staring down at its forelegs, which, for some reason, would not answer its call to move.

The rest of the pack, though, nearly a score strong, came in methodically, surrounding the panther in a deadly ring. Guenhwyvar looked all about for some escape, but the worgs did not rush frantically, leaving openings.

They worked in harmony, shoulder to shoulder, tightening the ring.

*   *   *   *   *

The leading orcs milled about the tangle of bent trees, looking for some way through. Some had begun to make progress, but the whole of the trap was interconnected, and any one of a dozen trip wires would send all the pines springing up.

One of the orcs found Montolio's net, then, the hard way. It stumbled over a rope, fell facedown on the net, then went high into the air, one of its companions caught beside it. Neither of them could have imagined how much better off they were than those they had left behind, particularly the orc unsuspectingly straddling the knife-set rope. When the trees sprang up, so did this devilish trap, gutting the creature and lifting it head over heels into the air.

Even those orcs not caught by the secondary traps did not fare well. Tangled branches, bristling with prickly pine needles, shot up all about them, sending a few on a pretty fair ride and scratching and disorienting the others.

Even worse for the orcs, Montolio used the sound of the rushing trees as his signal to open fire. Arrow after arrow whistled down the sheltered run, more hitting the mark than not. One orc lifted its spear to throw, then caught one arrow in the face and another in the chest. Another beast turned and fled, crying "Bad magic!" frantically.

To those crossing the rock wall, the screamer seemed to fly, its feet kicking above the ground. Its startled companions understood when the orc came back down in a heap, a quivering arrow shaft protruding from its back.

Drizzt, still on his tenuous perch, didn't have time to marvel at the efficient execution of Montolio's well-laid plans. From the west, the giant was now on the move and, back the other way, the two remaining worg-riders had settled enough to resume their charges, torches held high.

* * * * *

The ring of snarling worgs tightened. Guenhwyvar could smell their stinking breath. The panther could not hope to charge through the thick ranks, nor could the cat get over them quickly enough to flee.

Guenhwyvar found another route. Hind paws tamped down on Caroak's still-twitching body and the panther arrowed straight up into the air, twenty feet and more. Guenhwyvar caught the maple's lowest branch with long front claws, hooked on, and pulled itself up. Then the panther disappeared into the boughs, leaving the frustrated pack howling and growling.

Guenhwyvar reappeared quickly though, out from the side and back to the ground, and the pack took up the pursuit. The panther had come to know this terrain quite well over the last few weeks and now Guenhwyvar had figured out exactly where to lead the wolves.

They ran along a ridge, with a dark and brooding emptiness on their left flank. Guenhwyvar marked well the boulders and the few scattered trees. The panther couldn't see the chasm's opposite bank and had to trust fully in its memory. Incredibly fast, Guenhwyvar pivoted suddenly and sprang out into the night, touching down lightly across the wide way and speeding off toward the grove. The worgs would have a long jump—too long for most of them—or a long way back around if they meant to follow.

They inched up snarling and scratching at the ground. One poised on the lip and meant to try the leap, but an arrow exploded into its side and destroyed its determination.

Worgs were not stupid creatures, and the sight of the arrow put them on the defensive. The ensuing shower by Kellindil and his kin was more than they expected. Dozens of arrows whistled in, dropping the worgs where they stood. Only a few escaped that barrage, and they promptly scattered to the corners of the night.

* * * * *

Drizzt called upon another magical trick to stop the torch-bearers. Faerie fire, harmless dancing flames, appeared suddenly below the torch fires, rolling down the wooden instrument to lick at the orcs' hands. Faerie fire did not burn—was not even warm—but when the orcs saw the flames engulfing their hands, they were far from rational.

One of them threw its torch out wide, and the jerking motion cost it its seat. It tumbled down in the grass, and the worg turned yet another time and snarled in frustration.

The other orc simply dropped its torch, which fell on top of its mount's head. Sparks and flames erupted from the worg's thick coat, stinging its eyes and ears, and the beast went crazy. It dropped into a headlong roll, bouncing right over the startled orc.

The orc staggered back to its feet, dazed and bruised and holding its arms out wide as if in apology. The singed worg wasn't interested in hearing any, however. It sprang straight in and clamped its powerful jaws on the orc's face.

Drizzt didn't see any of it. The drow could only hope that his trick had worked, for as soon as he had cast the spell, he released his foothold on the crossbow and let the torn branch carry him down to the ground.

Two orcs, finally seeing a target, rushed at the drow as he landed, but as soon as Drizzt's hands were free of the branch, they held his scimitars. The orcs came in, oblivious, and Drizzt slapped their weapons aside and cut them down. The drow waded through more scattered resistance as he made his way to his prepared spot. A grim smile found his face when at last he felt the ranseur's metal shaft under his bare feet. He remembered the giants back in Maldobar that had slain the innocent family, and he took comfort that now he would kill another of their evil kin.

"*Mangura bok woklok!*" Drizzt cried, placing one foot on the root fulcrum and the other on the butt of the hidden weapon.

* * * * *

Montolio smiled when he heard the drow's call, gaining confidence in the proximity of his powerful ally. His bow sang out a few more times, but the ranger sensed that the orcs were coming in at him in a roundabout way, using the thick trees as cover. The ranger waited, baiting them in. Then, just before they closed, Montolio dropped his bow, whipped out his sword and slashed the rope at his side, right below a huge knot. The severed rope rolled up into the air, the knot catching on a fork in the lowest branch, and Montolio's shield, empowered with one of Drizzt's darkness spells, dropped down to hang at precisely the right height for the ranger's waiting arm.

Darkness held little influence over the blind ranger, but the few orcs that had come in at Montolio found themselves in a precarious position. They jostled and swung wildly—one cut down its own brother—while Montolio calmly sorted out the melee and went to methodical work. In the matter of a minute, four of the five who had come in were dead or dying and the fifth had taken flight.

Far from sated, the ranger and his portable ball of darkness followed, searching for voices or sounds that would lead him to more orcs. Again came the cry that made Montolio smile.

* * * * *

"*Mangura bok woklok!*" Drizzt yelled again. An orc tossed a spear at the drow, which Drizzt promptly swatted aside. The distant orc was now unarmed, but Drizzt would not pursue, determinedly holding his position.

"*Mangura bok woklok!*" Drizzt cried again. "Come in, stupid block head!" This time the giant, approaching the wall in Montolio's direction, heard the words. The great monster hesitated a moment, regarding the drow curiously.

Drizzt didn't miss the opportunity. "*Mangura bok woklok!*"

With a howl and a stamp that shook the earth, the giant kicked a hole in the rock wall and strode toward Drizzt.

"*Mangura bok woklok!*" Drizzt said for good measure, angling his feet properly.

The giant broke into a dead run, scattering terrified orcs before it and slamming its stone and its club together angrily. It sputtered a thousand curses at Drizzt in those few seconds, words that the drow would never decipher. Three times the drow's height and many times his weight, the giant loomed over Drizzt, and its rush seemed as though it would surely bury Drizzt where he calmly stood.

When the giant got only two long strides from Drizzt, committed fully to its collision course, Drizzt dropped all of his weight onto his back foot. The ranseur's butt dropped into the hole. Its tip angled up.

Drizzt leaped back at the moment the giant plowed into the ranseur. The weapon's tip and hooked barbs disappeared into the giant's belly, drove upward through its diaphragm and into its heart and lungs. The metal shaft bowed and seemed as if it would break as its butt end was driven a foot and more into the ground.

The ranseur held, and the giant was stopped cold. It dropped its club and rock, reached helplessly for the metal shaft with hands that had not the strength to even close around it. Huge eyes bulged in denial, in terror, and in absolute surprise. The great mouth opened wide and contorted weirdly, but could not even find the wind to scream.

Drizzt, too, almost cried out, but caught the words before he uttered them. "Amazing," he said, looking back to where Montolio was fighting, for the cry he nearly shouted was a praise to the goddess Mielikki. Drizzt shook his head helplessly and smiled, stunned by the acute perceptions of his not-so-blind companion.

With those thoughts in mind and a sense of righteousness in his heart, Drizzt ran up the shaft and slashed at the giant's throat with both weapons. He continued on, stepping right on the giant's shoulder and head and then leaping off toward a group of watching orcs, whooping as he went.

The sight of the giant, their bully, quivering and gasping, had already unnerved the orcs, but when this ebony-skinned and wild-eyed drow monster leaped at them, they broke rank altogether. Drizzt's charge got him to the closest two, and he promptly cut them down and charged on.

Twenty feet to the drow's left, a ball of blackness rolled out of the trees, leading a dozen frightened orcs before it. The orcs knew that to fall within that impenetrable globe was to fall within the blind hermit's reach and to die.

* * * * *

Two orcs and three worgs, all that remained of the torch-bearers, regrouped and slipped quietly toward the grove's eastern edge. If they could get in behind the enemy, they believed the battle still could be won.

The orc farthest to the north never even saw the rushing black form. Guenhwyvar plowed it down and charged on, confident that that one would never rise again.

A worg was next in line. Quicker to react than the orc, the worg spun and faced the panther, its teeth bared and jaws snapping.

Guenhwyvar snarled, pulling up short right before it. Great claws came in alternately in a series of slaps. The worg could not match the cat's speed. It swung its jaws from side to side, always a moment too late to catch up to the darting paws. After only five slaps, the worg was defeated. One eye had closed forever, its tongue, half torn, lolled helplessly out one side of its mouth, and its lower jaw was no longer in line with its upper. Only the presence of other targets saved the worg, for when it turned and fled the way it had come, Guenhwyvar, seeing closer prey, did not follow.

* * * * *

Drizzt and Montolio had flushed most of the invading force back out over the rock wall. "Bad magic!" came the general orc cry, voices edged on desperation. Hooter and his owl companions aided the growing frenzy, flapping down all of a sudden in orc faces, nipping with a talon or beak, then rushing off again into the sky. Still another orc discovered one of the traps as it tried to flee. It went down howling and shrieking, its cries only heightening its companions' terror.

"No!" Roddy McGristle cried in disbelief. "Ye've let two beat up yer whole force!"

Graul's glare settled on the burly man.

"We can turn 'em back," Roddy said. "If they see ye, they'll go back to the fight." The mountain man's appraisal was not off the mark. If Graul and Roddy had made their entrance then, the orcs, still numbering more than fifty, might have regrouped. With most of their traps exhausted, Drizzt and Montolio would have been in a sore position indeed! But the orc king had seen another brewing problem to the north and had decided, despite Roddy's protests, that the old man and the dark elf simply weren't worth the effort.

Most of the orcs in the field heard the newest danger before they saw it, for Bluster and his friends were a noisy lot. The largest obstacle the bears found as they rolled through the orc ranks was picking out a single target in the mad rush. They swatted orcs as they passed, then chased them into the copse and beyond, all the way back to their holes by the river. It was high spring; the air was charged with energy and excitement, and how these playful bears loved to swat orcs!

* * * * *

The whole horde of rushing bodies swarmed right past the fallen quickling. When Tephanis awoke, he found that he was the only one alive on the blood-soaked field. Growls and shouts wafted in from the west, the fleeing band, and sounds of battle still sounded in the ranger's grove. Tephanis knew that his part in the battle, minor though it had been, was over. Tremendous pain rolled up the sprite's leg, more pain than he had ever known. He looked down to his torn foot and to his horror realized that the only way out of the wicked trap was to complete the gruesome cut, losing the end of his foot and all five of his toes in the process. It was not a difficult job—the foot was hanging by a thin piece of skin—and Tephanis did not hesitate, fearing that the drow would come out at any moment and find him.

The quickling stifled his scream and covered the wound with his torn shirt, then ambled—slowly—off into the trees.

* * * * *

The orc crept along silently, glad for the covering noises of the fight between the panther and a worg. All thoughts of killing the old man or the drow had flown from this orc now; it had seen its comrades chased away by a pack of bears. Now the orc only wanted to find a way out, not an easy feat in the thick, low tangle of pine branches.

It stepped on some dry leaves as it came into one clear area and froze at the resounding crackle. The orc glanced to the left, then slowly brought its head back around to the right. All of a sudden, it jumped and spun, expecting an attack from the rear. But all was clear as far as it could tell and all, except for the distant panther growls and worg yelps, was quiet. The orc let out a profound sigh of relief and sought the trail once again.

It stopped suddenly on instinct and threw its head way back to look up. A dark form crouched on a branch just above the orc's head, and the silvery flash shot down before the orc could begin to react. The curve of the scimitar's blade proved perfect for slipping around the orc's chin and diving into its throat.

The orc stood very still, arms wide and twitching, and tried to scream, but the whole length of its larynx was torn apart. The scimitar came out in a rush and the orc fell backward into death.

Not so far away, another orc finally extracted itself from the hanging net and quickly cut free its buddy. The two of them, enraged and not as anxious to run away without a fight, crept in quietly.

"In the dark," the first explained as they came through one thicket and found the landscape blotted out by an impenetrable globe. "Deep."

Together, the orcs raised their spears and threw, grunting savagely with the effort. The spears disappeared into the dark globe, dead center, one banging into a metallic object but the other striking something softer.

The orcs' cries of victory were cut short by two twangs of a bowstring. One of the creatures lurched forward, dead before it hit the ground, but the other, stubbornly holding its footing, managed to look down to its chest, to the protruding point of an arrowhead. It lived long enough to see Montolio casually stride past and disappear into the darkness to retrieve his shield.

Drizzt watched the old man from a distance, shaking his head and wondering.

* * * * *

"It is ended," the elven scout told the others when they caught up to him among the boulders just south of Mooshie's Grove.

"I am not so certain," Kellindil replied, looking curiously back to the west and hearing the echoes of bear growls and orc screams. Kellindil suspected that something beyond Graul was behind this attack and, feeling somewhat responsible for the drow, he wanted to know what it might be.

"The ranger and drow have won the grove," the scout explained.

"Agreed," said Kellindil, "and so your part is ended. Go back, all of you, to the campsite."

"And will you join us?" one of the elves asked, though he

had already guessed the answer.

"If the fates decree it," Kellindil replied. "For now, I have other business to attend."

The others did not question Kellindil further. Rarely did he come to their realm and never did he remain with them for long. Kellindil was an adventurer; the road was his home. He set off at once, running to catch up to the fleeing orcs, then paralleling their movements just south of them.

* * * * *

"Ye let just two of them beat ye!" Roddy griped when he and Graul had a moment to stop and catch their breath. "Two of them!"

Graul's answer came in the swing of a heavy club. Roddy partially blocked the blow, but its weight knocked him backward.

"Ye're to pay for that!" the mountain man growled, tearing Bleeder from his belt. A dozen of Graul's minions appeared beside the orc king then and immediately understood the situation.

"Yous has brought ruin to us!" Graul snapped at Roddy. Then to his orcs, he shouted, "Kill him!"

Roddy's dog tripped the closest of the group and Roddy didn't wait for the others to catch up. He turned and sprinted off into the night, using every trick he knew to get ahead of the pursuing band.

His efforts were quickly successful—the orcs really didn't want any more battles this night—and Roddy would have been wise to stop looking over his shoulder.

He heard a rustle up ahead and turned just in time to catch the pommel of a swinging sword squarely in the face. The weight of the blow, multiplied by Roddy's own momentum, dropped the mountain man straight to the ground and into unconsciousness.

"I am not surprised," Kellindil said over the writhing body.

❧ 19 ❧

Separate Ways

Eight days had done nothing to ease the pain in Tephanis's foot. The sprite ambled about as best he could, but whenever he broke into a sprint, he inevitably veered to one side and more often than not crashed into a bush or, worse, the unbending trunk of a tree.

"Will-you-please-quit-growling-at-me, stupid-dog!" Tephanis snapped at the yellow canine he had been with since the day after the battle. Neither had become comfortable around the other. Tephanis often lamented that this ugly mutt was in no way akin to Caroak.

But Caroak was dead; the quickling had found the winter wolf's torn body. Another companion gone, and now the sprite was alone again. "Alone-except-for-you, stupid-dog!" he lamented.

The dog bared its teeth and growled.

Tephanis wanted to slice its throat, wanted to run up and down the length of the mangy animal, cutting and slashing at every inch. He saw the sun riding low in the sky, though, and knew that the beast might soon prove valuable.

"Time-for-me-to-go!" the quickling spouted. Faster than the dog could react, Tephanis darted by it, grabbed at the rope he had hung about the dog's neck, and zipped three complete circuits of a nearby tree. The dog went after him, but Tephanis easily kept out of its reach until the leash snapped taut, flipping the dog right over. "Be-back-soon, you-stupid-thing!"

Tephanis sped along the mountain paths, knowing that this night might be his last chance. The lights of Maldobar burned in the far distance, but it was a different light, a campfire, that guided the quickling. He came upon the small camp just a few minutes later, glad to see that the elf was not around.

He found Roddy McGristle sitting at the base of a huge tree, his arms pulled behind him and tied at the wrists around the trunk. The mountain man seemed a wretched thing—as wretched as the dog—but Tephanis was out of options. Ulgulu and Kempfana were dead, Caroak was dead, and Graul, after the disaster at the grove, had actually placed a bounty on the quickling's head.

That left only Roddy—not much of a choice, but Tephanis had no desire to survive on his own ever again. He sped, unnoticed, to the back of the tree and whispered in the mountain man's ear. "You-will-be-in-Maldobar-tomorrow."

Roddy froze at the unexpected, squeaky voice.

"You will be in Maldobar tomorrow," Tephanis said again, as slowly as he could.

"Go away," Roddy growled at him, thinking that the sprite was teasing him.

"You-should-be-kinder-to-me, oh-you-should!" Tephanis snapped right back. "The-elf-means-to-imprison-you, you-know. For-crimes-against-the-blind-ranger."

"Shut yer mouth," McGristle growled, louder than he had intended.

"What are you about?" came Kellindil's call from not so far away.

"There, you-have-done-it-now, silly-man!" Tephanis whispered.

"I told ye to go away!" Roddy replied.

"I-might, and-then-where-would-you-be? In-prison?" Tephanis said angrily. "I-can-help-you-now, if-you-want-my-help."

Roddy was beginning to understand. "Untie my hands," he ordered.

"They-already-are-untied," Tephanis replied, and Roddy found the sprite's words to be true. He started to rise but changed his mind abruptly as Kellindil entered the camp.

"Keep-still," Tephanis advised. "I-will-distract-your-captor."

Tephanis had moved as he spoke the words and Roddy heard only an unintelligible murmur. He kept his hands behind him, though, seeing no other course available with the heavily armed elf approaching.

"Our last night on the road," Kellindil remarked, dropping by the fire the coney he had shot for a meal. He moved in front of Roddy and bent low. "I will send for Lady Falconhand once we have arrived in Maldobar," he said. "She names Montolio DeBrouchee as a friend and will be interested to learn of the events in the grove."

"What do ye know?" Roddy spat at him. "The ranger was a friend o' mine, too!"

"If you are a friend of orc king Graul, then you are no friend of the ranger in the grove," Kellindil retorted.

Roddy had no immediate rebuttal, but Tephanis supplied one. A buzzing noise came from behind the elf and Kellindil, dropping a hand to his sword, spun about.

"What manner of being are you?" he asked the quickling, his eyes wide in amazement.

Kellindil never learned the answer, for Roddy came up suddenly behind him and slammed him to the ground. Kellindil was a seasoned fighter, but in close he was no match for the sheer brawn of Roddy McGristle. Roddy's huge and dirty hands closed on the slender elf's throat.

"I-have-your-dog," Tephanis said to Roddy when the foul business was done. "Tied-it-to-a-tree."

"Who are ye?" Roddy asked, trying to hide his elation, both for his freedom and for the knowledge that his dog still lived. "And what do ye want with me?"

"I-am-a-little-thing, you-can-see-that-to-be-true," Tephanis explained. "I-like-keeping-big-friends."

Roddy considered the offer for a moment. "Well, ye've earned it," he said with a laugh. He found Bleeder, his trusted axe, among the dead elf's belongings and rose up huge and grim-faced. "Come on then, let's get back to the mountains. I've a drow to deal with."

A sour expression crossed the quickling's delicate features, but Tephanis hid it before Roddy could notice. Tephanis had no desire to go anywhere near the blind ranger's grove. Aside from the fact that the orc king had placed a bounty on his head, he knew that the other elves might get suspicious if Roddy showed up without Kellindil. More than that, Tephanis found the pain in his head and foot even more acute at the mere thought of facing the dark elf again.

"No!" the sprite blurted. Roddy, not used to being disobeyed, eyed him dangerously.

"No-need," Tephanis lied. "The-drow-is-dead, killed-by-a-worg."

Roddy didn't seem convinced.

"I-led-you-to-the-drow-once," Tephanis reminded him.

Truly Roddy was disappointed, but he no longer doubted the quickling. If it hadn't been for Tephanis, Roddy knew, he never would have located Drizzt. He would be more than a hundred miles away, sniffing around Morueme's Cave and spending all of his gold on dragon lies. "What about the blind ranger?" Roddy asked.

"He-lives, but-let-him-live," Tephanis replied. "Many-powerful-friends-have-joined-him." He led Roddy's gaze to Kellindil's body. "Elves, many-elves."

Roddy nodded his assent. He had no real grudge against Mooshie and had no desire to face Kellindil's kin.

They buried Kellindil and all of the supplies they couldn't take with them, found Roddy's dog, and set out later that same night for the wide lands to the west.

*   *   *   *   *

Back at Mooshie's grove, the summer passed peacefully and productively, with Drizzt coming into the ways and methods of a ranger even more easily than optimistic Montolio had believed. Drizzt learned the name for every tree or bush in the region, and every animal, and more importantly, he learned how to learn, how to observe the clues that Mielikki gave him. When he came upon an animal that he had not encountered before, he found that simply by watching its movements and actions he could quickly discern its intent, demeanor, and mood.

"Go and feel its coat," Montolio whispered to him one day in the gray and blustery twilight. The old ranger pointed across a field, to the tree line and the white flicking of a deer's tail. Even in the dim light, Drizzt had trouble seeing the deer, but he sensed its presence, as Montolio obviously had.

"Will it let me?" Drizzt whispered back. Montolio smiled and shrugged.

Drizzt crept out silently and carefully, following the shadows along the edge of the meadow. He chose a northern, downwind approach, but to get north of the deer, he had to come around from the east. He knew his error when he was still two dozen yards from the deer. It lifted its head suddenly, sniffed, and flicked its white tail.

Drizzt froze and waited for a long moment while the deer resumed its grazing. The skittish creature was on the alert now, and as soon as Drizzt took another measured step, the deer bolted away.

But not before Montolio, taking the southern approach, had gotten close enough to pat its rump as it ran past.

Drizzt blinked in amazement. "The wind favored me!" he protested to the smug ranger.

Montolio shook his head. "Only over the last twenty yards, when you came north of the deer," he explained. "West was better than east until then."

"But you could not get north of the deer from the west," Drizzt said.

"I did not have to," Montolio replied. "There is a high bluff back there," he pointed to the south. "It cuts the wind at this angle—swirls it back around."

"I did not know."

"You have to know," Montolio said lightly. "That is the trick of it. You have to see as a bird might and look down upon all the region before you choose your course."

"I have not learned to fly," Drizzt replied sarcastically.

"Nor have I!" roared the old ranger. "Look above you."

Drizzt squinted as he turned his eyes to the gray sky. He made out a solitary form, gliding easily with great wings held wide to catch the breeze.

"A hawk," the drow said.

"Rode the breeze from the south," Montolio explained, "then banked west on the breaking currents around the bluff. If you had observed its flight, you might have suspected the change in terrain."

"That is impossible," Drizzt said helplessly.

"Is it?" Montolio asked, and he started away—to hide his smile. Of course the drow was correct; one could not tell the topography of the terrain by the flight patterns of a hawk. Montolio had learned of the shifting wind from a certain sneaky owl who had slipped in at the ranger's bidding right after Drizzt had started out across the meadow, but Drizzt didn't have to know that. Let the drow consider the fib for a while, the old ranger decided. The contemplation, recounting all he had learned, would be a valuable lesson.

"Hooter told you," Drizzt said a half-hour later, on the trail back to the grove. "Hooter told you of the wind and told you of the hawk."

"You seem sure of yourself."

"I am," Drizzt said firmly. "The hawk did not cry—I have become aware enough to know that. You could not see the bird, and I know that you did not hear the rush of wind over its wings, whatever you may say!"

Montolio's laughter brought a smile of confirmation to the drow's face.

"You have done well this day," the old ranger said.

"I did not get near the deer," Drizzt reminded him.

"That was not the test," Montolio replied. "You trusted in your knowledge to dispute my claims. You are sure of the lessons you have learned. Now hear some more. Let me tell you a few tricks when approaching a skittish deer."

They talked all the way back to the grove and far into the night after that. Drizzt listened eagerly, absorbing every word as he was let in on still more of the world's wondrous secrets.

A week later, in a different field, Drizzt placed one hand on the rump of a doe, the other on the rump of its speckle-coated fawn. Both animals lit out at the unexpected touch, but Montolio "saw" Drizzt's smile from a hundred yards away.

Drizzt's lessons were far from complete when the summer waned, but Montolio no longer spent much time instructing the drow. Drizzt had learned enough to go out and learn on his own, listening and watching the quiet voices and subtle signs of the trees and the animals. So caught up was Drizzt in his unending revelations that he hardly noticed the profound changes in Montolio. The ranger felt much older now. His back would hardly straighten on chill mornings and his hands often went numb. Montolio remained stoic about it all, hardly one for self-pity and hardly lamenting what he knew was to come.

He had lived long and fully, had accomplished much, and had experienced life more vividly than most men ever would.

"What are your plans," he said unexpectedly to Drizzt one night as they ate their dinner, a vegetable stew that Drizzt had concocted.

The question hit Drizzt hard. He had no plans beyond the present, and why should he, with life so easy and enjoyable—more so than it had ever been for the beleaguered drow renegade? Drizzt really didn't want to think about the question, so he threw a biscuit at Guenhwyvar to change the subject. The panther was getting a bit too comfortable on Drizzt's bedroll, wrapping up in the blankets to the point where Drizzt worried that the only way to get Guenhwyvar out of the tangle would be to send it back to the astral plane.

Montolio was persistent. "What are your plans, Drizzt Do'Urden?" the old ranger said again firmly. "Where and how will you live?"

"Are you throwing me out?" Drizzt asked.

"Of course not."

"Then I will live with you," Drizzt replied calmly.

"I mean after," Montolio said, growing flustered.

"After what?" Drizzt asked, thinking that Mooshie knew something he did not.

Montolio's laughter mocked his suspicions. "I am an old man," the ranger explained, "and you are a young elf. I am older than you, but even if I were a babe, your years would far outdistance my own. Where will Drizzt Do'Urden go when Montolio DeBrouchee is no more?"

Drizzt turned away. "I do not . . ." he began tentatively. "I will stay here."

"No," Montolio replied soberly. "You have much more before you than this, I hope. This life would not do."

"It has suited you," Drizzt snapped back, more forcefully than he had intended.

"For five years," Montolio said calmly, taking no offense. "Five years after a life of adventure and excitement."

"My life has not been so quiet," Drizzt reminded him.

"But you are still a child," Montolio said. "Five years is not five hundred, and five hundred is what you have remaining. Promise me now that you will reconsider your course when I am no more. There is a wide world out there, my friend, full of pain, but filled with joy as well. The former keeps you on the path of growth, and the latter makes the journey tolerable.

"Promise me now," Montolio said, "that when Mooshie is no more, Drizzt will go and find his place."

Drizzt wanted to argue, to ask the ranger how he was so certain that this grove was not Drizzt's 'place.' A mental scale dipped and leveled, then dipped again within Drizzt at that moment. He weighed the memories of Maldobar, the farmers' deaths, and all the memories before that of the trials he had faced and the evils that had so persistently followed him. Against this, Drizzt considered his heartfelt desire to go back out in the world. How many other Mooshies might he find? How many friends? And how empty would be this grove when he and Guenhwyvar had it to themselves?

Montolio accepted the silence, knowing the drow's confusion. "Promise me that when the time is upon you, you will at least consider what I have said."

Trusting in Drizzt, Montolio did not have to see his friend's affirming nod.

* * * * *

The first snow came early that year, just a light dusting from broken clouds that played hide-and-seek with a full moon. Drizzt, out with Guenhwyvar, reveled in the seasonal change, enjoyed the reaffirmation of the endless cycle. He was in high spirits when he bounded back to the grove, shaking the snow from the thick pine branches as he picked his way in.

The campfire burned low; Hooter sat still on a low branch and even the wind seemed not to make a sound. Drizzt looked to Guenhwyvar for some explanation, but the panther only sat by the fire, somber and still.

Dread is a strange emotion, a culmination of too-subtle clues that brings as much confusion as fear.

"Mooshie?" Drizzt called softly, approaching the old ranger's den. He pushed aside the blanket and used it to screen the light from the embers of the dying campfire, letting his eyes slip into the infrared spectrum.

He remained there for a very long time, watching the last wisps of heat depart from the ranger's body. But if Mooshie was cold, his contented smile emanated warmth.

Drizzt fought back many tears over the next few days, but whenever he remembered that last smile, the final peace that had come over the aged man, he reminded himself that the tears were for his own loss and not for Mooshie.

Drizzt buried the ranger in a cairn beside the grove, then spent the winter quietly, tending to his daily chores and wondering. Hooter came by less and less frequently, and on one occasion the departing look Hooter cast at Drizzt told the drow beyond doubt that the owl would never return to the grove.

In the spring, Drizzt came to understand Hooter's sentiments. For more than a decade, he had been searching for a home, and he had found one with Montolio. But with the ranger gone, the grove no longer seemed so hospitable. This was Mooshie's place, not Drizzt's.

"As I promised," Drizzt mumbled one morning. Montolio had asked him to consider his course carefully when the ranger was no more, and Drizzt now held to his word. He had become comfortable in the grove and was still accepted here, but the grove was no longer his home. His home was out there, he knew, out in that wide world that Montolio had assured him was "full of pain, but filled with joy as well."

Drizzt packed a few items—practical supplies and some of the ranger's more interesting books—belted on his scimitars, and slung the longbow over his shoulder. Then he took a final walk around the grove, viewing one last time the rope bridges, the armory, the brandy barrel and trough, the tree root where he had stopped the charging giant, the sheltered run where Mooshie had made his stand. He called Guenhwyvar, and the panther understood as soon as it arrived.

They never looked back as they moved down the mountain trail, toward the wide world of pains and joys.

❧ Part 5 ❧

Sojourn

How different the trail seemed as I departed Mooshie's Grove from the road that had led me there. Again I was alone, except when Guenhwyvar came to my call. On this road, though, I was alone only in body. In my mind I carried a name, the embodiment of my valued principles. Mooshie had called Mielikki a goddess; to me she was a way of life.

She walked beside me always along the many surface roads I traversed. She led me out to safety and fought off my despair when I was chased away and then hunted by the dwarves of Citadel Adbar, a fortress northeast of Mooshie's Grove. Mielikki, and my belief in my own value, gave me the courage to approach town after town throughout the northland. The receptions were always the same: shock and fear that quickly turned to anger. The more generous of those I encountered told me simply to go away; others chased me with weapons bared. On two occasions I was forced to fight, though I managed to escape without anyone being badly injured.

The minor nicks and scratches were a small price to pay. Mooshie had bidden me not to live as he had, and the old ranger's perceptions, as always, proved true. On my journeys throughout the northland I retained something—hope—that I never would have held if I had remained a hermit in the evergreen grove. As each new village showed on the horizon, a tingle of anticipation quickened my steps. One day, I was determined, I would find acceptance and find my home.

It would happen suddenly, I imagined. I would approach

a gate, speak a formal greeting, then reveal myself as a dark elf. Even my fantasy was tempered by reality, for the gate would not swing wide at my approach. Rather, I would be allowed guarded entry, a trial period much like the one I endured in Blingdenstone, the svirfneblin city. Suspicions would linger about me for many months, but in the end, principles would be seen and accepted for what they were; the character of the person would outweigh the color of his skin and the reputation of his heritage.

I replayed that fantasy countless times over the years. Every word of every meeting in my imagined town became a litany against the continued rejections. It would not have been enough, but always there was Guenhwyvar, and now there was Mielikki.

— Drizzt Do'Urden

♣ 20 ♣

Years and Miles

The Harvest Inn in Westbridge was a favorite gathering place for travelers along the Long Road that stretched between the two great northern cities of Waterdeep and Mirabar. Aside from comfortable bedding at reasonable rates, the Harvest offered Derry's Tavern and Eatery, a renowned story-swapping bar where on any night of any week a guest might find adventurers from regions as varied as Luskan and Sundabar. The hearth was bright and warm, the drinks were plentiful, and the yarns woven in Derry's were ones that would be told and retold all across the realms.

Roddy kept the cowl of his worn traveling cloak pulled low about him, hiding his scarred face, as he tore into his mutton and biscuits. The old yellow dog sat on the floor beside him, growling, and every now and then Roddy absently dropped it a piece of meat.

The ravenous bounty hunter rarely lifted his head from the plate, but Roddy's bloodshot eyes peered suspiciously from the shadows of his cowl. He knew some of the ruffians gathered in Derry's this night, personally or by reputation, and he wouldn't trust them any more than they, if they were wise, would trust him.

One tall man recognized Roddy's dog as he passed the table and stopped, thinking to greet the bounty hunter. The tall man walked away silently, though, realizing that miserable McGristle wasn't really worth the effort. No one knew exactly what had happened those years before in the mountains near Maldobar, but Roddy had come out of that region deeply scarred, physically and emotionally. Always a surly one, McGristle now spent more time growling than talking.

Roddy gnawed a bit longer then dropped the thick bone down to his dog and wiped his greasy hands on his cloak, inadvertently brushing back the side of his cowl that hid his gruesome scars. Roddy quickly pulled the cowl back down, his gaze darting about for anyone who might have noticed. A single disgusted glance had cost several men their lives where Roddy's scars were concerned.

No one seemed to notice, though, not this time. Most of those who weren't busily eating were over at the bar, arguing loudly.

"Never was it!" one man growled.

"I told you what I saw!" another shot back. "And I told you right!"

"To yer eyes!" the first shouted back, and still another put in, "Ye'd not know one if ye seen one!" Several of the men closed in, bumping chest to chest.

"Stand quiet!" came a voice. A man pushed out of the throng and pointed straight at Roddy, who, not recognizing the man, instinctively dropped his hand to Bleeder, his well-worn axe.

"Ask McGristle!" the man cried. "Roddy McGristle. He knows about dark elves better than any."

A dozen conversations sprouted up at once as the whole group, looking like some amorphous rolling blob, slid over toward Roddy. Roddy's hand was off Bleeder again, crossing fingers with the other one on the table in front of him.

"Ye're McGristle, are ye?" the man asked Roddy, showing the bounty hunter a good measure of respect.

"Might that I am," Roddy replied calmly, enjoying the attention. He hadn't been surrounded by a group so interested in what he had to say since the Thistledown clan had been found murdered.

"Aw," a disgruntled voice piped in from somewhere in the back, "what's he know about dark elves."

Roddy's glare sent those in front back a step, and he no-

ticed the movement. He liked the feeling, liked being important again, respected.

"Drow elf killed my dog," he said gruffly. He reached
down and yanked up the old yellow hound's head, display-
ing the scar. "And dented this one's head. Damned dark
elf—" he said deliberately, easing the cowl back from his
face—"gave me this." Normally Roddy hid the hideous scars,
but the crowd's gasps and mumbles sounded immensely
satisfying to the wretched bounty hunter. He turned to the
side, gave them a full view, and savored the reaction for as
long as he could.

"Black-skinned and white-haired?" asked a short, fat-bellied man, the one who had begun the debate back at the bar
with his own tale of a dark elf.

"Would have to be if he was a dark elf," Roddy huffed
back. The man looked about triumphantly.

"That is what I tried to tell them," he said to Roddy. "They
claim that I saw a dirty elf, or an orc maybe, but I knew it
was a drow!"

"If ye see a drow," Roddy said grimly and deliberately,
weighing every word with importance, "then ye know ye
seen a drow. And ye'll not forget that ye seen a drow! And
let any man that doubts yer words go and find a drow for
himself. He'll come back to ye with a word of bein' sorry!"

"Well, I seen a dark elf," the man proclaimed. "I was camping in Lurkwood, north of Grunwald. Peaceful enough
night, I thought, so I let the fire up a bit to beat the cold
wind. Well, in walked this stranger without a warning,
without a word!"

Every man in the group hung on the words now, hearing
them in a different light now that the drow-scarred stranger had somewhat confirmed the tale.

"Without a word, or a bird call, or nothing!" the fat-bellied man went on. "He had his cloak pulled low, suspicious,
so I said to him, 'What are you about?'

"'Searching for a place that my companions and I may
camp the night,' he answered, calm as you may. Seemed reasonable enough to me, but I still did not like that low cowl.

'Pull back your hood then,' I told him. 'I share nothing without seeing a man's face.' He considered my words a minute, then he moved his hands up, real slow,"—the man imitated the movement dramatically, glancing around to ensure that he had everyone's attention.

"I needed to see nothing more!" the man cried suddenly, and everyone, though they had heard the same tale told the same way only a moment before, jumped back in surprise. "His hands were as black as coal and as slender as an elf's. I knew then, but I know not how I knew so surely, that it was a drow before me. A drow, I say, and let any man who doubts my words go and find a dark elf for himself!"

Roddy nodded his approval as the fat-bellied man stared down his former doubters. "Seems I've heard too much about dark elves lately," the bounty hunter grumbled.

"I've heared of just the one," another man piped in. "Until we spoke to you, I mean, and heard of your battle. That makes two drow in six years."

"As I said," Roddy remarked grimly, "seems I've heard too much about dark—" Roddy never finished as the group exploded into exaggerated laughter around him. It seemed like the grand old times to the bounty hunter, the days when everyone about him hung tense on his every word.

The only man who wasn't laughing was the fat-bellied storyteller, too shook up from his own recounting of his meeting with the drow. "Still," he said above the commotion, "when I think of those purple eyes staring out at me from under that cowl!"

Roddy's smile disappeared in the blink of an eye. "Purple eyes?" he barely managed to gasp. Roddy had encountered many creatures that used infravision, the heat-sensing sight most common among denizens of the Underdark, and he knew that normally, such eyes showed as dots of red. Roddy still remembered vividly the purple eyes looking down at him when he was trapped under the maple tree. He knew then, and he knew now, that those strange-hued orbs were a rarity even among the dark elves.

Those in the group closest to Roddy stopped their laughing, thinking that Roddy's question shed doubt on the truth of the man's tale.

"They were purple," the fat-bellied man insisted, though there was little conviction in his shaky voice. The men around him waited for Roddy's agreement or rebuttal, not knowing whether or not to laugh at the storyteller.

"What weapons did the drow wield?" Roddy asked grimly, rising ominously to his feet.

The man thought for a moment. "Curved swords," he blurted.

"Scimitars?"

"Scimitars," the other agreed.

"Did the drow say his name?" Roddy asked, and when the man hesitated, Roddy grabbed him by the collar and pulled him over the table. "Did the drow say his name?" the bounty hunter said again, his breath hot on the fat-bellied man's face.

"No . . . er, uh, Driz . . ."

"Drizzit?"

The man shrugged helplessly, and Roddy threw him back to his feet. "Where?" the bounty hunter roared. "And when?"

"Lurkwood," the quivering, full-bellied man said again. "Three weeks ago. Drow's going to Mirabar with the Weeping Friars, I would guess." Most of the crowd groaned at the mention of the fanatic religious group. The Weeping Friars were a ragged band of begging sufferers who believed—or claimed to believe—that there was a finite amount of pain in the world. The more suffering they took on themselves, the friars said, the less remained for the rest of world to endure. Nearly everyone scorned the order. Some were sincere, but some begged for trinkets, promising to suffer horribly for the good of the giver.

"Those were the drow's companions," the fat-bellied man continued. "They always go to Mirabar, go to find the cold, as winter comes on."

"Long way," someone remarked.

"Longer," said another. "The Weeping Friars always take

the tunnel route."

"Three hundred miles," the first man who had recognized Roddy put in, trying to calm the agitated bounty hunter. But Roddy never even heard him. His dog in tow, he spun away and stormed out of Derry's, slamming the door behind him and leaving the whole group mumbling to each other in absolute surprise.

"It was Drizzit that took Roddy's dog and ear," the man went on, now turning his attention to the group. He had no previous knowledge of the strange drow's name; he merely had made an assumption based on Roddy's reaction. Now the group flowed around him, holding their collective breath for him to tell them of the tale of Roddy McGristle and the purple-eyed drow. Like any proper patron of Derry's, the man didn't let lack of real knowledge deter him from telling the tale. He hooked his thumbs into his belt and began, filling in the considerable blanks with whatever sounded appropriate.

A hundred more gasps and claps of appreciation and startled delight echoed on the street outside of Derry's that night, but Roddy McGristle and his yellow dog, their wagon wheels already thick in the mud of the Long Road, heard none of them.

"Hey, what-are-you-doing?" came a weary complaint from a sack behind Roddy's bench. Tephanis crawled out. "Why-are-we-leaving?"

Roddy twisted about and took a swipe, but Tephanis, even sleepy-eyed, had no trouble darting out of harm's way.

"Ye lied to me, ye cousin to a kobold!" Roddy growled. "Ye told me that the drow was dead. But he's not! He's on the road to Mirabar, and I mean to catch him!"

"Mirabar?" Tephanis cried. "Too-far, too-far!" The quickling and Roddy had passed through Mirabar the previous spring. Tephanis thought it a perfectly miserable place, full of grim-faced dwarves, sharp-eyed men, and a wind much too cold for his liking. "We-must-go-south-for-the-winter. South-where-it-is-warm!"

Roddy's ensuing glare silenced the sprite. "I'll forget what ye did to me," he snarled, then he added an ominous warn-ing, "if we get the drow." He turned from Tephanis then, and the sprite crawled back into his sack, feeling miserable and wondering if Roddy McGristle was worth the trouble.

Roddy drove through the night, bending low to urge his horse onward and muttering "Six years!" over and over.

* * * * *

Drizzt huddled close to the fire that roared out of an old ore barrel the group had found. This would be the drow's seventh winter on the surface, but still he remained un-comfortable in the chill. He had spent decades, and his peo-ple had lived for many millennia, in the seasonless and warm Underdark. Although winter was still months away, its approach was evident in the chill winds blowing down from the Spine of the World Mountains. Drizzt wore only an old blanket, thin and torn, over his clothes, chain mail, and weapon belt.

The drow smiled when he noticed his companions fidget-ing and huffing over who got the next draw on a bottle of wine they had begged and how much the last drinker had taken. Drizzt was alone at the barrel now; the Weeping Fri-ars, while not actually shunning the drow, didn't often go near him. Drizzt accepted this and knew that the fanatics appreciated his companionship for practical, if not aesthet-ic, reasons. Some of the band actually enjoyed attacks by the various monsters of the land, viewing them as opportu-nities for some true suffering, but the more pragmatic of the group appreciated having the armed and skilled drow around for protection.

The relationship was acceptable to Drizzt, if not fulfilling. He had left Mooshie's Grove years ago filled with hope, but hope tempered by the realities of his existence. Time after time, Drizzt had approached a village only to be put out be-hind a wall of harsh words, curses, and drawn weapons. Every time, Drizzt shrugged away the snubbing. True to his ranger spirit—for Drizzt was indeed a ranger now, in training as well as in heart—he accepted his lot stoically.

The last rejection had shown Drizzt that his resolve was wearing thin, though. He had been turned away from Luskan, on the Sword Coast, but not by any guards, for he had never even approached the place. Drizzt's own fears had kept him away, and that fact had frightened him more than any swords he had ever faced. On the road outside the city, Drizzt had met up with this handful of Weeping Friars, and the outcasts had tentatively accepted him, as much because they had no means to keep him out as because they were too full of their own wretchedness to care about any racial differences. Two of the group had even thrown themselves at Drizzt's feet, begging him to unleash his "dark elf terrors" and make them suffer.

Through the spring and summer, the relationship had evolved with Drizzt serving as silent guardian while the friars went about their begging and suffering ways. All in all, it was quite distasteful, even sometimes deceitful, to the principled drow, but Drizzt had found no other options.

Drizzt stared into the leaping flames and considered his fate. He still had Guenhwyvar at his call and had put his scimitars and bow to gainful use many times. Every day he told himself that beside the somewhat helpless fanatics, he was serving Mielikki, and his own heart, well. Still, he did not hold the friars in high regard and did not call them friends. Watching the five men now, drunk and slobbering all over each other, Drizzt suspected that he never would.

"Beat me! Slash me!" one of the friars cried suddenly, and he ran over toward the barrel, stumbling into Drizzt. Drizzt caught him and steadied him, but only for a moment.

"Loosh your dwow whickedniss on me head!" the dirty, unshaven friar sputtered, and his lanky frame tumbled down in an angular heap.

Drizzt turned away, shook his head, and unconsciously dropped a hand into his pouch to feel the onyx figurine, needing the touch to remind him that he was not truly alone. He was surviving, fighting an endless and lonely battle, but was far from contented. He had found a place, perhaps, but not a home.

"Like the grove without Montolio," the drow mused. "Never a home."

"Did you say something?" asked a portly friar, Brother Mateus, coming over to collect his drunken companion. "Please excuse Brother Jankin, friend. He has imbibed too much, I fear."

Drizzt's helpless smile told that he had taken no offense, but his next words caught Brother Mateus, the leader and most rational member—if not the most honest—of the group, off guard.

"I will complete the trip to Mirabar with you," Drizzt explained, "then I will leave."

"Leave?" asked Mateus, concerned.

"This is not my place," Drizzt explained.

"Ten-Towns ish the place!" Jankin blurted.

"If anyone has offended you . . ." Mateus said to Drizzt, taking no heed of the drunken man.

"No one," Drizzt said and smiled again. "There is more for me in this life, Brother Mateus. Do not be angry, I beg, but I am leaving. It was not a decision I came to lightly."

Mateus took a moment to consider the words. "As you choose," he said, "but might you at least escort us through the tunnel into Mirabar?"

"Ten-Towns!" Jankin insisted. "Thast the place fer sufferin'! You'd like it, too, drow. Land o' rogues, where a rogue might find hish place!"

"Often there are rakes in the shadows who would prey on unarmed friars," Mateus interrupted, giving Jankin a rough shake.

Drizzt paused a moment, transfixed on Jankin's words. Jankin had collapsed, though, and the drow looked up to Mateus. "Is that not why you take the tunnel route into the city?" Drizzt asked the portly friar. The tunnel was normally reserved for mine carts, rolling down from the Spine of the World, but the friars always went through it, even in situations such as this, when they had to make a complete circuit of the city just to get to the long route's entrance. "To fall victim and suffer?" Drizzt continued. "Surely the road is clear and more convenient with winter still months away." Drizzt did not like the tunnel to Mirabar. Any wanderers they met on that road would be too close for the drow to hide his identity. Drizzt had been accosted there on both his previous trips through.

"The others insist that we go through the tunnel, though it is many miles out of our way," replied Mateus, a sharp edge to his tone. "But I prefer more personal forms of suffering and would appreciate your company through to Mirabar."

Drizzt wanted to scream at the phony friar. Mateus considered missing a single meal a harsh suffering and only used his facade because many gullible people handed coins to the cloaked fanatics, more often than not just to be rid of the smelly men.

Drizzt nodded and watched as Mateus hauled Jankin away. "Then I leave," he whispered under his breath. He could tell himself over and over that he was serving his goddess and his heart by protecting the seemingly helpless band, but their behavior often flew in the face of those words.

"Dwow! Dwow!" Brother Jankin slobbered as Mateus dragged him back to the others.

☙ 21 ☙

Hephaestus

Tephanis watched the party of six—the five friars and Drizzt—make their slow way toward the tunnel on the western approach to Mirabar. Roddy had sent the quickling ahead to scout out the region, telling Tephanis to turn the drow, if he found the drow, back toward Roddy. "Bleeder'll be taking care of that one," Roddy had snarled, slapping his formidable axe across his palm.

Tephanis wasn't so sure. The sprite had watched Ulgulu, a master arguably more powerful than Roddy McGristle, dispatched by the drow, and another mighty master, Caroak, had been torn apart by the drow's black panther. If Roddy got his wish and met the drow in battle, Tephanis might soon be searching for yet another master.

"Not-this-time, drow," the sprite whispered suddenly, an idea coming to mind. "This-time-I-get-you!" Tephanis knew the tunnel to Mirabar—he and Roddy had used it the winter before last, when snow had buried the western road—and had learned many of its secrets, including one that the sprite now planned to use to his advantage.

He made a wide circuit around the group, not wanting to alert the sharp-eared drow, and still made the tunnel entrance long before the others. A few minutes later, the sprite was more than a mile in, picking at an intricate lock, one that seemed clumsy to the skilled quickling, on a portcullis crank.

* * * * *

Brother Mateus led the way into the tunnel, with another friar at his side and the remaining three completing a shielding circle around Drizzt. Drizzt had requested this so that he could remain inconspicuous if anyone happened by. He kept his cloak pulled up tightly and his shoulders hunched. He stayed low in the middle of the group.

They met no other travelers and moved along the torch-lit passage at a steady pace. They came to an intersection and Mateus stopped abruptly, seeing the raised portcullis to a passage on the right side. A dozen steps in, an iron door swung wide, and the passage beyond that was pitch black, not torch-lit like the main tunnel.

"How curious," Mateus remarked.

"Careless," another corrected. "Let us pray that no other travelers, who might not know the way as well as we, happen by here and take the wrong path!"

"Perhaps we should close the door," still another offered.

"No," Mateus quickly interjected. "There may be some down there, merchants perhaps, who would not be so pleased if we followed that plan."

"No!" Brother Jankin cried suddenly and ran to the front of the group. "It is a sign! A sign from God! We are beckoned, my brethren, to Phaestus, the ultimate suffering!"

Jankin turned to charge down the tunnel, but Mateus and one other, hardly surprised by Jankin's customarily wild outburst, immediately sprang upon him and bore him to the ground.

"Phaestus!" Jankin cried wildly, his long and shaggy black hair flying all about his face. "I am coming!"

"What is it?" Drizzt had to ask, having no idea of what the friars were talking about, though he thought he recognized the reference. "Who, or what, is Phaestus?"

"Hephaestus," Brother Mateus corrected.

Drizzt did know the name. One of the books he had taken from Mooshie's Grove was of dragon lore, and Hephaestus, a venerable red dragon living in the mountains northwest of Mirabar, had an entry.

"That is not the dragon's real name, of course," Mateus

went on between grunts as he struggled with Jankin. "I do not know that, nor does anyone else anymore." Jankin twisted suddenly, throwing the other monk aside, and promptly stomped down on Mateus's sandal.

"Hephaestus is an old red dragon who has lived in the caves west of Mirabar for as long as anyone, even the dwarves, can remember," explained another friar, Brother Herschel, one less engaged than Mateus. "The city tolerates him because he is a lazy one and a stupid one, though I would not tell him so. Most cities, I presume, would choose to tolerate a red if it meant not fighting the thing! But Hephaestus is not much for pillaging—none can recall the last time he even came out of his hole—and he even does some ore-melting for hire, though the fee is steep."

"Some pay it, though," added Mateus, having Jankin back under control, "especially late in the season, looking to make the last caravan south. Nothing can separate metal like a red dragon's breath!" His laughter disappeared quickly as Jankin slugged him, dropping him to the ground.

Jankin bolted free, for just a moment. Quicker than anyone could react, Drizzt threw off his cloak and rushed after the fleeing monk, catching him just inside the heavy iron door. A single step and twisting maneuver put Jankin down hard on his back and took the wild-eyed friar's breath away.

"Let us get by this region at once," the drow offered, staring down at the stunned friar. "I grow tired of Jankin's antics—I might just allow him to run down to the dragon!"

Two of the others came over and gathered Jankin up, then the whole troupe turned to depart.

"Help!" came a cry from farther down the dark tunnel.

Drizzt's scimitars came out in his hands. The friars all gathered around him, peering down into the gloom.

"Do you see anything?" Mateus asked the drow, knowing that Drizzt's night vision was much keener than his own.

"No, but the tunnel turns a short way from here," Drizzt replied.

"Help!" came the cry again. Behind the group, around the corner in the main tunnel, Tephanis had to suppress his laughter. Quicklings were adept ventriloquists, and the biggest problem Tephanis had in deceiving the group was keeping his cries slow enough to be understood.

Drizzt took a cautious step in, and the friars, even Jankin, sobered by the distress call, followed right behind. Drizzt motioned for them to go back, even as he suddenly realized the potential for a trap.

But Tephanis was too quick. The door slammed with a resounding thud and before the drow, two steps away, could push through the startled friars, the sprite already had the door locked. A moment later, Drizzt and the friars heard a second crash as the portcullis came down.

Tephanis was back out in the daylight a few minutes later, thinking himself quite clever and reminding himself to keep a puzzled expression when he explained to Roddy that the drow's party was nowhere to be found.

* * * * *

The friars grew tired of yelling as soon as Drizzt reminded them that their screams might arouse the occupant at the other end of the tunnel. "Even if someone happens by the portcullis, he will not hear you through this door," the drow said, inspecting the heavy portal with the single candle Mateus had lit. A combination of iron, stone, and leather, and perfectly fitted, the door had been crafted by dwarves. Drizzt tried pounding on it with the pommel of a scimitar, but that produced only a dull thud that went no farther than the screams.

"We are lost," groaned Mateus. "We have no way out, and our stores are not too plentiful."

"Another sign!" Jankin blurted suddenly, but two of the friars knocked him down and sat on him before he could run off toward the dragon's den.

"Perhaps there is something to Brother Jankin's thinking," Drizzt said after a long pause.

Mateus looked at him suspiciously. "Are you thinking that our stores would last longer if Brother Jankin went to meet

Hephaestus?" he asked.

Drizzt could not hold his laughter. "I have no intention of sacrificing anyone," he said and looked at Jankin struggling under the friars. "No matter how willing! But we have only one way out, it would seem."

Mateus followed Drizzt's gaze down the dark tunnel. "If you plan no sacrifices, then you are looking the wrong way," the portly friar huffed. "Surely you are not thinking to get past the dragon!"

"We shall see," was all that the drow answered. He lit another candle from the first one and moved a short distance down the tunnel. Drizzt's good sense argued against the undeniable excitement he felt at the prospect of facing Hephaestus, but it was an argument that he expected simple necessity to overrule. Montolio had fought a dragon, Drizzt remembered, had lost his eyes to a red. The ranger's memories of the battle, aside from his wounds, were not so terrible. Drizzt was beginning to understand what the blind ranger had told him about the differences between survival and fulfillment. How valuable would be the five hundred years Drizzt might have left to live?

For the friar's sake, Drizzt did hope that someone would come along and open the portcullis and door. The drow's fingers tingled with promised thrills, though, when he reached into his sack and pulled out a book on dragon lore he had taken from the grove.

The drow's sensitive eyes needed little light, and he could make out the script with only minor difficulty. As he suspected, there was an entry for the venerable red who lived west of Mirabar. The book confirmed that Hephaestus was not the dragon's real name, rather the name given to it in reference to some obscure god of blacksmiths.

The entry was not extensive, mostly tales from the merchants who went in to hire the dragon for its breath, and other tales of merchants who apparently said the wrong thing or haggled too much about the cost—or perhaps the dragon was merely hungry or in a foul mood—for they never came back out. Most importantly to Drizzt, the entry confirmed the friar's description of the beast as lazy and somewhat stupid. According to the notes, Hephaestus was overly proud, as dragons usually were, and able to speak the common tongue, but "lacking in the area of suspicious insight normally associated with the breed, particularly with venerable reds."

"Brother Herschel is attempting to pick the lock," Mateus said, coming over to Drizzt. "Your fingers are nimble. Would you give it a try?"

"Neither Herschel nor I could get through that lock," Drizzt said absently, not looking up from the book.

"At least Herschel is trying," Mateus growled, "and not huddled off by himself wasting candles and reading some worthless tome!"

"Not so worthless to any of us who mean to get out of here alive," Drizzt said, still not looking up. He had the portly friar's attention.

"What is it?" Mateus asked, leaning closely over Drizzt's shoulder, even though he could not read.

"It tells of vanity," Drizzt replied.

"Vanity? What does vanity have to do . . ."

"Dragon vanity," Drizzt explained. "A very important point, perhaps. All dragons possess it in excess, evil ones more than good ones."

"Wielding claws as long as swords and breath that can melt a stone, well they should!" grumbled Mateus.

"Perhaps," Drizzt conceded, "but vanity is a weakness—do not doubt—even to a dragon. Several heroes have exploited this trait to a dragon's demise."

"Now you're thinking of killing the thing?" Mateus gawked.

"If I must," Drizzt said, again absently. Mateus threw up his hands and walked away, shaking his head to answer the questioning stares of the others.

Drizzt smiled privately and returned to his reading. His plans were taking definite form now. He read the entire entry several times, committing every word of it to memory.

Three candles later, Drizzt was still reading and the friars were growing impatient and hungry. They prodded Mateus, who stood, hiked his belt up over his belly, and strode toward Drizzt.

"More vanity?" he asked sarcastically.

"Done with that part," Drizzt answered. He held up the book, showing Mateus a sketch of a huge black dragon curled up around several fallen trees in a thick swamp. "I am learning now of the dragon that may aid our cause."

"Hephaestus is a red," Mateus remarked scornfully, "not a black."

"This is a different dragon," Drizzt explained. "Mergandevinasander of Chult, possibly a visitor to converse with Hephaestus."

Brother Mateus was at a complete loss. "Reds and blacks do not get on well," he snipped, his skepticism obvious. "Every fool knows that."

"Rarely do I listen to fools," Drizzt replied, and again the friar turned and walked away, shaking his head.

"There is something more that you do not know, but Hephaestus most probably will," Drizzt said quietly, too low for anyone to hear. "Mergandevinasander has purple eyes!" Drizzt closed the book, confident that it had given him enough understanding to make his attempt. If he had ever witnessed the terrible splendor of a venerable red before, he would not have been smiling at that moment. But both ignorance and memories of Montolio bred courage in the young drow warrior who had so little to lose, and Drizzt had no intention of giving in to starvation for fear of some unknown danger. He wouldn't go forward either, not yet.

Not until he had time to practice his best dragon voice.

* * * * *

Of all the splendors Drizzt had seen in his adventurous life, none—not the great houses of Menzoberranzan, the cavern of the illithids, even the lake of acid—began to approach the awe-inspiring spectacle of the dragon's lair. Mounds of gold and gems filled the huge chamber in rolling waves, like the wake of some giant ship on the sea. Weapons and armor, gleaming magnificently, were piled all about, and the abundance of crafted items—chalices, goblets and the like—could have fully stocked the treasure rooms of a hundred rich kings.

Drizzt had to remind himself to breathe when he looked upon the splendor. It wasn't the riches that held him so—he cared little for material things—but the adventures that such wondrous items and wealth hinted at tugged Drizzt in a hundred different directions. Looking at the dragon's lair belittled his simple survival on the road with the Weeping Friars and his simple desire to find a peaceful and quiet place to call his home. He thought again of Montolio's dragon tale, and of all the other adventurous tales the blind ranger had told him. Suddenly he needed those adventures for himself.

Drizzt wanted a home, and he wanted to find acceptance, but he realized then, looking at the spoils, that he also desired a place in the books of the bards. He hoped to travel roads dangerous and exciting and even write his own tales.

The chamber itself was immense and uneven, rolling back around blind corners. The whole of it was dimly lit in a smoky, reddish golden glow. It was warm, uncomfortably so when Drizzt and the others took the time to consider the source of that heat.

Drizzt turned back to the waiting friars and winked, then pointed down to his left, to the single exit. "You know the signal," he mouthed silently.

Mateus nodded tentatively, still wondering if it had been wise to trust the drow. Drizzt had been a valuable ally to the pragmatic friar on the road these last few months, but a dragon was a dragon.

Drizzt surveyed the room again, this time looking past the treasures. Between two piles of gold he spotted his target, and that was no less splendid than the jewels and gems. Lying in the valley of those mounds was a huge, scaled tail, red-gold like the hue of the light, swishing slightly and rhythmically back and forth, each swipe piling the gold deeper around it.

Drizzt had seen pictures of dragons before; one of the wizard masters in the Academy had even created illusions of the various dragon types for the students to inspect. Nothing, though, could have prepared the drow for this moment, his first view of a living dragon. In all the known realms there was nothing more impressive, and of all the dragon types, huge reds were perhaps the most imposing.

When Drizzt finally managed to tear his gaze from the tail, he sorted out his path into the chamber. The tunnel exited high on the side of a wall, but a clear trail led down to the floor. Drizzt studied this for a long moment, memorizing every step. Then he scooped two handfuls of dirt into his pockets, removed an arrow from his quiver, and placed a darkness spell over it. Carefully and quietly, Drizzt picked his blind steps down the trail, guided by the continuing swish of the scaly tail. He nearly stumbled when he reached the first pile of gems and heard the tail come to an abrupt stop.

"Adventure," Drizzt reminded himself quietly, and he went on, concentrating on his mental image of his surroundings. He imagined the dragon rearing up before him, seeing through his darkness-globe disguise. He winced instinctively, expecting a burst of flame to engulf him and shrivel him where he stood. But he pressed on, and when he at last came over the gold pile, he was glad to hear the easy, thunderlike, breathing of the slumbering dragon.

Drizzt started up the second mound slowly, letting a spell of levitation form in his thoughts. He didn't really expect the spell to work very well—it had been failing more completely each time he attempted it. Any help he could get would add to the effect of his deception. Halfway up the mound, Drizzt broke into a run, spraying coins and gems with every step. He heard the dragon rouse, but didn't slow, drawing his bow as he went.

When he reached the ridge, he leaped out and enacted the levitation, hanging motionless in the air for a split second before the spell failed. Then Drizzt dropped, firing the bow and sending the darkness globe soaring across the chamber.

He never would have believed that a monster of such size could be so nimble, but when he crashed heavily onto a pile of goblets and jeweled trinkets, he found himself staring into the face of a very angry beast.

Those eyes! Like twin beams of damnation, their gaze latched onto Drizzt, bored right through him, impelled him to fall on his belly and grovel for mercy, and to reveal every deception, to confess every sin to Hephaestus, this god-thing. The dragon's great, serpentine neck angled slightly to the side, but the gaze never let go of the drow, holding him as firmly as one of Bluster the bear's hugs.

A voice sounded faintly but firmly in Drizzt's thoughts, the voice of a blind ranger spinning tales of battle and hero-ism. At first, Drizzt hardly heard it, but it was an insistent voice, reminding Drizzt in its own special way that five oth-er men depended on him now. If he failed, the friars would die.

This part of the plan was not too difficult for Drizzt, for he truly believed in his words. "Hephaestus!" he cried in the common tongue. "Can it be, at long last? Oh, most magnifi-cent! More magnificent than the tales, by far!"

The dragon's head rolled back a dozen feet from Drizzt, and a confused expression came into those all-knowing eyes, revealing the facade. "You know of me?" Hephaestus boomed, the dragon's hot breath blowing Drizzt's white mane behind him.

"All know of you, mighty Hephaestus!" Drizzt cried, scrambling to his knees but not daring to stand. "It was you whom I sought, and now I have found you and am not dis-appointed!"

The dragon's terrible eyes narrowed suspiciously. "Why would a dark elf seek Hephaestus, Destroyer of Cockleby, Devourer of Ten Thousand Cattle, He Who Crushed Anga-lander the Stupid Silver, He Who . . ." It went on for many minutes, with Drizzt bearing the foul breath stoically, all the while feigning enchantment with the dragon's listing of his many wicked accomplishments. When Hephaestus was done, Drizzt had to pause a moment to remember the initial question.

His real confusion only added to the deception at the time. "Dark elf?" he asked as if he didn't understand. He looked up at the dragon and repeated the words, even more confused. "Dark elf?"

The dragon looked all around, his gaze falling like twin beacons across the treasure mounds, then lingering for some time on Drizzt's blackness globe, halfway across the room. "I mean you!" Hephaestus roared suddenly, and the force of the yell knocked Drizzt over backward. "Dark elf!"

"Drow?" Drizzt said, recovering quickly and daring now to stand. "No, not I." He surveyed himself and nodded in sudden recognition. "Yes, of course," he said. "So often do I forget this mantle I wear!"

Hephaestus issued a long, low, increasingly impatient growl and Drizzt knew he had better move quickly.

"Not a drow," he said. "Though soon I might be if Hephaestus cannot help me!" Drizzt could only hope that he had piqued the dragon's curiosity. "You have heard of me, I am sure, mighty Hephaestus. I am, or was and hope to be again, Mergandevinasander of Chult, an old black of no small fame."

"Mergandevin . . . ?" Hephaestus began, but the dragon let the word trail away. Hephaestus had heard of the black, of course; dragons knew the names of most of the other dragons in all the world. Hephaestus knew, too, as Drizzt had hoped he would, that Mergandevinasander had purple eyes.

To aid him through the explanation, Drizzt recalled his experiences with Clacker, the unfortunate pech who had been transformed by a wizard into the form of a hook horror. "A wizard defeated me," he began somberly. "A party of adventurers entered my lair. Thieves! I got one of them, though, a paladin!"

Hephaestus seemed to like this little detail, and Drizzt, who had just thought of it, congratulated himself silently.

"How his silvery armor sizzled under the acid of my breath!"

"Pity to so waste him," Hephaestus interjected. "Paladins do make such fine meals!"

Drizzt smiled to hide his uneasiness at the thought. How would a dark elf taste? he could not help but wonder with the dragon's mouth so very near. "I would have killed them all—and a fine treasure take it would have been—but for that wretched wizard! It was he that did this terrible thing to me!" Drizzt looked at his drow form reprovingly.

"Polymorph?" Hephaestus asked, and Drizzt noted a bit of sympathy—he prayed—in the voice.

Drizzt nodded solemnly. "An evil spell. Took my form, my wings, and my breath. Yet I remained Mergandevinasander in thought, though . . ." Hephaestus widened his eyes at the pause, and the pitiful, confused look that Drizzt gave actually backed the dragon up.

"I have found this sudden affinity to spiders," Drizzt muttered. "To pet them and kiss them . . ." So that is what a disgusted red dragon looks like, Drizzt thought when he glanced back up at the beast. Coins and trinkets tinkled all throughout the room as an involuntary shudder coursed through the dragon's spine.

* * * * *

The friars in the low tunnel couldn't see the exchange, but they could make out the conversation well enough and understood what the drow had in mind. For the first time that any of them could recall, Brother Jankin was stricken speechless, but Mateus managed to whisper a few words, echoing their shared sentiments.

"He has got a measure of fortitude, that one!" The portly friar chuckled, and he slapped a hand across his own mouth, fearing that he had spoken too loudly.

* * * * *

"Why have you come to me?" Hephaestus roared angrily. Drizzt skidded backward under the force but managed to hold his balance this time.

"I beg, mighty Hephaestus!" Drizzt pleaded. "I have no choice. I traveled to Menzoberranzan, the city of drow, but this wizard's spell was powerful, they told me, and they could do nothing to dispel it. So I come to you, great and powerful Hephaestus, renowned for your abilities with spells of transmutation. Perhaps one of my own kind . . ."

"A black?" came the thunderous roar, and this time, Drizzt did fall. "Your own kind?"

"No, no, a dragon," Drizzt said quickly, retracting the apparent insult and hopping back to his feet—thinking that he might be running soon. Hephaestus's continuing growl told Drizzt that he needed a diversion, and he found it behind the dragon, in the deep scorch marks along the walls and back of a rectangular alcove. Drizzt figured this was where Hephaestus earned his considerable pay melting ores. The drow couldn't help but shudder as he wondered how many unfortunate merchants or adventurers might have found their end between those blasted walls.

"What caused such a cataclysm?" Drizzt cried in awe. Hephaestus dared not turn away, suspecting treachery. A moment later, though, the dragon realized what the dark elf had noticed and the growl disappeared.

"What god has come down to you, mighty Hephaestus, and blessed you with such a spectacle of power? Nowhere in all the realms is there stone so torn! Not since the fires that formed the world . . ."

"Enough!" Hephaestus boomed. "You who are so learned does not know the breath of a red?"

"Surely fire is the means of a red," Drizzt replied, never taking his gaze from the alcove, "but how intense might the flames be? Surely not so as to wreak such devastation!"

"Would you like to see?" came the dragon's answer in a sinister, smoking hiss.

"Yes!" Drizzt cried, then, "No!" he said, dropping into a fetal curl. He knew he was walking a tentative line here, but he knew it was a necessary gamble. "Truly I would desire to witness such a blast, but truly I fear to feel its heat."

"Then watch, Mergandevinasander of Chult!" Hephaestus roared. "See your better!" The sharp intake of the dragon's breath pulled Drizzt two steps forward, brought his white hair stinging around into his eyes, and nearly tore the blanket-cloak from his back. On the mound behind him, coins toppled forward in a noisy rush.

Then the dragon's serpentine neck swung about in a long and wide arc, putting the great red's head in line with the alcove.

The ensuing blast stole the air from the chamber; Drizzt's lungs burned and his eyes stung, both from the heat and the brightness. He continued to watch, though, as the dragon fire consumed the alcove in a roaring, thunderous blaze. Drizzt noted, too, that Hephaestus closed his eyes tightly when he breathed his fire.

When the conflagration was finished, Hephaestus swung back triumphantly. Drizzt, still looking at the alcove, at the molten rock running down the walls and dripping from the ceiling, did not have to feign his awe.

"By the gods!" he whispered harshly. He managed to look back at the dragon's smug expression. "By the gods," he said again. "Mergandevinasander of Chult, who thought himself supreme, is humbled."

"And well he should be!" Hephaestus boomed. "No black is the equal of a red! Know that now, Mergandevinasander. It is a fact that could save your life if ever a red comes to your door!"

"Indeed," Drizzt promptly agreed. "But I fear that I shall have no door." Again he looked down at his form and scowled with disdain. "No door beyond one in the city of dark elves!"

"That is your fate, not mine," Hephaestus said. "But I shall take pity on you. I shall let you depart alive, though that is more than you deserve for disturbing my slumber!"

This was the critical moment, Drizzt knew. He could have taken Hephaestus up on the offer; at that moment, he wanted nothing more than to be out of there. But his principles and Mooshie's memory wouldn't let him go. What of his companions in the tunnel? he reminded himself. And what of the adventures for the bards' books?

"Devour me then," he said to the dragon, though he could hardly believe the words as he spoke them. "I who have known the glory of dragonkind cannot be content with life as a dark elf."

Hephaestus's huge maw inched forward.

"Alas for all the dragonkind!" Drizzt wailed. "Our numbers ever decreasing, while the humans multiply like vermin. Alas for the treasures of dragons, to be stolen by wizards and paladins!" The way he spat that last word gave Hephaestus pause.

"And alas for Mergandevinasander," Drizzt continued dramatically, "to be struck down thus by a human wizard whose power outshines even that of Hephaestus, mightiest of dragonkind!"

"Outshines!" Hephaestus cried, and the whole chamber trembled under the power of that roar.

"What am I to believe?" Drizzt yelled back, somewhat pitifully compared to the dragon's volume. "Would Hephaestus not aid one of his own diminishing kind? Nay, that I cannot believe, that the world shall not believe!" Drizzt aimed a pointed finger at the ceiling above him, preaching for all he was worth. He did not have to be reminded of the price of failure. "They will say, one and all from all the wide realms, that Hephaestus dared not try to dispel the wizard's magic, that the great red dared not reveal his weakness against so powerful a spell for fear that his weakness would invite that same wizard-led party to come north for another haul of dragon plunder!

"Ah!" Drizzt shouted, wide-eyed. "But will not Hephaestus's perceived surrender also give the wizard and his nasty thieving friends hope of such plunder? And what dragon possesses more to steal than Hephaestus, the red of rich Mirabar?"

The dragon was at a loss. Hephaestus liked his way of life,

sleeping on treasures ever-growing from high-paying merchants. He didn't need the likes of heroic adventurers poking around in his lair! Those were the exact sentiments Drizzt had been counting on.

"Tomorrow!" the dragon roared. "This day I contemplate the spell and tomorrow Mergandevinasander shall be a black once more! Then he shall depart, his tail aflame, if he dares utter one more blasphemous word! Now I must take my rest to recall the spell. You shall not move, dragon in drow form. I smell you where you are and hear as well as anything in all the world. I am not as sound a sleeper as many thieves have wished!"

Drizzt did not doubt a word of it, of course, so while things had gone as well as he had hoped, he found himself in a bit of a mess. He couldn't wait a day to resume his conversation with the red, nor could his friends. How would proud Hephaestus react, Drizzt wondered, when the dragon tried to counter a spell that didn't even exist? And what, Drizzt told himself as he neared panic, would he do if Hephaestus actually did change him into a black dragon?

"Of course, the breath of a black has advantages over a red's," Drizzt blurted as Hephaestus swung away.

The red came back at him in a frightening flash and with frightening fury.

"Would you like to feel my breath?" Hephaestus snarled. "How great would come your boasts then, I must wonder?"

"No, not that," Drizzt replied. "Take no insult, mighty Hephaestus. Truly the spectacle of your fires stole my pride! But the breath of a black cannot be underestimated. It has qualities beyond even the power of a red's fire!"

"How say you?"

"Acid, O Hephaestus the Incredible, Devourer of Ten Thousand Cattle," Drizzt replied. "Acid clings to a knight's armor, digs through in lasting torment."

"As dripping metal might?" Hephaestus asked sarcastically. "Metal melted by a red's fire?"

"Longer, I fear," Drizzt admitted, dropping his gaze. "A red's breath comes in a burst of destruction, but a black's lingers, to the enemy's dismay."

"A burst?" Hephaestus growled. "How long can your breath last, pitiful black? Longer can I breath, I know!"

"But . . ." Drizzt began, indicating the alcove. This time, the dragon's sudden intake pulled Drizzt several steps forward and nearly whipped him from his feet. The drow kept his wits enough to cry out the appointed signal, "Fires of the Nine Hells!" as Hephaestus swung his head back in line with the alcove.

*　*　*　*　*

"The signal!" Mateus said above the tumult. "Run for your lives! Run!"

"Never!" cried the terrified Brother Herschel, and the others, except for Jankin, didn't disagree.

"Oh, to suffer so!" the shaggy-haired fanatic wailed, stepping from the tunnel.

"We have to! On our lives!" Mateus reminded them, catching Jankin by the hair to keep him from going the wrong way.

They struggled at the tunnel exit for several seconds and then the other friars, realizing that perhaps their only hope soon would pass them by, burst out of the tunnel and the whole group tumbled out and down the sloping path from the wall. When they recovered, they were surely in a fix, and they danced about aimlessly, not sure of whether to climb back up to the tunnel or light out for the exit. Their desperate scrambling hardly made any headway up the slope, especially with Mateus still trying to rein in Jankin, so the exit was the only way. Tripping all over themselves, the friars fled across the room.

Even their terror did not prevent each of them, even Jankin, from scooping up a pocketful of baubles as he passed.

*　*　*　*　*

Never had there been such a blast of dragon fire! Hephaestus, eyes closed, roared on and on, disintegrating the stone in the alcove. Great gouts of flame burst out into the room—Drizzt was nearly overcome by the heat—but the angry dragon did not relent, determined to humble the annoying visitor once and for all.

The dragon peeked once, to witness the effects of his display. Dragons knew their treasure rooms better than anything in the world, and Hephaestus did not miss the image of five fleeting figures darting across the main chamber toward the exit.

The breath stopped abruptly and the dragon swung about. "Thieves!" he roared, splitting stone with his thunderous voice.

Drizzt knew that the game was up.

The great, spear-filled maw snapped at the drow. Drizzt stepped to the side and leaped, having nowhere else to go. He caught one of the dragon's horns and rode up with the beast's head. Drizzt managed to scramble on top of it and held on for all his life as the outraged dragon tried to shake him free. Drizzt reached for a scimitar but found a pocket instead, and he pulled out a handful of dirt. Without the slightest hesitation, the drow flung the dirt down into the dragon's evil eye.

Hephaestus went berserk, snapping his head violently, up and down and all about. Drizzt held on stubbornly, and the devious dragon discerned a better method.

Drizzt understood Hephaestus's intent as the head shot up into the air at full speed. The ceiling was not so high— not compared with Hephaestus's serpentine neck. It was a long fall, but a preferable fate by far, and Drizzt dropped off just before the dragon's head slammed into the rock.

Drizzt dizzily regained his feet as Hephaestus, hardly slowed by the crushing impact, sucked in his breath. Luck saved the drow, and not for the first or the last time, as a considerable chunk of stone fell from the battered ceiling and crashed into the dragon's head. Hephaestus's breath blurted out in a harmless puff and Drizzt darted with all speed over the treasure mound, diving down behind.

Hephaestus roared in rage and loosed the rest of his breath, without thinking, straight for the mound. Gold coins melted together; enormous gemstones cracked under the pressure. The mound was fully twenty feet thick and tightly packed, but Drizzt, against the opposite side, felt his back aflame. He jumped out from the pile, leaving his cloak smoking and meshed with molten gold.

Out came Drizzt, scimitars drawn, as the dragon reared. The drow rushed straight in bravely, stupidly, whacking away with all his strength. He stopped, stunned, after only two blows, both scimitars ringing painfully in his hands; he might as well have banged them against a stone wall!

Hephaestus, head high, had paid the attack no heed. "My gold!" the dragon wailed. Then the beast looked down, his lamplight gaze boring through the drow once more. "My gold!" Hephaestus said again, wickedly.

Drizzt shrugged sheepishly, then he ran.

Hephaestus snapped his tail about, slamming it into yet another mound of treasure and showering the room in flying gold and silver coins and gemstones. "My gold!" the dragon roared over and over as he slammed his way through the tight piles.

Drizzt fell behind another mound. "Help me, Guenhwyvar," he begged, dropping the figurine.

"I smell you, thief!" The dragon purred—as if a thunderstorm could purr—not far from Drizzt's mound.

In response, the panther came to the top of the mound, roared in defiance, then sprang away. Drizzt, down at the bottom, listened carefully, measuring the steps, as Hephaestus rushed forward.

"I shall chew you apart, shape-changer!" the dragon bellowed, and his gaping mouth snapped down at Guenhwyvar.

But teeth, even dragon teeth, had little effect on the insubstantial mist that Guenhwyvar suddenly became.

Drizzt managed to pocket a few baubles as he rushed out, his retreat covered by the din of the frustrated dragon's tantrum. The chamber was large and Drizzt was not quite gone when Hephaestus recovered and spotted him. Confused but no less enraged, the dragon roared and started after Drizzt.

In the goblin tongue, knowing from the book that Hephaestus spoke it but hoping that the dragon wouldn't know he knew, Drizzt yelled, "When the stupid beast follows me out, come out and get the rest!"

Hephaestus skidded to a stop and spun about, eyeing the low tunnel that led to the mines. The stupid dragon was in a frightful fit, wanting to munch on the imposing drow but fearing a robbery from behind. Hephaestus stalked over to the tunnel and slammed his scaly head into the wall above it, for good measure, then moved back to think things over.

The thieves had made the exit by now, the dragon knew; he would have to go out under the wide sky if he wanted to catch them—not a wise proposition at this time of year, considering the dragon's lucrative business. In the end, Hephaestus settled the dilemma as he settled every problem: He vowed to thoroughly eat the next merchant party that came his way. His pride restored in that resolution, one that he undoubtedly would forget as soon as he returned to his sleep, the dragon moved back about his chamber, repiling the gold and salvaging what he could from the mounds he inadvertently had melted.

❧ 22 ❧

Homeward Bound

"You got us through!" Brother Herschel cried. All of the friars except Jonkin threw a great hug on Drizzt as soon as the drow caught up to them in a rocky vale west of the dragon lair's entrance.

"If ever there is a way that we can repay you . . . !"

Drizzt emptied his pockets in response, and five sets of eager eyes widened as gold trinkets and baubles rolled forth, glittering in the afternoon sun. One gem in particular, a two-inch ruby, promised wealth beyond anything the friars had ever known.

"For you," Drizzt explained. "All of it. I have no need of treasures."

The friars looked about guiltily, none of them willing to reveal the booty stored in his own pockets. "Perhaps you should keep a bit," Mateus offered, "if you still plan to strike out on your own."

"I do," Drizzt said firmly.

"You cannot stay here," reasoned Mateus. "Where will you go?"

Drizzt really hadn't given it much thought. All he really knew was that his place was not among the Weeping Friars. He pondered a while, recalling the many dead-end roads he had traveled. A thought popped into his head.

"You said it," Drizzt remarked to Jankin. "You named the place a week before we entered the tunnel."

Jankin looked at him curiously, hardly remembering.

"Ten-Towns," Drizzt said. "Land of rogues, where a rogue might find his place."

"Ten-Towns?" Mateus balked. "Surely you should reconsider your course, friend. Icewind Dale is not a welcoming place, nor are the hardy killers of Ten-Towns."

"The wind is ever blowing," Jankin added with a wistful look in his dark and hollow eyes, "filled with stinging sand and an icy bite. I will go with you!"

"And the monsters!" added one of the others, slapping Jankin on the back of the head. "Tundra yeti and white bears, and fierce barbarians! No, I would not go to Ten-Towns if Hephaestus himself tried to chase me there!"

"Well the dragon might," said Herschel, glancing nervously back toward the not-so-distant lair. "There are some farmhouses nearby. Perhaps we could stay there the night and get back to the tunnel tomorrow."

"I'll not go with you," Drizzt said again. "You name Ten-Towns an unwelcoming place, but would I find any warmer reception in Mirabar?"

"We will go to the farmers this night," Mateus replied, reconsidering his words. "We will buy you a horse there, and the supplies you will need. I do not wish you to go away at all," he said, "but Ten-Towns seems a good choice—" He looked pointedly at Jankin—"for a drow. Many have found their place there. Truly it is a home for he who has none."

Drizzt understood the sincerity in the friar's voice and appreciated Mateus's graciousness. "How do I find it?" he asked.

"Follow the mountains," Mateus replied. "Keep them always at your right hand's reach. When you get around the range, you have entered Icewind Dale. Only a single peak marks the flat land north of the Spine of the World. The towns are built around it. May they be all that you hope!"

With that, the friars prepared to leave. Drizzt clasped his hands behind his head and leaned back against the valley wall. It was indeed time for his parting with the friars, he knew, but he could not deny both the guilt and loneliness that the prospect offered. The small riches they had taken from the dragon's lair would greatly change his companions' lives, would give them shelter and all the necessities, but wealth could do nothing to alter the barriers that Drizzt faced.

Ten-Towns, the land that Jankin had named a house for the homeless, a gathering ground for those who had nowhere else to go, brought the drow a measure of hope. How many times had fate kicked him? How many gates had he approached hopefully only to be turned away at the tip of a spear? This time will be different, Drizzt told himself, for if he could not find a place in the land of rogues, where then might he turn?

For the beleaguered drow, who had spent so very long running from tragedy, guilt, and prejudices he could not escape, hope was not a comfortable emotion.

*   *   *   *   *

Drizzt camped in a small copse that night while the friars went into the small farming village. They returned the next morning leading a fine horse, but with one of their group conspicuously absent.

"Where is Jankin?" Drizzt asked, concerned.

"Tied up in a barn," Mateus replied. "He tried to get away last night, to go back . . ."

"To Hephaestus," Drizzt finished for him.

"If he is still in a mind for it this day, we might just let him go," added a disgusted Herschel.

"Here is your horse," Mateus said, "if the night has not changed your mind."

"And here is a new wrap," offered Herschel. He handed Drizzt a fine, fur-lined cloak. Drizzt knew how uncharacteristically generous the friars were being, and he almost changed his mind. He could not dismiss his other needs, though, and he would not satisfy them among this group.

To display his resolve, the drow moved straight to the animal, meaning to climb right on. Drizzt had seen a horse before, but never so close. He was amazed by the beast's sheer strength, the muscles rippling along the animal's neck, and he was amazed, too, by the height of the animal's back.

He spent a moment staring into the horse's eyes, communicating his intent as best he could. Then, to everyone's shock, even Drizzt's, the horse bent low, allowing the drow to climb easily into the saddle.

"You have a way with horses," remarked Mateus. "Never did you mention that you were a skilled rider."

Drizzt only nodded and did his very best to remain in the saddle when the horse started into a trot. It took the drow many moments to figure out how to control the beast and he had circled far to the east—the wrong way—before he managed to turn about. Throughout the circuit, Drizzt tried hard to keep up his facade, and the friars, never ones for horses themselves, merely nodded and smiled.

Hours later, Drizzt was riding hard to the west, following the southern edge of the Spine of the World.

* * * * *

"The Weeping Friars," Roddy McGristle whispered, looking down from a stony bluff at the band as they made their way back toward Mirabar's tunnel later that same week.

"What?" Tephanis gawked, rushing from his sack to join Roddy. For the very first time, the sprite's speed proved a liability. Before he even realized what he was saying, Tephanis blurted, "It-cannot-be! The-dragon . . ."

Roddy's glare fell over Tephanis like the shadow of a thundercloud.

"I-mean-I-assumed . . ." Tephanis sputtered, but he realized that Roddy, who knew the tunnel better than he and knew, too, the sprite's ways with locks, had pretty much guessed the indiscretion.

"Ye took it on yerself to kill the drow," Roddy said calmly.

"Please, my-master," Tephanis replied. "I-did-not-mean . . . I-feared-for-you. The-drow-is-a-devil, I-say! I-sent-them-down-the-dragon's-tunnel. I-thought-that-you . . ."

"Forget it," Roddy growled. "Ye did what ye did, and no more about it. Now get in yer sack. Mighten that we can fix what ye done, if the drow's not dead."

Tephanis nodded, relieved, and zipped back into the sack. Roddy scooped it up and called his dog to his side.

"I'll get the friars talking," the bounty hunter vowed, "but first . . ." Roddy whipped the sack about, slamming it into the stone wall.

"Master!" came the sprite's muffled cry.

"Ye drow-stealin . . ." Roddy huffed, and he beat the sack mercilessly against the unyielding stone. Tephanis squirmed for the first few whacks, even managed to begin a tear with his little dagger. But then the sack darkened with wetness and the sprite struggled no more.

"Drow-stealing mutant," Roddy mumbled, tossing the gory package away. "Come on, dog. If the drow's alive, the friars'll know where to find him."

* * * * *

The Weeping Friars were an order dedicated to suffering, and a couple of them, particularly Jankin, had indeed suffered much in their lives. None of them, though, had ever imagined the level of cruelty they found at the hands of wild-eyed Roddy McGristle, and before an hour had passed, Roddy, too, was driving hard to the west along the southern edge of the mountain range.

* * * * *

The cold eastern wind filled his ears with its endless song. Drizzt had heard it every second since he had rounded the western edge of the Spine of the World and turned north and then east, into the barren stretch of land named for this wind, Icewind Dale. He accepted the mournful groan and the wind's freezing bite willingly, for to Drizzt the rush of air came as a gust of freedom.

Another symbol of that freedom, the sight of the wide sea, came as the drow rounded the mountain range. Drizzt had visited the shoreline once, on his passage to Luskan, and now he wanted to pause and go the few miles to its shores again. But the cold wind reminded him of the impending winter, and he understood the difficulty he would find in traveling the dale once the first snows had fallen.

Drizzt spotted Kelvin's Cairn, the solitary mountain on the tundra north of the great range, the first day after he had turned into the dale. He made for it anxiously, visualizing its singular peak as the marking post to the land he would call home. Tentative hope filled him whenever he focused on that mountain.

He passed several small groups, solitary wagons or a handful of men on horseback, as he neared the region of Ten-Towns along the caravan route, a southwestern approach. The sun was low in the west and dim, and Drizzt kept the cowl of his fine cloak pulled low, hiding his ebony skin. He nodded curtly as each traveler passed.

Three lakes dominated the region, along with the peak of rocky Kelvin's Cairn, which rose a thousand feet above the broken plain and was capped with snow even through the short summer. Of the ten towns that gave the area its name, only the principle city, Bryn Shander, stood apart from the lakes. It sat above the plain, on a short hill, its flag whipping defiantly against the stiff wind. The caravan route, Drizzt's trail, led to this city, the region's principle marketplace.

Drizzt could tell from the rising smoke of distant fires that several other communities were within a few miles of the city on the hill. He considered his course for a moment, wondering if he should go to one of these smaller, more secluded towns instead of continuing straight on to the principle city.

"No," the drow said firmly, dropping a hand into his pouch to feel the onyx figurine. Drizzt kicked his horse ahead, up the hill to the walled city's forbidding gates.

"Merchant?" asked one of the two guards standing bored before the iron-bound portal. "Ye're a bit late in the year for trading."

"No merchant," Drizzt replied softly, losing a good measure of his nerve now that the hour was upon him. He reached up slowly to his hood, trying to keep his trembling hand moving.

"From what town, then?" the other guard asked. Drizzt dropped his hand back, his courage deflected by the blunt question.

"From Mirabar," he answered honestly, and then, before he could stop himself and before the guards posed another distracting question, he reached up and pulled back his hood.

Four eyes popped wide and hands immediately dropped to belted swords.

"No!" Drizzt retorted suddenly. "No, please." A weariness came into both his voice and his posture that the guards could not understand. Drizzt had no strength left for sense-less battles of misunderstanding. Against a goblin horde or a marauding giant, the drow's scimitars came easily into his hands, but against one who only battled him because of misperceptions, his blades weighed heavily indeed.

"I have come from Mirabar," Drizzt continued, his voice growing steadier with each syllable, "to Ten-Towns to reside in peace." He held his hands out wide, offering no threat.

The guards hardly knew how to react. Neither of them had ever seen a dark elf—though they knew beyond doubt that Drizzt was one—or knew more about the race than fireside tales of the ancient war that had split the elven peoples apart.

"Wait here," one of the guards breathed to the other, who didn't seem to appreciate the order. "I will go inform Spokesman Cassius." He banged on the iron-bound gate and slipped inside as soon as it was opened wide enough to let him through. The remaining guard eyed Drizzt unblinking, his hand never leaving his sword hilt.

"If you kill me, a hundred crossbows will cut you down," he declared, trying but utterly failing to sound confident.

"Why would I?" Drizzt asked innocently, keeping his hands wide apart and his posture unthreatening. This en-counter had gone well so far, he believed. In every other village he had dared approach, those first seeing him had fled in terror or chased him with bared weapons.

The other guard returned a short time later with a small and slender man, clean-shaven and with bright blue eyes that scanned continuously, taking in every detail. He wore fine clothes, and from the respect the two guards showed the man, Drizzt knew at once that he was of high rank.

He studied Drizzt for a long while, considering every move and every feature. "I am Cassius," he said at length, "Spokesman of Bryn Shander and Principle Spokesman of Ten-Towns' Ruling Council."

Drizzt dipped a short bow. "I am Drizzt Do'Urden," he said, "of Mirabar and points beyond, now come to Ten-Towns."

"Why?" Cassius asked sharply, trying to catch him off guard.

Drizzt shrugged. "Is a reason required?"

"For a dark elf, perhaps," Cassius replied honestly.

Drizzt's accepting smile disarmed the spokesman and quieted the two guards, who now stood protectively close to his sides. "I can offer no reason for coming, beyond my desire to come," Drizzt continued. "Long has been my road, Spokesman Cassius. I am weary and in need of rest. Ten-Towns is the place of rogues, I have been told, and do not doubt that a dark elf is a rogue among the dwellers of the surface."

It seemed logical enough, and Drizzt's sincerity came through clearly to the observant spokesman. Cassius dropped his chin in his palm and thought for a long while. He didn't fear the drow, or doubt the elf's words, but he had no intention of allowing the stir that a drow would cause in his city.

"Bryn Shander is not your place," Cassius said bluntly, and Drizzt's lavender eyes narrowed at the unfair proclamation. Undaunted, Cassius pointed to the north. "Go to Lonelywood, in the forest on the northern banks of Maer Dualdon," he offered. He swung his gaze to the southeast. "Or to Good Mead or Dougan's Hole on the southern lake, Redwaters. These are smaller towns, where you will cause less stir and find less trouble."

"And when they refuse my entry?" Drizzt asked. "Where then, fair spokesman? Out in the wind to die on the empty plain?"

"You do not know—"

"I know," Drizzt interrupted. "I have played this game many times. Who will welcome a drow, even one who has forsaken his people and their ways and who desires nothing more than peace?" Drizzt's voice was stern and showed no self-pity, and Cassius again understood the words to be true.

Truly Cassius sympathized. He himself had been a rogue once and had been forced to the ends of the world, to forlorn Icewind Dale, to find a home. There were no ends farther than this; Icewind Dale was a rogue's last stop. Another thought came to Cassius then, a possible solution to the dilemma that would not nag at his conscience.

"How long have you lived on the surface?" Cassius asked, sincerely interested.

Drizzt considered the question for a moment, wondering what point the spokesman meant to make. "Seven years," he replied.

"In the northland?"

"Yes."

"Yet you have found no home, no village to take you in," Cassius said. "You have survived hostile winters and, doubtless, more direct enemies. Are you skilled with those blades you hang on your belt?"

"I am a ranger," Drizzt said evenly.

"An unusual profession for a drow," Cassius remarked.

"I am a ranger," Drizzt said again, more forcefully, "well trained in the ways of nature and in the use of my weapons."

"I do not doubt," Cassius mused. He paused, then said, "There is a place offering shelter and seclusion." The spokesman led Drizzt's gaze to the north, to the rocky slopes of Kelvin's Cairn. "Beyond the dwarven vale lies the mountain," Cassius explained, "and beyond that the open tundra. It would do Ten-Towns well to have a scout on the mountain's northern slopes. Danger always seems to come from that direction."

"I came to find my home," Drizzt interrupted. "You offer me a hole in a pile of rock and a duty to those whom I owe nothing." In truth, the suggestion appealed to Drizzt's ranger spirit.

"Would you have me tell you that things are different?" Cassius replied. "I'll not let a wandering drow into Bryn Shander."

"Would a man have to prove himself worthy?"

"A man does not carry so grim a reputation," Cassius replied evenly, without hesitation. "If I were so magnanimous, if I welcomed you on your words alone and threw my gates wide, would you enter and find your home? We both know better than that, drow. Not everyone in Bryn Shander would be so open-hearted, I promise. You would cause an uproar wherever you went and, whatever your demeanor and intent, you would be forced into battles.

"It would be the same in any of the towns," Cassius went on, guessing that his words had struck a chord of truth in the homeless drow. "I offer you a hole in a pile of rock, within the borders of Ten-Towns, where your actions, good or bad, will become your reputation beyond the color of your skin. Does my offer seem so shallow now?"

"I shall need supplies," Drizzt said, accepting the truth of Cassius's words. "And what of my horse? I do not think the slopes of a mountain are a proper place for such a beast."

"Trade your horse then," Cassius offered. "My guard will get a fair price and return here with the supplies you will need."

Drizzt thought about the suggestion for a moment, then handed the reins to Cassius.

The spokesman left then, thinking himself quite clever. Not only had he averted any immediate trouble, he had convinced Drizzt to guard his borders, all in a place where Bruenor Battlehammer and his clan of grim-faced dwarves could certainly keep the drow from causing any trouble.

* * * * *

Roddy McGristle pulled his wagon into a small village nestled in the shadows of the mountain range's western end. Snow would come soon, the bounty hunter knew, and he had no desire to be caught halfway up the dale when it began. He'd stay here with the farmers and wait out the winter. Nothing could leave the dale without passing this area, and if Drizzt had gone there, as the friars had revealed, he had nowhere left to run.

* * * * *

Drizzt set out from the gates that night, preferring the darkness for his journey, despite the cold. His direct approach to the mountain took him along the eastern rim of the rocky gorge that the dwarves had claimed as their home. Drizzt took extra care to avoid any guards the bearded folk might have set. He had encountered dwarves only once before, when he had passed Citadel Adbar on his earliest wanderings out of Mooshie's Grove, and it had not been a pleasant experience. Dwarven patrols had chased him off without waiting for any explanations, and they had dogged him through the mountains for many days.

For all his prudence in getting past the valley, though, Drizzt could not ignore a high mound of rocks he came upon, a climb with steps cut into the piled stones. He was less than halfway to the mountain, with several miles and hours of night still to go, but Drizzt moved up the detour, step over step, enchanted by the widening panorama of town lights about him.

The climb was not high, only fifty feet or so, but with the flat tundra and clear night Drizzt was afforded a view of five cities: two on the banks of the lake to the east, two to the west on the largest lake, and Bryn Shander, on its hillock a few miles to the south.

How many minutes passed Drizzt did not know, for the sights sparked too many hopes and fantasies for him to notice. He had been in Ten-Towns for barely a day, but already he was feeling comfortable with the sights, with knowing that thousands of people about the mountain would hear of him and possibly come to accept him.

A grumbling, gravelly voice shook Drizzt from his contemplations. He dropped into a defensive crouch and circled behind a rock. The stream of complaints marked the coming figure clearly. He was wide-shouldered and about a foot shorter than Drizzt, though obviously heavier than the drow. Drizzt knew it was a dwarf even before the figure paused to adjust its helmet—by slamming its head into a stone.

"Dagnaggit blasted," the dwarf muttered, "adjusting" the helmet a second time.

Drizzt was certainly intrigued, but he was also smart enough to realize that a grumbling dwarf wouldn't likely welcome an uninvited drow in the middle of a dark night. As the dwarf moved for yet another adjustment, Drizzt skipped off, running lightly and silently along the side of the trail. He passed close by the dwarf but then was gone with no more rustle than the shadow of a cloud.

"Eh?" the dwarf mumbled when he came back up, this time satisfied with his headgear's fit. "Who's that? What're ye about?" He went into a series of short, spinning hops, eyes darting alertly all about.

There was only the darkness, the stones, and the wind.

❧ 23 ❧

A Memory Come To Life

The season's first snow fell lazily over Icewind Dale, large flakes drifting down in mesmerizing zigzag dances, so different from the wind-whipped blizzards most common to the region. The young girl, Catti-brie, watched it with obvious enchantment from the doorway of her cavern home, the hue of her deep-blue eyes seeming even purer in the reflection of the ground's white blanket.

"Late in comin', but hard when it gets here," grumbled Bruenor Battlehammer, a red-bearded dwarf, as he came up behind Catti-brie, his adopted daughter. "Suren to be a hard season, as are all in this place for white dragons!"

"Oh, me Daddy!" replied Catti-brie sternly. "Stop yer whining! Suren 'tis a beautiful fall, and harmless enough without the wind to drive it."

"Humans," huffed the dwarf derisively, still behind the girl. Catti-brie could not see his expression, tender toward her even as he grumbled, but she didn't need to. Bruenor was nine parts bluster and one part grouch, by Catti-brie's estimation.

Catti-brie spun on the dwarf suddenly, her shoulder-length, auburn locks twirling about her face. "Can I go out to play?" she asked, a hopeful smile on her face. "Oh, please, me Daddy!"

Bruenor forced on his best grimace. "Go out!" he roared. "None but a fool'd look for an Icewind Dale winter as a place for playin'! Show some sense, girl! The season'd freeze yer bones!"

Catti-brie's smile disappeared, but she refused to surrender so easily. "Well said for a dwarf," she retorted, to Bruenor's horror. "Ye're well enough fit for the holes and the less ye see o' the sky, the more ye're smiling! But I've a long winter ahead, and this might be me last chance to see the sky. Please, Daddy?"

Bruenor could not hold his snarling visage against his daughter's charm, but he did not want her to go out. "I'm fearing there's something prowlin' out there," he explained, trying to sound authoritative. "Sensed it on the climb a few nights back, though I never seen it. Mighten be a white lion, or a white bear. Best to . . ." Bruenor never finished, for Catti-brie's disheartened look more than destroyed the dwarf's imagined fears.

Catti-brie was no novice to the dangers of the region. She had lived with Bruenor and his dwarven clan for more than seven years. A raiding goblin band had killed Catti-brie's parents when she was only a toddler, and, though she was human, Bruenor had taken her in as his own.

"Ye're a hard one, me girl," Bruenor said in answer to Catti-brie's relentless, sorrow-filled expression. "Go out and find yer play, then, but don't ye be goin' too far! On yer word, ye spirited filly, keep the caves in sight and a sword and horn on yer belt."

Catti-brie rushed over and planted a wet kiss on Bruenor's cheek, which the taciturn dwarf promptly wiped away, grumbling at the girl's back as she disappeared into the tunnel. Bruenor was the leader of the clan, as tough as the stone they mined. But every time Catti-brie planted an appreciative kiss on his cheek, the dwarf realized he had given in to her.

"Humans!" the dwarf growled again, and he stomped down the tunnel to the mine, thinking to batter a few pieces of iron, just to remind himself of his toughness.

* * * * *

It was easy for the spirited young girl to rationalize her disobedience when she looked back across the valley from the lower slopes of Kelvin's Cairn, more than three miles from Bruenor's front door. Bruenor had told Catti-brie to keep the caves in sight, and they were, or at least the wider terrain around them was, from this high vantage point.

But Catti-brie, happily sliding down one bumpy expanse, soon found a flaw in not heeding to her experienced father's warnings. She had come to the bottom, a delightful ride, and was briskly rubbing the stinging chill out of her hands, when she heard a low and ominous growl.

"White lion," Catti-brie mouthed silently, remembering Bruenor's suspicion. When she looked up, she saw that her father's guess had not quite hit the mark. It was indeed a great feline the girl saw looking down at her from a bare, stony mound, but the cat was black, not white, and a huge panther, not a lion.

Defiantly, Catti-brie pulled her knife from its sheath. "Keep yerself back, cat!" she said, only the slightest tremor in her voice, for she knew that fear invited attack from wild animals.

Guenhwyvar flattened its ears and plopped to its belly, then issued a long and resounding roar that echoed throughout the stony region.

Catti-brie could not respond to the power in that roar, or to the very long and abundant teeth the panther showed. She searched around for some escape but knew that no matter which way she ran she could not get beyond the panther's first mighty spring.

"Guenhwyvar!" came a call from above. Catti-brie looked back up the snowy expanse to see a slender, cloaked form picking a careful route toward her. "Guenhwyvar!" the newcomer called again. "Be gone from here!"

The panther growled a throaty reply, then bounded away, leaping the snow-covered boulders and springing up small cliffs as easily as if it were running across a smooth and flat field.

Despite her continuing fears, Catti-brie watched the departing panther with sincere admiration. She had always loved animals and had often studied them, but the interplay of Guenhwyvar's sleek muscles was more majestic than anything she had ever imagined. When she at last came out of her trance, she realized that the slender figure was right behind her. She whirled about, knife still in hand.

The blade dropped from her grasp and her breathing halted abruptly as soon as she looked upon the drow.

Drizzt, too, found himself stunned by the encounter. He wanted to make certain that the girl was all right, but when he looked upon Catti-brie, all thoughts of his purpose faded away in a flood of memories.

She was about the same age as the sandy-haired boy on the farm, Drizzt noted initially, and that thought inevitably brought back the agonizing memories of Maldobar. When Drizzt looked more closely, though, into Catti-brie's eyes, his thoughts were sent flying back further into his past, to his days marching alongside his dark kin. Catti-brie's eyes possessed that same joyful and innocent sparkle that Drizzt had seen in the eyes of an elven child, a girl he had rescued from the savage blades of his raiding kin. The memory overwhelmed Drizzt, sent him whirling back to that bloody glade in the elven wood, where his brother and fellow drow had brutally slaughtered an elven gathering. In the frenzy, Drizzt had almost killed the elven child, had almost put himself forever on that same dark road that his kin so willingly followed.

Drizzt shook himself free of the recollection and reminded himself that this was a different child of a different race. He meant to speak a greeting, but the girl was gone.

That damning word, "drizzit," echoed in the drow's thoughts several times as he made his way back to the cave he had set up as his home on the mountain's northern face.

*   *   *   *   *

That same night, the onslaught of the season began in full. The cold eastern wind blowing off the Reghed Glacier drove the snow into high, impassable drifts.

Catti-brie watched the snow forlornly, fearing that many

weeks might pass before she could again go to Kelvin's
Cairn. She hadn't told Bruenor or any of the other dwarves
about the drow, for fear of punishment and that Bruenor
would drive the drow away. Looking at the piling snow,
Catti-brie wished that she had been braver, had remained
and talked to the strange elf. Every howl of the wind
heightened that wish and made the girl wonder if she had
lost her only chance.

* * * * *

"I'm off to Bryn Shander," Bruenor announced one morning more than two months later. An unexpected break had
come in Icewind Dale's normal seven-month winter, a rare
January thaw. Bruenor eyed his daughter suspiciously for a
long moment. "Ye're meanin' to go out yerself this day?" he
asked.

"If I may," Catti-brie answered. "The caves're tight around
me and the wind's not so cold."

"I'll get a dwarf or two to go with ye," Bruenor offered.

Catti-brie, thinking that now might be her chance to go
back to investigate the drow, balked at the notion. "They're
all for mendin' their doors!" she retorted, more sharply
than she intended. "Don't ye be botherin' them for the likes
of meself!"

Bruenor's eyes narrowed. "Ye've too much stubbornness
in ye."

"I get it from me dad," Catti-brie said with a wink that shot
down any more forthcoming arguments.

"Take care, then," Bruenor began, "and keep—"

". . . the caves in sight!" Catti-brie finished for him.
Bruenor spun about and stomped out of the cave, grumbling helplessly and cursing the day he had ever taken a
human in for a daughter. Catti-brie only laughed at the unending facade.

Once again it was Guenhwyvar who first encountered
the auburn-haired girl. Catti-brie had set straight out for
the mountain and was making her way around its western-

most trails when she spotted the black panther above her, watching her from a rock spur.

"Guenhwyvar," the girl called, remembering the name the drow had used. The panther growled lowly and dropped from the spur, moving closer.

"Guenhwyvar?" Catti-brie said again, less certain, for the panther was only a few dozen strides away. Guenhwyvar's ears came up at the second mention of the name and the cat's taut muscles visibly relaxed.

Catti-brie approached slowly, one deliberate step at a time. "Where's the dark elf, Guenhwyvar?" she asked quietly. "Can ye take me to him?"

"And why would you want to go to him?" came a question from behind.

Catti-brie froze in her tracks, remembering the smooth-toned, melodic voice, then turned slowly to face the drow. He was only three steps behind her, his lavender-eyed gaze locking onto hers as soon as they met. Catti-brie had no idea of what to say, and Drizzt, absorbed again by memories, stood quiet, watching and waiting.

"Be ye a drow?" Catti-brie asked after the silence became unbearable. As soon as she heard her own words, she privately berated herself for asking such a stupid question.

"I am," Drizzt replied. "What does that mean to you?"

Catti-brie shrugged at the strange response. "I've heard that drow be evil, but ye don't seem so to me."

"Then you have taken a great risk in coming out here all by yourself," Drizzt remarked. "But fear not," he quickly added, seeing the girl's sudden uneasiness, "for I am not evil and will bring no harm to you." After the months alone in his comfortable but empty cave, Drizzt did not want this meeting to end quickly.

Catti-brie nodded, believing his words. "Me name's Catti-brie," she said. "Me dad is Bruenor, King o' Clan Battlehammer."

Drizzt cocked his head curiously.

"The dwarves," Catti-brie explained, pointing back to the valley. She understood Drizzt's confusion as soon as she spoke the words. "He's not me real dad," she said. "Bruenor took me in when I was just a babe, when me real parents were . . ."

She couldn't finish, and Drizzt didn't need her to, understanding her pained expression.

"I am Drizzt Do'Urden," the drow interjected. "Well met, Catti-brie, daughter of Bruenor. It is good to have another to talk with. For all these weeks of winter, I have had only Guenhwyvar, there, when the cat is around, and my friend does not say much, of course!"

Catti-brie's smile nearly took in her ears. She glanced over her shoulder to the panther, now reclining lazily in the path. "She's a beautiful cat," Catti-brie remarked.

Drizzt did not doubt the sincerity in the girl's tone, or in the admiring gaze she dropped on Guenhwyvar. "Come here, Guenhwyvar," Drizzt said, and the panther stretched and slowly rose. Guenhwyvar walked right beside Catti-brie, and Drizzt nodded to answer her unspoken but obvious desire. Tentatively at first, but then firmly, Catti-brie stroked the panther's sleek coat, feeling the beast's power and perfection. Guenhwyvar accepted the petting without complaint, even bumped into Catti-brie's side when she stopped for a moment, prodding her to continue.

"Are you alone?" Drizzt asked.

Catti-brie nodded. "Me dad said to keep the caves in sight." She laughed. "I can see them well enough, by me thinkin'!"

Drizzt looked back into the valley, to the far rock wall several miles away. "Your father would not be pleased. This land is not so tame. I have been on the mountain for only two months, and I have fought twice already shaggy white beasts I do not know."

"Tundra yeti," Catti-brie replied. "Ye must be on the northern side. Tundra yeti don't come around the mountain."

"Are you so certain?" Drizzt asked sarcastically.

"I've not ever seen one," Catti-brie replied, "but I'm not fearing them. I came to find yerself, and now I have."

"You have," said Drizzt, "and now what?"

Catti-brie shrugged and went back to petting Guenhwyvar's sleek coat.

"Come," Drizzt offered. "Let us find a more comfortable place to talk. The glare off the snow stings my eyes."

"Ye're used to the dark tunnels?" Catti-brie asked hopefully, eager to hear tales of lands beyond the borders of Ten-Towns, the only place Catti-brie had ever known.

Drizzt and the girl spent a marvelous day together. Drizzt told Catti-brie of Menzoberranzan and Catti-brie answered his tales with stories of Icewind Dale, of her life with the dwarves. Drizzt was especially interested in hearing about Bruenor and his kin, since the dwarves were his closest, and most-feared, neighbors.

"Bruenor talks rough as stone, but I'm knowin' him better than all that!" Catti-brie assured the drow. "He's a right fine one, and so's the rest o' the clan."

Drizzt was glad to hear it, and glad, too, that he had made this connection, both for the implications of having such a friend and even more so because he truly enjoyed the charming and spirited lass's company. Catti-brie's energy and zest for life verily bubbled over. In her presence, the drow could not recall his haunting memories, could only feel good about his decision to save the elven child those many years before. Catti-brie's singsong voice and the careless way she flipped her flowing hair about her shoulders lifted the burden of guilt from Drizzt's back as surely as a giant could have hoisted a rock.

Their tales could have gone on all that day and night, and for many weeks afterward, but when Drizzt noticed the sun riding low along the western horizon, he realized that the time had come for the girl to head back to her home.

"I will take you," Drizzt offered.

"No," Catti-brie replied. "Ye best not. Bruenor'd not understand, and ye'd get me in a mountain o' trouble. I can get back, don't ye be worrying! I know these trails better'n yerself, Drizzt Do'Urden, and ye couldn't keep up to me if ye tried!"

Drizzt laughed at the boast but almost believed it. He and the girl set out at once, moving to the mountain's southernmost spur and then saying their good-byes with promises that they would meet again during the next thaw, or in the spring if none came sooner.

Truly the girl was skipping lightly when she entered the dwarven complex, but one look at her surly father stole a measure of her delight. Bruenor had gone to Bryn Shander that morning on business with Cassius. The dwarf wasn't thrilled to learn that a dark elf had made a home so close to his door, but he guessed that his curious—too curious—daughter would think it a grand thing.

"Keep yerself away from the mountain," Bruenor said as soon as he noticed Catti-brie, and then she was in despair.

"But me Dad—" she tried to protest.

"On yer word, girl!" the dwarf demanded. "Ye'll not set foot on that mountain again without me permission! There's a dark elf there, by Cassius's telling. On yer word!"

Catti-brie nodded helplessly, then followed Bruenor back to the dwarven complex, knowing she would have a hard time changing her father's mind, but knowing, too, Bruenor held views far from justified where Drizzt Do'Urden was concerned.

* * * * *

Another thaw came a month later and Catti-brie heeded her promise. She never put one foot on Kelvin's Cairn, but from the valley trails around it, she called out to Drizzt and to Guenhwyvar. Drizzt and the panther, looking for the girl with the break in the weather, were soon beside her, in the valley this time, sharing more tales and a picnic lunch that Catti-brie had packed.

When Catti-brie got back to the dwarven mines that evening, Bruenor suspected much and asked her only once if she had kept her word. The dwarf had always trusted his daughter, but when Catti-brie answered that she had not been on Kelvin's Cairn, his suspicions did not diminish.

❧ 24 ❧

Revelations

Bruenor ambled along the lower slopes of Kelvin's Cairn for the better part of the morning. Most of the snow was melted now with spring thick in the air, but stubborn pockets still made the trails difficult. Axe in one hand and shield, emblazoned with the foaming mug standard of Clan Battlehammer, in the other, Bruenor trudged on, spitting curses at every slick spot, at every boulder obstacle, and at dark elves in general.

He rounded the northwesternmost spur of the mountain, his long, pointed nose cherry-red from the biting wind and his breath coming hard. "Time for a rest," the dwarf muttered, spotting a stone alcove sheltered by high walls from the relentless wind.

Bruenor wasn't the only one who had noticed the comfortable spot. Just before he reached the ten-foot-wide break in the rock wall, a sudden flap of leathery wings brought a huge, insectlike head rising up before him. The dwarf fell back, startled and wary. He recognized the beast as a remorhaz, a polar worm, and was not so eager to jump in against it.

The remorhaz came out of the cubby in pursuit, its snakelike, forty-foot-long body rolling out like an ice-blue ribbon behind it. Multifaceted bug eyes, shining bright white, honed in on the dwarf. Short, leathery wings kept the creature's front half reared and ready to strike while dozens of scrambling legs propelled the remainder of the long torso.

Bruenor felt the increasing heat as the agitated creature's

back began to glow, first to a dull brown, then brightening to red.

"That'll stop the wind for a bit!" the dwarf chuckled, realizing that he could not outrun the beast. He stopped his retreat and waved his axe threateningly.

The remorhaz came straight in, its formidable maw, large enough to swallow the diminutive target whole, snapping down hungrily.

Bruenor jumped aside and angled his shield and body to keep the maw from snapping off his legs, while slamming his axe right between the monster's horns.

The wings beat ferociously, lifting the head back up. The remorhaz, hardly injured, poised to strike again quickly, but Bruenor beat it to the spot. He snatched his bulky axe with his shield hand, drew a long dagger, and dove forward, right between the monster's first set of legs.

The great head came down in a rush, but Bruenor had already slipped under the low belly, the beast's most vulnerable spot. "Ye get me point?" Bruenor chided, driving the dagger up between the scale ridge.

Bruenor was too tough and too well armored to be seriously injured by the worm's thrashing, but then the creature began to roll, meaning to put its glowing-hot back on the dwarf.

"No, ye don't, ye confused dragon-worm-bird-bug!" Bruenor howled, scrambling to keep away from the heat. He came to the creature's side and heaved with all his strength, tumbling the off-balance remorhaz right over.

Snow sputtered and sizzled when the fiery back touched down. Bruenor kicked and swatted his way past the thrashing legs to get to the vulnerable underside. The dwarf's many-notched axe smashed in, opening a wide and deep gash.

The remorhaz coiled and snapped its long body to and fro, throwing Bruenor to the side. The dwarf was up in an instant, but not quickly enough, as the polar worm rolled at him. The searing back caught Bruenor on the thigh as he tried to leap away, and the dwarf came out limping, grabbing at his smoking leather leggings.

Then they faced off again, both showing considerably more respect for the other.

The maw gaped; with a quick snap, Bruenor's axe took a tooth from it and deflected it aside. The dwarf's wounded leg buckled with the blow, though, and a stumbling Bruenor could not get out of the way. A long horn hooked Bruenor under the arm and hurled him far to the side.

He crashed amid a small field of rocks, recovered, and purposely banged his head against a large stone to adjust his helmet and knock the dizziness away.

The remorhaz left a trail of blood, but it did not relent. The huge maw opened and the creature hissed, and Bruenor promptly chucked a stone down its gullet.

* * * * *

Guenhwyvar alerted Drizzt to the trouble down at the northwestern spur. The drow had never seen a polar worm before, but as soon as he spotted the combatants, from a ridge high above, he knew that the dwarf was in trouble. Lamenting that he had left his bow back in the cave, Drizzt drew his scimitars and followed the panther down the mountainside as quickly as the slippery trails would allow.

* * * * *

"Come on, then!" the stubborn dwarf roared at the remorhaz, and indeed the monster did charge. Bruenor braced himself, meaning to get in at least one good shot before becoming worm food.

The great head came down at him, but then the remorhaz, hearing a roar from behind, hesitated and looked away.

"Fool move!" the dwarf cried in glee, and Bruenor slashed with his axe at the monster's lower jaw, splitting it cleanly between two great incisors. The remorhaz screeched in pain; its leathery wings flapped wildly, trying to get the head out of the wicked dwarf's reach.

Bruenor hit it again, and then a third time, each blow cutting huge creases in the maw and driving the head down.

"Think ye're to bite at me, eh?" the dwarf cried. He lashed out with his shield hand and grabbed at a horn as the remorhaz head began to rise again. A quick jerk turned the monster's head at a vulnerable angle and the knotted muscles in Bruenor's arm snapped viciously, cleaving his mighty axe into the polar worm's skull.

The creature shuddered and thrashed for a second longer, then lay still, its back still glowing hotly.

A second roar from Guenhwyvar took the proud dwarf's eyes from his kill. Bruenor, injured and tentative, looked up to see Drizzt and the panther fast approaching, the drow with both scimitars drawn.

"Come on!" Bruenor roared at them both, misunderstanding their charge. He banged his axe against his heavy shield. "Come on and feel me blade!"

Drizzt stopped abruptly and called for Guenhwyvar to do the same. The panther continued to stalk, though, ears flattened.

"Be gone, Guenhwyvar!" Drizzt commanded.

The panther growled indignantly one final time and sprang away.

Satisfied that the cat was gone, Bruenor snapped his glare on Drizzt, standing at the other end of the fallen polar worm.

"Yerself and me, then?" the dwarf spat. "Ye got the belly to face me axe, drow, or do little girls be more to yer likin'?"

The obvious reference to Catti-brie brought an angry light to Drizzt's eyes, and his grasp on his weapons tightened.

Bruenor swung his axe easily. "Come on," he chided derisively. "Ye got the belly to come and play with a dwarf?"

Drizzt wanted to scream out for all the world to hear. He wanted to spring over the dead monster and smash the dwarf, deny the dwarf's words with sheer and brutal force, but he couldn't. Drizzt couldn't deny Mielikki and couldn't betray Mooshie. He had to sublimate his rage once again, had to take the insults stoically and with the realization that he, and his goddess, knew the truth of what lay in his heart.

The scimitars spun into their sheaths and Drizzt walked away, Guenhwyvar coming up beside him.

Bruenor watched the pair go curiously. At first he thought the drow a coward, but then, as the excitement of the battle gradually diminished, Bruenor came to wonder about the drow's intent. Had he come down to finish off both combatants, as Bruenor had first assumed? Or had he, possibly, come down to Bruenor's aid?

"Nah," the dwarf muttered, dismissing the possibility. "Not a dark elf!"

The walk back was long for the limping dwarf, giving Bruenor many opportunities to replay the events around the northwestern spur. When he finally arrived back at the mines, the sun had long set and Catti-brie and several dwarves were gathered, ready to go out to look for him.

"Ye're hurt," one of the dwarves remarked. Catti-brie immediately imagined a fight between Drizzt and her father.

"Polar worm," the dwarf explained casually. "Got him good, but got a bit of a burn for me effort."

The other dwarves nodded admiringly at their leader's battle prowess—a polar worm was no easy kill—and Catti-brie sighed audibly.

"I saw the drow!" Bruenor growled at her, suspecting the source of that sigh. The dwarf remained confused about his meeting with the dark elf, and confused, too, about where Catti-brie fit into all of this. Had Catti-brie actually met the dark elf? he wondered.

"I seen him, I did!" Bruenor continued, now speaking more to the other dwarves. "Drow and the biggest an' blackest cat me eyes ever set on. He came down for me, just as I dropped the worm."

"Drizzt would not!" Catti-brie interrupted before her father could get into his customary story-telling roll.

"Drizzt?" Bruenor asked, and the girl turned away, realizing that her lie was up. Bruenor let it go—for the moment.

"He did, I say!" the dwarf continued. "Came in at me with both his blades drawn! I chased that one an' the cat off!"

"We could hunt him down," offered one of the dwarves. "Run him off the mountain!" The others nodded and mumbled their agreement, but Bruenor, still struggling with the drow's intent, cut them short.

"He's got the mountain," Bruenor told them. "Cassius gave it to him, and we need no trouble with Bryn Shander. As long as the drow stays put and stays outa our way, we'll leave him be.

"But," Bruenor continued, eyeing Catti-brie directly, "ye're not to speak to, ye're not to go near, that one again!"

"But—" Catti-brie started futilely.

"Never!" Bruenor roared. "I'll have yer word now, girl, or by Moradin, I'll have that dark elf's head!"

Catti-brie hesitated, horribly trapped.

"Tell me!" Bruenor demanded.

"Ye have me word," the girl mumbled, and she fled back to the dark shelter of the cave.

*　*　*　*　*

"Cassius, Spokesman o' Bryn Shander, sent me yer way," the gruff man explained. "Says ye'd know the drow if any would."

Bruenor glanced around his formal audience hall to the many other dwarves in attendance, none of them overly impressed by the rude stranger. Bruenor dropped his bearded chin into his palm and yawned widely, determined to remain outside this apparent conflict. He might have bluffed the crude man and his smelly dog out of the halls without further bother, but Catti-brie, sitting at her father's side, shuffled uneasily.

Roddy McGristle did not miss her revealing movement. "Cassius says ye must've seen the drow, him bein' so close."

"If any of me people have," Bruenor replied absently, "they've spoke not a bit of it. If yer drow's about, he's been no bother."

Catti-brie looked curiously at her father and breathed easier.

"No bother?" Roddy muttered, a sly look coming into his eye. "Never is, that one." Slowly and dramatically, the mountain man peeled back his hood, revealing his scars. "Never a bother, until ye don't expect what ye get!"

"Drow give ye that?" Bruenor asked, not overly alarmed or impressed. "Fancy scars—better'n most I seen."

"He killed my dog!" Roddy growled.

"Don't look dead to me," Bruenor quipped, drawing chuckles from every corner.

"My other dog," Roddy snarled, understanding where he stood with this stubborn dwarf. "Ye care not a thing for me, and well ye shouldn't. But it's not for myself that I'm hunting this one, and not for any bounty on his head. Ye ever heared o' Maldobar?"

Bruenor shrugged.

"North o' Sundabar," Roddy explained. "Small, peaceable place. Farmers all. One family, the Thistledowns, lived on the side o' town, three generations in a single house, as good families will. Bartholemew Thistledown was a good man, I tell ye, as his pa afore him, an' his children, four lads and a filly—much like yer own—standing tall and straight with a heart of spirit and a love o' the world."

Bruenor suspected where the burly man was leading, and by Catti-brie's uncomfortable shifting beside him, he figured that his perceptive daughter knew as well.

"Good family," Roddy mused, feigning a wispy, distant expression. "Nine in the house." The mountain man's visage hardened suddenly and he glared straight at Bruenor. "Nine died in the house," he declared. "Hacked by yer drow, and one ate up by his devil cat!"

Catti-brie tried to respond, but her words came out in a garbled shriek. Bruenor was glad of her confusion, for if she had spoken clearly, her argument would have given the mountain man more than Bruenor wanted him to know. The dwarf laid a hand across his daughter's shoulders, then answered Roddy calmly. "Ye've come to us with a dark tale.

Ye shook me daughter, and I'm not for liking me daughter shook!"

"I beg yer forgivings kingly dwarf," Roddy said with a bow, "but ye must be told of the danger on yer door. Drow's a bad one, and so's his devil cat! I want no repeating o' the Maldobar tragedy."

"And ye'll get none in me halls," Bruenor assured him. "We're not simple farmers, take to yer heart. Drow won't be botherin' us any more'n ye've bothered us already."

Roddy wasn't surprised that Bruenor wouldn't help him, but he knew well that the dwarf, or at least the girl, knew more about Drizzt's whereabouts than they had let on. "If not for me, then for Bartholemew Thistledown, I beg ye, good dwarf. Tell me if ye know where I might find the black demon. Or if ye don't know, then give me some soldiers to help me sniff him out."

"Me dwarves've much to do with the melt," Bruenor explained. "Can't be spared chasin' another's fiends." Bruenor really didn't care one way or another for Roddy's gripe with the drow, but the mountain man's story did confirm the dwarf's belief that the dark elf should be avoided, particularly by his daughter. Bruenor actually might have helped Roddy and been done with it, more to get them both out of his valley than for any moral reasons, but he couldn't ignore Catti-brie's obvious distress.

Roddy unsuccessfully tried to hide his anger, looking for some other option. "Where would ye go if ye was runnin', King Bruenor?" he asked. "Ye know the mountain better'n any living, so Cassius told me. Where should I look?"

Bruenor found that he liked seeing the unpleasant human so distressed. "Big valley," he said cryptically. "Wide mountain. Lot o' holes." He sat quiet for a long moment, shaking his head.

Roddy's facade blew away altogether. "Ye'd help the murderin' drow?" he roared. "Ye call yerself a king, but ye'd . . ."

Bruenor leaped up from his stone throne, and Roddy backed away a cautious step and dropped a hand to Bleeder's handle.

"I've the word o' one rogue against another rogue!" Bruenor growled at him. "One's as good—as bad!—as the other, by me guess!"

"Not by a Thistledown's guess!" Roddy cried, and his dog, sensing his outrage, bared its teeth and growled menacingly.

Bruenor looked at the strange, yellow beast curiously. It was getting near dinnertime and arguments did so make Bruenor hungry! How might a yellow dog fill his belly? he wondered.

"Have ye nothing more to give to me?" Roddy demanded.

"I could give ye me boot," Bruenor growled back. Several well-armed dwarven soldiers moved in close to make certain that the volatile human didn't do anything foolish. "I'd offer ye supper," Bruenor continued, "but ye smell too bad for me table, and ye don't seem the type what'd be takin' a bath."

Roddy yanked his dog's rope and stormed away, banging his heavy boots and slamming through each door he came upon. At Bruenor's nod, four soldiers followed the mountain man to make certain that he left without any unfortunate incidents. In the formal audience hall, the others laughed and howled about the way their king had handled the human.

Catti-brie didn't join in on the mirth, Bruenor noted, and the dwarf thought he knew why. Roddy's tale, true or not, had instilled some doubts in the girl.

"So now ye have it," Bruenor said to her roughly, trying to push her over the edge in their running argument. "The drow's a hunted killer. Now ye'll take me warnings to heart, girl!"

Catti-brie's lips disappeared in a bitter bite. Drizzt had not told her much about his life on the surface, but she could not believe that this drow whom she had come to know would be capable of murder. Neither could Catti-brie deny the obvious: Drizzt was a dark elf, and to her more experienced father, at least, that fact alone gave credence to Mc-Gristle's tale.

"Ye hear me, girl?" Bruenor growled.

"Ye've got to get them all together," Catti-brie said suddenly. "The drow and Cassius, and ugly Roddy McGristle. Ye've got to—"

"Not me problem!" Bruenor roared, cutting her short. Tears came quickly to Catti-brie's soft eyes in the face of her father's sudden rage. All the world seemed to turn over before her. Drizzt was in danger, and more so was the truth about his past. Just as stinging to Catti-brie, her father, whom she had loved and admired for all her remembered life, seemed now to turn a deaf ear to the calls for justice.

In that horrible moment, Catti-brie did the only thing an eleven-year-old could do against such odds—she turned from Bruenor and fled.

*　*　*　*　*

Catti-brie didn't really know what she meant to accomplish when she found herself running along the lower trails of Kelvin's Cairn, breaking her promise to Bruenor. Catti-brie could not refuse her desire to come, though she had little to offer Drizzt beyond a warning that McGristle was looking for him.

She couldn't sort through all the worries, but then she stood before the drow and understood the real reason she had ventured out. It was not for Drizzt that she had come, though she wanted him safe. It was for her own peace.

"Ye never speaked o' the Thistledowns of Maldobar," she said icily in greeting, stealing the drow's smile. The dark expression that crossed Drizzt's face clearly showed his pain.

Thinking that Drizzt, by his melancholy, had accepted blame for the tragedy, the wounded girl spun and tried to flee. Drizzt caught her by the shoulder, though, turned her about, and held her close. He would be a damned thing indeed if this girl, who had accepted him with all her heart, came to believe the lies.

"I killed no one," Drizzt whispered above Catti-brie's sobs, "except the monsters that slew the Thistledowns. On my word!" He recounted the tale then, in full, even telling of his flight from Dove Falconhand's party.

"And now I am here," he concluded, "wishing to put the experience behind me, though never, on my word, shall I ever forget it!"

"Ye weave two tales apart," Catti-brie replied. "Yerself an' McGristle, I mean."

"McGristle?" Drizzt gasped as though his breath had been blasted from his body. Drizzt hadn't seen the burly man in years and had thought Roddy to be a thing of his distant past.

"Came in today," Catti-brie explained. "Big man with a yellow dog. He's hunting ye."

The confirmation overwhelmed Drizzt. Would he ever escape his past? he wondered. If not, how could he ever hope to find acceptance?

"McGristle said ye killed them," Catti-brie continued.

"Then you have our words alone," Drizzt reasoned, "and there is no evidence to prove either tale." The ensuing silence seemed to go for hours.

"Never did like that ugly brute." Catti-brie sniffed, and she managed her first smile since she had met McGristle.

The affirmation of their friendship struck Drizzt profoundly, but he could not forget the trouble that was now hovering all about him. He would have to fight Roddy, and maybe others if the bounty hunter could stir up resentment—not a difficult task considering Drizzt's heritage. Or Drizzt would have to run away, again accept the road as his home.

"What'll ye do?" Catti-brie asked, sensing his distress.

"Do not fear for me," Drizzt assured her, and he gave her a hug as he spoke, one that he knew might be his way of saying good-bye. "The day grows long. You must get back to your home."

"He'll find ye," Catti-brie replied grimly.

"No," Drizzt said calmly. "Not soon anyway. With Guenhwyvar by my side, we will keep Roddy McGristle away until I can figure my best course. Now, be off! The night comes swiftly and I do not believe that your father would appreciate your coming here."

The reminder that she would have to face Bruenor again set Catti-brie in motion. She bid Drizzt farewell and turned away, then rushed back up to the drow and threw a hug around him. Her step was lighter as she moved back down the mountain. She hadn't resolved anything for Drizzt, at least as far as she knew, but the drow's troubles seemed a distant second compared to her own relief that her friend was not the monster some claimed him to be.

The night would be dark indeed for Drizzt Do'Urden. He had thought McGristle a long-distant problem, but the menace was here now, and none save Catti-brie had jumped to his defense.

He would have to stand alone—again—if he meant to stand at all. He had no allies beyond Guenhwyvar and his own scimitars, and the prospects of battling McGristle—win or lose—did not appeal to him.

"This is no home," Drizzt muttered to the frosty wind. He pulled out the onyx figurine and called to his panther companion. "Come, my friend," he said to the cat. "Let us be away before our adversary is upon us."

Guenhwyvar kept an alert guard while Drizzt packed up his possessions, while the road-weary drow emptied his home.

❧ 25 ❧

Dwarven Banter

Catti-brie heard the growling dog, but she had no time to react when the huge man leaped out from behind a boulder and grabbed her roughly by the arm. "I knowed ye knowed!" McGristle cried, putting his foul breath right in the girl's face.

Catti-brie kicked him in the shin. "Ye let me go!" she retorted. Roddy was surprised that she had no trace of fear in her voice. He gave her a good shake when she tried to kick him again.

"Ye came to the mountain for a reason," Roddy said evenly, not relaxing his grip. "Ye came to see the drow—I knowed that ye was friends with that one. Seen it in yer eyes!"

"Ye know not a thing!" Catti-brie spat in his face. "Ye talk in lies."

"So the drow told ye his story o' the Thistledowns, eh?" Roddy replied, easily guessing the girl's meaning. Catti-brie knew then that she had erred in her anger, had given the wretch confirmation of her destination.

"The drow?" Catti-brie said absently. "I'm not for guessing what ye're speaking about."

Roddy's laughter mocked her. "Ye been with the drow, girl. Ye've said it plain enough. And now ye're goin' to take me to see him."

Catti-brie sneered at him, drawing another rough shake.

Roddy's grimace softened then, suddenly, and Catti-brie liked even less the look that came into his eye. "Ye're a spirited girl, ain't ye?" Roddy purred, grabbing Catti-brie's other shoulder and turning her to face him squarely. "Full o' life, eh? Ye'll take me to the drow, girl, don't ye doubt. But mighten be there's other things we can do first, things to show ye not to cross the likes o' Roddy McGristle." His caress on Catti-brie's cheek seemed ridiculously grotesque, but horribly and undeniably threatening, and Catti-brie thought she would gag.

It took every bit of Catti-brie's fortitude to face up to Roddy at that moment. She was only a young girl but had been raised among the grim-faced dwarves of Clan Battlehammer, a proud and rugged group. Bruenor was a fighter, and so was his daughter. Catti-brie's knee found Roddy's groin, and as his grip suddenly relaxed, the girl brought one hand up to claw at his face. She kneed him a second time, with less effect, but Roddy's defensive twist allowed her to pull away, almost free.

Roddy's iron grip tightened suddenly around her wrist, and they struggled for just a moment. Then Catti-brie felt an equally rough grab at her free hand, and before she could understand what had happened, she was pulled from Roddy's grasp and a dark form stepped by her.

"So ye come to face yer fate," Roddy snarled delightedly at Drizzt.

"Run off," Drizzt told Catti-brie. "This is not your affair." Catti-brie, shaken and terribly afraid, did not argue.

Roddy's gnarled hands clenched Bleeder's handle. The bounty hunter had faced the drow in battle before and had no intention of trying to keep up with that one's agile steps and twists. With a nod, he loosed his dog.

The dog got halfway to Drizzt, was just about to leap at him, when Guenhwyvar buried it, rolling it far to the side. The dog came back to its feet, not seriously wounded but backing off several steps every time the panther roared in its face.

"Enough of this," Drizzt said, suddenly serious. "You have pursued me through years and leagues. I salute your resilience, but your anger is misplaced, I tell you. I did not kill the Thistledowns. Never would I have raised a blade against them!"

"To Nine Hells with the Thistledowns!" Roddy roared back. "Ye think that's what this is about?"

"My head would not bring you your bounty," Drizzt retorted.

"To Nine Hells with the gold!" Roddy yelled. "Ye took my dog, drow, an' my ear!" He banged a dirty finger against the side of his scarred face.

Drizzt wanted to argue, wanted to remind Roddy that it was he who had initiated the fight, and that his own axe swing had felled the tree that had torn his face. But Drizzt understood Roddy's motivation and knew that mere words would not soothe. Drizzt had wounded Roddy's pride, and to a man like Roddy that injury far outweighed any physical pain.

"I want no fight," Drizzt offered firmly. "Take your dog and be gone, on your word alone that you'll pursue me no longer."

Roddy's mocking laughter sent a shudder up Drizzt's spine. "I'll chase ye to the ends o' the world, drow!" Roddy roared. "And I'll find ye every time. No hole's deep enough to keep me from ye. No sea's wide enough! I'll have ye, drow. I'll have ye now or, if ye run, I'll have ye later!"

Roddy flashed a yellow-toothed smile and cautiously stalked toward Drizzt. "I'll have ye drow," the bounty hunter growled again quietly. A sudden rush brought him close and Bleeder swiped across wildly. Drizzt hopped back.

A second strike promised similar results, but Roddy, instead of following through, came with a deceptively quick backhand that glanced Drizzt's chin.

He was on Drizzt in an instant, his axe whipping furiously every which way. "Stand still!" Roddy cried as Drizzt deftly sidestepped, hopped over, or ducked under each blow. Drizzt knew that he was taking a dangerous chance in not countering the wicked blows, but he hoped that if he could tire the burly man, he might still find a more peaceful solution.

Roddy was agile and quick for a big man, but Drizzt was far quicker, and the drow believed that he could play the game a good while longer.

Bleeder came in a side swipe, diving across at Drizzt's chest. The attack was a feint, with Roddy wanting Drizzt to duck under so that he might kick the drow in the face.

Drizzt saw through the deception. He leaped instead of ducked, turned a somersault above the cutting axe, and came down lightly, even closer to Roddy. Now Drizzt did wade in, punching with both scimitar hilts straight into Roddy's face. The bounty hunter staggered backward, feeling warm blood rolling out of his nose.

"Go away," Drizzt said sincerely. "Take your dog back to Maldobar, or wherever it is that you call home."

If Drizzt believed that Roddy would surrender in the face of further humiliation, he was badly mistaken. Roddy bellowed in rage and charged straight in, dipping his shoulder in an attempt to bury the drow.

Drizzt pounded his weapon hilts down onto Roddy's dipped head and launched himself into a forward roll right over Roddy's back. The bounty hunter went down hard but came quickly to his knees, drawing and firing a dagger at Drizzt even as the drow turned back.

Drizzt saw the silvery flicker at the last instant and snapped a blade down to deflect the weapon. Another dagger followed, and another after that, and each time, Roddy advanced a step on the distracted drow.

"I'm knowing yer tricks, drow," Roddy said with an evil grin. Two quick steps brought him right up to Drizzt and Bleeder again sliced in.

Drizzt dove into a sidelong roll and came up a few feet away. Roddy's continuing confidence began to unnerve Drizzt; he had hit the bounty hunter with blows that would have dropped most men, and he wondered how much damage the burly human could withstand. That thought led Drizzt to the inevitable conclusion that he might have to start hitting Roddy with more than his scimitar hilts.

Again Bleeder came from the side. This time, Drizzt did

not dodge. He stepped within the arc of the axe blade and blocked with one weapon, leaving Roddy open for a strike with the other scimitar. Three quick right jabs closed one of Roddy's eyes, but the bounty hunter only grinned and charged, catching hold of Drizzt and bearing the lighter combatant to the ground.

Drizzt squirmed and slapped, understanding that his conscience had betrayed him. In such close quarters, he could not match Roddy's strength, and his limited movements destroyed his advantage of speed. Roddy held his position on top and maneuvered one arm to chop down with Bleeder.

A yelp from his yellow dog was the only warning he got, and that didn't register enough for him to avoid the panther's rush. Guenhwyvar bowled Roddy off Drizzt, slamming him to the ground. The burly man kept his wits enough to swipe at the panther as it continued past, nicking Guenhwyvar on the rear flank.

The stubborn dog came rushing in, but Guenhwyvar recovered, pivoted right around Roddy, and drove it away.

When Roddy turned back to Drizzt, he was met by a savage flurry of scimitar blows that he could not follow and could not counter. Drizzt had seen the strike on the panther and the fires in his lavender eyes no longer indicated compromise. A hilt smashed Roddy's face, followed by the flat of the other blade. A foot kicked his stomach, his chest, and then his groin in what seemed a single motion. Impervious, Roddy accepted it all with a snarl, but the enraged drow pressed on. One scimitar caught again under the axe head, and Roddy moved to charge, thinking to bear Drizzt to the ground once more.

Drizzt's second weapon struck first, though, slicing across Roddy's forearm. The bounty hunter recoiled, grasping at his wounded limb as Bleeder fell to the ground.

Drizzt never slowed. His rush caught Roddy off guard and several kicks and punches left the man reeling. Drizzt then leaped high into the air and kicked straight out with both feet, connecting squarely on Roddy's jaw and dropping him heavily to the ground. Still Roddy shrugged it off and tried to rise, but this time, the bounty hunter felt the edges of two scimitars come to rest on opposite sides of his throat.

"I told you to be on your way," Drizzt said grimly, not moving his blades an inch but letting Roddy feel the cold metal acutely.

"Kill me," Roddy said calmly, sensing a weakness in his opponent, "if ye got the belly for it!"

Drizzt hesitated, but his scowl did not soften. "Be on your way," he said with as much calm as he could muster, calm that denied the coming trial he knew he would face.

Roddy laughed at him. "Kill me, ye black-skinned devil!" he roared, bulling his way, though he remained on his knees, toward Drizzt. "Kill me or I'll catch ye! Not for doubtin', drow. I'll hunt ye to the corners o' the world and under it if need!"

Drizzt blanched and glanced at Guenhwyvar for support.

"Kill me!" Roddy cried, bordering on hysteria. He grabbed Drizzt's wrists and pulled them forward. Lines of bright blood appeared on both sides of the man's neck. "Kill me as ye killed my dog!"

Horrified, Drizzt tried to pull away, but Roddy's grip was like iron.

"Ye got not the belly for it?" the bounty hunter bellowed. "Then I'll help ye!" He jerked the wrists sharply against Drizzt's pull, cutting deeper lines, and if the crazed man felt pain, it did not show through his unyielding grin.

Waves of jumbled emotions assaulted Drizzt. He wanted to kill Roddy at that moment, more out of stupefied frustration than vengeance, and yet he knew that he could not. As far as Drizzt knew, Roddy's only crime was an unwarranted hunt against him and that was not reason enough. For all that he held dear, Drizzt had to respect a human life, even one as wretched as Roddy McGristle's.

"Kill me!" Roddy shouted over and over, taking lewd pleasure in the drow's growing disgust.

"No!" Drizzt screamed in Roddy's face with enough force to silence the bounty hunter. Enraged to a point where he could not contain his trembling, Drizzt did not wait to see if Roddy would resume his insane cry. He drove a knee into Roddy's chin, pulled his wrists free of Roddy's grasp, then slammed his weapon hilts simultaneously into the bounty hunter's temples.

Roddy's eyes crossed, but he did not swoon, stubbornly shaking the blow away. Drizzt slammed him again and again, finally beating him down, horrified at his own actions and at the bounty hunter's continuing defiance.

When the rage had played itself out, Drizzt stood over the burly man, trembling and with tears rimming his lavender eyes. "Drive that dog far away!" he yelled to Guenhwyvar. Then he dropped his bloodied blades in horror and bent down to make sure that Roddy was not dead.

* * * * *

Roddy awoke to find his yellow dog standing over him. Night was fast falling and the wind had picked up again. His head and arm ached, but he dismissed the pain, wanting only to resume his hunt, confident now that Drizzt would never find the strength to kill him. His dog caught the scent at once, leading back to the south, and they set off. Roddy's nerve dissipated only a little when they came around a rocky outcropping and found a red-bearded dwarf and a girl waiting for him.

"Ye don't be touchin' me girl, McGristle," Bruenor said evenly. "Ye just shouldn't be touchin' me girl."

"She's in league with the drow!" Roddy protested. "She told the murdering devil of my comin'!"

"Drizzt's not a murderer!" Catti-brie yelled back. "He never did kill the farmers! He says ye're saying that just so others'll help ye to catch him!" Catti-brie realized suddenly that she had just admitted to her father that she had met with the drow. When Catti-brie had found Bruenor, she had told him only of McGristle's rough handling.

"Ye went to him," Bruenor said, obviously wounded. "Ye lied to me, an' ye went to the drow! I telled ye not to. Ye said ye wouldn't . . ."

Bruenor's lament stung Catti-brie profoundly, but she held fast to her beliefs. Bruenor had raised her to be honest, but that included being honest to what she knew was right. "Once ye said to me that everyone gets his due," Catti-brie retorted. "Ye told me that each is different and each should be seen for what he is. I've seen Drizzt, and seen him true, I tell ye. He's no killer! And he's—" She pointed accusingly at McGristle—"a liar! I take no pride in me own lie, but never could I let Drizzt get caught by this one!"

Bruenor considered her words for a moment, then wrapped one arm about her waist and hugged her tightly. His daughter's deception still stung, but the dwarf was proud that his girl had stood up for what she believed. In truth, Bruenor had come out here, not looking for Catti-brie, whom he believed was sulking in the mines, but to find the drow. The more he recounted his fight with the remorhaz, the more Bruenor became convinced that Drizzt had come down to help him, not to fight him. Now, in light of recent events, few doubts remained.

"Drizzt came and pulled me free of that one," Catti-brie went on. "He saved me."

"Drow's got her mixed," Roddy said, sensing Bruenor's growing attitude and wanting no fight with the dangerous dwarf. "He's a murderin' dog, I say, and so would Bartholemew Thistledown if a dead man could!"

"Bah!" Bruenor snorted. "Ye don't know me girl or ye'd be thinking the better than to call her a liar. And I told ye before, McGristle, that I don't like me daughter shook! Me thinkin's that ye should be gettin' outa me valley. Me thinkin's that ye should be goin' now."

Roddy growled and so did his dog, which sprung between the mountain man and the dwarf and bared its teeth at Bruenor. Bruenor shrugged, unconcerned, and growled back at the beast, provoking it further.

The dog lurched at the dwarf's ankle, and Bruenor promptly put a heavy boot in its mouth and pinned its bottom jaw to the ground. "And take yer stinkin' dog with ye!"

Bruenor roared, though in admiring the dog's meaty flank, he was thinking again that he might have better use for the surly beast.

"I go where I choose, dwarf!" Roddy retorted. "I'm gonna get me a drow, and if the drow's in yer valley, then so am I!"

Bruenor recognized the clear frustration in the man's voice, and he took closer note then of the bruises on Roddy's face and the gash on his arm. "The drow got away from ye," the dwarf said, and his chuckle stung Roddy acutely.

"Not for long," Roddy promised. "And no dwarf'll stand in my way!"

"Get along back to the mines," Bruenor said to Catti-brie. "Tell the others I mighten be a bit late for dinner." The axe came down from Bruenor's shoulder.

"Get him good," Catti-brie mumbled under her breath, not doubting her father's prowess in the least. She kissed Bruenor atop his helmet, then rushed off happily. Her father had trusted her; nothing in all the world could be wrong.

*   *   *   *   *

Roddy McGristle and his three-legged dog left the valley a short while later. Roddy had seen a weakness in Drizzt and thought he could win against the drow, but he saw no such signs in Bruenor Battlehammer. When Bruenor had Roddy down, a feat that hadn't taken very long, Roddy did not doubt for a second that if he had asked the dwarf to kill him, Bruenor gladly would have complied.

From the top of the southern climb, where he had gone for his last look at Ten-Towns, Drizzt watched the wagon roll out of the vale, suspecting that it was the bounty hunter's. Not knowing what it all meant, but hardly believing that Roddy had undergone a change of heart, Drizzt looked down at his packed belongings and wondered where he should turn next.

The lights of the towns were coming on now, and Drizzt watched them with mixed emotions. He had been on this climb several times, enchanted by his surroundings and thinking he had found his home. How different now was this view! McGristle's appearance had given Drizzt pause and reminded him that he was still an outcast, and ever to be one.

"Drizzit," he mumbled to himself, a damning word indeed. At that moment, Drizzt did not believe he would ever find a home, did not believe that a drow who was not in heart a drow had a place in all the realms, surface or Underdark. The hope, ever fleeting in Drizzt's weary heart, had flown altogether.

"Bruenor's Climb, this place is called," said a gruff voice behind Drizzt. He spun about, thinking to flee, but the red-bearded dwarf was too close for him to slip by. Guenhwyvar rushed to the drow's side, teeth bared.

"Put yer pet away, elf," Bruenor said. "If cat tastes as bad as dog, I'll want none of it!

"My place, this is," the dwarf went on, "me bein' Bruenor and this bein' Bruenor's Climb!"

"I saw no sign of ownership," Drizzt replied indignantly, his patience exhausted from the long road that now seemed to grow longer. "I know your claim now, and so I will leave. Take heart, dwarf. I shall not return."

Bruenor put a hand up, both to silence the drow and to stop him from leaving. "Just a pile o' rocks," he said, as close to an apology as Bruenor had ever given. "I named it as me own, but does that make it so? Just a damned piled o' rocks!"

Drizzt cocked his head at the dwarf's unexpected rambling.

"Nothin's what it seems, drow!" Bruenor declared. "Nothin'! Ye try to follow what ye know, ye know? But then ye find that ye know not what ye thought ye knowed! Thought a dog'd be tastin' good—looked good enough—but now me belly's cursing me every move!"

The second mention of the dog sparked a sudden revelation concerning Roddy McGristle's departure. "You sent him away," Drizzt said, pointing down to the route out of the vale. "You drove McGristle off my trail."

Bruenor hardly heard him, and certainly wouldn't have admitted the kind-hearted deed, in any case. "Never trusted humans," he said evenly. "Never know what one's about, and when ye find out, too many's the time it's too late for fixin'! But always had me thoughts straight about other folks. An elf's an elf, after all, and so's a gnome. And orcs are straight-out stupid and ugly. Never knew one to be otherways, an' I known a few!" Bruenor patted his axe, and Drizzt did not miss his meaning.

"So was me thoughts about the drow," Bruenor continued. "Never met one—never wanted to. Who would, I ask? Drow're bad, mean-hearted, so I been told by me dad an' by me dad's dad, an' by any who's ever told me." He looked out to the lights of Termalaine on Maer Dualdon in the west, shook his head, and kicked a stone. "Now I heared a drow's prowlin' about me valley, and what's a king to do? Then me daughter goes to him!" A sudden fire came into Bruenor's eyes, but it mellowed quickly, almost as if in embarrassment, as soon as he looked at Drizzt. "She lies in me face—never has she done that afore, and never again if she's a smart one!"

"It was not her fault," Drizzt began, but Bruenor waved his hands about wildly to dismiss the whole thing.

"Thought I knowed what I knowed," Bruenor continued after a short pause, his voice almost a lament. "Had the world figured, sure enough. Easy to do when ye stay in yer own hole."

He looked back to Drizzt, straight into the dim shine of the drow's lavender eyes. "Bruenor's Climb?" the dwarf asked with a resigned shrug. "What's it mean, drow, to put a name on a pile o' rocks? Thought I knowed, I did, an' thought a dog'd taste good." Bruenor rubbed a hand over his belly and frowned. "Call it a pile o' rocks then, an' I've no claim on it more'n yerself! Call it Drizzt's Climb then, an' ye'd be kicking me out!"

"I would not," Drizzt replied quietly. "I do not know that I could if I wished to!"

"Call it what ye will!" Bruenor cried, suddenly distressed. "And call a dog a cow—that don't change the way the thing'll taste!" Bruenor threw up his hands, flustered, and turned away, stomping down the rock path, grumbling with every step.

"And ye be keepin' yer eyes on me girl," Drizzt heard Bruenor snarl above his general grumbles, "if she's so orc-headed as to keep goin' to the stinkin' yeti an' worm-filled mountain! Be knowin' that I hold yerself . . ." The rest faded away as Bruenor disappeared around a bend.

Drizzt couldn't begin to dig his way through that rambling dialogue, but he didn't need to put Bruenor's speech in perfect order. He dropped a hand on Guenhwyvar, hoping that the panther shared the suddenly wondrous panoramic view. Drizzt knew then that he would sit up on the climb, Bruenor's Climb, many times and watch the lights flicker to life, for, adding up all that the dwarf had said, Drizzt surmised one phrase clearly, words he had waited so many years to hear:

Welcome home.

❧ Epilogue ❧

Of all the races in the known realms, none is more confusing, or more confused, than humans. Mooshie convinced me that gods, rather than being outside entities, are personifications of what lies in our hearts. If this is true, then the many, varied gods of the human sects—deities of vastly different demeanors—reveal much about the race.

If you approach a halfling, or an elf, or a dwarf, or any of the other races, good and bad, you have a fair idea of what to expect. There are exceptions, of course; I name myself as one most fervently! But a dwarf is likely to be gruff, though fair, and I have never met an elf, or even heard of one, that preferred a cave to the open sky. A human's preference, though, is his own to know—if even he can sort it out.

In terms of good and evil, then, the human race must be judged most carefully. I have battled vile human assassins, witnessed human wizards so caught up in their power that they mercilessly destroyed all other beings in their paths, and seen cities where groups of humans preyed upon the unfortunate of their own race, living in kingly palaces while other men and women, and even children, starved and died in the gutters of the muddy streets. But I have met other humans—Catti-brie, Mooshie, Wulfgar, Agorwal of Termalaine—whose honor could not be questioned and whose contributions to the good of the realms in their short life spans will outweigh that of most dwarves and elves who might live a half a millennium and more.

They are indeed a confusing race, and the fate of the world comes more and more into their ever-reaching hands. It may prove a delicate balance, but certainly not a dull one. Humans encompass the spectrum of character more fully than any other beings; they are the only "goodly" race that wages war upon itself—with alarming frequency.

The surface elves hold out hope in the end. They who have lived the longest and seen the birth of many centuries take faith that the human race will mature to goodness, that the evil in it will crush itself to nothingness, leaving the world to those who remain.

In the city of my birth I witnessed the limitations of evil, the self-destruction and inability to achieve higher goals, even goals based upon the acquisition of power. For this reason, I, too, will hold out hope for the humans, and for the realms. As they are the most varied, so too are humans the most malleable, the most able to disagree with that within themselves that they learn to be false.

My very survival has been based upon my belief that there is a higher purpose to this life: that principles are a reward in and of themselves. I cannot, therefore, look forward in despair, but rather with higher hopes for all in mind and with the determination that I might help to reach those heights.

This is my tale, then, told as completely as I can recall and as completely as I choose to divulge. Mine has been a long road filled with ruts and barriers, and only now that I have put so much so far behind me am I able to recount it honestly.

I will never look back on those days and laugh; the toll was too great for humor to seep through. I do often remember Zaknafein, though, and Belwar and Mooshie, and all the other friends I have left behind.

I have often wondered, too, of the many enemies I have faced, of the many lives my blades have ended. Mine has been a violent life in a violent world, full of enemies to myself and to all that I hold dear. I have been praised for the perfect cut of my scimitars, for my abilities in battle, and I must admit that I have many times allowed myself to feel pride in those hard-earned skills.

Whenever I remove myself from the excitement and consider the whole more fully, though, I lament that things could not have been different. It pains me to remember Masoj Hun'ett, the only drow I ever killed; it was he who initiated our battle and he certainly would have killed me if I had not proven the stronger. I can justify my actions on that fated day, but never will I be comfortable with their necessity. There should be a better way than the sword.

In a world so filled with danger, where orcs and trolls loom, seemingly, around every bend in the road, he who can fight is most often hailed as the hero and given generous applause. There is more to the mantle of "hero," I say, than strength of arm or prowess in battle. Mooshie was a hero, truly, because he overcame adversity, because he never blinked at unfavorable odds, and mostly because he acted within a code of clearly defined principles. Can less be said of Belwar Dissengulp, the handless deep gnome who befriended a renegade drow? Or of Clacker, who offered his own life rather than bring danger to his friends?

Similarly, I name Wulfgar of Icewind Dale a hero, who adhered to principle above battle lust. Wulfgar overcame the misperceptions of his savage boyhood, learned to see the world as a place of hope rather than a field of potential conquests. And Bruenor, the dwarf who taught Wulfgar that important difference, is as rightful a king as ever there was in all the realms. He embodies those tenets that his people hold most dear, and they will gladly defend Bruenor with their very lives, singing a song to him even with their dying breaths.

In the end, when he found the strength to deny Matron Malice, my father, too, was a hero. Zaknafein, who had lost his battle for principles and identity throughout most of his life, won in the end.

None of these warriors, though, outshines a young girl I came to know when I first traveled across Ten-Towns. Of all the people I have ever met, none has held themselves to higher standards of honor and decency than Catti-brie. She has seen many battles, yet her eyes sparkle clearly with in-

nocence and her smile shines untainted. Sad will be the day, and let all the world lament, when a discordant tone of cynicism spoils the harmony of her melodic voice.

Often those who call me a hero speak solely of my battle prowess and know nothing of the principles that guide my blades. I accept their mantle for what it is worth, for their satisfaction and not my own. When Catti-brie names me so, then will I allow my heart to swell with the satisfaction of knowing that I have been judged for my heart and not my sword arm; then will I dare to believe that the mantle is justified.

And so my tale ends—do I dare to say? I sit now in comfort beside my friend, the rightful king of Mithril Hall, and all is quiet and peaceful and prosperous. Indeed this drow has found his home and his place. But I am young, I must remind myself. I may have ten times the years remaining as those that have already passed. And for all my present contentment, the world remains a dangerous place, where a ranger must hold to his principles, but also to his weapons.

Do I dare to believe that my story is fully told?

I think not.

—Drizzt Do'Urden

Fantasy Adventure

The Cleric Quintet

R. A. Salvatore

Book One
Canticle

High in the placid Snowflake Mountains lies a little-known conservatory for bards, priests, clerics, and others. Cloistered among his colleagues, a scholar-priest named Cadderly must contain a malevolent, consuming essence that's been uncorked, before his own brethren can turn against him. Cadderly must put his studies to the test and enter the catacombs far below to save his brothers and himself.

On sale in November 1991, Canticle is the first in a new five-book series of novels entitled The Cleric Quintet, set in the FORGOTTEN REALMS fantasy world from TSR, Inc. R. A. Salvatore is the author of the bestselling Icewind Dale and Dark Elf trilogies.

FANTASY ADVENTURE

▪ THE HARPERS ▪

A Force for Good in the Realms!

This open-ended series of stand-alone novels chronicles the Harpers' heroic battles against forces of evil, all for the peace of the Realms.

The Parched Sea
Troy Denning

The Zhentarim have sent an army to enslave the fierce nomads of the Great Desert. Only one woman, the outcast witch Ruha, sees the true danger—and only the Harpers can counter the evil plot. Available July 1991.

Elfshadow
Elaine Cunningham

Harpers are being murdered, and the trail leads to Arilyn Moonblade. Is she guilty or is she the next target? Arilyn must uncover the ancient secret of her sword's power in order to find and face the assassin.
Available October 1991.

Red Magic
Jean Rabe

One of the powerful and evil Red Wizards wants to control more than his share of Thay. While the mage builds a net of treachery, the Harpers put their own agents into action to foil his plans for conquest.
Available November 1991.

DragonLance® Saga

Meetings Sextet

Kindred Spirits

Mark Anthony and Ellen Porath

The reluctant paternal dwarven hero, Flint Fireforge, is invited to the elven kingdom of Qualinesti, where he meets a young, unhappy half-elf named Tanis. But when Laurana, the beauteous daughter of the elves' ruler, declares her love for Tanis, a deadly rival for her affections concocts a scenario fraught with risk and scandal for both the half-elf and his dwarven ally. On Sale April 1991.

Wanderlust

Mary Kirchoff and Steve Winter

Tasslehoff Burrfoot accidentally pockets one of Flint's copper bracelets and Tanis good-naturedly defends the top-knotted newcomer to Solace—triggering a thoroughly unpredictable tale, which includes a sinister stranger who has evil on his mind for the three new friends. On Sale September 1991.

Dark Heart

Tina Daniell

At long last, the story of the beautiful, dark-hearted Kitiara Uth Matar, from the birth of her twin brothers, the frail mage Raistlin and the warrior Caramon. Kitiara's increasing fascination with evil throws her into the company of a roguish stranger and an eerie mage whose fates are intermingled with her own. On Sale January 1992.

THE ALL NEW

The world's oldest science
fiction magazine ...

BEGINS IN MAY 1991

FANTASY ADVENTURE

The
Legacy

R. A. Salvatore

**The hero of the
FORGOTTEN REALMS® Dark Elf Trilogy
returns in TSR's first hardcover volume
by *New York Times* bestselling author
R. A. Salvatore!**

Life was good for Drizzt Do'Urden, better than
it ever had been for the beleaguered dark elf.
His dearest friend, the dwarf Bruenor, had
reclaimed his throne, and Wulfgar and Catti-
brie were to be wed in the spring. Even the
halfling Regis had returned. All the friends were
united in the safety and prosperity of Mithril
Hall. But Drizzt had not achieved this state of
peace without leaving powerful enemies in his
wake. Lloth, the dreaded Spider Queen deity of
the evil dark elves, counted herself among them
and vowed to take vengeance on Drizzt.

On sale in October 1992.